THE BEST OF BAGEHOT

THE BEST OF
BAGEHOT

EDITED WITH AN INTRODUCTION BY

RUTH DUDLEY EDWARDS

HAMISH HAMILTON · LONDON

HAMISH HAMILTON LTD

Published by the Penguin Group
Penguin Books Ltd, 27 Wrights Lane, London w8 5tz, England
Penguin Books USA Inc., 375 Hudson Street, New York, New York 10014, USA
Penguin Books Australia Ltd, Ringwood, Victoria, Australia
Penguin Books Canada Ltd, 10 Alcorn Avenue, Toronto, Ontario, Canada m4v 3b2
Penguin Books (NZ) Ltd, 182–190 Wairau Road, Auckland 10, New Zealand

Penguin Books Ltd, Registered Offices: Harmondsworth, Middlesex, England

First published 1993

1 3 5 7 9 10 8 6 4 2

Typeset by Datix International Limited, Bungay, Suffolk
Filmset in 11/14 pt Monophoto Bembo
Printed in England by Clays Ltd, St Ives plc

A CIP catalogue record for this book is available from the British Library

ISBN 0–241–13287–8

TO DAVID GORDON

CONTENTS

INTRODUCTION

He hated dullness, apathy, pomposity, the time-worn phrase,
the greasy platitude. His writings are an armoury of offensive
weapons against pompous fools.

—Augustine Birrell, 1901

I fell in love with Walter Bagehot while writing the history of *The
Economist*, of which he was editor from 1861 to 1877.

Although he lived to be only fifty-one, Bagehot left behind him a
body of work which fills fifteen substantial and rather forbidding-
looking volumes.* As I settled down to read them I felt sorry for
myself. Within a very short time I realized I was in the company
of an exciting and enriching intelligence and an irreverent and
beguiling personality. By the end of the first volume, which
includes his hilarious essay on the ostensibly solemn topic of Edward
(*Decline and Fall of the Roman Empire*) Gibbon, I was in love. I
developed the habit of ringing friends to read them choice extracts;
photocopied pages of Bagehot landed through their letter-boxes; at
dinner parties no one was safe.

Usually the initial response was surprise that Bagehot was funny
and made one think. Most people vaguely saw him as a solemn
Victorian worthy who said grave things about the constitution.
Many of them had never even heard of him, or could not
pronounce his name.† Few had any idea of the vast range of his
work or realized that the distinguishing feature of all his thinking
was his fascination with human behaviour.

Yet for over a century, people in the public eye have been singing
Bagehot's praises. Here is a sample:

1858. MATTHEW ARNOLD (*à propos* his early literary essays): '[They]

---

* *The Collected Works of Walter Bagehot* (*WB*), edited by Norman St John-Stevas
and published by The Economist, 1966–1986.
† 'Bajot', the 'g' being soft, as in 'badger'.

I

seem to me to be of the very first quality, showing not talent only, but a concern for the *simple truth* which is rare in English literature as it is in English politics and English religion.'

1877. LORD GRANVILLE, ex-Foreign Secretary: 'I consider his loss to be a great loss to politics, to economics, to literature, and the community. As Mr Cobden once said of Mr Gladstone, that he rolled out figures with the same charm as other men declaimed beautiful poetry, so Mr Bagehot gave a peculiar flavour and charm to his writings on the driest subject.'

1881. W. E. GLADSTONE: 'A man of most remarkable gifts, and among them was a singular discernment as to public characters, and a not less excellent faculty for embodying the results in literary form.'

1898. WOODROW WILSON: 'Walter Bagehot was a wit as well as a seer − one of the most original and audacious wits that the English race has produced.'

1914. LORD BRYCE: 'You felt he was hunting for truth, and you enjoyed the sense that he allowed you to be his companion in the chase.'

1938. G. M. YOUNG: '[In searching for the greatest Victorian mind] we are looking for a man who was in and of his age, and who could have been of no other: a man with sympathy to share, and genius to judge, its sentiments and movements; a man not too illustrious or consummate to be companionable, but one, nevertheless, whose ideas took root and are still bearing; whose influence, passing from one fit mind to another, could transmit, and can still impart, the most precious element in Victorian civilization, its robust and masculine sanity. Such a man there was: and I award the place to Walter Bagehot . . . Of the Victorian mind, by which I mean the kind of intelligence that one learns to look for and recognize in the years of his maturity, say, from 1846 when he was twenty to 1877 when he died, the characteristics that most impress me are capaciousness and energy. It had room for so many ideas, and threw them about as lustily as a giant baby playing skittles. The breadth and vigour of Bagehot's mind appear on every page he has left, and they were, we know, not less conspicuous in his conversation and the conduct of affairs. But what was peculiarly his own was the perfect management of all this energy and all these resources.'

1943. WALT ROSTOW: 'His views on the trade cycle . . . incorporate his special gifts of generalization. One never loses touch with the institutions Bagehot is describing, nor the people who infuse them. Few latter-day cycle theorists, even those who have explicitly dealt with the so-called "psychological factors", have permitted themselves such a bland and relevant observation as: "All people are most credulous when they are most happy."'

1965. SIR WILLIAM HALEY: '[In his literary essays] he had sense, shrewdness, taste, sympathy, imagination, and an equal regard for the world of practice and feeling . . . He showed us that to be serious was not to be dull, and to be gay was not to be trivial.'

1968. PEREGRINE WORSTHORNE (on the historical essays): 'Although most of these essays were written more than a hundred years ago . . . they are more truly revealing about British politics . . . than most of what is being written in the newspapers and journals at the present time. It is no exaggeration to say that if extracts were now reprinted every week in the Sunday newspapers, the public would learn more about Harold Wilson, Enoch Powell and General de Gaulle and the rest than they do from reading . . . what they have perforce to read instead . . . [He] is such glorious fun to read. Under his spell the black clouds of confusion which make society seem so inexplicable and frightening begin to break up and one feels, most wonderful feeling of all, the sunshine of *understanding* breaking through.'

So why did Bagehot never become widely read? There seem to be a myriad reasons. One was his unpronounceable name, which made people reluctant to quote him. Another was his association with the nineteenth-century *Economist*, not many people's idea of an inspiring read. Yet another was the difficulty of categorizing a man who was a banker, editor, essayist, journalist and failed politician, who wrote *inter alia* on economics, education, history, law, literature, politics, religion and social psychology. His books cover an odd range of heavy-sounding subjects under deadly titles, those published during his lifetime being: *Estimates of Some Englishmen and Scotchmen*; *The English Constitution*; *A Practical Plan for Assimilating the English and American Money, as a Step Towards a Universal Money*; *Physics and Politics or Thoughts on the Application of the Principles of 'Natural Selection' and 'Inheritance' to Political Society* and *Lombard Street: a Description of the Money Market*. Then there is the tendency of self-important intellectuals to dismiss a man who wrote entertainingly and colloquially as lightweight and the assumption of this age of 'experts' that the polymath is by definition superficial, complemented by the arrogant and inaccurate presumption that academic progress will have long ago rendered Bagehot's ideas on all his areas of interest out-of-date. And modern readers are narrow; few are attracted by the notion of reading about both the money market and social Darwinism, the English constitution and the poetry of Shelley. Yet one of the glories of Bagehot is that each one of his areas of interest contributes to all the others: an article on discount houses may draw on poetry; an essay on Edward Gibbon brings in the money market.

In the 1960s, the distinguished historian Jacques Barzun considered why Bagehot remained 'a shadowy figure in that part of the public mind where reputations are considered settled' and put his finger on what was by then a key element: 'if a man has been dead nearly a hundred years and is "well-known" without being known well, a certain impatience arises at the mere mention of his name. It would be better for him to exchange his ambiguous position for one of complete obscurity. It is easier to pull Kierkegaard out of nowhere and establish his complex presence than to revise our judgements of those who have only half entered the Pantheon, whose nose and cheekbone only are showing'.

Barzun was introducing the historical volumes of *The Collected Works of Walter Bagehot*, *The Economist*'s stately tribute to its most revered name. Though well edited, beautifully produced, and a treasure-chest for those prepared to open them, the fifteen uniform navy-blue volumes did little to attract the unconverted. Like the editor of the *Works*, Norman St John-Stevas (now Lord St John of Fawsley), the paper's luminaries sought to bring their great man to a wider public. Prime Ministers and ex-Prime Ministers were hauled in to pay tribute. In 1967 Harold Wilson unveiled a blue plaque on 12

Upper Belgrave Street, where Bagehot lived from 1861 to 1870; Edward Heath spoke at the launch of the political volumes in 1974, while Harold Macmillan did the honours in 1978 for the economic and Margaret Thatcher for the miscellaneous and last volumes in 1986.

Perhaps such attention from the great and the old merely serves to give an impression of Bagehot as the object of veneration of an 'army of fogies' (one of his appellations for the Conservative Party). It is an unfortunate fate for someone whose gaiety and boyishness persisted throughout his life, yet it has helped to distance him further from those who might be induced to sample him not for his common sense, which the respectable continually stress in an off-putting way, but for his sheer ability to invigorate his readers in any generation. One of his contemporaries observed that one seldom asked Bagehot a question 'without his answer making you either think or laugh, or both think and laugh together'. His writings have the same effect.

It is rare to find any attentive reader of Bagehot who does not develop an enormous affection for him: as a later *Economist* editor put it simply, he was 'a wonderful man'. Yet his devoted admirers face enormous obstacles to their evangelism. It is a frustration akin to that of the man who believes he has found the secret of life but cannot persuade anyone to listen to it. Here is my effort to spread the light.

I do not intend to waste space that might be Bagehot's, but a brief biography is necessary. Superficially, his life seems uneventful. He was born in 1826 in Langport, a prosperous Somerset town, into a background of banking and trading. He was educated at the nonconformist Bristol College and University College, London, where he performed brilliantly. He travelled a little, was called to the Bar but as a career opted instead for provincial banking with freelance writing as a hobby. In 1855, with his great friend Richard Holt Hutton, later editor first of *The Economist* and then of the *Spectator*, he founded the *National Review*.

Bagehot's desire to write about economics brought him into the ambit of the Liberal politician James Wilson, who had founded *The Economist* in 1843, and in 1858 he married Eliza, eldest of the six Wilson girls; their childless marriage was happy. Wilson went to India in 1859 as Financial Member of the Council and died there the following year, leaving Bagehot in charge of his family affairs and his paper. The following year Bagehot took over from Holt Hutton and until his death in 1877 simultaneously edited *The Economist* and managed a bank branch. He was respected in the City and in political circles, where his wise and non-partisan advice was sought by both Conservative and Liberal Chancellors of the Exchequer.

Behind these rather dull facts was a life of unusual intellectual and emotional intensity, beginning with his mother's madness. When his parents married, Thomas Bagehot was twenty-eight; Edith, ten years his senior, was a beautiful widow with three sons. Together they had two children, but the first died at three years of age. While Walter was very young one of his half-brothers died and another was killed in an accident; the survivor and eldest was feeble-minded. Edith, a woman of great wit and *joie de vivre*, was driven into the first of her bouts of insanity. 'Every trouble in life is a joke compared to madness,' Walter Bagehot was often to say. It was to dominate most of his life, for Edith predeceased him by only seven years. Yet he was passionately attached to her, for she was a remarkable woman and their minds were very similar. 'There is nothing like "speaking the truth from the heart" even where people differ,' she wrote to him once, 'and between parents and children these are the only discussions which really make correspondence interesting and valuable for time and eternity.' So when the following year she wrote him some deluded letters, he responded honestly and critically.

If she was yeast, her husband Thomas was ballast. Dependable, affectionate and well grounded in history, philosophy and politics, he guided his son's reading and general education. To the sixteen-year-old Walter he wrote that education was like a tree: 'The roots must be deep and firm if the trunk is to grow high and its branches spread widely, and all its parts must grow together.' Between the two of them, Bagehot had the best of educations: his intellect and emotions were in harmony. Sensitive, perceptive and with a remorseless eye for the incongruous and the absurd, he cast a detached and sardonic eye on his fellow-man. His friend Hutton likened him to a naturalist: a better comparison might be a lepidopterist.

Bagehot had in abundance what he considered a prerequisite for genius – 'an experiencing nature'. An example was the effect on him of spending a few months in France in 1851, where his visit luckily coincided with Louis Napoleon's *coup d'état*, an event which he thoroughly enjoyed and on which he published a series of letters whose apparent frivolity maddened many respectable people. But the letters had much more to them than provocative wit: they showed a young man ruminating on the conflict between order and liberty and the contrasts between England and France in a truly original way.

Bagehot always, said James Bryce, 'made a new cut into things'. More than that, because all his observations on the world are rooted in his fascination with human behaviour, many of his observations have an extraordinary timelessness. This, as well as his humour and the sparkle of his mind, wins him new admirers in every generation – admirers who, unlike him, care that he should be appreciated by posterity. 'I am afraid I am callous, possibly proud, and do not care for mere general reputation,' he wrote once to Eliza. 'Of course it wd. be a pleasure if it shd. come, but it is a thing which no sane man ought to make necessary to his happiness, or think of but as a temporary luxury, even if it shd. come to him. First-rate fame – the fame of great productive artists – is a matter of ultimate certainty, but no other fame is. Posterity cannot take up little people, there are so many of them.' He was not a little person; his first-rate fame will come.

R.D.E.

ACKNOWLEDGEMENTS

I am grateful to everyone who took an interest in this book, particularly to Penny Butler, who put in a lot of work as my enthusiastic and wise unofficial editor and persuaded me to cast off the restrictions of the thematic approach. Pippa Allen and Melinda Rees efficiently typed out an enormous number of selections from Bagehot for use here and in *The Pursuit of Reason: The Economist, 1843–1993*. (I have inevitably drawn heavily on what I wrote about Bagehot in *The Pursuit of Reason*.) At *The Economist*, Rupert Pennant-Rea, Hugo Meynell and Sarah Child eased the book's conception, Helen Alexander provided me with much-needed resources and Helen Mann helped me as unstintingly as she helps everyone. My publisher, Andrew Franklin, was his usual brilliant and infuriating self. Christine Collins copy-edited the manuscript and was of great assistance. My agent, Felicity Bryan, continues to be wonderful. Carol Scott has been filing, typing and researching as well as solving my practical problems and calming me for over two years: without her, I doubt if I would have finished anything.

Of the many friends who humoured me by enthusing about their enforced diet of Bagehot, Nina Clarke, Gordon Lee, James McGuire, Jill Neville, Una O'Donoghue and George Watson deserve special thanks.

The book is dedicated to David Gordon, chief executive of *The Economist* until April 1993. Not only did he voluntarily give me the moral and practical support I needed to produce both this anthology and the history of the paper, but he made good jokes too. Besides, we enjoy Bagehot for the same reasons.

METHOD

This should have more properly been called *A Highly Subjective Selection of Some of My Favourite Examples of the Writing of Bagehot*, but the marketing department refused to wear it.

Items in this anthology range in length from nine to 14,000 words. After much thought, I decided not to cut the articles, essays and the chapter from *The English Constitution*, for part of the pleasure of Bagehot lies in his discursiveness and his asides; however, where the surgery could be done neatly, I have extracted passages, paragraphs and one-liners from longer pieces.

After much agonizing, I decided simply to arrange the material in alphabetical order rather than divide it by discipline (economics, history, literature) or themes (business, education, human character, religion, trade). This has produced what I hope is a pleasingly random effect. It is the only way of avoiding losing readers for the categories they think they are not interested in. A section called 'Business' is doomed to repel many, who may, just may, read something called 'Businessmen and Theoreticians' if they come across it accidentally. I plead with readers to abandon their prejudices. 'The Special Dangers of High Commercial Developments' may sound like a yawn. In fact it is the best explanation I've seen for why Robert Maxwell ruined his business. 'The Gains of the World by the Two Last Wars in Europe' is a brilliant analysis of the balance of power.

Favouring clarity above pedantry, I have very occasionally changed a word without acknowledging the fact and cut something out without leaving an ellipsis.

All text save 'The Proposed College for Women' comes from *The Collected Works of Walter Bagehot* (*WB*); for all substantial extracts I give the location in *WB* and the year and location of first publication, even if the version in *WB* is slightly amended because of Bagehot's second thoughts. For short, untitled extracts and aphorisms, sources in *WB* are given on pages 270–71

R.D.E.

9

The academies are asylums of the ideas and the taste of the last age.

All established customs will find grave people to defend them, and ingenious reasons are soon found for them.

An ambassador is not simply an aent; he is also a spectacle. He is sent abroad for show as well as for substance

Any aid to a present bad bank is the surest mode of preventing the establishment of a future good bank.

As a rule, and particular cases excepted, every new destructive invention is a great evil; it causes new expense, and renders useless old and valued implements.

ABSENCE OF REPOSE

Tranquillity can never be the lot of those who rule nations. Glory they may have; the praise of men; the approbation of their own consciences; the happiness which springs from the full occupation of every faculty and every hour; the intense interest with which dealing with great affairs vivifies the whole of existence; the supreme felicity of all allotted to men – that of feeling that they have lived the life and may die the death of the truest benefactors of their race. All these rewards they may aspire to; but *repose*, a sense of enduring security, comfortable and confident relaxation of 'having attained', of being safe in port, of everything 'being made snug', which enables a man to say to his soul, 'Soul! thou hast much peace laid up for many years: eat, drink, be merry, and sleep;' – these blessings are not for either sovereigns or statesmen, at least not for those of Europe in modern days.

(*WB*, xiv, 268, from 'The State of Europe', *National Review*, 1864)

ADMINISTRATION

[Sir Robert Peel] was a great administrator. Civilization requires this. In a simple age work may be difficult, but it is scarce. There are fewer people, and everybody wants fewer things. The mere tools of civilization seem in some sort to augment work. In early times, when a despot wishes to govern a distant province, he sends down a satrap on a grand horse, with other people on little horses; and very little is heard of the satrap again unless he send back some of the little people to tell what he has been doing. No great labour of superintendence is possible. Common rumour and casual complaints are the sources of intelligence. If it seem certain that the province is in a bad state, satrap No. 1 is recalled, and satrap No. 2 sent out in his stead. In civilized countries the process is different. You erect a *bureau* in the province you want to govern; you make it write letters and copy letters; it sends home eight reports per diem to the head *bureau* in St Petersburg. Nobody does a sum in the province without somebody doing the same sum in the capital, to 'check him', and see that he does it correctly. The consequence of this is, to throw on the heads of departments an amount of reading and labour which can only be accomplished by the greatest natural aptitude, the most efficient training, the most firm and regular industry. Under a free government it is by no means better, perhaps in some respects it is worse. It is true that many questions which, under the French despotism, are referred to Paris, are settled in England on the very spot where they are to be done, without reference to London at all. But as a set-off, a constitutional administrator has to be always consulting others, finding out what this man or that man chooses to think; learning which form of error is believed by Lord B., which by Lord C.; adding up the errors of the alphabet, and seeing what portion of what he thinks he ought to do, they will all of them together allow him to do. Likewise, though the personal freedom and the individual discretion which free governments allow to their subjects seem at first likely to diminish the work which those governments have to do, it may be doubted whether it does so really and in the end. Individual discretion strikes out so many more pursuits, and some supervision must be maintained over each of those pursuits. No despotic government would consider the police force of London enough to keep down, watch, and superintend such a population; but then no despotic government would have such a city as London to keep down. The freedom of growth allows the possibility of growth; and though liberal governments take so much less in proportion upon them, yet the scale of operations is so much enlarged by the continual exercise of civil liberty, that the real work is ultimately perhaps as immense. While a despotic government is regulating ten per cent of ten men's actions, a free government has to regulate one per cent of a hundred men's actions.

(*WB*, iii, 253–4, from The Character of 'Sir Robert Peel',
National Review, 1856)

ADOLESCENCE

Most boys are conceited; most boys have a wonderful belief in their own power. 'At sixteen,' says Mr Disraeli, 'everyone believes he is the most peculiar man who ever lived.' And there is certainly no difficulty in imagining Mr Disraeli thinking so. The difficulty is not to entertain this proud belief, but to keep it; not to have these lofty visions, but to hold them. Manhood comes, and with it come the plain facts of the world. There is no illusion in them; they have a distinct teaching: 'The world,' they say definitely, 'does not believe in you. You fancy you have a call to a great career, but no one else even imagines that you fancy it. You do not dare to say it out loud.' Before the fear of ridicule and the touch of reality the illusions of youth pass away, and with them goes all intellectual courage. We have no longer the hardihood; we have scarcely the wish to form our own creed, to think our own thought, to act upon our own belief; we try to be sensible, and we end in being ordinary; we fear to be eccentric, and we end in being commonplace.

(*WB*, iii, 127, from 'William Pitt', *National Review*, 1861)

AGE

An old man of the world has no great objects, no telling enthusiasm, no large proposals, no noble reforms; his advice is that of the old banker, 'Live, sir, from day to day, and don't trouble yourself!' Years of acquiescing in proposals as to which he has not been consulted, of voting for measures which he did not frame, and in the wisdom of which he often did not believe, of arguing for proposals from half of which he dissents, – usually de-intellectualize a parliamentary states-man before he comes to half his power.

(*WB*, iii, 144, from 'William Pitt', *National Review*, 1861)

AMERICAN IMMATURITY

It was the first time that the experiment had been tried of letting a nation of freemen, and of free men in the highest phase of civilization, grow and expand quite without any resisting or constraining force to limit and compress and mould it into the shapes which a society of nations necessarily imposes. It was supposed that the political life of this people would grow like a forest tree, all the more rich and free and magnificent for not being jostled by a number of competing neighbours. So many of the miseries of Europe had obviously arisen from the fierce competitions and rivalries of nations, – so much freedom had been extinguished simply because it was incompatible with the genius of neighbouring powers, that at that time the idea of a continent over which a single nation might spread and stretch at pleasure, without encountering a single formidable rival, had in it a peculiar attraction for the Liberal party. Here it was thought all the conditions of political freedom were combined in the most perfect harmony. No Liberal politician of really thoughtful intellect, however, is so well satisfied on this head now. Very many – amongst whom we must reckon ourselves – have come to the conclusion that it is with young nations much as it is with young children: – if they are brought up in close association with each other, they will fight much and create the most dreadful disturbances in their youth, and yet they will on the whole grow up into more various, more interesting, and better disciplined forms of mature life than 'only children' educated at home. The constant action and reaction of different tempers, different talents, different tastes, is, on the whole, an advantage, a great advantage, to their originality of character – a great advantage also to their self-knowledge. Liberal politicians, who are far from wishing to see the dull uniformity of American life broken by the successful inauguration of so great a national evil as a slave empire, yet admit freely that the experiment of one nation for one continent has turned out on the whole far from well. The American nation has very much the sort of faults which 'only children' are said to have. It has no correct measure of its own strength. Having never entered into close competition with any other nation, it indulges in that infinite braggadocio which a public school so soon rubs out of a conceited boy.

(*WB*, iv, 97–8, from 'The "Monroe Doctrine" in 1823 and 1863',
The Economist, 1863)

ARID INTELLECTUALS

There are a whole class of minds which prefer the literary delineation of objects to the actual eyesight of them. To some life is difficult. An insensible nature, like a rough hide, resists the breath of passing things; an unobserving retina in vain depicts whatever a quicker eye does not explain. But anyone can understand a book; the work is done, the facts observed, the formulae suggested, the subjects classified. Of course, it needs labour, and a following fancy, to peruse the long lucubrations and descriptions of others; but a fine detective sensibility is unnecessary; type is plain, an earnest attention will follow it and know it. To this class Mr Macaulay belongs: and he has characteristically maintained that dead authors are more fascinating than living people. 'These friendships,' he tells us, 'are exposed to no danger from the occurrences by which other attachments are weakened or dissolved. Time glides on; fortune is inconstant; tempers are soured; bonds which seemed indissoluble are daily sundered by interest, by emulation, or by caprice. But no such cause can affect the silent converse which we hold with the highest of human intellects. That placid intercourse is disturbed by no jealousies or resentments. These are the old friends who are never seen with new faces; who are the same in wealth and in poverty, in glory and in obscurity. With the dead there is no rivalry; in the dead there is no change. Plato is never sullen; Cervantes is never petulant; Demosthenes never comes unseasonably; Dante never stays too long. No difference of political opinion can alienate Cicero; no heresy can excite the horror of Bossuet.' But Bossuet is dead; and Cicero was a Roman; and Plato wrote in Greek. Years and manners separate us from the great. After dinner, Demosthenes *may* come unseasonably; Dante might stay too long. *We* are alienated from the politician, and have a horror of the theologian. Dreadful idea, having Demosthenes for an intimate friend! He had pebbles in his mouth; he was always urging action; he spoke such good Greek; we cannot dwell on it, – it is too much. Only a mind impassive to our daily life, unalive to bores and evils, to joys and sorrows, incapable of the deepest sympathies, a prey to print, could imagine it. The mass of men have stronger ties and warmer hopes. The exclusive devotion to books tires. We require to love and hate, to act and live.

(*WB*, i, 401–2, from 'Mr Macaulay', *National Review*, 1856)

'THE ASSASSINATION OF MR LINCOLN'*

The murder of Mr Lincoln is a very great and very lamentable event, perhaps the greatest and most lamentable which has occurred since the *coup d'état*, if not since Waterloo. It affects directly and immensely the welfare of the three most powerful countries in the world, America, France, and England, and it affects them all for evil. Time, circumstances, and agent have all conspired as by some cruel perversity to increase the mischief and the horror of an act which at any moment, or under any circumstances, would have been most mischievous and horrible. It is not merely that a great man has passed away, but he has disappeared at the very time when his special greatness seemed almost essential to the world, when his death would work the widest conceivable evil, when the chance of replacing him, even partially, approached nearest to zero, and he has been removed

* Bagehot made amends here for having misread and grossly underestimated Lincoln until late in his career.

in the very way which almost alone among causes of death could have doubled the political injury entailed by the decease itself. His death destroys one of the strongest guarantees for continued peace between his country and the external world, while his murder diminishes almost indefinitely the prospects of reconciliation between the two camps into which that country has for four years been divided. At the very instant of all others, when North and South had most reason to see in his character a possibility of reunion, and to dread the accession of his inevitable successor, a Southerner murders him to place that successor in his chair, gives occasion for an explosion of sectional hate, and makes a man who has acknowledged that hate master of armies which can give to that hate an almost limitless expression in act. At the very moment when the dread of war between the Union and Western Europe seemed, after inflicting incessant injury for four years, about to die away, a murderer deprives us of the man who had most power and most will to maintain peace, and thereby enthrones another whose tendencies are at best an unknown quantity, but who is sure, from inexperience, to sway more towards violence than his predecessor. The injury done alike to the North, to the South, and to the world, is so irremediable, the consequences of the act may be so vast, and are certainly so numerous, that it is with some diffidence we attempt to point out the extent of the American loss, and the result that loss may produce.

The greatness of the American loss seems to us to consist especially in this. To guide and moderate a great revolution, and heal up the wounds created by civil war, it is essential that the government should be before all things strong. If it is weak it is sure either to be violent, or to allow some one of the jarring sections of the community to exhibit violence unrestrained, to rely on terror as the French convention, under a false impression of its own dangers, did, or to permit a party to terrorize, as the first ministry of Louis XVIII did. The 'Reign of Terror' and the 'Terreur Blanc' were alike owing, one to an imaginary the other to a real weakness on the part of the governing power. There are so many passions to be restrained, so many armed men to be dealt with, so many fanatic parties to convince, so many private revenges to check, so many extra legal acts to do, that nothing except an irresistible government can ever hope to secure the end which every government by instinct tries to attain, namely, external order. Now, the difficulty of creating a strong government in America is almost insuperable. The people in the first place dislike government, not this or that administration, but government in the abstract, to such a degree that they have invented a quasi philosophical theory, proving that government, like war or harlotry, is a 'necessary evil'. Moreover, they have constructed a machinery in the shape of states, specially and deliberately calculated to impede central action, to stop the exercise of power, to reduce government, except so far as it is expressed in arrests by the parish constable, to an impossibility. They have an absolute parliament, and though they have a strong executive, it is, when opposed to the people, or even when in advance of the people, paralysed by a total absence of friends. To make this weakness permanent they have deprived even *themselves* of absolute power, have first forbidden themselves to change the Constitution, except under circumstances which never occur, and have then, through the machinery of the common schools, given to that Constitution the moral weight of a religious document. The construction of a strong government, therefore, *i.e.* of a government able to do great acts very quickly, is really impossible, except in one event. The head of the executive may, by an infinitesimal chance, be a man so exactly representative of the people, that his acts always represent their thoughts, so shrewd that he can steer his way amidst the legal difficulties piled deliberately in his path, and so good that he desires power only for the national ends. The chance of obtaining such a man was, as we say, infinitesimal; but the United States, by a good fortune, of which they will one day be cruelly sensible, had obtained him. Mr Lincoln, by a rare combination of qualities – patience, sagacity, and honesty – by a still more rare sympathy, not with the best of his nation but the best average of his nation, and by a moderation rarest of all, had attained such vast moral authority that he could make all the hundred wheels of the Constitution move in one direction without exerting any physical force. For example, in order to secure the constitutional prohibition of slavery, it is absolutely essential that some *forty-eight* separate representative bodies, differing in modes of election, in geographical interests, in education, in prejudices, should harmoniously and strongly co-operate, and so immense was Mr Lincoln's influence – an influence, it must be remembered, unsupported in this case by power – that had he lived, that co-operation, of which statesmen might well despair, would have been a certainty. The President had, in fact, attained to the very position – the dictatorship – to use a bad description, required by revolutionary times. At the same time, this vast authority, not having been seized illegally, and being wielded by a man radically good – who for example really reverenced civil liberty and could tolerate venomous opposition – could never be directed to ends wholly disapproved by the ways of those who conferred it. It was, in fact, the authority which nations find it so very hard to secure, which only Italy and America have in our time secured, – a good and benevolent, but resistless temporary despotism. That despotism, moreover, was exercised by a man whose brain was a very great one. We do not know in history such an example of the growth of a ruler in wisdom as was exhibited by Mr Lincoln. Power and responsibility visibly widened his mind and elevated his character. Difficulties, instead of irritating him as they do most men, only increased his reliance on patience; opposition, instead of ulcerating, only made him more tolerant and determined. The very style of his public papers altered, till the very man who had written in an official despatch about 'Uncle Sam's web feet', drew up his final inaugural in a style which extorted from critics so hostile as the *Saturday Reviewers*, a burst of involuntary admiration. A good but benevolent temporary despotism, wielded by a wise man, was the very instrument the wisest would have desired for the United States; and in losing Mr Lincoln, the Union has lost it. The great authority attached by law to the President's office reverts to Mr Johnson, but the far greater moral authority belonging to Mr Lincoln disappears. There is no longer any person in the Union whom the Union dare or will trust to do exceptional acts, to remove popular generals, to override crotchetty states, to grant concessions to men in arms, to act when needful, as in the *Trent* case, athwart the popular instinct.

2. The consequences of this immense loss can as yet scarcely be conjectured, for the one essential datum, the character of the President, is not known. It is probable that that character has been considerably

misrepresented. Judging from information necessarily imperfect, we have formed an *ad interim* opinion that Mr Johnson is very like an average Scotch tradesman, very shrewd, very pushing, very narrow, and very obstinate, inclined to take the advice of anyone with more *knowledge* than himself, but unable to act on it when opposed to certain central convictions, not oppressive, but a little indifferent if his plans result in oppression, and subject to fits of enthusiasm as hard to deal with as fits of drunkenness. Should this estimate prove correct, we shall have in the United States a government absolutely resolved upon immediate abolition, whatever its consequences, foolish or wise according to the character of its advisers, very incapable of diplomacy, which demands above all things knowledge, very firm, excessively unpopular with its own agents, and liable to sudden and violent changes of course, so unaccountable as almost to appear freaks. Such a government will find it difficult to overcome the thousand difficulties presented by the organization of the states, by the bitterness of partisans, or by the exasperated feelings of the army, and will be driven, we fear, to overcome them by violence, or at least to deal with them in a spirit of unsparing rigour. It is, therefore, we conceive, *prima facie* probable that the South will be slower to come in, and much less ready to settle down when it has come in, than it would have been under Mr Lincoln; and this reluctance will be increased by the consciousness that the North has at length obtained a plausible excuse for relentless severity. It will also be much more ready to escape its difficulties by foreign war. Beyond those two somewhat vague propositions, there are as yet too few data whatever for judgement. Least of all are there data to decide whether the North will adhere to the policy of moderation. Upon the whole we think they will, the average American showing in politics that remarkable lenity which arises from perfect freedom, and the consequent absence of fear; but he is also excitable, and it is on the first direction of that excitement that everything will depend. If it takes the direction of vengeance, Mr Johnson, whose own mind has been embittered against the planters by family injuries, may break loose from his Cabinet; but if, as is much more probable, it takes the direction of over reverence for the policy of the dead, he must coerce his own tendencies until time and the sobering effect of great power have extinguished them.

He is certainly a strong man, though of rough type, and the effect of power on the strong is usually to soften.

(*WB*, iv, 407–11, from *The Economist*, 1865)

AUTO-DIDACTS

In our notion the object of a university education is to train intellectual men for the pursuits of an intellectual life. For though education by training or reading will not make people quicker or cleverer or more inventive, yet it will make them soberer. A man who finds out for himself all that he knows is rarely remarkable for calmness; the excitement of the discovery, and a weak fondness for his own investigations, a parental inclination to believe in their excessive superiority, combine to make the self-taught and original man dogmatic, decisive, and detestable. He comes to you with a notion that Noah discarded in the ark, and attracts attention to it, as if it were a stupendous novelty of his own. A book-bred man rarely does this; he knows that his notions are old notions, that his favourite theories are the rejected axioms of long deceased people: he is too well aware how much may be said for every side of everything to be very often overweeningly positive on any point.

(*WB*, vii, 345, from 'Oxford', *Prospective Review*, 1852)

Being a bachelor, he was a kind of amateur in life, and did not really care.

The being without an opinion is so painful to human nature that most people will leap to hasty opinion rather than undergo it.

The best history is but like the art of Rembrandt; it casts a vivid light on certain selected causes, and those which were best and greatest; it leaves all the rest in shadow and unseen.

A bureaucracy is sure to think that its duty is to augment official power, official business, or official members, rather than to leave free the energies of mankind; it overdoes the quantity of government, as well as impairs its quality.

Business is really more agreeable than pleasure; it interests the whole mind, the aggregate nature of man more continuously, and more deeply. But it does not *look* as if it did.

BARTER

The air and the sunlight – the riches of nature – are nothing in political economy, because everyone can have them, and therefore no one will give anything for them. 'Wealth' is not such for economic purposes, unless it is scarce and transferable, and so desirable that someone is anxious to give something else for it. The business of the science is not with the general bounty of nature to all men, but with the privileged possessions – bodily and mental powers included – which some have, and which others have not.

Unluckily when we come to inquire what makes these things exchange for more or less of value, one among another, we find ourselves in the middle of a question which involves many and difficult elements, and which requires delicate handling. Most of the difficulties which are felt in reflecting on the entire subject are owing to a deficient conception of the primitive ingredient. And this will surprise no one conversant with the history of science, for most errors in it have been introduced at the beginning, just as the questions which a child is apt to ask are in general the ones which it is hardest to answer.

It is usual to begin treating the subject by supposing a state of barter, and this is in principle quite right, for 'money' is a peculiar commodity which requires explanation, and the simplest cases of exchange take place without it. But it is apt to be forgotten that a state of barter is not a very easy thing fully to imagine. The very simplicity which renders it useful in speculation makes it more and more unlike our present complex experience. Happily, though barter has died out of the adult life of civilized communities, there remains an age when we, most of us, had something to do with it. To schoolboys money is always a scarce and often a brief possession, and they are obliged to eke out the want by simpler expedients. The memories of most of us may help them in the matter, though their present life certainly will not.

Suppose, then, that one boy at school has a ham sent him from home (those who object to trivial illustrations must be sent back to the Platonic Socrates to learn that they are of the most special use in the most difficult matters, and be set to read the history of philosophy that they may learn what becomes of the pomposity which neglects them), and suppose that another boy has cake, and that each has more of his own than he cares for and lacks something of the other, what are the proportions in which they will exchange? If boy A likes his own ham scarcely at all, or not very much, and if he is very fond of cake, he will be ready to barter a great deal of it against a little of boy B's cake; and if boy B is fond of cake too and does not care so much for ham, cake will be at a premium, and a very little of it will go a great way in the transaction, especially if the cake is a small one and the ham a big one; but if, on the contrary, both boys care much for ham, and neither much for cake, and also the ham be small and the cake large, then the ham will be at a premium, the cake at a discount, and both sides of the exchange will be altered. The use of this simplest of all cases is that you see the inevitable complexity of, and that you cannot artificially simplify, the subject. There are in every exchange, as we here see, no less than six elements which more or less affect it in general: first, the quantities of the two commodities, and next, two feelings in each exchanger – first, his craving for the commodity of the other, and secondly his liking or disinclination for his own. In every transaction, small or great, you will be liable to blunder unless you consider all six.

The introduction of money introduces in this respect no new element.

(*WB*, xi, 302–3, from 'Adam Smith and Our Modern Economy', first published in *Economic Studies*, 1880)

BISHOPS

In general we observe that those become most eminent in the sheep-fold who partake most eminently of the qualities of the wolf. Nor is this surprising. The church is ... a congregation of men, faithful indeed, but faithful in various degrees. In every corporation or combination of men, no matter for what purpose collected, there are certain secular qualities which attain eminence as surely as oil rises above water. Attorneys are for the world, and the world is for attorneys. Activity, vigour, sharp-sightedness, tact, boldness, watchfulness, and such as these, raise a man in the church as certainly as in the State; so long as there is wealth and preferment in the one, they will be attained a good deal as wealth and office are in the other. The *prowling* faculties will have their way. Those who hunger and thirst after riches will have riches, and those who hunger not, will not.

(*WB*, i, 218, from 'Bishop Butler', *National Review*, 1854)

BOOMS

The mercantile community will have been unusually fortunate if during the period of rising prices it has not made great mistakes. Such a period naturally excites the sanguine and the ardent; they fancy that the prosperity they see will last always, that it is only the beginning of a greater prosperity. They altogether over-estimate the demand for the article they deal in, or the work they do. They all in their degree – and the ablest and the cleverest the most – work much more than they should, and trade far above their means. Every great crisis reveals the excessive speculations of many houses which no one before suspected, and which commonly indeed had not begun, or had not carried very far, those speculations till they were tempted by the daily rise of price and the surrounding fever . . .

The good times too, of high price almost always engender much fraud. All people are most credulous when they are most happy; and when much money has just been made, when some people are really making it, when most people think they are making it, there is a happy opportunity for ingenious mendacity. Almost everything will be believed for a little while, and long before discovery the worst and most adroit deceivers are geographically or legally beyond the reach of punishment. But the harm they have done diffuses harm, for it weakens credit still farther.

(*WB*, ix, 127, from *Lombard Street*, 1873)

BUREAUCRATS

In a public office, it would be indecorous to rush like a mighty wind. Yet it would be a great error to imagine that, in so large a department of human life, no expedient to economize thought and to dispense, *pro tanto*, with the pain of reflection, had been discovered and adopted. That resource is what are called business habits. There is such a thing as the pomp of order. In every public office there is a grave official personage, who is always neat, whose papers are always filed, whose handwriting is always regular, who is considered a monster of experience, who can minute any proceeding, and docket any document. There is no finer or more saving investment of exertion than the formation of such habits. Under their safeguard, you may omit anything, and commit every blunder. The English people never expect anyone to be original. If it can be said, 'The gentleman whose conduct is so harshly impugned is a man of long experience, who is not wont to act hastily – who is remarkable for official precision – in whom many Secretaries of State have placed much reliance,' that will do; and it will not be too anxiously inquired what such a man has done. The immense probability is that he has done nothing. He is well aware that, so long as he can say anything is 'under consideration', he is safe – and so long as he is safe, he is happy.

(*WB*, vi, 92, from 'Thinking Government', *Saturday Review*, 1856)

EDMUND BURKE

Although [Edmund Burke] had rather a coarse, incondite temperament, not finely susceptible to the best influences, to the most exquisite beauties of the world in which he lived, he yet lived in that world thoroughly and completely. He did not take an interest, as a poet does, in the sublime because it is sublime, in the beautiful because it is beautiful; but he had the passions of more ordinary men in a degree, and of an intensity, which ordinary men may be most thankful that they have not. In no one has the intense faculty of intellectual hatred – the hatred which the absolute dogmatist has for those in whom he incarnates and personifies the opposing dogma – been fiercer and stronger: he, if any man, cast himself upon his time.

(*WB*, i, 417, from 'Mr Macaulay', *National Review*, 1856)

BUSINESSMEN AND THEORETICIANS

Years ago I heard Mr Cobden say at an Anti-Corn Law League meeting that 'political economy was the highest study of the human mind, for that the physical sciences required by no means so hard an effort'. An orator cannot be expected to be exactly precise, and of course political economy is in no sense the highest study of mind – there are others which are much higher, for they are concerned with things much nobler than wealth or money; nor is it true that the effort of mind which political economy requires is nearly as great as that required for the abstruser theories of physical science, for the theory of gravitation, or the theory of natural selection; but, nevertheless, what Mr Cobden meant had – as was usual with his first-hand mind – a great fund of truth. He meant that political economy –

effectual political economy, political economy which in complex problems succeeds – is a very difficult thing; something altogether more abstruse and difficult, as well as more conclusive, than that which many of those who rush in upon it have a notion of. It is an abstract science which labours under a special hardship. Those who are conversant with its abstractions are usually without a true contact with its facts; those who are in contact with its facts have usually little sympathy with and little cognisance of its abstractions. Literary men who write about it are constantly using what a great teacher calls 'unreal words' – that is, they are using expressions with which they have no complete vivid picture to correspond. They are like physiologists who have never dissected; like astronomers who have never seen the stars; and, in consequence, just when they seem to be reasoning at their best, their knowledge of the facts falls short. Their primitive picture fails them, and their deduction altogether misses the mark – sometimes, indeed, goes astray so far, that those who live and move among the facts, boldly say that they cannot comprehend 'how anyone can talk such nonsense'. While, on the other hand, these people who live and move among the facts often, or mostly, cannot of themselves put together any precise reasonings about them. Men of business have a solid judgement – a wonderful guessing power of what is going to happen – each in his own trade; but they have never practised themselves in reasoning out their judgements and in support-ing their guesses by argument; probably if they did so some of the finer and correcter parts of their anticipations would vanish. They are like the sensible lady to whom Coleridge said, 'Madam, I accept your conclusion, but you must let me find the logic for it.' Men of business can no more put into words much of what guides their life than they could tell another person how to speak their language. And so the 'theory of business' leads a life of obstruction, because theorists do not see the business, and the men of business will not reason out the theories. Far from wondering that such a science is not completely perfect, we should rather wonder that it exists at all.

(*WB*, xi, 226–7, from 'The Postulates of English Political Economy',
Fortnightly Review, 1876)

Civilized ages inherit the human nature which was victorious in barbarous ages, and that nature is, in many respects, not at all suited to civilized circumstances.

The commanding element in life and history is a great person. One Napoleon is worth fifty common generals; he can do far more, and what he does will be infinitely better remembered. No cabinet can effectually rule this country if it is a cabinet only – if it is not itself ruled by a great prime minister.

Commerce is like war; its result is patent. Do you make money or do you not make it? There is as little appeal from figures as from battles.

A common language, as far as our present experience goes, is hardly ever a bond of friendship, but it is very often, and naturally, a source of irritation to both the communities that speak it. Every trivial and disparaging remark passed upon one nation by another in a language common to both rubs the sores of wounded vanity.

Credit in business is like loyalty in government. You must take what you can find of it, and work with it if possible.

Credit – the disposition of one man to trust another – is singularly varying. In England, after a great calamity everybody is suspicious of everybody; as soon as that calamity is forgotten, everybody again confides in everybody.

Culture always diminishes intensity.

CALVINISM

What can be worse for people than to hear in their youth arguments, alike clamorous and endless, founded on ignorant interpretations of inconclusive words? As soon as they come to years of discretion all instructed persons cease to take part in such discussions, and often they say nothing at all on the great problems of human life and destiny. Sometimes the effect goes farther; those subjected to this training become not only silent but careless. There is nothing like Calvinism for generating indifference. The saying goes that the Scotchmen are those who believe most or least; and it is most natural that it should be so, for they have been so hurt and pestered with religious stimulants, that it is natural they should find total abstinence from them both pleasant and healthy.

(*WB*, iii, 110–11, from 'Adam Smith as a Person', *Fortnightly Review*, 1876)

THE CAPITALIST

The capitalist is the motive power in modern production, in the 'great commerce'. He settles what goods shall be made, and what not; what brought to market, and what not. He is the general of the army; he fixes on the plan of operations, organizes its means, and superintends its execution. If he does this well, the business succeeds and continues; if he does it ill, the business fails and ceases. Everything depends on the correctness of the unseen decisions, on the secret sagacity of the determining mind. And I am careful to dwell on this, though it is so obvious, and though no man of business would think it worth mentioning, because books forget it – because the writers of books are not familiar with it. They are taken with the conspicuousness of the working classes; they hear them say, it is we who made Birmingham, we who made Manchester, but you might as well say that it was the compositors who made *The Times* newspaper. No doubt the craftsmen were necessary to both, but of themselves they were insufficient to either. The printers do not settle what is to be printed; the writers even do not settle what is to be written. It is the editor who settles everything. He creates *The Times* from day to day; on his power of hitting the public fancy its prosperity and power rest; everything depends on his daily bringing to the public exactly what the public wants to buy; the rest of Printing House Square – all the steam-presses, all the type, all the staff, clever as so many of them are, are but implements which he moves.

In the very same way the capitalist edits the 'business'; it is he who settles what commodities to offer to the public; how and when to offer them, and all the rest of what is material. This monarchical structure of money business increases as society goes on, just as the corresponding structure of war business does, and from the same causes. In primitive times a battle depends as much on the prowess of the best fighting men, of some Hector or some Achilles, as on the good science of the general. But nowadays it is a man at the far end of a telegraph wire – a Count Moltke, with his head over some papers – who sees that the proper persons are slain, and who secures the victory. So in commerce. The primitive weavers are separate men with looms apiece, the primitive weapon makers separate men with flints apiece; there is no organized action, no planning, contriving, or foreseeing in either trade, except on the smallest scale; but now the whole is an affair of money and management; of a thinking man in a dark office, computing the prices of guns or worsteds. No doubt in some simple trades these essential calculations can be verified by several persons – by a board of directors, or something like it. But these trades, as the sagacity of Adam Smith predicted, and as painful experience now shows, are very few; the moment there comes anything difficult or complicated, the board 'does not see its way', and then, except it is protected by a monopoly, or something akin to monopoly, the individual capitalist beats it out of the field. But the details of this are not to my present purpose. The sole point now material is that the transference of capital from employment to employment involves the pre-existence of employment, and this pre-existence involves that of 'employers': of a set of persons – one or many, though usually one – who can effect the transfer of that capital from employment to employment, and can manage it when it arrives at the employment to which it is taken.

And this management implies knowledge. In all cases successful production implies the power of adapting means to ends, of making what you want as you want it. But after the division of labour has arisen, it implies much more than this; it then requires, too, that the producer should know the wants of the consumer, a man whom he mostly has never seen, whose name probably he does not know, very likely even speaking another language, living according to other habits, and having scarcely any point of intimate relation to the producer, except a liking for what he produces. And if a person who does not see is to suit another who is not seen, he must have much head-knowledge, an acquired learning in strange wants as well as of the mode of making things to meet them. A person possessing that knowledge is necessary to the process of transferring capital, for he alone can use it when the time comes, and if he is at the critical instant not to be found, the change fails, and the transfer is a loss and not a gain.

(*WB*, xi, 264–5, from 'The Postulates of English Political Economy',
Fortnightly Review, 1876)

CATHOLICISM

[Catholicism] advertises itself by its bold pretension; it says it is a king, a prophet, a supernatural agency; it can bind and loose; it has authority to speak; it has a lesson to teach; it teaches an unearthly morality; it tells men not to form ties in the world, not to go out of the world, not to be comfortable and rich, but to be poor and holy; to live as saints in convents, not to live as men in the world. This is a lesson which eager men learn readily, which imaginative men love to hear. It gets rid of the tameness of life, of the poorness of human duties, of the petty definiteness of ordinary existence. A superhuman morality will always be acceptable to aspiring youth; they will run to hear it, they will long to obey and practise it. Catholicism advertises for men with spiritual ambition, and she bids higher than any other creed.

(*WB*, ii, 275–6, from 'French Religiousness and M. Renan', *Spectator*,
1863)

CAVALIERS

The chill nature of the most brilliant among English historians [Macaulay] is shown in his defective dealing with the passionate eras of our history. He has never been attracted, or not proportionably attracted, by the singular mixture of heroism and slavishness, of high passion and base passion, which mark the Tudor period. The defect is apparent in his treatment of a period on which he has written powerfully – the time of the civil wars. He has never in the highest manner appreciated either of the two great characters – the Puritan and the Cavalier – which are the form and life of those years. What historian, indeed, has ever estimated the Cavalier character? There is Clarendon – the grave, rhetorical, decorous lawyer – piling words, congealing arguments, – very stately, a little grim. There is Hume – the Scotch metaphysician – who has made out the best case for such people as never were, for a Charles who never died, for a Strafford who would never have been attainted, – a saving, calculating north-countryman, – fat, impassive, – who lived on eightpence a day. What have these people to do with an enjoying English gentleman? It is easy for a *doctrinaire* to bear a *post-mortem* examination, – it is much the same whether he be alive or dead; but not so with those who live during their life, whose essence is existence, whose being is in anima-tion. There seem to be some characters who are not made for history, as there are some who are not made for old age. A Cavalier is always young. The buoyant life arises before us rich in hope, strong in vigour, irregular in action; men young and ardent, framed in the 'prodigality of nature'; open to every enjoyment, alive to every passion; eager, impulsive; brave without discipline; noble without principle; prizing luxury, despising danger, capable of high sentiment, but in each of whom the

> Addiction was to courses vain,
> His companies unlettered, rude, and shallow,
> His hours filled up with riots, banquets, sports;
> And never noted in him any study,
> Any retirement, any sequestration
> From open haunts and popularity.

We see these men setting forth or assembling to defend their king and church; and we see it without surprise; a rich daring loves danger; a deep excitability likes excitement. If we look around us, we may see what is analogous. Some say that the battle of the Alma was won by the 'uneducated gentry'; the 'uneducated gentry' would be Cavaliers now. The political sentiment is part of the character. The essence of Toryism is enjoyment. Talk of the ways of spreading a wholesome Conservatism throughout this country: give painful lectures, distribute weary tracts (and perhaps this is as well – you may be able to give an argumentative answer to a few objections, you may diffuse a distinct notion of the dignified dullness of politics); but as far as communicating and establishing your creed are concerned – try a little pleasure. The way to keep up old customs is, to enjoy old customs; the way to be satisfied with the present state of things is, to enjoy that state of things. Over the 'Cavalier' mind this world passes with a thrill of delight; there is an exultation in a daily event, zest in the 'regular thing', joy at an old feast. Sir Walter Scott is an example of this. Every habit and practice of old Scotland was inseparably in his mind associated with genial enjoyment. To propose to touch one of her institutions, to abolish one of those practices, was to touch a personal pleasure – a point on which his mind reposed, a thing of memory and hope. So long as this world is this world, will a buoyant life be the proper source of an animated Conservatism. – The 'church-and-king' enthusiasm has even a deeper connection with the Cavaliers. Carlyle has said in his vivid way, 'Two or three young gentlemen have said, "Go to, I will *make* a religion."' This is the exact opposite of what the irregular enjoying man can think or conceive. What! is he, with his untrained mind and his changeful heart and his ruleless practice, to create a creed? Is the gushing life to be asked to construct a cistern? Is the varying heart to be its own master, the evil practice its own guide? Sooner will a ship invent its own rudder, devise its own pilot, than the eager being will find out the doctrine which is to restrain him. The very intellect is a type of the confusion of the soul. It has little arguments on a thousand subjects, hearsay sayings, original flashes, small and bright, struck from the heedless mind by the strong impact of the world. And it has nothing else. It has no systematic knowledge; it has a hatred of regular attention. What can an understanding of this sort do with refined questioning or subtle investigation? It is obliged in a sense by its very nature to take what comes; it is overshadowed in a manner by the religion to which it is born; its conscience tells it that it owes obedience to something; it craves to worship something; that something, in both cases, it takes from the past. 'Thou hast not chosen me, but I have chosen thee,' might his faith say to a believer of this kind. A certain bigotry is altogether natural to him. His creed seems to him a primitive fact, as certain and evident as the stars. – The political faith (for it is a faith) of these persons is of a kind analogous. The virtue of loyalty assumes in them a passionate aspect, and overflows, as it were, all the intellect which belongs to the topic. This virtue, this need of our nature, arises, as political philosophers tell us, from the conscious necessity which man is under of obeying an external moral rule. We feel that we are by nature and by the constitution of all things under an obligation to conform to a certain standard, and we seek to find or to establish in the sphere without an authority which shall enforce it, shall aid us in compelling others and also in mastering ourselves. When a man impressed with this principle comes in contact with the institution of civil government as it now exists and as it has always existed, he finds what he wants – he discovers an authority; and he feels bound to submit to it. We do not, of course, mean that all this takes place distinctly and consciously in the mind of the person; on the contrary, the class of minds most subject to its influence are precisely those which have in general the least defined and accurate consciousness of their own operations, or of what befalls them. In matter of fact, they find themselves under the control of laws and of a polity from the earliest moment that they can remember, and they obey it from habit and custom years before they know why. Only in later life, when distinct thought is from an outward occurrence forced upon them, do they feel the necessity of some such power; and in proportion to their passionate and impulsive disposition they feel it the more. The law has in a less degree on them the same effect which military discipline has in a greater. It braces them to defined duties, and subjects them to a known authority. Quieter minds find this authority in an internal conscience; but in riotous natures its still small voice is lost if it be not echoed in loud harsh tones from the firm and outer world:

Their breath is agitation, and their life
A storm whereon they ride.

From without they crave a bridle and a curb. The doctrine of
non-resistance is no *accident* of the Cavalier character, though it seems
at first sight singular in an eager tumultuous disposition. So inconsistent is human nature, that it proceeds from the very extremity of that
tumult. They know that they cannot allow themselves to question the
authority which is upon them; they feel its necessity too acutely, their
intellect is untrained in subtle disquisitions, their conscience fluctuating,
their passions rising. They are sure that if they once depart from that
authority, their whole soul will be in anarchy. As a riotous state tends to
fall under a martial tyranny, a passionate mind tends to subject itself to
an extrinsic law – to enslave itself to an outward discipline. 'That is what
the king says, boy, and that was ever enough for Sir Henry Lee.' An
hereditary monarchy is, indeed, the very embodiment of this principle.
The authority is so defined, so clearly vested, so evidently intelligible; it
descends so distinctly from the past, it is imposed so conspicuously from
without. Anything free refers to the people; anything elected seems self-
chosen. 'The divinity that doth hedge a king' consists in his evidently
representing an unmade, unchosen, hereditary duty.

The greatness of this character is not in Mr Macaulay's way, and
its faults are. Its license affronts him; its riot alienates him. He is for
ever contrasting the dissoluteness of Prince Rupert's horse with the
restraint of Cromwell's pikemen. A deep enjoying nature finds no
sympathy. The brilliant style passes forward: we dwell on its brilliancy, but it is cold. He has no tears for that warm life, no tenderness
for that extinct joy. The ignorance of the Cavalier, too, moves his
wrath: 'They were ignorant of what every schoolgirl knows.' Their
loyalty to their sovereign is the devotion of the Egyptians to the god
Apis, who selected 'a calf to adore'. Their non-resistance offends the
philosopher: their license is commented on with the tone of a precisian.
Their indecorum does not suit the dignity of the narrator. Their rich
free nature is unappreciated; the tingling intensity of their joy is
unnoticed. In a word, there is something of the schoolboy about the
Cavalier – there is somewhat of a schoolmaster about the historian.

(*WB*, i, 405-8, from 'Mr Macaulay', *National Review*, 1856)

The Wealth of Nations, which was published in 1776, is this year just a hundred years old, and the English Political Economy Club gave on Wednesday a dinner in celebration of the fact, at which they had the remarkable honour of entertaining the French Minister of Finance, who came from Paris for the purpose, and who made on the occasion a most admirable and suitable speech. No compliment could have been more suitable for a dinner in celebration of the beginning of the most effectual of political philosophies, and the one which has by far the most affected the intercourse of nations.

Nothing beforehand, – nothing if we look at the matter with the eyes, say, of the year 1770, could have seemed more unlikely than that Adam Smith should have succeeded in such an achievement. Political economy is, above all things, the theory of business, and if ever there was an eminent man who pre-eminently was not a man of business it was Adam Smith. He was a bookish student who never made a sixpence, who was unfit for all sorts of affairs, and whose absence of mind is hardly credible. He once astonished a sentinel who did him some kind of military salute by drawing himself up and giving with perfect gravity a facsimile salute in return. On another occasion, when he had to put his signature to an official document, instead of doing so he copied with slow and elaborate care the name of the person who had signed before him. And these acts are but specimens of his life. If the townsmen of Kirkcaldy – the little place where *The Wealth of Nations* was written – had been told to select the townsman who was most unlikely, as far as externals went, to tell this world how to make money, most likely they would have selected Adam Smith, whose writings have, in fact, caused more money to be made and prevented more money from being wasted, than those of any other author.

That there had been various preceding political economies, more than the common world much remembers, rather enhances the wonder. Unquestionably, many hardheaded men, and some sects of writers, can be mentioned who approached more or less nearly to the general doctrines now accepted as the true theory of commerce. What sort of 'natural selection', then, made Adam Smith's political economy so much more successful than that of all others? Why was this most unlikely-looking Scotch student the 'favoured' philosopher whose name was to be annexed for all time to the true theory of trade?

One great piece of good fortune to Adam Smith was his time. Historians of science remark that most great discoveries are based on large collections of new facts. And this was the case with trade in the eighteenth century. There was then a much vaster, a much wider, and much more varied commerce than the world had ever seen in any preceding time. And its contents were catalogued and were commented upon in a quantity and with an accuracy which there had been nothing like before. 'Political Arithmetic', as statistics were then called, was no doubt then very small in comparison with the mass of figures to which it has grown now; but still it existed, and existed for the first time – at least, in any connected bulk – and that existence was a sign of the recent extension of commerce and of the changed place it began to take in men's minds. Adam Smith was singularly fortunate among philosophers, for he had a new world to explain and new data for explaining it.

And he had also a world to conquer. The new commerce which had grown up had done so in spite of any law which could be framed to prevent it – not that such had been in the least the intention of legislators. On the contrary, they were most anxious to develop trade, and to make the nations rich which were subject to them; but they had pursued a wrong, though very natural, method. Seemingly, the most obvious person to consult on matters of trade, is the trader; the person who, at first sight, seems likely to know most about a thing, is the person who makes it; and, accordingly, the European governments had taken counsel with the producer. But, unhappily, the producer was just the wrong person to consult. What he wanted was a high price for his article, and a monopoly of the market in which to sell it; and the laws he recommended were inevitably framed, more or less, to obtain his wishes; whereas, the interest of the nations which the governments were trustees for, and which they were sincerely desirous to serve, was a 'low price', unrestricted competition from abroad, and a freedom for everyone to buy or sell everything at home. The legislative success of Adam Smith's philosophy has transcended that of all other philosophers very much from this. He found a world in which the interests of the buyer were supposed to be secured by laws, framed at the suggestion of the seller, and he was able to show, not by mere elaborate argument – though he gave that too – but also by an unsurpassed store of living illustrations, that these laws worked ill, and were sure to do so, because they were framed in the wrong person's interest. To use a homely illustration, Adam Smith was so fortunate as to find a world in 'which the cat had the custody of the cream', and to have had unprecedented facilities for showing the absurdity of the arrangement.

And when we look more closely at the matter, we find notwithstanding the outside impression, that he was a person singularly fitted to do this. He belonged to what – calling the group from the representative most familiar to us – we may call 'the Macaulay type of Scotchmen'. He possessed in combination, – exactly that power of lucid exposition, that eager interest in his subject, that immense power of illustrating it from all quarters, and that hard kind of predominant – we might almost say – intolerant common sense, of which every reader of Mr Trevelyan's excellent biography will just now have in his mind an almost perfect specimen. Many persons are now deterred from reading *The Wealth of Nations* by the dullness of modern books of political economy, but most of it really consists of some of the most striking and graphic writing in the language. And its defect, like that of several other great works of the eighteenth century, is rather that it tries to make its subject more interesting than it ought to be, and not to dwell on the dull standpoints of the truth, though these are often the most important parts of all. But perhaps for its peculiar time and purpose this defect was almost a merit. It gained a hearing from the mass of mankind, who always think they ought to be able to understand even the most complex subjects with little effort, and so brought home approximate truth to those most concerned in its application. A student familiar with abstractions may prefer teaching like Ricardo's, which begins in dry principles, and which goes with unabbreviated reasoning to conclusions that are as dry. But such students are very rare. Teaching like Adam Smith's, imperfect and external as from its method it is, vitally changes the minds and maxims of thousands to whom an abstract treatise is intolerable.

Three other circumstances, too, helped Adam Smith. First – he was educated in England – educated, we mean, as a young man; and though Oxford may have taught him little of book learning in comparison with what she ought, as he always said she did, she gave him – for he lived there several years – a sort of familiarity with English things, and of sympathy with English life, which the Scotchmen of that day often wanted. Anyone who will compare Hume's way of treating an English subject with Adam Smith's, will at once feel the contrast. Hume without disguise hates the whole thing; Adam Smith – though, no doubt, even in him there are unextinguished vestiges of the old feud between the countries – abounds in kindly understanding, and seems always to remember that he spent a happy youth in England, though possibly not one of the elaborate book-training which he coveted.

Secondly – Adam Smith lived for years in Glasgow, then even a commercial city of intelligence, and was a member of a club of merchants, 'in which the express design was to inquire into the nature and principles of trade in all its branches, and to communicate their knowledge on that subject to each other'. A set of strongheaded merchants, trained as the Scotchmen have ever since the Reformation been, in abstract reasoning, would be sure to argue out something near to Free-trade – and tradition preserves the name of a certain 'Provost Cochrane', to whom Adam Smith always said he was under great obligations. This club and the atmosphere of Glasgow life, probably taught him more than he was aware of, not so much in the way of definite ideas and conclusions, as in the way of 'putting business things', so that men of business can understand them – an art which a man cannot learn in his study, for books will never teach it, but which Adam Smith pre-eminently possessed, and which is an essential prerequisite to his characteristic work. Lastly – Adam Smith resided in France a considerable time in middle life, which not only brought him into contact with the French *Economistes*, who had like him, a Free-trade doctrine, and traces of whose influence curiously leavening the original Scotch substance of the thought, are everywhere to be found in *The Wealth of Nations*, but also generally widened his culture, excited his mind, and in those days of the old *régime*, introduced him to an almost complete specimen of commercial morbid anatomy on the greatest scale, showing how a treasury which ought to be full might be made empty, and how a nation which ought to have been rich and happy might be made and kept poor and miserable.

As far as England is concerned, most of the legislative effects of the work of Adam Smith are complete. He thought the adoption of a Free-trade legislation as unlikely as the creation of a 'Utopia', but yet it has been established. The fetters in which pre-existing laws bound our commerce, have been removed, and the result is that we possess the greatest, the most stable, and the most lucrative commerce which the world has ever seen. Deep as was Adam Smith's conviction of the truth of his principles, the history of England for the last thirty years would have been almost inconceivable to him. Thirty years ago Carlyle and Arnold had nearly convinced the world of the irrecoverable poverty of our lower classes. The 'condition of England question', as they termed it, was bringing us fast to ruin. But, in fact, we were on the eve of the greatest prosperity which we have ever seen, or perhaps any other nation. And it was to the repeal of the Corn Laws in 1846, and to the series of changes of which this was the type, and the most important, that we owe this wonderful contrast. The nature and the direction of the result Adam Smith would have unquestionably accepted; but the magnitude and the rapidity – the 'figures and the pace' – would have been far beyond his imagination. Even to us, with the aid of our modern experience of large transactions, they are amazing, and no mind trained in the comparatively slow and small school of the eighteenth century, would, a hundred years since, have been able to think them possible.

In almost all other countries much remains to be done in the alteration of the laws in the way that Adam Smith would have suggested. The English race have gone into many countries, and have there done many wonderful things, but they have not been able to take their Free-trade principles with them. Everywhere 'Protection' rises like a weed from the soil; the wish to consult, and the habit of being guided by the producer, are as strong in the United States in

1876 as ever they were in England in 1776; and almost all our colonies partake the same spirit. Probably no one can over-estimate the loss of wealth and the diminution of happiness which this unhappy ignorance causes. A rational tariff in America would have done more indirectly to make American industry stable and prosperous, and directly to advance the growth of wealth and industry, than anything else which could be named. And yet an irrational and pernicious tariff seems fixed upon the United States for many years.

In Europe there has not been for many years any symptom of commercial progress so good as the presence of M. Léon Say – the French Finance Minister – at Adam Smith's festival. The circumstances of France are for the moment very difficult; a very large revenue must be raised, and in this case, as in all similar ones, much of it will have to be raised not in the best way. But it is much that the guidance of such immense affairs should be in the hands of one who is thoroughly imbued with wise opinions, and much that they should no longer be at the mercy of M. Thiers, the last statesman in Europe, perhaps, who avers that he is 'a Protectionist on principle', and who only wishes that the 'tall chimnies' of some favoured producer should smoke and thrive, no matter at what cost to the consumer, or at what ruin to other industries.

And though in England the legislative work of Adam Smith has nearly come to an end, there is much else which we have yet to learn from him, – at any rate, from the spirit of his teacher, if not from its letter. Though a political economist, he was not a mere economist – or, rather, he was the antithesis of one as we now think of him. Great as his work has been, he said, with much melancholy, not long before his death, 'I meant to have done more.' *The Wealth of Nations* was but a part of a much larger work in which he meant to treat something like what we should now call the 'evolution' of human society and of human improvement. He discovered, as it has been put, 'the natural progress of opulence while looking for the natural progress of all things'. And he was disappointed to think that he finished so little of so great a scheme. In this critics, instructed by longer experience, will not agree with him. These great plans are the bane of philosophy; 'the master mind', as has been profoundly said, 'shows itself in limitation', and, fortunate as Adam Smith was in many ways, it is his greatest good fortune that fate constrained and compelled him to it. But, nevertheless, this wider design in which *The Wealth of Nations* began, is one of its peculiar features and one which we nowadays much want Adam Smith to complete. The world is too much divided between economists, who think only of 'wealth', and sentimentalists, who are never so sure they are right as when they differ from what political economy teaches. Now of course it is true that there are some things, though not many things, more important than money, and a nation may well be called on to abandon the maxims which would produce the most money, for others which would promote some of these better ends. The case is much like that of health in the body. There are unquestionable circumstances in which a man may be called on to endanger and to sacrifice his health at some call of duty. But for all that bodily health is a most valuable thing, and the advice of the physician as to the best way of keeping it is very much to be heeded, and in the same way, though the wealth is occasionally to be foregone, and the ordinary rules of industry abandoned, yet still national wealth is in itself and in its connections a great end, and economists who teach us how to arrive at it are most useful. Nor were they ever so useful as now, when there is a tendency to magnify the occasional exceptions to their doctrines into the rule. Their teaching, being based on hard fact, is often most painful to human nature, and accordingly in every age a whole race of socialists will gainsay and oppose it. They are like pleasant doctors who teach people to eat and drink too much, only they have higher pretensions, and say you must not think of health only; there are things which are higher than health, and so they appeal at once to the higher aspirations of humanity and to its lower weaknesses. We must not be deluded into thinking that the characteristic work of Adam Smith is over because the laws of which he disapproved are repealed. Perhaps there never was a time in which we more needed to combine a stern and homely sagacity resembling his, with the far-reaching aims and ample knowledge for which he was so remarkable.

(*WB*, iii, 113–19, *The Economist*, 1876)

RICHARD COBDEN

Mr Cobden was very anomalous in two respects. He was a *sensitive* agitator. Generally, an agitator is a rough man of the O'Connell type, who says anything himself, and lets others say anything. You 'peg into me and I will peg into you, and let us see which will win', is his motto. But Mr Cobden's habit and feeling was utterly different. He never spoke ill of anyone. He arraigned principles, but not persons ... Very rarely, if even ever in history, has a man achieved so much by his words – been victor in what was thought at the time to be a class struggle – and yet spoken so little evil as Mr Cobden ...

This sensitive nature is one marked peculiarity in Mr Cobden's career as an agitator, and another is that he was an agitator *for men of business*. Generally speaking, occupied men charged with the responsibilities and laden with the labour of grave affairs are jealous of agitation. They know how much may be said against anyone who is responsible for anything. They know how unanswerable such charges nearly always are, and how false they easily may be. A capitalist can hardly help thinking, 'Suppose a man was to make a speech against *my* mode of conducting my own business, how much he would have to say.' Now it is an exact description of Mr Cobden that by the personal magic of a single-minded practicability, he made men of business abandon this objection. He made them rather like the new form of agitation. He made them say, 'How businesslike, how wise, just what it would have been right to do.'

(*WB*, iii, 294–5, from 'Mr Cobden', *The Economist*, 1865)

COLONIAL GOVERNMENT

A colonial governor is a ruler who has no permanent interest in the colony he governs; who perhaps had to look for it in the map when he was sent thither; who takes years before he really understands its parties and its controversies; who, though without prejudice himself, is apt to be a slave to the prejudices of local people near him; who inevitably, and almost laudably, governs not in the interest of the colony, which he may mistake, but in his own interest, which he sees and is sure of. The first desire of a colonial governor is not to get into a 'scrape', not to do anything which may give trouble to his superiors – the Colonial Office – at home, which may cause an untimely and dubious recall, which may hurt his after career. He is sure to leave upon the colony the feeling that they have a ruler who only half knows them, and does not so much as half care for them. We hardly appreciate this common feeling in our colonies, because *we* appoint *their* sovereign; but we should understand it in an instant if, by political metamorphosis, the choice were turned the other way – if *they* appointed *our* sovereign.

(*WB*, v, 354, from *The English Constitution*, 1867)

CONSCIENCE

The source of [the religion of superstition] is in the conscience. The moral principle (whatever may be said to the contrary by complacent thinkers) is really to most men a principle of fear. The delights of a good conscience may be reserved for better beings, but few men who know themselves will say that they have often felt them by vivid and actual experience. A sensation of shame, of reproach, remorse, of sin (to use the word we instinctively shrink from because it expresses the meaning), is what the moral principle really and practically thrusts on most men. Conscience is the condemnation of ourselves. We expect a penalty. As the Greek proverb teaches, 'where there is shame there is fear'; where there is the deep and intimate anxiety of guilt – the feeling which has driven murderers, and other than murderers, forth to wastes, and rocks, and stones, and tempests – we see, as it were, in a single complex and indivisible sensation, the pain and sense of guilt, and the painful anticipation of its punishment. How to be free from this is the question. How to get loose from this – how to be rid of the secret tie which binds the strong man and cramps his pride, and makes him angry at the beauty of the universe – which will not let him go forth like a great animal, like the king of the forest, in the glory of his might, but restrains him with an inner fear and a secret foreboding, that if he do but exalt himself he shall be abased; if he do but set forth his own dignity, he will offend ONE who will deprive him of it. This, as has often been pointed out, is the source of the bloody rites of heathendom. You are going to battle, you are going out in the bright sun with dancing plumes and glittering spear; your shield shines, and your feathers wave, and your limbs are glad with the consciousness of strength, and your mind is warm with glory and renown, – with coming glory and unobtained renown, – for who are you to hope for these – who are *you* to go forth proudly against the pride of the sun, with your secret sin and your haunting shame, and your real fear? First lie down and abase yourself – strike your back with hard stripes – cut deep with a sharp knife as if you would eradicate the consciousness – cry aloud – put ashes on your head – bruise yourself with stones, then perhaps God may pardon you; or, better still, so runs the incoherent feeling, give him something, your ox, your ass, whole hecatombs, if you are rich enough, anything, it is but a chance – you do not know what will please him – at any rate, what you love best yourself – that is most likely – your first-born son, then, after such gifts and such humiliation, he may be appeased – he may let you off – he may without anger let you go forth Achilles-like in the glory of your shield – he may *not* send you home as he would else, the victim of rout and treachery, with broken arms and foul limbs, in weariness and humiliation.

Of course it is not this kind of fanaticism that we impute to a prelate of the English Church: human sacrifices are not respectable, and Achilles was not rector of Stanhope. But though the costume and circumstances of life change, the human heart does not; its feelings remain. The same anxiety, the same consciousness of personal sin, which lead in barbarous times to what has been described, show themselves in civilized life as well. In this quieter period, their great manifestation is scrupulosity, a care about the ritual of life, an attention to meats and drinks, and cups and washings. Being so unworthy as we are, feeling what we feel, abased as we are abased, who shall say that these are beneath us? In ardent imaginative youth they may seem so, but let a few years come, let them dull the will or contract the heart, or stain the mind – then the consequent feeling will be, as full experience shows, not that a ritual is too mean, too low, too degrading for human nature, but that it is a mercy we have to do no more – that we have only to wash in Jordan – that we have not even to go out into the unknown distance to seek for Abana and Pharpar, rivers of Damascus. We have no right to judge, we cannot decide, we must do what is laid down for us, – we fail daily even in this, – we must never cease for a moment in our scrupulous anxiety to omit by no tittle and to exceed by no iota.

(*WB*, i, 226–8, from 'Bishop Butler', *National Review*, 1854)

THE CONSTITUTIONAL STATESMAN

A constitutional statesman is in general a man of common opinions and uncommon abilities. The reason is obvious. When we speak of a free government, we mean a government in which the sovereign power is divided, in which a single decision is not absolute, where argument has an office. The essence of the 'gouvernement des avocats', as the Emperor Nicholas called it, is that you must persuade so many persons. The appeal is not to the solitary decision of a single statesman; not to Richelieu or Nesselrode alone in his closet; but to the jangled mass of men, with a thousand pursuits, a thousand interests, a thousand various habits. Public opinion, as it is said, rules; and public opinion is the opinion of the average man. Fox used to say of Burke: 'Burke is a wise man; but he is wise too soon.' The average man will not bear this. He is a cool, common person, with a considerate air, with figures in his mind, with his own business to attend to, with a set of ordinary opinions arising from and suited to ordinary life. He can't bear novelty or originalities. He says: 'Sir, I never heard such a thing *before* in my life'; and he thinks this a *reductio ad absurdum*. You may see his taste by the reading of which he approves. Is there a more splendid monument of talent and industry than *The Times*? No wonder that the average man – that anyone – believes in it. As Carlyle observes: 'Let the highest intellect able to write epics try to write such a leader for the morning newspapers, it cannot do it; the highest intellect will fail.' But did you ever see anything there you had never seen before? Out of the million articles that everybody has read, can any one person trace a single marked idea to a single article? Where are the deep theories, and the wise axioms, and the everlasting sentiments which the writers of the most influential publication in the world have been the first to communicate to an ignorant species? Such writers are far too shrewd. The two million, or whatever number of copies it may be, they publish, are not purchased because the buyers wish to know new truth. The purchaser desires an article which he can appreciate at sight; which he can lay down and say: 'An excellent article, very excellent; exactly *my own* sentiments.' Original theories give trouble; besides, a grave man on the Coal Exchange does not desire to be an apostle of novelties among the contemporaneous dealers in fuel; – he wants to be provided with remarks he can make on the topics of the day which will not be known *not* to be his; that are not too profound; which he can fancy the paper only reminded him of. And just in the same way, precisely as the most popular political paper is not that which is abstractedly the best or most instructive, but that which most exactly takes up the minds of men where it finds them, catches the floating sentiment of society, puts it in such a form as society can fancy would convince another society which did not believe, – so the most influential of constitutional statesmen is the one who most felicitously expresses the creed of the moment, who administers it, who embodies it in laws and institutions, who gives it the highest life it is capable of, who induces the average man to think: 'I could not have done it any better, if I had had time myself.'

(*WB*, iii, 242–3, from 'The Character of Sir Robert Peel',
National Review, 1856)

Decorum is the essence, pomposity the advantage, of tutors.

The discovery of a law of nature is very like the discovery of a murder. In the one case you arrest a suspected person, and in the other you isolate a suspected cause.

Discretion is a quality seldom appreciated till it is lost.

THE DANGER OF LENDING TO SEMI-CIVILIZED COUNTRIES

Many persons have not a distinct perception of the risk of lending to a country in a wholly different state of civilization. They can hardly imagine the difficulties with which such a country struggles, and the dangers to which it is exposed. They forget that national good faith is a rare and recent thing, and they expect to find it where the condition of its existence cannot be found. Take the case of Egypt: we have no doubt that the present agents for the loan in England expect it will be paid; we have no doubt that the present Viceroy is a man of intelligence, and that he will wish to keep faith with his creditors; we have no doubt that the natural resources of Egypt are enormous: it was its wonderful fertility that gave it its place in the world. But how little do facts like these, or others like them, prove that a debt will be paid, or that interest on it will be paid when new borrowings cease to be possible.

The primary conditions of national good faith are three – a continuous polity; a fixed political morality; and a constant possession of money. But it is difficult to prove that Egypt, or Turkey, or any oriental power, possesses these. Take the first: the polity of Egypt is not continuous, but *dis*continuous. Egypt is ruled by a foreign dynasty of absolute monarchs, each of whom has his own character, his own ends, and his own means; each of whom may dislike what his predecessor did, and may in turn begin something which his own successors may disapprove of in turn. M. Lesseps, a judge naturally partial, described this to Mr Senior:

'It is true', said Lesseps, 'that he attempted to force some improvements for which the country was not ripe. An uneducated man, seeing the enormous superiority of Europeans, may be forgiven for not having estimated accurately the relative importance of the different elements of that superiority. He sought for it too much in material causes, in our manufactures, and in our commerce. But it is not true that he ignored, or even neglected, the moral and intellectual sources of our greatness. He founded many hundreds of schools for one factory.

'Abbas Pasha hated knowledge and schools, as he hated everything European. He discouraged the schools, and, if he had lived, Egypt would have relapsed into utter ignorance. Saïd Pasha has not yet had time to repair much of the harm done by his predecessor, but he is doing so more quickly than was even hoped by those who know how much he has to do, and how few there are to assist him. He has suppressed two schools in Cairo, and for sufficient reasons. One was the medical school, in which it had become a trade to deliver fraudulent certificates of ill health as exemptions from military service. He is educating a set of young medical men, but not in a school. The other was a military school, which Abbas Pasha had turned into a seminary of the most atrocious vices.'

Even, therefore, while the present family exists, the policy of the country is changeable, because it shifts with the will of each monarch; and the dynasty may be changed too. Mehemet Ali, the founder, was an illiterate man of genius who could not write, and who could barely read. He massacred the Mamelukes and established himself. But in the east, such kingdoms fall as easily as they rise. No one who lends money to Egypt can foresee who will be its permanent rulers.

Upon the point of repayment a change may be critical. Monarch B. may say, 'I do not want to pay the debts of Monarch A. *I* never had the money. This country never was the better for the money; it was spent on palaces which I do not care for, or upon women who are now dead, or upon foolish enterprises which were only advantageous to European charlatans. I will not throw good money after bad.' No doubt it would be for the permanent interest of the country to pay its debts, but it may not be easy to make a short-sighted and selfish despot comprehend it; and it is not easy to show that it is for his present interest. He will think, 'I have this large sum of ready money now, which I can spend as I like, and to please myself. Shall I send it away to these foreigners? No doubt it is said that if I do, the foreigners may a year or two hence lend me a larger sum. But how do I know that? Who can tell what notions such people may take up? Till three or four years ago they would not lend at all, and three or four years hence they may refuse to lend. Besides, the present money is enough. I can live well enough within the revenue, as it is: I do not want to borrow any more, and there is no reason why I should pay what someone else borrowed.'

Of course, this is immoral. But our notion of continuous political morality is very modern, and hardly penetrates to oriental despotisms. Where there is a vigorous life in the people, there may be a continuous public feeling. France has often changed her rulers, but each new ruler recognizes the debts of the old rulers, just as he recognizes his treaties; he accepts the burdens as well as acquires the powers. But an eastern monarch disregards the treaties of those whom he overthrew. In his idea 'he is the state', and those treaties were not made with him. Oriental monarchs have had very little experience of national debts: till very lately, no one thought of lending to such persons upon such terms; but in general, they would disregard the debts of their predecessors, just as they disregard their treaties.

No doubt, under a good administration, the Egyptian exchequer would overflow, but a good administration is scarcely possible in such a country. One of Mr Senior's informants puts the difficulties plainly:

'I proposed to the Viceroy', said Mougel Bey, 'either to erect for him a steam mill which would perform the same service much better, at half the expense, or to erect one myself if he would contract to let me grind for him at half the cost at which he grinds for himself. But so many interests are opposed to my plan that it has not yet been adopted. In the first place, there are about five hundred persons employed about the mills, well paid, and with little to do, whom the change would deprive of their business; and secondly, there are a few persons of great influence to whom the present system is convenient. Not more than three fourths of the wheat that is sent to the mills returns from them. The deficiency is supplied by beans, or oats, or sand. Some part of the profit finds its way as hush money to the subordinate officers, but the bulk goes to the heads of the military departments. Our visitor, the Minister of Marine Affairs, gets his share.'

'Is he a man of ability?' I asked.

'Of great ability', answered Mougel, 'in his own peculiar business, that of getting money. But he has neither knowledge nor talent for any other purpose. He began life as a common sailor: in a Mussulman country, no special instruction is supposed to be necessary for command. He rose from before the mast, and now administers the Egyptian navy. Luckily, there is not enough of it for him to do much harm.

'It is only gradually', he continued, 'that one learns the extent of the abuses in an absolute government. When I was making those docks I found the expense of obtaining Puzzuoli cement from Italy considerable. A sample of clay fit for the purpose was brought to me, and I ascertained that it was to be found at Gourry, a village on the Nile, which you will pass as you go up. I went thither, sent for the chief man, or Sheich, and told him that I understood that there was in the lands of his village the clay of which I showed him a specimen. His countenance fell, and he assured me that the whole bed had been worked out. I walked over the village, and soon found that the stratum, instead of being exhausted, was, in fact, almost inexhaustible. Half the land belonging to the village consisted of it. Thereupon, I ordered him to provide within a fixed time a certain number of bricks.

'As soon as I heard that they were ready I went to look at them, but found them unburnt. "We cannot," said the Sheich, "burn bricks in this village, except when the Nile is at its lowest: at present it fills our kilns. We are forced to send our clay to Upper Egypt, if it is to be burnt." I looked at his kilns, and, in fact, they were full of water. But, as they stood many feet above the level of the Nile, and the Nile was then increasing, it was obvious that the water had been deposited, not by the Nile, but by the villagers.'

With an administration in this state, and a people in this state, no gifts of nature can always ensure a full treasury.

As to the present loan, it may be said that though all that we say be true; though the Egyptian population may be dishonest; though the government may be unstable; though a new dynasty may neglect old claims, yet that the lenders may be safe in reliance upon their security. But bad as the notion of security for foreign loans is in general – and we have often shown that it is bad, and why – we do not remember a case in which it is as bad as this. The Pasha is going to buy an estate, and he says he will *himself* hold the estate as a security. A kind of fictitious separation is, indeed, set up between the Viceroy of Egypt and the government; but this is mere imagination.

In an unlimited despotism, there is nothing but the despot; all comes from him; all centres in him; nothing controls him. And if he does not choose to pay, who can get at the land which he keeps – the 'security' which is relied on?

It seems a truism to say that no lender to a country can be safe unless he knows something about that country. But in practice it is a paradox. We lend to countries whose condition we do not know, and whose want of civilization we do not consider, and, therefore, we lose our money.

(*WB*, x, 419, *The Economist*, 1867)

DECOROUS DULLNESS

A great part of the 'best' English people keep their mind in a state of decorous dullness. They maintain their dignity; they get obeyed; they are good and charitable to their dependants. But they have no notion of *play* of mind; no conception that the charm of society depends on it. They think cleverness an antic, and have a constant though needless horror of being thought to have any of it. So much does this stiff dignity give the tone, that the few Englishmen capable of social brilliancy mostly secrete it. They reserve it for persons whom they can trust, and whom they know to be capable of appreciating its *nuances*.

(*WB*, v, 264, from *The English Constitution*, 1867)

DEFENCE

Everyone who has visited the Star and Garter is aware that at the moment of ordering dinner there is little use in suggesting difficulties. Anyone who should attempt a calculation of expense, a budget for the evening, would be marked *bore* at once. The effective orator just then is the trusted epicure that knows dishes and sauces and wines. The popular impulse sets strong for a good dinner; he who can satisfy that impulse is the hero of the instant; and who so attempts to stay it may hurt other people's temper, but will hardly keep his own. The time for objection is later. There is always a financial reaction at the epoch of the *bill*; then, and not till then, has the antagonist of luxury the chance of attention.

Great things and small things are just the same. When military men or naval men, or, far worse, enthusiastic amateurs of war by sea

or land, insist on the necessity of such and such things No. 1, or such
and such things No. 2, or such and such things No. 19 (for they will
go on as long as you let them) – it is of no use objecting. They say:
'England is not safe without these things. Would you endanger our
country? Would you risk our homes and families? Would you not
like to be secure yourself?' Such rhetoric is unanswerable for the best
of all reasons, that it half-convinces oneself. The time of objection is
when you see the *bill*. On a sudden the history of late years then
strikes you very vividly. First, the Admiralty took away some money
with which it made wooden ships; and then it 'discovered its error',
and acknowledged that wooden sailing ships were useless; so it asked
for additional money and made wooden *steam* ships with much *éclat*.
And I for one was convinced it would be all right, and that England
was now safe. But in less than a year the Admiralty discovered its
error again, and pronounced all wooden ships, whether steam or
sailing ships, to be useless; so it abstracted further money and
constructed 'ironplated ships', the *Warrior* and that sort of thing,
which cost almost fabulous sums apiece; and now 'the Admiralty is
discovering its error' again, or something like it, for it wants more
money, and is making what I must call naval *nondescripts* – a sort of
Merrimacs and Monitors – things more like an ugly insect than a
ship, and which seem to me capable of infinite varieties, just as insects
are. I know (though it is a matter of prophecy, I am as sure of it as if
it had happened) that as soon as we have made one sort of these ugly
and indescribable things, we shall be told it is of no use, and that we
must make another more ill-favoured and indescribable still.

(*WB*, viii, 45–6, from 'Count Your Enemies and Economise on
Your Expenditure', pamphlet, 1862)

DICKENS AND THACKERAY

The phrase 'household book' has, when applied to the works of Mr
Dickens, a peculiar propriety. There is no contemporary English
writer whose works are read so generally through the whole house,
who can give pleasure to the servants as well as to the mistress, to the
children as well as to the master. Mr Thackeray without doubt
exercises a more potent and plastic fascination within his sphere, but

that sphere is limited. It is restricted to that part of the middle class which gazes inquisitively at the 'Vanity Fair' world. The delicate touches of our great satirist have, for such readers, not only the charm of wit, but likewise the interest of valuable information; he tells them of the topics which they want to know. But below this class there is another and far larger, which is incapable of comprehending the idling world or of appreciating the accuracy of delineations drawn from it . . . which only cares for or knows of its own multifarious, industrial, fig-selling world, – and over these also Mr Dickens has power.

(*WB*, ii, 78, from 'Charles Dickens', *National Review*, 1858)

DIPLOMATIC RELATIONS

The recognition of a new government by other governments generally means, and always ought to mean this, and this only: that the government in question is really strong enough and stable enough to act on behalf of the country, with such authority and such power to compel obedience as governments ought to exert. If that be so, then the only effect of not recognizing such a government is to introduce an unwarrantable confusion into the dealings between the two nations. If you decline to recognize the real manager of a company, you cannot transact the business which may arise between you and that company in the ordinary way; and you induce other people, moreover, to suppose that the manager of that company has not the authority and position which ought to belong to a manager. Precisely similar is the result of not recognizing a government which is really governing, and the only one which is really governing, the nation. It prevents the commercial and other social transactions between the two nations from taking place under the most regular and satisfactory conditions, and being protected by the full guarantees of civilized European habits, and it induces other governments to treat with needless distrust and suspicion a government which is thus openly ignored by a powerful state. The sole justifiable reason for refusing to recognize a government is that that government does not really enforce order and wield authority. When that is so, when there are several competitors for the functions of government, or when, though there are no other competitors, the government of the moment has so little real control of the people that it is defied with impunity and can look only for a short life, it is right, as well as inevitable, for settled governments to withhold their recognition till some authority emerges from the chaos with adequate claims on their respect. By recognizing every ephemeral power that chooses to call itself a government, foreign states might be drawn into the unpleasant position of receiving injuries and grievances from a power quite too weak to be called to account; nay, so weak that it may have disappeared long before any indemnity can be demanded from it. And worse, an appearance of recognition might lead other states into treating it with a confidence that it did not deserve. For this reason it has been the wholesome practice of all self-respecting governments to await the signs of real power – the evidence of adequate political responsibility – before entering into relations with new-born or revolutionary governments.

No doubt, however, there have been occasional instances in which the withdrawal of political recognition has been used as a kind of diplomatic penalty, or mode of indicating quasi-belligerence, in the case of petty states which have acted in a way displeasing to the government which thus withdrew their envoy. That, as it seems to us, unless really meant as the preliminary of war, is a very unwise sort of proceeding, borrowed, without any justification, from the rules which guide the intercourse of society.

(*WB*, viii, 265–6, from 'Prince Bismarck and Spain', *The Economist*, 1875)

DISCIPLINE

The most important matters for the labouring classes, as for all others, are restraining discipline over their passions and an effectual culture of their consciences. In recent times these wants are more pressing than ever. Great towns are depots of temptation, and, unless care be taken, corrupters of all deep moral feeling. The passions also act with more violence than elsewhere in the intervals of a monotonous occupation, and owing to the increasing division of labour the industrial tasks of mankind are every day becoming more and more monotonous.

(*WB*, xi, 193, from 'Principles of Political Economy', *Prospective Review*, 1848)

DISRAELI

It has been Mr Disraeli's misfortune throughout his main political career to lead a party of very strong prejudices and principles, without feeling himself any cordial sympathy with either the one or the other. No doubt that is precisely the fact which has enabled him on most great emergencies to be of use to his party. His completely external intelligence has been to them what the elephant driver's – the mahout's – is to the elephant, comparatively insignificant as a force, but so familiar with all the habits of the creature which his sagacity has to guide, and so entirely, if it only knew, at its mercy, that all his acuteness is displayed in contriving to turn the creature's habits and instincts to his own end, profit, and advantage, – which, however, cannot be done without also carefully preserving the creature itself from great dangers, and guarding it against the violence of its own passions.

(*WB*, iii, 496, from 'Mr Disraeli's Administration', *The Economist*, 1868)

DULL GOVERNMENT

Parliament is a great thing, but it is not a cheerful thing. Just reflect on the existence of Mr SPEAKER. First, a small man speaks to him – then a shrill man speaks to him – then a man who cannot speak *will* speak to him. He leads a life of 'passing tolls', joint-stock companies, and members out of order. Life is short, but the forms of the House are long. Mr Ewart complains that a multitude of members, including the Prime Minister himself, actually go to sleep. The very morning paper feels the weight of this leaden *régime*. Even in the dullest society you hear complaints of the dullness of Parliament – of the representative tedium of the nation.

That an Englishman should grumble is quite right, but that he should grumble at gravity is hardly right. He is rarely a lively being himself, and he should have a sympathy with those of his kind. And he should further be reminded that his criticism is out of place – that dullness in matters of government is a good sign, and not a bad one – that, in particular, dullness in parliamentary government is a test of its excellence, an indication of its success. The truth is, all the best business is a little dull. If you go into a merchant's counting-house, you see steel pens, vouchers, files, books of depressing magnitude, desks of awful elevation, staid spiders, and sober clerks moving among the implements of tedium. No doubt, to the parties engaged, much of this is very attractive. 'What,' it has been well said, 'are technicalities to those without, are realities to those within.' To every line in those volumes, to every paper on those damp files, there has gone doubt, decision, action – the work of a considerate brain, the touch of a patient hand. Yet even to those engaged, it is commonly the least interesting business which is the best. The more the doubt, the greater the liability to error – the longer the consideration, generally the worse the result – the more the pain of decision, the greater the likelihood of failure. In Westminster Hall, they have a legend of a litigant who stopped his case because the lawyers said it was 'interesting'. 'Ah,' he remarked afterwards, 'they were going up to the "Lords" with it, and I should never have seen my money.' To parties concerned in law, the best case is a plain case. To parties concerned in trade, the best transaction is a plain transaction – the sure result of familiar knowledge; in political matters, the best sign that things are going well is that there should be nothing difficult – nothing requiring deep contention of mind – no anxious doubt, no sharp resolution, no lofty and patriotic execution. The opportunity for these qualities is the danger of the commonwealth. You cannot have a Chatham in time of peace – you cannot storm a Redan in Somersetshire. There is no room for glorious daring in periods of placid happiness.

And if this be the usual rule, certainly there is nothing in the nature of parliamentary government to exempt it from its operation. If business is dull, business wrangling is no better. It is dull for an absolute minister to have to decide on passing tolls, but it is still duller to hear a debate on them – to have to listen to the two extremes and the *via media*. One honourable member considers that the existing ninepence ought to be maintained; another thinks it ought to be abolished; and a third – the independent thinker – has statistics of his own, and suggests that fourpence-halfpenny would 'attain the maximum of revenue with the minimum of inconvenience' – only he could wish there were a decimal coinage to 'facilitate the calculations of practical pilots'. Of course this is not the highest specimen of parliamentary speaking. Doubtless, on great questions, when the public mind is divided, when the national spirit is roused, when powerful interests are opposed, when large principles are working their way, when deep difficulties press for a decision, there is an opportunity for noble eloquence. But these very circumstances are the signs, perhaps of calamity, certainly of political difficulty and national doubt. The national spirit is not roused in happy times – powerful interests are not divided in years of peace – the path of great principles is marked through history by trouble, anxiety, and conflict. An orator requires a topic. 'Thoughts that breathe and words that burn' will not suit the 'liability of joint-stock companies' – you cannot shed tears over a 'toll'. Where can there be a better proof of national welfare than that Disraeli cannot be sarcastic, and that Lord Derby fails in a diatribe? Happy is the country which is at peace within its borders – yet stupid is the country when the opposition is without a cry.

Moreover, when parliamentary business is a bore, it is a bore which cannot be overlooked. There is much torpor secreted in the *bureaux* of an absolute government, but no one hears of it – no one knows of its existence. In England it is different. With pains and labour – by the efforts of attorneys – by the votes of freeholders – you collect more than six hundred gentlemen; and the question is, what are they to do? As they come together at a specific time, it would seem that they do so for a specific purpose – but what it is they do not know. It is the business of the Prime Minister to discover it for them. It is extremely hard on an effervescent First Lord to have to set people down to mere business – to bore them with slow reforms – to explain details they cannot care for – to abolish abuses they never heard of – to consume the hours of the night among the perplexing details of an official morning. But such is the Constitution. The Parliament is assembled – some work must be found for it – and this is all that there is. The details which an autocratic government most studiously conceals are exposed in open day – the national sums are done in public – finance is made the most of. If the war had not intervened, who knows that by this time Parliament would not be commonly considered 'The Debating Board of Trade'? Intelligent foreigners can hardly be brought to understand this. It puzzles them to imagine how any good or smooth result can be educed from so much jangling, talking, and arguing. M. de Montalembert has described amazement as among his predominant sensations in England. He felt, he says, as if he were in a manufactory – where wheels rolled, and hammers sounded, and engines crunched – where all was certainly noise, and where all seemed to be confusion – but from which, nevertheless, by a miracle of industrial art, some beautiful fabric issued, soft, complete, and perfect. Perhaps this simile is too flattering to the neatness of our legislation, but it happily expresses the depressing noise and tedious din by which its results are really arrived at.

As are the occupations, so are the men. Different kinds of government cause an endless variety in the qualities of statesmen. Not a little of the interest of political history consists in the singular degree in which it shows the mutability and flexibility of human nature. After various changes, we are now arrived at the business statesman – or rather, the business speaker. The details which have to be alluded to, the tedious reforms which have to be effected, the long figures which have to be explained, the slow arguments which require a reply – the heaviness of subjects, in a word – have caused a corresponding weight in our oratory. Our great speeches are speeches of exposition – our eloquence is an eloquence of detail. No one can read or hear the speeches of our ablest and most enlightened statesmen without being struck with the contrast which they exhibit – we do not say to the orations of antiquity (which were delivered under circumstances too different to allow of a comparison), but to the great parliamentary displays of the last age – of Pitt, or Fox, or Canning. Differing from each other as the latter do in most of their characteristics, they all fall exactly within Sir James Mackintosh's definition of parliamentary oratory – 'animated and continuous after-dinner conversation'. They all have a gentlemanly effervescence and lively agreeability. They are suitable to times when the questions discussed were few, simple, and large – when detail was not – when the first requisite was a pleasant statement of obvious considerations. We are troubled – at least our orators are troubled – with more complex and difficult topics. The patient exposition, the elaborate minuteness, the exhaustive disquisition, of modern parliamentary eloquence, would formerly have been out of place – they are now necessary on complicated subjects, which require the exercise of a laborious intellect, and a discriminating understanding. We have not gained in liveliness by the change, and those who remember the great speakers of the last age are the loudest in complaining of our tedium. The old style still lingers on the lips of Lord Palmerston; but it is daily yielding to a more earnest and practical, to a sober *before*-dinner style.

It is of no light importance that these considerations should be recognized, and their value carefully weighed. It has been the bane of many countries which have tried to obtain freedom, but failed in the attempt, that they have regarded popular government rather as a means of intellectual excitement than as an implement of political work. The preliminary discussion was more interesting than the consequent action. They found it pleasanter to refine arguments than to effect results – more glorious to expand the mind with general ratiocination than to contract it to actual business. They wished, in a word, to have a popular government, without, at the same time, having a dull government. The English people have never yet forgotten what some nations have scarcely ever remembered – that politics are a kind of business – that they bear the characteristics, and obey the laws, inevitably incident to that kind of human action. Steady labour and dull material – wrinkles on the forehead and figures on the tongue – these are the English admiration. We may prize more splendid qualities on uncommon occasions, but these are for daily wear. You cannot have an era per annum – if every year had something memorable for posterity, how would posterity ever remember it? Dullness is our line, as cleverness is that of the French. Woe to the English people if they ever forget that, all through their history, heavy topics and tedious talents have awakened the admiration and engrossed the time of their Parliament and their country.

(*WB*, vi, 81–5, from *Saturday Review*, 1856)

The English Premier is a tenant-at-will, but the American President has obtained a *lease for years*.

Every new person you know is an intellectual burden because you may see them again, and must be able to recognize and willing to converse with them.

Every public man wins or loses by the balance which there is in his favour, but there are two ways of gaining that balance. Some statesmen have almost nothing put to their debit, so that all which they do, be it ever so little, goes with only slight deduction to their credit; others have a good deal put to their debit, but then, on the other hand, an immense sum is every now and then paid to their credit. Mr Gladstone is of the latter class; he 'turns over', as we should say in the City, 'a very large amount' and at the end of the year the balance to his advantage is most considerable, after charging him with all that he ought to be charged with.

ECONOMISTS

No real English gentleman, in his secret soul, was ever sorry for the death of a political economist: he is much more likely to be sorry for his life. There is an idea that he has something to do with statistics; or, if that be exploded, that he is a person who writes upon 'value': says that rent is – you cannot very well make out what; talks excruciating currency; he may be useful as drying machines are useful; but the notion of crying about him is absurd. You might as well cry at the death of a cormorant. Indeed how he can die is very odd. You would think a man who could digest all that arid matter; who really preferred 'sawdust without butter'; who liked the tough subsistence of rigid formulae, might defy by intensity of internal constitution all stomachic or lesser diseases. However they do die, and people say that the dryness of the Sahara is caused by a deposit of similar bones.

(*WB*, i, 324, from 'The First Edinburgh Reviewers', *National Review*, 1855)

EDUCATED IGNORANCE

It is of immense importance that there should be among the more opulent and comfortable classes a large number of minds trained by early discipline to this habitual restraint and sobriety. The very ignorance of such people is better than the best knowledge of half mankind. An uneducated man has no notion of being without an opinion: he is distinctly aware whether Venus is inhabited, and knows as well as Mr Cobden what is to be found in *all* the works of Thucydides; but his opinionated ignorance is rather kept in check, when people as strong-headed as himself, as rich, as respectable, and much better taught, are continually avowing that they don't at all know any of the points on which he is ready to decide. And when those who are careful *have* opinions, they are in general able to bear the temperate discussion of them. Education cannot ensure infallibility, but it most certainly ensures deliberation and patience. It forms the opinions of people that can form the opinions of others.

(*WB*, vii, 345–6, from 'Oxford', *Prospective Review*, 1852)

ENGLISH INSULARITY

The foreign policy of England has for many years been, according to the judgement now in vogue, inconsequent, fruitless, casual; aiming at no distinct pre-imagined end, based on no steadily preconceived principle. I have not room to discuss with how much or how little abatement this decisive censure should be accepted. However, I en-tirely concede that our recent foreign policy has been open to very grave and serious blame. But would it not have been a miracle if the English people, directing their own policy, and being what they are, had directed a good policy? Are they not above all nations divided from the rest of the world, insular both in situation and in mind, both for good and for evil? Are they not out of the current of common European causes and affairs? Are they not a race contemptuous of others? Are they not a race with no special education or culture as to the modern world, and too often despising such culture? Who could expect such a people to comprehend the new and strange events of foreign places? So far from wondering that the English Parliament has been inefficient in foreign policy, I think it is wonderful, and another sign of the rude, vague imagination that is at the bottom of our people, that we have done so well as we have.

(*WB*, v, 337–8, from *The English Constitution*, 1867)

ENGLISHNESS

Lord Althorp embodies all the characteristic virtues which enable Englishmen to effect well and easily great changes in politics: their essential fairness, their 'large roundabout common sense', their courage, and their disposition rather to give up something than to take the uttermost farthing. But on the other hand also he has all the characteristic English defects: their want of intellectual and guiding principle, their even completer want of the culture which would give that principle, their absorption in the present difficulty, and their hand-to-mouth readiness to take what solves it without thinking of other consequences. And I am afraid the moral of those times is that these English qualities as a whole – merits and defects together – are better suited to an early age of politics than to a later. As long as materials are deficient, these qualities are most successful in hitting off simple expedients, in adapting old things to new uses, and in extending ancient customs; they are fit for instantaneous little creations, and admirable at bit-by-bit growth. But when, by the incessant application of centuries, these qualities have created an accumulated mass of complex institutions, they are apt to fail, unless aided by others very different. The instantaneous origination of obvious expedients is of no use when the field is already covered with the heterogeneous growth of complex past expedients; bit-by-bit development is out of place unless you are sure which bit should and which bit should not be developed; the extension of customs may easily mislead when there are so many customs; no immense and involved subject can be set right except by faculties which can grasp what is immense and scrutinize what is involved. But mere common sense is here matched with more than it can comprehend, like a schoolboy in the differential calculus; – and absorption in the present difficulty is an evil, not a good, for what is wanted is that you should be able to see many things at once, and take in their bearings, not fasten yourself on one thing. The characteristic danger of great nations, like the Romans or the English, which have a long history of continuous creation, is that they may at last fail from not comprehending the great institutions which they have created.

(*WB*, iii, 202–3, from 'Lord Althorp and the Reform Act of 1832',
Fortnightly Review, 1876)

The favourite theorist of yesterday is punished today because the millennium is not yet come.

The first duty of society is the preservation of society. By the sound work of old-fashioned generations – by the singular painstaking of the slumberers in churchyards – by dull care – by stupid industry, a certain social fabric somehow exists – people contrive to go out to their work, and to find work to employ them actually until the evening, body and soul are kept together, and this is what mankind have to show for their six thousand years of toil and trouble.

FAILURE OF NERVE

A great nation very rarely hears two sides of anything which deeply concerns it – never, perhaps, of anything which most concerns it. Even parliamentary government – the best expedient for effectual and instructive discussion which the world has ever seen – fails in the most critical cases. Generally a parliament is divided into two great parties, and these are always more or less opposed to one another. If the ministry take one side, the opposition, by custom and bias of mind, always takes the contrary side, and so both sides are argued before the nation; but in a case affecting the nation's honour, or what is thought to be such, no party dares to take the side which is, or is said to be, opposed to that honour. The Whigs in the great French war opposed what was said to be necessary to the honour and existence of England, and by that course, from being a very powerful party, they were reduced so low that 'a hackney coach could hold them all'. No party will ever dare to tell the nation the truth on what most deeply and closely concerns it. And as a nation never hears anything against its own side, it naturally comes to believe that side to be unassailable and incontrovertible. In a quarrel between nations each thinks its own side so, and therefore the controversy must be fought out by 'steel and gunpowder' – words not being possible.

(*WB*, viii, 193, from 'No More Guarantees', *The Economist*, 1870)

THE FATE OF THE CENTRE PARTY

You can no more expect different generations to have exactly the same political opinions, to obey exactly the same laws, to love exactly the same institutions, than you can expect them to wear identical clothes, own identical furniture, or have identical manners. In both cases there will no doubt be much which is common to the two generations, but the similarity will be enhanced by contrast; the identity will be assured by differences. Unhappily, laws and institutions are not changed so easily as furniture and manners. The things of the individual can be changed by the individual, but the things of the community – at least in free states – can only be changed by the community; and communities are heavy to move. The necessary agents are many, and slow to gain. In consequence, all these states are liable to acute spasms of innovating energy. The force which ought to have acted daily and hourly has long been effectually resisted every day and every hour; at last it breaks forth with pent-up power; it frightens everyone, and for the minute seems as if it might destroy anything. This catastrophic innovating rage is, for the instant of its action, the predominant force in politics, and a statesman who gains its support need look for no other and care for no other.

But the misfortune of the left centre – or moderate Liberals – is that they cannot rely on gaining the support of either of these great powers. They are in sympathy neither with the intense Conservative force, nor with the intense innovating. They are 'betwixt and between', and make distinctions which no one heeds; they live in a debatable land, which each party attacks and neither defends; they have the sympathy of neither party, but the enmity of both . . .

In quiet times, moderate politicians have certainly not to fear either death or exile. But they have not only to fear, but to expect, that Conservatives like Mr Disraeli – the head of one power – will sneer at them as 'stray philosophers'; that Liberals like Mr Bright – the head of the other power – will deny that they are 'robust politicians'. They will have the consolations of philosophy, and they have a confident perception of truth attained; but they must do without conspicuous power and the 'worship of those with whom you sit at meat'; they must endure the tedium of inaction, and bear the constant sense of irritating helplessness. Though they are the best of rulers for the world, they are the last persons to be likely to rule.

The fate of the left centre – the moderate Liberals – is the harder, because that of the right centre – the moderate Conservatives – who differ from them so little, is so very much better. The world will accept from them that which it would never dream of accepting from their rivals. If the moderate Conservatives choose to propose moderate Liberal measures, they are certain to pass them. The Liberals must support them on principle and even the extreme Conservatives rarely try to oppose them, and still more rarely do so effectually. The most extreme Conservative is usually aware that some change must be carried sometimes and he is disposed to think that perhaps the changes that his own friends incline to may be those changes. At any rate he does not see where he can get so little change. If he leave the alliance of the moderate Conservative, he must either stand alone, which is impotence, or ally himself with Liberals, which is hateful. For one who wants to change nothing, to combine with those who want to change more, against those who wish to change less, is ridiculous. Accordingly the moderate Conservatives have almost always a game at their disposal if they are wise enough to perceive it. All that they concede, the attacking force will accept, and whatever they choose to concede, the rest of the defending force must allow. In two ways the Conservatives in happy states are likely to have a preponderance of power: first, because that happiness is an indication that in the main the existing institutions are suitable, and that very much organic change is not wanted; and secondly, because Conservatives, if they only knew it, have the greatest advantage in making the changes which have to be made.

(*WB*, vii, 229–31, from 'The Chances for a Long Conservative Régime in England', *Fortnightly Review*, 1878)

THE FELICITIES OF FRENCH

The characteristic aloofness of the Gothic mind, its tendency to devote itself to what is not present, is represented in composition by a want of care in the pettinesses of style. A certain clumsiness pervades all tongues of German origin. Instead of the language having been sharpened and improved by the constant keenness of attentive minds, it has been habitually used obtusely and crudely. Light, loquacious Gaul has for ages been the contrast. If you take up a pen just used by a good writer, for a moment you seem to write rather well. A language long employed by a delicate and critical society is a treasure of dextrous felicities. It is crystallized *esprit*.

(*WB*, ii, 22, from 'Béranger', *National Review*, 1857)

FOREIGN LITERATURE

The use of foreign literature is like the use of foreign travel. It imprints in early and susceptible years a deep impression of great and strange, and noble objects; but we cannot live with these. They do not resemble our familiar life; they do not bind themselves to our intimate affection; they are picturesque and striking, like strangers and wayfarers, but they are not of our home, or homely; they cannot speak to our 'business and bosoms'; they cannot touch the hearth of the soul. It would be better to have no outlandish literature in the mind than to have it the principal thing. We should be like accomplished vagabonds without a country, like men with a hundred acquaintances and no friends. We need an intellectual possession analogous to our own life; which reflects, embodies, improves it; on which we can repose; which will recur to us in the placid moments – which will be a latent principle even in the acute crises of our life. Let us be thankful if our researches in foreign literature enable us, as rightly used they will enable us, better to comprehend our own. Let us venerate what is old, and marvel at what is far. Let us read our own books. Let us understand ourselves.

(*WB*, i, 264, from 'William Cowper', *National Review*, 1855)

FRENCH INFLUENCE

The French have in some manner or other put their mark on all the externals of European life. The essence of every country remains little affected by their teaching; but in all the superficial embellishments of society they have enjoined the fashion; and the very language in which those embellishments are spoken of, shows at once whence they were derived. Something of this is doubtless due to the accidents of a central position, and an early and prolonged political influence; but more to a certain neatness of nature, a certain finish of the senses, which enables them more easily than others to touch lightly the light things of society, to see the *comme-il-faut*. 'I like,' said a good judge, 'to hear a Frenchman talk; he strikes a light.' On a hundred topics he gives the bright, sharp edge, where others have only a blunt approximation.

(*WB*, ii, 17, from 'Béranger', *National Review*, 1857)

THE FRENCH REVOLUTION AND ENGLAND

'If any person,' said Sir Samuel Romilly, the best of judges, for he lived through the times and was mixed up, heart and soul, in the matters he speaks of, 'if any person be desirous of having an adequate idea of the mischievous effects which have been produced in this country by the French Revolution and all its attendant horrors, he should attempt some reforms on humane and liberal principles. He will then find not only what a stupid dread of innovation, but what a savage spirit, it has infused into the minds of his countrymen.' And very naturally, for nothing is so cruel as fear. A whole generation in England, and indeed in Europe, was so frightened by the Reign of

Terror that they thought it could only be prevented by another Reign of Terror. The Holy Alliances, as they were then called, meant this and worked for this. Though we had not in name such an alliance in England, we had a state of opinion which did the work of one without one. Nine-tenths of the English people were above all things determined to put down 'French principles', and unhappily 'French principles' included what we should all now consider obvious improvements and rational reforms. They would not allow the most cruel penal code which any nation ever had to be mitigated; they did not wish justice to be questioned; they would not let the mass of the people be educated, or at least only so that it came to nothing; they would not alter anything which came down from their ancestors, for in their terror they did not know but there might be some charmed value even in the most insignificant thing; and after what they had seen happen in France, they feared that if they changed a single iota all else would collapse.

Upon this generation, too, came the war passion. They waged, and in the main – though with many errors – waged with power and spirit, the war with Napoleon; and they connected this with their horror of liberal principles in a way which is now very strange to us, but which was very powerful then. We know now that Napoleon was the head of a conservative reaction, a bitter and unfeeling reaction, just like that of the contemporary English; but the contemporary English did not know this. To the masses of them he was *Robespierre à cheval*, as someone called him – a sort of Jacobin waging war, in some occult way, for liberty and revolution, though he called himself Emperor. Of course the educated few gradually got more or less to know that Napoleon hated Jacobins and revolution, and liberty too, as much as it is possible to hate them; but the ordinary multitude, up to the end of the struggle, never dreamed of it. Thus in an odd way the war passion of the time strengthened its conservative feeling; and in a much more usual way it did so too, for it absorbed men's minds in the story of battles and the glory of victories, and left no unoccupied thought for gradual improvement and dull reform at home. A war time, also, is naturally a harsh time; for the tale of conflicts which sometimes raises men above pain, also tends to make men indifferent to it; the familiarity of the idea ennobles but also hardens.

(*WB*, iii, 209–10, from 'Lord Althorp and the Reform Act of 1832',
Fortnightly Review, 1876)

The great pleasure in life is doing what people say you cannot do.

A great Premier must add the vivacity of an idle man to the assiduity of a very laborious one.

The greatest defect of the House of Commons is that it has no leisure. The life of the house is the worst of all lives – a life of distracting routine.

THE GAINS OF THE WORLD BY THE TWO LAST WARS IN EUROPE

There is no need to fear that there will not be writing enough as to the two last wars in Europe – the Italian war of 1859 and the German war of 1866. The daily events which bring the latter to its close fill our newspapers and haunt our conversation. But there is great danger that under the cloud of detail the principal results may not be seen; that, according to the German saying, we may be unable to see the wood for looking at the trees; that the shillings and pence may draw off our attention from the pounds. We therefore propose to set down very barely and concisely the principal gains and losses of Europe and the world by these two wars – looking to broad results and not anxiously scrutinizing minutiae – neither extenuating the disadvantages of recent changes nor exaggerating their good consequences.

First, there is a plain, immense, and unprecedented step towards a great improvement in the substantial structure of nations. Nations are becoming *indestructible*. Both Italy as it is, and north Germany as it will be, are incapable of destruction. No probable military or political force will ever attempt to destroy them. Other nations may quarrel with them, fight them, beat them or be beaten by them, but they will not attempt to annihilate them. Many of the elements out of which these new permanent states are made had long been labelled for ruin. No one could suppose that the Duchy of Parma, the Grand Duchy of Tuscany, the Grand Duchy of Hesse, or the Kingdom of Hanover were likely to be lasting constituents of the European system. Hardly one of the small German states, and no one of the Italian, had the physical vigour which ensures longevity, or the vigorous intellectual life which makes longevity desirable. No one wished they would live for ever, and no one thought they would, though few were so sanguine as to hope that they would perish so very soon. Two states incapable of annihilation have taken the place of many states very capable of it and in the last degree exposed to it. And there is no greater security for the peace of the world. The existence of perishable states is like the unprotected exposure of tempting goods. Both almost solicit the hand of the spoiler. Half the wars in history are caused by the desire of strong states to annex weak states. Of the three last wars in Europe, the Russian was caused by the desire of the Czar to enter on the inheritance of the 'sick man'; the Italian and the German wars, whatever their nominal excuses, were, in fact, caused by the movement of 'nationalities' which is only suggested and only made possible by the existence of weak-lived States. Of all imaginable guarantees for the peace of the world, none would be so great as the palpable impossibility that one State should destroy another. Until this is so, the logic of facts will refute the logic of the Peace Society. The Peace Society says that all international disputes are capable of an arbitration, but no state will ever submit to arbitration the question of its own existence; and so long as the real motive of a war is the wish of the stronger to root out the weaker, it is idle to arbitrate upon nominal pretexts. The condition of Europe most unfavourable to war, is one in which the great majority of states are preserved from annihilation by their intrinsic vigour, and the few remaining destruct-ible ones are preserved by the common interest, the common respect, and the common guarantee of all the stronger powers.

Nearly connected with this great improvement in the structure of nations is a second. The European world is now, with exceptions and abatements it is true, but still upon the whole likely, to be made up of great nations. The process which is effecting that result is, it is true, still in progress; as yet its results are incomplete, but still its tendency is evident, and two of its great achievements are conspicuous. We have made two great nations – the Italian and the north German nation – within ten years; and mere size is not in the present state of the world a matter of secondary importance to any people. It has been said, perhaps with exaggeration, 'that the knell of small nations has sounded', but what is certainly true is, that the animation of small nations has declined. Great states for years past have been rising round them, and though they manage well their own matters, they do not mingle in the mighty strife of Europe, or elevate their subjects by conscious participation in momentous transactions. They are like the Greek republics after the rise of the Macedonian monarchy; they may feel that they have more ideas, or better civilization, or clearer judgement than the great powers, but these are matters of dispute and argument. What is certain is, that they have 'few cannons'. The demoralizing sensation of being 'nobody' has come upon them, and their spirit, life, and energy are not and cannot be what they once were. We do not wish to root out all the little states from Europe; there are some which, from situation, national character, and curious history, will long remain there. But still for a long time since it has been, and henceforward will even more be, a great gain to be born of a great nation. Politics, as centuries roll on, will probably fill less and less of the energies of mankind, and so the size of your nation will come to matter less and less; but in the present, and all the near future, the magnifying effect of a great career will ennoble powerful nations, and the deteriorating consequences of a petty life will render small nations more and more ignoble. Nor is the diffused participation in elevating excitement the only advantage the world reaps from an augmentation in the number of great nations. There are coarser advantages of a more economical kind. There is a saving in the mental cost of governing mankind. A lot of small states absorb into politics a needless mass of considerable minds, and their concentration into one sets at liberty a large number of them. If every county in England were independent, the minds wanted for a parliament for each, a ministry for each, a bureaucracy for each, would be incalculably greater than the minds now used in governing England. And the work would be worse done. Small politics debase the mind just as large politics improve it. The many small governments of Italy and Germany waste far more of the highest class of mind upon the work of government than the two single large states which will replace them; and the effect of the new politics will be to raise and rouse the minds engaged in them, while the effect of the minute old sort was often to cramp and lower them. The same principle runs through other ramifications. Thus it would indeed be bold to prophesy that a lessening of armies and a diminution of military expenditure would be the result of the creation of more great nations. We can hardly foresee enough for that. But we can foresee that there will be an increase in the utility of armies. The small German armies in the present war have been almost useless; the substantial strife was decided between Austria and Prussia in a single pitched battle, and the miscellaneous victories of Prussia over the lesser states only added to the number of her trophies and to the cost of her victories, but helped no one and harmed no one. Hereafter, every north German soldier at least will be substantially Prussian, and he will be used as part of a single great army, instead of being wasted amid the discordant action of many minute ones. And as is the utility of an army in war, so is the ennobling effect of war upon it. To have a real share in a great victory, so to say, aggrandises the souls of all concerned in it; but to have an infinitesimal participation in useless skirmishes wearies all and debases many, by confining them to plunder and licence.

A third result of these wars is an increase in the number of homogeneous nations, and the longer our experience of politics is, and the more careful our study of it, the higher will be our estimate of the importance of this characteristic. Much nonsense is talked as to the principle of nationalities, as about all approximate practical precepts which claim to be first philosophical principles, but one thing is obvious. It is a great advantage to a nation to be composed of human beings who understand one another, and a great disadvantage to be composed of such as do not understand each other. And heterogeneous compounds can scarcely understand one another. The various nations, all of which were till lately, and many of which still are, combined in the Empire of Austria, never could have a real national life. They were casually connected because accidents of descent and birth had subjected them to the same sovereign, but they had no knowledge of each other, care for or fellow-feeling with one another. The many attempts since 1855 to introduce a better system of Austrian government always failed on this account. It was impossible to introduce a system of representative government because one great section of the nation would not send members to it, and because the members who did come were sent from so many nations, spoke so many languages, and were animated by such different thoughts. The rights of a Czech were not the rights of a Hungarian; the rights of a Croat were not the rights of an Italian. *Divide et impera* was the old maxim of despotic statesmen; but for liberal and even semi-liberal statesmen unity is all but necessary, and division all but fatal. Under very peculiar conditions a nation like Switzerland may maintain a free life, though three languages are spoken in its Parliament, and though more than three races make up its population. But that example shows how strong a force is necessary to produce so anomalous a result, and how incomplete that result is when produced. The Swiss states were scarcely kept together by plain common necessity and intense common enmity. They knew that their league was necessary; that hated enemies were watching to break their unity; that if that unity were broken all would become slaves, and therefore, though often with much difficulty, that unity was always maintained. But no nation without the same extrinsic pressure could for twenty years have existed with elements so irreconcilable. And still that unity is very imperfect. A system of cantonal government is the life and essence of the whole polity, and yet that system maintains a state patriotism which often contradicts the national patriotism. 'My shirt is dearer to me than my coat,' said a Swiss statesman in 1846, meaning by that phrase to imply and justify his preference for the interest of his canton over the interest of his country. A federal government, especially in an area so minute, is an expedient for maintaining many centres of separation which tend to counteract the single centre of unity. The history of Switzerland, so far from proving that national homogeneity is not very conducive to national freedom, when well read proves the reverse; it proves that homogeneity is all but essential to any freedom and quite essential to the best freedom. An increase in the number of states, of which the subjects can really comprehend one another and really act with one another, is a probable sign of a great augmentation in the strength and number of free governments. Fifty years ago there was only one nation which could even *try* to form a free government, and that one – France – tried and failed. We now see how great her difficulties were – a hostile court, an incompetent aristocracy, an ignorant peasantry, large towns full of men depending upon uncertain trades, a literary class full of excellent intentions but without a true conception of practical politics, and overflowing with excessive and sanguine self-confidence. All the guides were blind and many of the people did not wish to be guided by them. The excitable and anxious French character, though not liable for all errors which have been charged to it, was nevertheless a perpetual cause of evil, which aggravated every calamity and darkened every good future. But though we may explain the failure of France, it was not the less a momentous and disastrous failure. It has created and diffused a sort of belief that free governments are much more difficult than they in truth are, and has led English-speaking persons, both here and in America, to pity other nations, and bless themselves that they have better political abilities than all foreigners, and especially than those 'poor French'. We shall now probably in the course of a few years have two great free nations – an Italian nation and a north German nation – and we may well hope that their conspicuous success may redeem the fatal effects of French failures, and bring even France itself back to a free, intellectual, and living government.

Lastly, it is evident (as we have often pointed out before) that the new map of Europe will be a better divided map than the old. The nations will be better balanced. This is in itself a great gain. The influence of France has for several years been far too great upon the Continent, and nothing but the singular ability with which the Emperor has exercised it has made it endurable. But that influence will be more effectually counterbalanced now. Not only in politics, but in literature and in society, Florence and Berlin will be living cities as London and Paris are living cities. France to a great extent, and England to some extent, will feel what so often happens to individuals in common life. In boyhood and early manhood a slight advantage in age, some four or five years, seems to give an almost incalculable advantage. A man of twenty-five has had a great start before one of twenty; he has perhaps left college, when the other is entering; at all events he had finished an important period of life which the other is just beginning. But after a few years this seeming inequality altogether changes: the man of forty has little or no advantage over the man of thirty-five; they do business one as well as another, and the fact that one began life a few years earlier is for all common purposes very trivial. Just so with nations – France and England had an early monopoly of certain advantages; they have been for many years the only two compact homogeneous powerful nations in Europe, and no one else has in many respects been comparable to them. But now other nations are beginning to share the same advantages, and in a few years all the effects of the first start will have faded away. North Germany and Italy will rival, equal, and perhaps excel, France and England in politics and literature, and in all by which one nation influences another. The preponderance of one or two nations is at an end; the day of many nations is beginning, and it is good for mankind that so it should be.

If we look out for set-offs which we are to reckon on the other side against these great gains, we shall hardly be able to find any. There is only one of signal magnitude, and the importance of that, though great now, will become less and less daily. We attach no importance to the recondite reason which French liberals have discovered for desiring the division of Germany. They say it is good that there should be many German nations, in order that a German liberal persecuted in one kingdom may have another to which he could fly. But no French liberal would be willing, for such a reason, to split up France. It would be very convenient to the enemies of the Emperor to be able to flee to Nancy or Marseilles; but they would not, therefore, be willing to endure the isolated existence of Lorraine or Provence. They know the blessing of unity to be so great that for themselves they would keep it at all hazards, and seem inclined to grudge it to any but themselves. Nor is much importance to be attached to the loss of old memories, old associations, and old objects of reverence, inevitable in the destruction of so many kingdoms and the fall of so many dynasties. Doubtless, in ignorant and out of the way rural places in Italy, a severe shock has been given to old habits of obedience; the old consecrated government is gone, and a new man-made government is put instead of it. Even in Germany many must feel the loss of their old rulers like the loss of household gods; they were, at any rate, familiar divinities if of rather homely make, and with but a narrow range of power. But in neither case is the accessary break of an inevitable revolution likely to destroy the continuity of civil society and the cement of social order; and therefore the effect is but slight now, and will be wholly forgotten everywhere in a few years. The most important set-off to the gains by the late war, is the bad example of the manner in which it was begun. It is impossible not to see in Bismarck a sort of cynical immorality – dangerous at all times, and perhaps peculiarly dangerous in the present age. We do not allude to his long contest with the Assembly on the structure of the army. That army has answered so well that Prussia has pardoned, and bystanders may pardon too, his far-seeing illegality. A political philosopher will admit that for such gigantic and sudden efforts a momentary dictator-ship has conclusive advantages over a parliamentary government. But none of these excuses can be pleaded for the treatment of Schleswig-Holstein. It is plain that Count Bismarck wanted a spark to fire his train; he wanted a war of some sort in Germany, and he used the duchies without hesitation and without scruple to provide a war. Prussia turned out the King of Denmark in the name of the Duke of Augustenburg or some other claimant of better right, and then divided the duchies between herself and Austria, who could have and claimed to have no right whatever. Then, as a capital expedient for kindling his coveted war, Bismarck quarrelled with Austria as to the division of the plunder. He began by robbing his *cestui que trust*, and ended by assaulting his co-trustee. Such shameless immorality may be hidden in the blaze of success, but the grave precedent of a great crime will be marked by history, and cast a shade over subsequent events.

(*WB*, viii, 154–60, *The Economist*, 1866)

THE GENERATION GAP

Every generation is unjust to the preceding generation; it respects its distant ancestors, but it thinks its fathers were 'quite wrong'. And this revolt of nature is a principal propelling force, and a power in civilization; for, without it, some set of strong men, consistently acting for a few generations, would soon stereotype the world. Yet this tendency is as unamiable as it is unfair, or even more unamiable. We enter into the fresh riches our fathers made for us, and at once we begin to say they are not the right sort; we enjoy and we grumble. We live in the house, and we say, 'If I had been the builder, that corner would not have stood out; if I could have had my way, the stairs would have been of oak; and how very obstinate my father always was about the smoke in the kitchen!' But we forget very likely that we are of a weaker force and more inefficient mind, and that, if we had had to build, probably there would have been no house at all.

(*WB*, vii, 388, from 'Matthew Arnold on the London University',
Fortnightly Review, 1868)

GENTLEMANLINESS

The gentlemanliness of our statesmen is no secondary excellence. It was said by Burke of a great nobleman of the last century that 'His virtues were his means'; that he accomplished by a gentle and high-minded honour what it would have been impossible to effect by coarse ability or impetuous disputation. If this great quality should die out from our political life, if it should be greatly diminished and permitted to sink gradually into decay, our political life will have lost a principal redeeming feature – our freedom will have lost one of its best securities – our statesmen will have lost the surest and best means of managing men.

(*WB*, vi, 122, from 'The Manners of Statesmen', *The Economist*,
1862)

EDWARD GIBBON★

A wit said of Gibbon's autobiography, that he did not know the difference between himself and the Roman Empire. He has narrated

---

★ A review of a new edition of Gibbon's *The History of the Decline and Fall of the Roman Empire*, with notes by Dean Milman and Guizot, the French politician and historian.

his 'progressions from London to Buriton, and from Buriton to London', in the same monotonous majestic periods that record the fall of states and empires. The consequence is, that a fascinating book gives but a vague idea of its subject. It may not be without its use to attempt a description of him in plainer though less splendid English.

The diligence of their descendant accumulated many particulars of the remote annals of the Gibbon family; but its real founder was the grandfather of the historian, who lived in the times of the 'South Sea'. He was a capital man of business according to the custom of that age – a dealer in many kinds of merchandise – like perhaps the 'complete tradesman' of Defoe, who was to understand the price and quality of *all* articles made within the kingdom. The preference, however, of Edward Gibbon, the grandfather, was for the article 'shares'; his genius, like that of Mr Hudson, had a natural tendency towards a commerce in the metaphysical and non-existent; and he was fortunate in the age on which his lot was thrown. It afforded many opportunities of gratifying that taste. Much has been written on panics and manias – much more than with the most outstretched intellect we are able to follow or conceive; but one thing is certain, that at particular times a great many stupid people have a great deal of stupid money. Saving people have often only the faculty of saving; they accumulate ably, and contemplate their accumulations with approbation; but what to do with them they do not know. Aristotle, who was not in trade, imagined that money is barren; and barren it is to quiet ladies, rural clergymen, and country misers. Several economists have plans for preventing improvident speculation; one would abolish Peel's Act, and substitute one-pound notes; another would retain Peel's Act, and make the calling for one-pound notes a capital crime: but our scheme is, not to allow any man to have a hundred pounds who cannot prove to the satisfaction of the Lord Chancellor that he knows what to do with a hundred pounds. The want of this easy precaution allows the accumulation of wealth in the hands of rectors, authors, grandmothers, who have no knowledge of business, and no idea except that their money now produces nothing, and ought and must be forced immediately to produce something. 'I wish,' said one of this class, 'for the largest immediate income, and I am therefore naturally disposed to purchase an *advowson*.' At intervals, from causes which are not to the present purpose, the money of these people – the blind capital (as we call it) of the country – is particularly large and craving; it seeks for someone to devour it, and there is 'plethora' – it finds someone, and there is 'speculation' – it is devoured, and there is 'panic'. The age of Mr Gibbon was one of these. The interest of money was very low, perhaps under three per cent. The usual consequence followed; able men started wonderful undertakings; the ablest of all, a company 'for carrying on an undertaking of great importance, but no one to know what it was'. Mr Gibbon was not idle. According to the narrative of his grandson, he already filled a considerable position, was worth sixty thousand pounds, and had great influence both in Parliament and in the City. He applied himself to the greatest bubble of all – one so great, that it is spoken of in many books as the cause and parent of all contemporary bubbles – the South-Sea Company – the design of which was to reduce the interest on the national debt, which, oddly enough, it did reduce, and to trade exclusively to the South Sea or Spanish America, where of course, it hardly did trade. Mr Gibbon became a director, sold and bought, traded and prospered; and was considered, perhaps with truth, to have obtained much money. The bubble was essentially a fashionable one. Public intelligence and the quickness of communication did not then as now at once spread pecuniary information and misinformation to secluded districts; but fine ladies, men of fashion – the London world – ever anxious to make as much of its money as it can, and then wholly unwise (it is not now very wise) in discovering how the most *was* to be made of it – 'went in' and speculated largely. As usual, all was favourable so long as the shares were rising; the price was at one time very high, and the agitation very general; it was, in a word, the railway mania in the South Sea. After a time, the shares 'hesitated', declined, and fell; and there was an outcry against everybody concerned in the matter, very like the outcry against the οἱ περὶ Hudson in our own time. The results, however, were very different. Whatever may be said, and, judging from the late experience, a good deal is likely to be said, as to the advantages of civilization and education, it seems certain that they tend to diminish a simple-minded energy. The Parliament of 1720 did not, like the Parliament of 1847, allow itself to be bored and incommoded by legal minutiae, nor did it forego the use of plain words. A committee reported the discovery of 'a train of the deepest villainy and fraud *hell* ever contrived to ruin a nation'; the directors of the company were arrested, and Mr Gibbon among the rest; he was compelled to give in a list of his effects: the general wish was that a retrospective act should be immediately passed, which would impose on him penalties something like, or even more severe than those now enforced on Paul and Strahan. In the end, however, Mr Gibbon escaped with a parliamentary conversation upon his affairs. His estate amounted to 140,000*l.*; and as this was a great sum, there was an obvious suspicion that he was a great criminal. The scene must have been very curious. 'Allowances of twenty pounds or one shilling were facetiously voted. A vague report that a director had formerly been concerned in another project by which some unknown persons had lost their money, was admitted as a proof of his actual guilt. One man was ruined because he had dropped a foolish speech that his horses should feed upon gold; another because he was grown so proud, that one day, at the Treasury, he had refused a civil answer to persons far above him.' The vanity of his descendant is evidently a little tried by the peculiar severity with which his grandfather was treated. Out of his hundred and forty thousand pounds it was only proposed that he should retain fifteen; and on an amendment even this was reduced to ten thousand. Yet there is some ground for believing that the acute energy and practised pecuniary power which had been successful in obtaining so large a fortune, were likewise applied with science to the inferior task of retaining some of it. The historian indeed says, 'On these ruins,' the 10,000*l.* aforesaid, 'with the skill and credit of which Parliament had not been able to deprive him, my grandfather erected the edifice of a new fortune: the labours of sixteen years were amply rewarded; and I have reason to believe that the second structure was not much inferior to the first.' But this only shows how far a family feeling may bias a sceptical judgement. The credit of a man in Mr Gibbon's position could not be very lucrative; and his skill must have been enormous to have obtained so much at the end of his life, in such circumstances, in so few years. Had he been an early Christian, the narrative of his descendant would have contained an insidious hint, 'that pecuniary property *may* be so secreted as to defy the awkward approaches of political investigation'. That he died rich is certain for two generations lived solely ·on the property he bequeathed.

The son of this great speculator, the historian's father, was a man to spend a fortune quietly. He is not related to have indulged in any particular expense, and nothing is more difficult to follow than the pecuniary fortunes of deceased families; but one thing is certain, that the property which descended to the historian – making every allowance for all minor and subsidiary modes of diminution, such as daughters, settlements, legacies, and so forth – was enormously less than 140,000*l.*; and therefore if those figures are correct, the second generation must have made itself very happy out of the savings of the past generation, and without caring for the poverty of the next. Nothing that is related of the historian's father indicates a strong judgement or an acute discrimination; and there are some scarcely dubious signs of a rather weak character.

Edward Gibbon, the great, was born on the 27th of April, 1737. Of his mother we hear scarcely anything; and what we do hear is not remarkably favourable. It seems that she was a faint inoffensive woman, of ordinary capacity, who left a very slight trace of her influence on the character of her son; who did little and died early. The real mother, as he is careful to explain, of his understanding and education was her sister, and his aunt, *Mrs* Catherine Porten, according to the speech of that age, a maiden lady of much vigour and capacity, and for whom her pupil really seems to have felt as much affection as was consistent with a rather easy and cool nature. There is a panegyric on her in the *Memoirs*; and in a long letter upon the occasion of her death, he deposes: 'To her care I am indebted in earliest infancy for the preservation of my life and health . . . To her instructions I owe the first rudiments of knowledge, the first exercise of reason, and a taste for books, which is still the pleasure and glory of my life; and though she taught me neither language nor science, she was certainly the most useful preceptor I ever had. As I grew up, an intercourse of thirty years endeared her to me as the faithful friend and the agreeable companion. You have seen with what freedom and confidence we lived,' &c. &c. To a less sentimental mind, which takes a more tranquil view of aunts and relatives, it is satisfactory to find that somehow he could not write to her. 'I wish,' he continues, 'I had as much to applaud and as little to reproach in my behaviour towards Mrs Porten since I left England; and when I reflect that my letters would have soothed and comforted her decline, I feel' what an ardent nephew would naturally feel at so unprecedented an event. Leaving his maturer years out of the question – a possible rhapsody of affectionate eloquence – she seems to have been of the greatest use to him in infancy. His health was very imperfect. We hear much of rheumatism, and lameness, and weakness; and he was unable to join in work and play with ordinary boys. He was moved from one school to another, never staying anywhere very long, and owing what knowledge he obtained rather to a strong retentive understanding than to any external stimulants or instruction. At one place he gained an acquaintance with the Latin elements at the price of 'many tears and some blood'. At last he was consigned to the instruction of an elegant clergyman, the Rev. Philip Francis, who had obtained notoriety by a metrical translation of Horace, the laxity of which is even yet complained of by construing schoolboys, and who, with a somewhat Horatian taste, went to London as often as he could, and translated *invisa negotia* as 'boys to beat'.

In school-work, therefore, Gibbon had uncommon difficulties and unusual deficiencies; but these were much more than counterbalanced by a habit which often accompanies a sickly childhood, and is the commencement of a studious life, the habit of desultory reading. The instructiveness of this is sometimes not comprehended. S. T. Coleridge used to say that he felt a great superiority over those who had not read – and fondly read – fairy tales in their childhood; he thought they wanted a sense which he possessed, the perception, or appercep- tion – we do not know which he used to say it was – of the unity and wholeness of the universe. As to fairy tales, this is a hard saying; but as to desultory reading it is certainly true. Some people have known a time in life when there was no book they could not read. The fact of its being a book went immensely in its favour. In early life there is an opinion that the obvious thing to do with a horse is to ride it; with a cake, to eat it; with sixpence, to spend it. A few boys carry this further, and think the natural thing to do with a book is to read it. There is an argument from design in the subject: if the book was not meant for that purpose, for what purpose was it meant? Of course, of any understanding of the works so perused there is no question or idea. There is a legend of Bentham, in his earliest childhood, climbing to the height of a huge stool and sitting there evening after evening with two candles engaged in the perusal of Rapin's history. It might as well have been any other book. The doctrine of utility had not then dawned on its immortal teacher; *cui bono* was an idea unknown to him. He would have been ready to read about Egypt, about Spain, about the coals in Borneo, the teak-wood in India, the current in the river Mississippi, on natural history or human history, on theology or morals, on the state of the dark ages or the state of the light ages, – on Augustulus or Lord Chatham, – on the first century or the seventeenth, – on the moon, the millennium, or the whole duty of man. Just then, reading is an end in itself. At that time of life you no more think of a future consequence, of the remote, the very remote possibility of deriving knowledge from the perusal of a book, than you expect so great a result from spinning a peg-top. You spin the top, and you read the book; and these scenes of life are exhausted. In such studies, of all prose perhaps the best is history. One page is so like another; battle No. 1 is so much on a par with battle No. 2. Truth may be, as they say, stranger than fiction, abstractedly; but in actual books, novels are certainly odder and more astounding than correct history. It will be said, what is the use of this? Why not leave the reading of great books till a great age? Why plague and perplex childhood with complex facts remote from its experience and inapprehensible by its imagination? The reply is, that though in all great and combined facts there is much which childhood cannot thoroughly imagine, there is also in very many a great deal which can only be truly apprehended for the first time at that age. Catch an American of thirty; – tell him about the battle of Marathon; what will he be able to comprehend of all that *you* mean by it; of all that halo which early impression and years of remembrance have cast around it? He may add up the killed and wounded, estimate the missing, and take the dimensions of Greece and Athens; but he will not seem to care much. He may say, 'Well, sir, perhaps it was a smart thing in that small territory; but it is a long time ago, and in *my* country James K. Burnup' did that which he will at length explain to you. Or try an experiment on yourself. Read the account of a Circassian victory, equal in numbers, in daring, in romance, to the old battle. Will you be able to feel about it at all in the same way? It is impossible. You cannot form a new set of associations; your mind is involved in pressing facts, your memory choked by a thousand details; the liveliness of fancy is gone with the childhood by which it was enlivened. Schamyl will never seem as great as Leonidas or Miltiades; Cnokemof, or whoever the Russian is, cannot be so imposing as Xerxes; the unpronounceable place cannot strike on your heart like Marathon or Plataea. Moreover, there is the further advantage which Coleridge shadowed forth in the remark we cited. Youth has a principle of consolidation. We begin with the whole. Small sciences are the labours of our manhood; but the round universe is the plaything of the boy. His fresh mind shoots out vaguely and crudely into the infinite and eternal. Nothing is hid from the depth of it: there are no boundaries to its vague and wandering vision. Early science, it has been said, begins in utter nonsense; it would be truer to say that it starts with boyish fancies. How absurd seem the notions of the first Greeks! Who could believe now that air or water was the principle, the pervading substance, the eternal material of all things? Such affairs will never explain a thick rock. And what a white original for a green and sky-blue world! Yet people disputed in those ages not whether it was either of those substances, but which of them it was. And doubtless there was a great deal, at least in quantity, to be said on both sides. Boys are improved; but some in our own day have asked 'Mamma, I say, what did God make the world of?' and several, who did not venture on speech, have had an idea of some one grey primitive thing, felt a difficulty as to how the red came, and wondered that marble could *ever* have been the same as moonshine. This is in truth the picture of life. We begin with the infinite and eternal, which we shall never apprehend; and these form a framework, a schedule, a set of co-ordinates to which we refer all which we learn later. At first, like the old Greek, 'we look up to the whole sky and are lost in the one and the all'; in the end we classify and enumerate, learn each star, calculate distances, draw cramped diagrams on the unbounded sky, write a paper on α Cygni and a treatise on ε Draconis, map special facts upon the indefinite void, and engrave precise details on the infinite and everlasting. So in history; somehow the whole comes in boyhood; the details later and in manhood. The wonderful series going far back to the times of old patriarchs with their flocks and herds, the keen-eyed Greek, the stately Roman, the watching Jew, the uncouth Goth, the horrid Hun, the settled picture of the unchanging East, the restless shifting of the rapid West, the rise of the cold and classical civilization, its fall, the rough impetuous middle ages, the vague warm picture of ourselves and home, – when did we learn these? Not yesterday nor today; but long ago, in the first dawn of reason, in the original flow of fancy. What we learn afterwards are but the accurate littlenesses of the great topic, the dates and tedious facts. Those who begin late learn only these; but the happy first feel the mystic associations and the progress of the whole.

There is no better illustration of all this than Gibbon. Few have begun early with a more desultory reading, and fewer still have described it so skilfully. 'From the ancient I leaped to the modern world: many crude lumps of Speed, Rapin, Mezeray, Davila, Machiavel, Father Paul, Bower, &c., I devoured like so many novels; and I swallowed with the same voracious appetite the descriptions of India and China, of Mexico and Peru. My first introduction to the historic scenes which have since engaged so many years of my life must be ascribed to an accident. In the summer of 1751 I accompanied my father on a visit to Mr Hoare's, in Wiltshire; but I was less delighted with the beauties of Stourhead than with discovering in the library a common book, the *Continuation of Echard's Roman History*, which is indeed executed with more skill and taste than the previous work. To me the reigns of the successors of Constantine were absolutely new; and I was immersed in the passage of the Goths over the Danube when the summons of the dinner-bell reluctantly dragged me from my intellectual feast. This transient glance served rather to irritate than to appease my curiosity: and as soon as I returned to Bath I procured the second and third volumes of Howell's *History of the World*, which exhibit the Byzantine period on a larger scale. Mahomet and his Saracens soon fixed my attention; and some instinct of criticism directed me to the genuine sources. Simon Ockley, an original in every sense, first opened my eyes; and I was led from one book to another till I had ranged round the circle of Oriental history. Before I was sixteen I had exhausted all that could be learned in English of the Arabs and Persians, the Tartars and Turks; and the same ardour urged me to guess at the French of D'Herbelot, and to construe the barbarous Latin of Pocock's *Abulfaragius.*' To this day the schoolboy-student of the *Decline and Fall* feels the traces of that schoolboy-reading. *Once,* he is conscious, the author like him felt, and solely felt, the magnificent progress of the great story and the scenic aspect of marvellous events.

A more sudden effect was at hand. However exalted may seem the praises which we have given to loose and unplanned reading, we are not saying that it is the sole ingredient of a good education. Besides this sort of education, which some boys will voluntarily and naturally give themselves, there needs, of course, another and more rigorous kind, which must be impressed upon them from without. The terrible difficulty of early life – the *use* of pastors and masters – really is, that they compel boys to a distinct mastery of that which they do not wish to learn. There is nothing to be said for a preceptor who is not dry. Mr Carlyle describes with bitter satire the fate of one of his heroes who was obliged to acquire whole systems of information in which he, the hero, saw no use, and which he kept as far as might be in a vacant corner of his mind. And this is the very point – dry language, tedious mathematics, a thumbed grammar, a detested slate, form gradually an interior separate intellect, exact in its information, rigid in its requirements, disciplined in its exercises. The two grow together, the early natural fancy touching the far extremities of the universe, lightly playing with the scheme of all things; the precise, compacted memory slowly accumulating special facts, exact habits, clear and painful conceptions. At last, as it were in a moment, the cloud breaks up, the division sweeps away; we find that in fact these exercises which puzzled us, these languages which we hated, these details which we despised, are the instruments of true thought, are the very keys and openings, the exclusive access to the knowledge which we loved.

In this second education the childhood of Gibbon had been very defective. He had never been placed under any rigid training. In his first boyhood he disputed with his aunt, 'that were I master of Greek and Latin, I must interpret to myself in English the thoughts of the original, and that such extemporary versions must be inferior to the elaborate translation of professed scholars: a silly sophism,' as he remarks, 'which could not easily be confuted by a person ignorant of any other language than her own'. Ill-health, a not very wise father, an ill-chosen succession of schools and pedagogues, prevented his acquiring exact knowledge in the regular subjects of study. His own description is the best – 'erudition that might have puzzled a doctor, and a degree of ignorance of which a schoolboy would have been ashamed'. The amiable Mr Francis, who was to have repaired the deficiency, went to London, and forgot him. With an impulse of discontent his father took a resolution, and sent him to Oxford at sixteen.

It is probable that a worse place could not have been found. The University of Oxford was at the nadir of her history and efficiency. The public professorial training of the middle ages had died away, and the intramural collegiate system of the present time had not begun. The University had ceased to be a teaching body, and had not yet become an examining body. 'The professors,' says Adam Smith, who had studied there, 'have given up almost the pretence of lecturing.' 'The examination,' said a great judge some years later, 'was a farce in my time. I was asked who founded University College; and I said, though the fact is now doubted, that King Alfred founded it; and *that* was the examination.' The colleges, deprived of the superintendence and watchfulness of their natural sovereign, fell, as Gibbon remarks, into 'port and prejudice'. The Fellows were a close corporation; they were chosen from every conceivable motive – because they were respectable men, because they were good fellows, because they were brothers of other Fellows, because their fathers had patronage in the church. Men so appointed could not be expected to be very diligent in the instruction of youth; many colleges did not even profess it; that of All Souls has continued down to our own time to deny that it has anything to do with it. Undoubtedly a person who came thither accurately and rigidly drilled in technical scholarship found many means and a few motives to pursue it. Some tutorial system probably existed at most colleges. Learning was not wholly useless in the church. The English gentleman has ever loved a nice and classical scholarship. But these advantages were open only to persons who had received a very strict training, and who were voluntarily disposed to discipline themselves still more. To the mass of mankind the University was a 'graduating machine'; the colleges, monopolist residences, – hotels without bells.

Taking the place as it stood, the lot of Gibbon may be thought rather fortunate. He was placed at Magdalen, whose fascinating walks, so beautiful in the later autumn, still recall the name of Addison, the example of the merits, as Gibbon is of the deficiencies, of Oxford. His first tutor was, in his own opinion, 'one of the best of the tribe'. 'Dr Waldegrave was a learned and pious man, of a mild disposition, strict morals, and abstemious life, who seldom mingled in the politics or the jollity of the college. But his knowledge of the world was confined to the University; his learning was of the last, rather than the present age; his temper was indolent; his faculties, which were not of the first rate, had been relaxed by the climate; and he was satisfied, like his fellows, with the slight and superficial discharge of an important trust. As soon as my tutor had sounded the insufficiency of his pupil in school-learning, he proposed that we should read every morning, from ten to eleven, the comedies of Terence. The sum of my improvement in the University of Oxford is confined to three or four Latin plays; and even the study of an elegant classic, which might have been illustrated by a comparison of ancient and modern theatres, was reduced to a dry and literal interpretation of the author's text. During the first weeks I constantly attended these lessons in my tutor's room; but as they appeared equally devoid of profit and pleasure, I was once tempted to try the experiment of a formal apology. The apology was accepted with a smile. I repeated the offence with less ceremony; the excuse was admitted with the same indulgence: the slightest motive of laziness or indisposition, the most trifling avocation at home or abroad, was allowed as a worthy impediment; nor did my tutor appear conscious of my absence or neglect. Had the hour of lecture been constantly filled, a single hour was a small portion of my academic leisure. No plan of study was recommended for my use; no exercises were prescribed for his inspection; and, at the most precious season of youth, whole days and weeks were suffered to elapse without labour or amusement, without advice or account.' The name of his second tutor is concealed in asterisks, and the sensitive conscience of Dean Milman will not allow him to insert a name 'which *Gibbon* thought proper to suppress'. The account, however, of the anonymous person is sufficiently graphic. 'Dr — well remembered that he had a salary to receive, and only forgot that he had a duty to perform. Instead of guiding the studies and watching over the behaviour of his disciple, I was never summoned to attend even the ceremony of a lecture; and excepting one voluntary visit to his rooms, during the eight months of his titular office the tutor and pupil lived in the same college as strangers to each other.' It added to the evils of this neglect, that Gibbon was much younger than most of the students; and that his temper, which was through life reserved, was then very shy. His appearance, too, was odd; 'a thin little figure, with a large head, disputing and arguing with the greatest ability'. Of course he was a joke among undergraduates; he consulted his tutor as to studying Arabic, and was seen buying *La Bibliothèque Orientale D'Herbelot*, and immediately a legend was diffused that he had turned Mahomedan. The random cast was not so far from the mark: cut off by peculiarities from the society of young people; deprived of regular tuition and systematic employment; tumbling about among crude masses of heterogeneous knowledge; alone with the heated brain of youth, – he did what an experienced man would expect – he framed a theory of all things. No doubt it seemed to him the most natural thing in the world. Was he to be the butt of ungenial wine-parties, or spend his lonely hours on shreds of languages? Was he not to know the *truth*? There were the old problems, the everlasting difficulties, the *moenia mundi*, the Hercules' pillars of the human imagination – 'fate, free-will, fore-knowledge absolute'. Surely these should come first; when we had learned the great landmarks, understood the guiding-stars, we might amuse ourselves with small points, and make a plaything of curious information. What particular theory the mind frames when in this state is a good deal matter of special accident. The *data* for considering these difficulties are not within its reach. Whether man be or be not born to solve the 'mystery of the knowable', he certainly is not born to solve it at seventeen, with the first hot rush of the untrained mind. The selection of Gibbon was remarkable: he became a Roman Catholic.

It seems now so natural that an Oxford man should take this step, that one can hardly understand the astonishment it created. Lord Sheffield tells us that the Privy Council interfered; and with good administrative judgement examined a London bookseller – some Mr Lewis – who had no concern in it. In the manor-house of Buriton it would have probably created less sensation if 'dear Edward' had announced his intention of becoming a monkey. The English have ever believed that the Papist is a kind of *creature*; and every sound mind would prefer a beloved child to produce a tail, a hide of hair, and a taste for nuts, in comparison with transubstantiation, wax-candles, and a belief in the glories of Mary.

What exact motives impelled Gibbon to this step cannot now be certainly known; the autobiography casts a mist over them; but from what appears, his conversion partly much resembled, and partly altogether differed from, the Oxford conversions of our own time. We hear nothing of the notes of a church, or the sin of the Reformation; and Gibbon had not an opportunity of even rejecting Mr Sewell's theory that it is 'a holy obligation to acquiesce in the opinions of your grandmother'. His memoirs have a halo of great names – Bossuet, the *History of Protestant Variations*, &c. &c. – and he speaks with becoming dignity of falling by a noble hand. He mentioned also to Lord Sheffield, as having had a preponderating influence over him, the works of Father Parsons, who lived in Queen Elizabeth's time. But in all probability these were secondary persuasions, justifications after the event. No young man, or scarcely any young man of seventeen, was ever converted by a systematic treatise, especially if written in another age, wearing an obsolete look, speaking a language which scarcely seems that of this world. There is an unconscious reasoning: 'The world has had this book before it so long, and has withstood it. There must be something wrong; it seems all right on the surface, but a flaw there must be.' The mass of the volumes, too, is unfavourable. 'All the paper-arguments in the world,' says the young convert in *Loss and Gain*, 'are unequal to giving one a view in a moment.' What the youthful mind requires is this short decisive argument, this view in a moment, this flash as it were of the understanding, which settles all, and diffuses a conclusive light at once and for ever over the whole. It is so much the pleasanter if the young mind can strike this view out for itself, from materials which are forced upon it from the controversies of the day; if it can find a certain solution of pending questions, and show itself wiser even than the wisest of its own, the very last age. So far as appears, this was the fortune of Gibbon. 'It was not long,' he says, 'since Dr Middleton's *Free Inquiry* had sounded an alarm in the theological world; much ink and much gall had been spilt in defence of the primitive miracles; and the two dullest of their champions were crowned with academic honours by the University of Oxford. The name of Middleton was unpopular; and his proscription very naturally led me to peruse his writings and those of his antagonists.' It is not difficult to discover in this work easy and striking arguments which might lead an untaught mind to the communion of Rome. As to the peculiar belief of its author there has been much controversy, with which we have not here the least concern; but the natural conclusion to which it would lead a simple intellect is, that all miracles are equally certain or equally uncertain. 'It being agreed, then,' says the acute controversialist, 'that in the original promise of these miraculous gifts there is no intimation of any particular period to which their continuance was limited, the next question is, by what sort of evidence the precise time of their duration is to be determined? But to this point one of the writers just referred to excuses himself, as we have seen, from giving any answer; and thinks it sufficient to declare in general that *the earliest fathers unanimously affirm them to have continued down to their times*. Yet he has not told us, as he ought to have done, to what age he limits the character of *the earliest fathers*; whether to the second or to the third century, or, with the generality of our writers, means also to include the fourth. But to whatever age he may restrain it, the difficulty at last will be to assign a reason why we must needs stop there. In the meanwhile, by his appealing thus to the *earliest fathers* only as unanimous on this article, a common reader would be apt to infer that the later fathers are more cold or diffident, or divided upon it; whereas the reverse of this is true, and the more we descend from those earliest fathers the more strong and explicit we find their successors in attesting the perpetual succession and daily exertion of the same miraculous powers in their several ages; so that if the cause must be determined by *the unanimous consent of fathers*, we shall find as much reason to believe that those powers were continued even to the latest ages as to any other, how early and primitive soever, after the days of the apostles. But the same writer gives us two reasons why he does not choose to say anything upon the subject of their duration; first, because *there is not light enough in history to settle it*; secondly, because *the thing itself is of no concern to us*. As to his first reason, I am at a loss to conceive what further light a professed advocate of the primitive ages and fathers can possibly require in this case. For as far as the church-historians can illustrate or throw light upon anything, there is not a single point in all history so constantly, explicitly, and unanimously affirmed by them all, as the continual succession of these powers through all ages, from the earliest father who first mentions them down to the time of the Reformation. Which same succession is still further deduced by persons of the most eminent character for their probity, learning, and dignity in the Romish church, to this very day. So that the only doubt which can remain with us is, whether the church-historians are to be trusted or not; for if any credit be due to them in the present case, it must reach either to all or to none; because the reason of believing them in any one age will be found to be of equal force in all, as far as it depends on the characters of the persons attesting, or the nature of the things attested.' In *terms* this and the whole of Middleton's argument is so shaped as to avoid including in its scope the miracles of Scripture, which are mentioned throughout with eulogiums and acquiescence, and so as to make you doubt whether the author believed them or not. This is exactly one of the pretences which the young strong mind delights to tear down. It would argue, 'This writer evidently *means* that the apostolic miracles have just as much evidence and no more than the popish or the patristic; and how strong' – for Middleton is a master of telling statement – 'he shows that evidence to be! I won't give up the apostolic miracles, I cannot; yet I must believe what has as much of historical testimony in its favour. It is no *reductio ad absurdum* that we must go over to the church of Rome; it is the most diffused of Christian creeds, the oldest of Christian churches.' And so the logic of the sceptic becomes, as often since, the most efficient instrument of the all-believing and all-determining church.

The consternation of Gibbon's relatives seems to have been enormous. They cast about what to do. From the experience of Oxford, they perhaps thought that it would be useless to have recourse to the Anglican clergy; this resource had failed. So they took him to Mr Mallet, a deist, to see if he could do anything; but he did nothing. Their next step was nearly as extraordinary. They placed him at Lausanne in the house of M. Pavilliard, a French Protestant minister. After the easy income, complete independence, and unlimited credit of an English undergraduate, he was thrown into a foreign country, deprived, as he says, by ignorance of the language both of 'speech and hearing', – in the position of a schoolboy, with a small allowance of pocket-money, and without the Epicurean comforts on which he already set some value. He laments the 'indispensable comfort of a servant', and the 'sordid and uncleanly table of Madame Pavilliard'. In our own day the watchful sagacity of Cardinal Wiseman would hardly allow a promising convert of expectations and talents to remain unsolaced in so pitiful a situation; we should hear soothing offers of flight or succour, some insinuation of a popish domestic and interesting repasts. But a hundred years ago the attention of the Holy See was very little directed to our English youth, and Gibbon was left to endure his position.

It is curious that he made himself comfortable. Though destitute of external comforts which he did not despise, he found what was the greatest luxury to his disposition, steady study and regular tuition. His tutor was, of course, to convert him if he could; but as they had no language in common, there was the preliminary occupation of teaching French. During five years both tutor and pupil steadily exerted themselves to repair the defects of a neglected and ill-grounded education. We hear of the perusal of Terence, Virgil, Horace, and Tacitus. Cicero was translated into French, and translated back again into Latin. In both languages the pupil's progress was sound and good. From letters of his which still exist, it is clear that he then acquired the exact and steady knowledge of Latin of which he afterwards made so much use. His circumstances compelled him to master French. If his own letters are to be trusted, he would be an example of his own doctrine, that no one is thoroughly master of more than one language at a time; they read like the letters of a

Frenchman trying and failing to write English. But perhaps there was a desire to magnify his continental progress, and towards the end of the time some wish to make his friends fear he was forgetting his own language.

Meantime the work of conversion was not forgotten. In some letters which are extant, M. Pavilliard celebrates the triumph of his logic. 'J'ai renversé,' says the pastor, 'l'infaillibilité de l'église; j'ai prouvé que jamais St Pierre n'a été chef des apôtres; que quand il l'aurait été, le pape n'est point son successeur; qu'il est douteux que St Pierre ait jamais été à Rome; mais supposé qu'il y ait été, il n'a pas été évêque de cette ville; que la transubstantiation est une invention humaine, et peu ancienne dans l'église,' &c., and so on through the usual list of Protestant arguments. He magnifies a little Gibbon's strength of conviction, as it makes the success of his own logic seem more splendid; but states two curious things, first, that Gibbon at least *pretended* to believe in the Pretender, and what is more amazing still – all but incredible – that he fasted. Such was the youth of the Epicurean historian!

It is probable, however, that the skill of the Swiss pastor was not the really operating cause of the event. Perhaps experience shows that the converts which Rome has made, with the threat of unbelief and the weapons of the sceptic, have rarely been permanent or advantageous to her. It is at best but a dangerous logic to drive men to the edge and precipice of scepticism, in the hope that they will recoil in horror to the very interior of credulity. Possibly men may show their courage – they may vanquish the *argumentum ad terrorem* – they may not find scepticism so terrible. This last was Gibbon's case. A more insidious adversary than the Swiss theology was at hand to sap his Roman Catholic belief. Pavilliard had a fair French library – not ill-stored in the recent publications of that age – of which he allowed his pupil the continual use. It was as impossible to open any of them and not come in contact with infidelity, as to come to England and not to see a green field. Scepticism is not so much a part of the French literature of that day as its animating spirit – its essence, its vitality. You can no more cut it out and separate it, than you can extract from Wordsworth his conception of nature, or from Swift his common sense. And it is of the subtlest kind. It has little in common with the rough disputation of the English deist, or the perplexing learning of the German theologian; but works with a tool more insinuating than either. It is, in truth, but the spirit of the world, which does not argue, but assumes; which does not so much elaborate as hints; which does not examine, but suggests. With the traditions of the church it contrasts traditions of its own; its technicalities are *bon sens, l'usage du monde, le fanatisme, l'enthousiasme*; to high hopes, noble sacrifices, awful lives, it opposes quiet ease, skilful comfort, placid sense, polished indifference. Old as transubstantiation may be, it is not older than Horace and Lucian. Lord Byron, in the well-known lines, has coupled the names of the two literary exiles on the Leman Lake. The page of Voltaire could not but remind Gibbon that the scepticism from which he had revolted was compatible with literary eminence and European fame – gave a piquancy to ordinary writing – was the very expression of caustic caution and gentlemanly calm.

The grave and erudite habits of Gibbon soon developed themselves. Independently of these abstruse theological disputations, he spent many hours daily – rising early and reading carefully – on classical and secular learning. He was not, however, wholly thus engrossed. There was in the neighbourhood of Lausanne a certain Mademoiselle Curchod, to whom he devoted some of his time. She seems to have been a morbidly rational lady; at least she had a grave taste. Gibbon could not have been a very enlivening lover; he was decidedly plain, and his predominating taste was for solid learning. But this was not all; she formed an attachment to M. Necker, afterwards the most slow of premiers, whose financial treatises can hardly have been agreeable even to a Genevese beauty. This was, however, at a later time. So far as appears, Gibbon was her first love. How extreme her feelings were one does not know. Those of Gibbon can scarcely be supposed to have done him any harm. However, there was an intimacy, a flirtation, an engagement – when, as usual, it appeared that neither had any money. That the young lady should procure any seems to have been out of the question; and Gibbon, supposing that he might, wrote to his father. The reply was unfavourable. Gibbon's mother was dead; Mr Gibbon senior was married again; and even in other circumstances would have been scarcely ready to encourage a romantic engagement to a lady with nothing. She spoke no English, too, and marriage with a person speaking only French is still regarded as a most unnatural event; forbidden, not indeed by the literal law of the church, but by those higher instinctive principles of our nature, to which the bluntest own obedience. No father could be expected to violate at once pecuniary duties and patriotic principles. Mr Gibbon senior forbade the match. The young lady does not seem to have been quite ready to relinquish all hope; but she had shown a grave taste, and fixed her affections on a sound and cold mind. 'I sighed,' narrates the historian, 'as a lover; but I obeyed as a son.' 'The letter in which Gibbon communicated to Mademoiselle Curchod the opposition of his father to their marriage,' says M. Suard, 'still exists in manuscript. The first pages are tender and melancholy, as might be expected from an unhappy lover; the latter became by degrees calm and reasonable; and the letter concludes with these words: *C'est pourquoi, mademoiselle, j'ai l'honneur d'être votre très humble et très obéissant serviteur, Edward Gibbon.*' Her father died soon afterwards, and 'she retired to Geneva, where, by teaching young ladies, she earned a hard subsistence for herself and her mother'; but the tranquil disposition of her admirer preserved him from any romantic display of sympathy and fidelity. He continued to study various readings in Cicero, as well as the passage of Hannibal over the Alps; and with those affectionate resources set sentiment at defiance. Yet thirty years later the lady, then the wife of the most conspicuous man in Europe, was able to suggest useful reflections to an aged bachelor, slightly dreaming of a superannuated marriage: 'Gardez-vous, monsieur, de former un de ces liens tardifs: le mariage qui rend heureux dans l'age mûr, c'est celui qui fut contracté dans la jeunesse. Alors seulement la réunion est parfaite, les goûts se communiquent, les sentimens se répandent, les idées deviennent communes, les facultés intellectuelles se modèlent mutuellement. Toute la vie est double, et toute la vie est une prolongation de la jeunesse; car les impressions de l'âme commandent aux yeux, et la beauté qui n'est plus conserve encore son empire; mais pour vous, monsieur, dans toute la vigueur de la pensée, lorsque toute l'existence est décidée, l'on ne pourroit sans un miracle trouver une femme digne de vous; et une association d'un genre imparfait rappelle toujours la statue d'Horace, qui joint à une belle tête le corps d'un stupide poisson. Vous êtes marié avec la gloire.' She was then a cultivated French lady, giving an account of the reception of the *Decline and Fall* at Paris, and expressing rather peculiar ideas on the style of Tacitus. The world had come round to her side, and she explains to her old lover rather well her happiness with M. Necker.

After living nearly five years at Lausanne, Gibbon returned to England. Continental residence has made a great alteration in many Englishmen; but few have undergone so complete a metamorphosis as Edward Gibbon. He left his own country a hot-brained and ill-taught youth, willing to sacrifice friends and expectations for a superstitious and half-known creed; he returned a cold and ac-complished man, master of many accurate ideas, little likely to hazard any coin for any faith: already, it is probable, inclined in secret to a cautious scepticism; placing thereby, as it were, upon a system the frigid prudence and unventuring incredulity congenial to his character. His change of character changed his position among his relatives. His father, he says, met him as a friend; and they continued thenceforth on a footing of 'easy intimacy'. Especially after the little affair of Mademoiselle Curchod, and the 'very sensible view he took in that instance of the matrimonial relation', there can be but little question that Gibbon was justly regarded as a most safe young man, singularly prone to large books, and a little too fond of French phrases and French ideas; but yet with a great feeling of common sense, and a wise preference of permanent money to transitory sentiment. His father allowed him a moderate, and but a moderate income, which he husbanded with great care, and only voluntarily expended in the purchase and acquisition of serious volumes. He lived an externally idle but really studious life, varied by tours in France and Italy; the toils of which, though not in description very formidable, a trifle tried a sedentary habit and somewhat corpulent body. The only English avocation which he engaged in was, oddly enough, war. It does not appear the most likely in this pacific country, nor does he seem exactly the man for *la grande guerre*; but so it was; and the fact is an example of a really Anglican invention. The English have discovered pacific war. We may not be able to kill people as well as the French, or fit out and feed distant armaments as neatly as they do;

but we are unrivalled at a quiet armament here at home which never kills anybody, and never wants to be sent anywhere. A 'constitutional militia' is a beautiful example of the mild efficacy of civilization, which can convert even the 'great manslaying profession' (as Carlyle calls it) into a quiet and dining association. Into this force Gibbon was admitted; and immediately, contrary to his anticipations, and very much against his will, was called out for permanent duty. The hero of the *corps* was a certain dining Sir Thomas, who used at the end of each new bottle to announce with increasing joy how much soberer he had become. What his fellow-officers thought of Gibbon's French predilections and large volumes it is not difficult to conjecture; and he complains bitterly of the interruption to his studies. However, his easy composed nature soon made itself at home; his polished tact partially concealed from the 'mess' his recondite pursuits, and he contrived to make the Hampshire armament of classical utility. 'I read,' he says, '"the Analysis of Caesar's Campaign in Africa". Every motion of that great general is laid open with a critical sagacity. A complete military history of his campaigns would do almost as much honour to M. Guichardt as to Caesar. This finished the *Mémoires*, which gave me a much clearer notion of ancient tactics than I ever had before. Indeed, my own military knowledge was of some service to me, as I am well acquainted with the modern discipline and exercise of a battalion. So that though much inferior to M. Folard and M. Guichardt, who had seen service, I am a much better judge than Salmasius, Casaubon, or Lipsius; mere scholars, who perhaps had never seen a battalion under arms.'

The real occupation of Gibbon, as this quotation might suggest, was his reading; and this was of a peculiar sort. There are many kinds of readers, and each has a sort of perusal suitable to his kind. There is the voracious reader, like Dr Johnson, who extracts with grasping appetite the large features, the mere essence of a trembling publication, and rejects the rest with contempt and disregard. There is the subtle reader, who pursues with fine attention the most imperceptible and delicate ramifications of an interesting topic, marks slight traits, notes changing manners, has a keen eye for the character of his author, is minutely attentive to every prejudice and awake to every passion, watches syllables and waits on words, is alive to the light air of nice associations which float about every subject – the motes in the bright sunbeam – the delicate gradations of the passing shadows. There is the stupid reader, who prefers dull books – is generally to be known by his disregard of small books and English books, but likes masses in modern Latin, *Graevius de torpore mirabili; Horrificus de gravitate sapientiae*. But Gibbon was not of any of these classes. He was what common people would call a matter-of-fact, and philosophers nowadays a *positive* reader. No disciple of M. Comte could attend more strictly to precise and provable phenomena. His favourite points are those which can be weighed and measured. Like the dull reader, he had perhaps a preference for huge books in unknown tongues: but, on the other hand, he wished those books to contain real and accurate information. He liked the firm earth of positive knowledge. His fancy was not flexible enough for exquisite refinement, his imagination too slow for light and wandering literature; but he felt no love of dullness in itself, and had a prompt acumen for serious eloquence. This was his kind of reflection. 'The author of the *Adventurer*, No. 127 (Mr Joseph Warton, concealed under the signature of Z), concludes his ingenious parallel of the ancients and moderns by the following remark: "That age will never again return, when a Pericles, after walking with Plato in a portico built by Phidias and painted by Apelles, might repair to hear a pleading of Demosthenes or a tragedy of Sophocles." It will never return, because it never existed. Pericles (who died in the fourth year of the LXXXIXth Olympiad. ant. Ch. 429, Dio. Sic. l. xii. 46) was confessedly the patron of Phidias, and the contemporary of Sophocles; but he could enjoy no very great pleasure in the conversation of Plato, who was born in the same year that he himself died ("Diogenes Laertius in Platone" v. Stanley's "History of Philosophy", p. 154). The error is still more extraordinary with regard to Apelles and Demosthenes, since both the painter and the orator survived Alexander the Great, whose death is above a century posterior to that of Pericles (in 323). And indeed, though Athens was the seat of every liberal art from the days of Themistocles to those of Demetrius Phalereus, yet no particular era will afford Mr Warton the complete synchronism he seems to wish for; as tragedy was deprived of her famous triumvirate before the arts of philosophy and eloquence had attained the perfection which they soon after received from the hands of Plato, Aristotle, and Demosthenes.'

And wonderful is it for what Mr Hallam calls 'the languid students of our present age' to turn over the journal of his daily studies. It is true, it seems to have been revised by himself; and so great a narrator would group effectively facts with which he was so familiar; but allowing any discount (if we may use so mean a word) for the skilful art of the impressive historian, there will yet remain in the *Extraits de mon Journal* a wonderful monument of learned industry. You may open them anywhere. '*Dissertation on the Medal of Smyrna*, by M. de Boze: replete with erudition and taste; containing curious researches on the pre-eminence of the cities of Asia. — *Researches on the Polypus*, by Mr Trembley. A new world: throwing light on physics, but darkening metaphysics. — Vegetius's *Institutions*. This writer on tactics has good general notions; but his particular account of the Roman discipline is deformed by confusion and anachronisms.' Or, 'I this day began a very considerable task, which was, to read Cluverius's *Italia Antiqua* in two volumes in folio, Leyden 1624, Elzevirs'; and it appears he did read it as well as begin it, which is the point where most enterprising men would have failed. From the time of his residence at Lausanne his Latin scholarship had been sound and good; and his studies were directed to the illustration of the best Roman authors; but it is curious to find on the 16th of August 1761, after his return to England, and when he was twenty-four years old, the following extract: 'I have at last finished the "Iliad". As I undertook it to improve myself in the Greek language, which I had totally neglected for some years past, and to which I never applied myself with a proper attention, I must give a reason why I began with Homer and that contrary to Le Clerc's advice. I had two: first, as Homer is the most ancient Greek author (excepting perhaps Hesiod) who is now extant; and as he was not only the poet, but the lawgiver, the theologian, the historian, and the philosopher, of the ancients, every succeeding writer is full of quotations from, or allusions to, his writings, which it would be difficult to understand without a previous knowledge of them. In this situation, was it not natural to follow the ancients themselves, who always began their studies by the perusal of Homer? Secondly, no writer ever treated such a variety of subjects. As every part of civil, military, or economical life is introduced into his poems, and as the simplicity of his age allowed him to call every thing by its proper name, almost the whole compass of the Greek tongue is comprised in Homer. I have so far met with the success I hoped for, that I have acquired a great facility in reading the language, and treasured up a very great stock of words. What I have rather neglected is, the grammatical construction of them, and especially the many various inflexions of the verbs. In order to acquire that dry but necessary branch of knowledge, I propose bestowing some time every morning on the perusal of the *Greek Grammar of Port Royal*, as one of the best extant. I believe that I read nearly one-half of Homer like a mere schoolboy, not enough master of the words to elevate myself to the poetry. The remainder I read with a good deal of care and criticism, and made many observations on them. Some I have inserted here; for the rest I shall find a proper place. Upon the whole, I think that Homer's few faults (for some he certainly has) are lost in the variety of his beauties. I expected to have finished him long before. The delay was owing partly to the circumstances of my way of life and avocations, and partly to my own fault; for while everyone looks on me as a prodigy of application, I know myself how strong a propensity I have to indolence.' Posterity will confirm the contemporary theory that he was a 'prodigy' of steady study. Those who know what the Greek language is, how much of the *Decline and Fall* depends on Greek authorities, how few errors the keen criticism of divines and scholars has been able to detect in his employment of them, will best appreciate the patient everyday labour which could alone repair the early neglect of so difficult an attainment.

It is odd how little Gibbon wrote, at least for the public, in early life. More than twenty-two years elapsed from his first return from Lausanne to the appearance of the first volume of his great work, and in that long interval his only important publication, if it can indeed be so called, was a French essay, *Sur l'Étude de la Littérature*, which contains some sensible remarks, and shows much regular reading; but which is on the whole a 'conceivable treatise', and would be wholly forgotten if it had been written by anyone else. It was little read in England, and must have been a serious difficulty to his friends in the militia; but the Parisians read it, or said they had read it, which is more in their way, and the fame of being a French author was a great aid to him in foreign society. It flattered, indeed, the French *literati* more than anyone can now fancy. The French had then the idea that it was uncivilized to speak any other language, and the notion of *writing* any other seemed quite a *bêtise*. By a miserable misfortune you might not know French, but at least you could conceal it assiduously; white paper anyhow might go unsoiled; posterity at least should not hear of such ignorance. The Parisian was to be the universal tongue. And it did not seem absurd, especially to those only slightly acquainted with foreign countries, that this might in part be so. Political eminence had given their language a diplomatic supremacy. No German literature existed as yet; Italy had ceased to produce important books. There was only England left to dispute the literary omnipotence; and such an attempt as Gibbon's was a peculiarly acceptable flattery, for it implied that her most cultivated men were beginning to abandon their own tongue, and to write like other nations in the cosmopolitan *lingua franca*. A few far-seeing observers, however, already contemplated the train of events which at the present day give such a preponderating influence to our own writers, and make it an arduous matter even to explain the conceivableness of the French ambition. Of all men living then or since, David Hume was the most likely from prejudice and habit to take an unfavourable view of English literary influence; he had more literary fame than he deserved in France, and less in England; he had much of the French neatness, he had but little of the English nature; yet his cold and discriminating intellect at once emancipated him from the sophistries which imposed on those less watchful. He wrote to Gibbon, 'I have only one objection, derived from the language in which it is written. Why do you compose in French, and carry faggots into the wood, as Horace says with regard to Romans who wrote in Greek? I grant that you have a like motive to those Romans, and adopt a language much more generally diffused than your native tongue; but have you not remarked the fate of those two ancient languages in the following ages? The Latin, though then less celebrated and confined to more narrow limits, has in some measure outlived the Greek, and is now more generally understood by men of letters. Let the French, therefore, triumph in the present diffusion of their tongue. Our solid and increasing establishments in America, where we need less dread the inundation of barbarians, promise a superior stability and duration to the English language.' The cool sceptic was correct. The great breeding people have gone out and multiplied; colonies in every clime attest our success; French is the *patois* of Europe; English is the language of the world.

Gibbon took the advice of his sagacious friend, and prepared himself for the composition of his great work in English. His studies were destined, however, to undergo an interruption. 'Yesterday morning,' he wrote to a friend, 'about half an hour after seven, as I was destroying an army of barbarians, I heard a double rap at the door, and my friend Mr Eliot was soon introduced. After some idle conversation, he told me that if I was desirous of being in parliament, he had an independent seat very much at my service.' The borough was Liskeard; and the epithet independent is, of course, ironical, Mr Eliot being himself the constituency of that place. The offer was accepted, and one of the most learned of members of parliament took his seat.

The political life of Gibbon is briefly described. He was a supporter of Lord North. That well-known statesman was, in the most exact sense, a representative man, – although representative of the class of persons most out of favour with the transcendental thinkers, who invented this name. Germans deny it, but in every country common opinions are very common. Everywhere, there exists the comfortable mass; quiet, sagacious, short-sighted, – such as the Jews whom Rabshakeh tempted by their vine and their fig-tree, such as the English with their snug dining-room and after-dinner nap, domestic happiness and Bullo coal; sensible, solid men, without stretching irritable reason, but with a placid, supine instinct; without originality and without folly; judicious in their dealings, respected in the world; wanting little, sacrificing nothing; good-tempered people in a word, 'caring for nothing until they are themselves hurt'. Lord North was one of this class. You could hardly make him angry. 'No doubt,' he said, tapping his fat sides, 'I am that odious thing a minister; and I believe other people wish they were so too.' Profound people look deeply for the maxims of his policy; and it being on the surface, of course they fail to find it. He did not what the mind but what the *body* of the community wanted to have done; he appealed to the real people, the large English commonplace herd. His abilities were great;

and with them he did what people with no abilities wished to do, and could not do. Lord Brougham has just published his Letters to the King, showing that which partial extracts had made known before, that North was quite opposed to the war he was carrying on; was convinced it could not succeed; hardly, in fact, wished it might. Why did he carry it on? *Vox populi*, the voice of well-dressed men commanded it to be done; and he cheerfully sacrificed American people, who were nothing to him, to English, who were something, and a king, who was much. Gibbon was the very man to support such a ruler. His historical writings have given him a posthumous eminence; but in his own time he was doubtless thought a sensible safe man, of ordinary thoughts and intelligible actions. To do him justice, he did not pretend to be a hero. You know, he wrote to his friend Deyverdun, 'que je suis entré au parliament sans patriotisme, sans ambition, et que toutes mes vues se bornoient à la place commode et honnête d'un *lord of trade*'. Wise in his generation was written on his brow. He quietly and gently supported the policy of his time.

Even, however, amid the fatigue of parliamentary attendance, – the fatigue, in fact, of attending a nocturnal and oratorical club, where you met the best people, who could not speak, as well as a few of the worst, who *would*, – Gibbon's history made much progress. The first volume, a quarto, one-sixth of the whole, was published in the spring of 1776, and at once raised his fame to a high point. Ladies actually read it – read about Boetica and Tarraconensis, the Roman legions and the tribunitian powers. Grave scholars wrote dreary commendations. 'The first impression,' he writes, 'was exhausted in a few days; a second and third edition were scarcely adequate to the demand; and the bookseller's property was twice invaded by the pirates of Dublin. My book was on every table' – tables must have been rather few in that age – 'and almost on every toilette; the historian was crowned by the taste or fashion of the day; nor was the general voice disturbed by the barking of any profane critic.' The noise penetrated deep into the unlearned classes. Mr Sheridan, who never read anything 'on principle', said that the crimes of Warren Hastings surpassed anything to be found in the 'correct sentences of Tacitus' or 'on the *luminous* page of Gibbon'. Someone seems to have been struck with the jet of learning, and questioned the great wit. 'I said,' he replied, '*voluminous*.'

History, it is said, is of no use; at least a great critic, who is understood to have in the press a very elaborate work in that kind, not long since seemed to allege that writings of this sort did not establish a theory of the universe, and were therefore of no avail. But whatever may be the use of this sort of composition in itself and abstractedly, it is certainly of great use relatively and to literary men. Consider the position of a man of that species. He sits beside a library fire, with nice white paper, a good pen, a capital style, every means of saying everything, but nothing to say; of course he is an able man; of course he has an active intellect, beside wonderful culture, but still one cannot always have original ideas. Every day cannot be an era; a train of new speculation very often will not be found; and how dull it is to make it your business to write, to stay by yourself in a room to write, and then to have nothing to say! It is dreary work mending seven pens, and waiting for a theory to 'turn up'. What a gain if something would happen! then one could describe it. Something has happened, and that something is history. On this account, since a sedate Greek discovered this plan for a grave immortality, a series of accomplished men have seldom been found wanting to derive a literary capital from their active and barbarous kindred. Perhaps when a Visigoth broke a head, he thought that that was all. Not so; he was making history; Gibbon has written it down.

The manner of writing history is as characteristic of the narrator as the actions are of the persons who are related to have performed them; often much more so. It may be generally defined as a view of one age taken by another; a picture of a series of men and women painted by one of another series. Of course, this definition seems to exclude contemporary history; but if we look into the matter carefully, is there such a thing? What are all the best and most noted works that claim the title – memoirs, scraps, materials – composed by men of like passions with the people they speak of, involved it may be in the same events describing them with the partiality and narrowness of eager actors; or even worse, by men far apart in a monkish solitude, familiar with the lettuces of the convent-garden, but hearing only faint dim murmurs of the great transactions which they slowly jot down in the barren chronicle: these are not to be named in the same short breath, or included in the same narrow word, with the equable, poised, philosophic narrative of the retrospective historian. In the great histories there are two topics of interest – the man as a type of the age in which he lives, – the events and manners of the age he is describing; very often almost all the interest is the contrast of the two.

You should do everything, said Lord Chesterfield, in minuet time. It was in that time that Gibbon wrote his history, and such was the manner of the age. You fancy him in a suit of flowered velvet, with a bag and sword, wisely smiling, composedly rounding his periods. You seem to see the grave bows, the formal politeness, the finished deference. You perceive the minuetic action accompanying the words: 'Give,' it would say, 'Augustus a chair: Zenobia, the humblest of your slaves: Odoacer, permit me to correct the defect in your attire.' As the slapdash sentences of a rushing critic express the hasty impatience of modern manners, so the deliberate emphasis, the slow acumen, the steady argument, the impressive narration bring before us what is now a tradition, the picture of the correct eighteenth-century gentleman, who never failed in a measured politeness, partly because it was due in propriety towards others, and partly because from his own dignity it was due most obviously to himself.

And not only is this true of style, but may be extended to other things also. There is no one of the many literary works produced in the eighteenth century more thoroughly characteristic of it than Gibbon's history. The special characteristic of that age is its clinging to the definite and palpable; it had a taste beyond everything for what is called solid information. In literature the period may be defined as that in which authors had ceased to write for students, and had not begun to write for women. In the present day no one can take up any book intended for general circulation, without clearly seeing that the writer supposes most of his readers will be ladies or young men; and that in proportion to his judgement, he is attending to their taste. Two or three hundred years ago books were written for professed and systematic students, – the class the fellows of colleges were designed to be, – who used to go on studying them all their lives. Between these there was a time in which the more marked class of literary consumers were strong-headed, practical men. Education had not become so general, or so feminine, as to make the present style –

what is called the 'brilliant style' – at all necessary; but there was enough culture to make the demand of common diffused persons more effectual than that of special and secluded scholars. A book-buying public had arisen of sensible men, who would not endure the awful folio style in which the schoolmen wrote. From peculiar causes, too, the business of that age was perhaps more free from the hurry and distraction which disable so many of our practical men now from reading. You accordingly see in the books of the last century what is called a masculine tone; a firm, strong, perspicuous narration of matter of fact, a plain argument, a contempt for everything which distinct definite people cannot entirely and thoroughly comprehend. There is no more solid book in the world than Gibbon's history. Only consider the chronology. It begins before the year ONE and goes down to the year 1453, and is a schedule or series of schedules of important events during that time. Scarcely any fact deeply affecting European civilization is wholly passed over, and the great majority are elaborately recounted. Laws, dynasties, churches, barbarians, appear and disappear. Everything changes; the old world – the classical civilization of form and definition – passes away, a new world of free spirit and inward growth emerges; between the two lies a mixed weltering interval of trouble and confusion, when everybody hates everybody, and the historical student leads a life of skirmishes, is oppressed with broils and feuds. All through this long period Gibbon's history goes with steady consistent pace; like a Roman legion through a troubled country – *haeret pede pes*; up hill and down hill, through marsh and thicket, through Goth or Parthian – the firm defined array passes forward – a type of order, and an emblem of civilization. Whatever may be the defects of Gibbon's history, none can deny him a proud precision and a style in marching order.

Another characteristic of the eighteenth century is its taste for dignified pageantry. What an existence was that of Versailles! How gravely admirable to see the *grand monarque* shaved, and dressed, and powdered; to look on and watch a great man carefully amusing himself with dreary trifles. Or do we not even now possess an invention of that age – the great eighteenth-century footman, still in the costume of his era, with dignity and powder, vast calves and noble mien? What a world it must have been when all men looked like that! Go and gaze with rapture at the footboard of a carriage, and say, Who would not obey a premier with such an air? Grave, tranquil, decorous pageantry is a part, as it were, of the essence of the last age. There is nothing more characteristic of Gibbon. A kind of pomp pervades him. He is never out of livery. He ever selects for narration those themes which look most like a levee; grave chamberlains seem to stand throughout; life is a vast ceremony, the historian at once the dignitary and the scribe.

The very language of Gibbon shows these qualities. Its majestic march has been the admiration – its rather pompous cadence the sport of all perusers. It has the greatest merit of an historical style; it is always going on; you feel no doubt of its continuing in motion. Many narrators of the reflective class, Sir Archibald Alison for example, fail in this; your constant feeling is, 'Ah! he is pulled up; he is going to be profound; he never will go on again.' Gibbon's reflections connect the events; they are not sermons between them. But, notwithstanding, the manner of the *Decline and Fall* is the last which should be recommended for strict imitation. It is not a style in which you can tell the truth. A monotonous writer is suited only to monotonous matter. Truth is of various kinds – grave, solemn, dignified, petty, low, ordinary; and a historian who has to tell the truth must be able to tell what is vulgar as well as what is great, what is little as well as what is amazing. Gibbon is at fault here. He *cannot* mention Asia *Minor*. The petty order of sublunary matters; the common gross existence of ordinary people; the necessary littlenesses of necessary life, are little suited to his sublime narrative. Men on *The Times* feel this acutely; it is most difficult at first to say many things in the huge imperial manner. And after all you cannot tell everything. 'How, sir,' asked a reviewer of Sydney Smith's life, 'do you say a "good fellow" in print?' 'Mr —,' replied the editor, 'you should not say it at all.' Gibbon was aware of this rule: he omits what does not suit him; and the consequence is, that though he has selected the most various of historical topics, he scarcely gives you an idea of variety. The ages change, but the varnish of the narration is the same.

It is not unconnected with this fault that Gibbon gives us but an indifferent description of individual character. People seem a good deal alike. The cautious scepticism of his cold intellect, which

disinclined him to every extreme, depreciates great virtues and extenu-
ates great vices; and we are left with a tame neutral character, capable
of nothing extraordinary, – hateful, as the saying is, 'both to God and
to the enemies of God'.

A great point in favour of Gibbon is the existence of his history.
Some great historians seem likely to fail here. A good judge was
asked which he preferred, Macaulay's *History of England* or Lord
Mahon's. 'Why,' he replied, 'you observe Lord Mahon has written
his history; and by what I see Macualay's will be written not only for
but *among* posterity.' Practical people have little idea of the practical
ability required to write a large book, and especially a large history.
Long before you get to the pen, there is an immensity of pure
business; heaps of material are strewn everywhere; but they lie in
disorder, unread, uncatalogued, unknown. It seems a dreary waste of
life to be analysing, indexing, extracting works and passages, in which
one per cent of the contents are interesting, and not half of that
percentage will after all appear in the flowing narrative. As an
accountant takes up a bankrupt's books filled with confused statements
of ephemeral events, the disorderly record of unprofitable speculations,
and charges this to that head, and that to this, – estimates earnings,
specifies expenses, demonstrates failures; so the great narrator, going
over the scattered annalists of extinct ages, groups and divides, notes
and combines, until from a crude mass of darkened fragments there
emerges a clear narrative, a concise account of the result and upshot of
the whole. In this art Gibbon was a master. The laborious research of
German scholarship, the keen eye of theological zeal, a steady criticism
of eighty years, have found few faults of detail. The account has been
worked right, the proper authorities consulted, an accurate judgement
formed, the most telling incidents selected. Perhaps experience shows
that there is something English in this talent. The Germans are more
elaborate in single monographs; but they seem to want the business-
ability to work out a complicated narrative, to combine a long
whole. The French are neat enough, and the style is very quick; but
then it is difficult to believe the facts; the account on its face seems too
plain and no true Parisian ever was an antiquary. The great classical
histories published in this country in our own time show that the
talent is by no means extinct; and they likewise show, what is also

evident, that this kind of composition is easier with respect to ancient than with respect to modern times. The barbarians burned the books; and though all the historians abuse them for it, it is quite evident that in their hearts they are greatly rejoiced. If the books had existed, they would have had to read them. Mr Macaulay has to peruse every book printed with long ʃ's; and it is no use after all; somebody will find some stupid MS., an old account-book of an 'ingenious gentleman', and with five entries therein destroy a whole hypothesis. But Gibbon was exempt from this; he could count the books the efficient Goths bequeathed; and when he had mastered them he might pause. Still it was no light matter, as anyone who looks at the books – awful folios in the grave Bodleian – will most certainly credit and believe. And he did it all himself; he never showed his book to any friend, or asked anyone to help him in the accumulating work, not even in the correction of the press. 'Not a sheet,' he says, 'has been seen by any human eyes, excepting those of the author and the printer; the faults and the merits are exclusively my own.' And he wrote most of it with one pen, which must certainly have grown erudite towards the end.

The nature of his authorities clearly shows what the nature of Gibbon's work is. History may be roughly divided into universal and particular; the first being the narrative of events affecting the whole human race, at least the main historical nations, the narrative of whose fortunes is the story of civilization; and the latter being the relation of events relating to one or a few particular nations only. Universal history, it is evident, comprises great areas of space and long periods of time; you cannot have a series of events visibly operating on all great nations without time for their gradual operation, and without tracking them in succession through the various regions of their power. There is no instantaneous transmission in historical causation; a long interval is required for universal effects. It follows, that universal history necessarily partakes of the character of a summary. You cannot recount the cumbrous annals of long epochs without condensation, selection, and omission; the narrative, when shortened within the needful limits, becomes concise and general. What it gains in time, according to the mechanical phrase, it loses in power. The particular history, confined within narrow limits, can show us the whole contents of these limits, explain its features of human interest, recount in graphic detail all its interesting transactions, touch the human heart with the power of passion, instruct the mind with patient instances of accurate wisdom. The universal is confined to a dry enumeration of superficial transactions; no action can have all its details; the canvas is so crowded that no figure has room to display itself effectively. From the nature of the subject, Gibbon's history is of the latter class; the sweep of the narrative is so wide; the decline and fall of the Roman empire being in some sense the most universal event which has ever happened, – being, that is, the historical incident which has most affected all civilized men, and the very existence and form of civilization itself, – it is evident that we must look rather for a comprehensive generality than a telling minuteness of delineation. The history of a thousand years does not admit the pictorial detail which a Scott or a Macaulay can accumulate on the history of a hundred. Gibbon has done his best to avoid the dryness natural to such an attempt. He inserts as much detail as his limits will permit; selects for more full description striking people and striking transactions; brings together at a single view all that relates to single topics; above all, by a regular advance of narration, never ceases to imply the regular progress of events and the steady course of time. None can deny the magnitude of such an effort. After all, however, these are merits of what is technically termed composition, and are analogous to those excellencies in painting or sculpture that are more respected by artists than appreciated by the public at large. The fame of Gibbon is highest among writers; those especially who have studied for years particular periods included in his theme (and how many those are; for in the East and West he has set his mark on all that is great for ten centuries!) acutely feel and admiringly observe how difficult it would be to say so much, and leave so little untouched; to compress so many telling points; to present in so few words so apt and embracing a narrative of the whole. But the mere unsophisticated reader scarcely appreciates this; he is rather awed than delighted; or rather, perhaps, he appreciates it for a little while, then is tired by the roll and glare; next on any chance – the creaking of an organ or the stirring of a mouse – in time of temptation he falls away. It has been said, the way to answer all objections to Milton is to take down the book and read him; the way to reverence Gibbon is not to read him at all, but look at him, from outside, in the bookcase, and think how much there is within; what a course of events, what a muster-roll of names, what a steady solemn sound! You will not like to take the book down; but you will think how much you could be delighted if you would.

It may be well, though it can be only in the most cursory manner, to examine the respective treatment of the various elements in this vast whole. The history of the *Decline and Fall* may be roughly and imperfectly divided into the picture of the Roman empire – the narrative of barbarian incursions – the story of Constantinople: and some few words may be hastily said on each.

The picture, – for so, from its apparent stability when contrasted with the fluctuating character of the later period, we may call it, – which Gibbon has drawn of the united empire has immense merit. The organization of the imperial system is admirably dwelt on; the manner in which the old republican institutions were apparently retained, but really altered, is compendiously explained; the mode in which the imperial will was transmitted to and carried out in remote provinces is distinctly displayed. But though the mechanism is admirably delineated, the dynamical principle, the original impulse, is not made clear. You never feel you are reading about the Romans. Yet no one denies their character to be most marked. Poets and orators have striven for the expression of it.

Mr Macaulay has been similarly criticized; it has been said, that notwithstanding his great dramatic power, and wonderful felicity in the selection of events on which to exert it, he yet never makes us feel that we are reading about Englishmen. The coarse clay of our English nature *cannot* be represented in so fine a style. In the same way, and to a much greater extent (for this is perhaps an unthankful criticism, if we compare Macaulay's description of anybody with that of any other historian), Gibbon is chargeable with neither expressing nor feeling the essence of the people concerning whom he is writing. There was, in truth, in the Roman people a warlike fanaticism, a puritanical essence, an interior, latent, restrained, enthusiastic religion, which was utterly alien to the cold scepticism of the narrator. Of course he was conscious of it. He indistinctly felt that at least there was something he did not like; but he could not realize or sympathize with it without a change of heart and nature. The old Pagan has a sympathy with the religion of enthusiasm far above the reach of the modern Epicurean.

It may indeed be said, on behalf of Gibbon, that the old Roman character was in its decay, and that only such slight traces of it were remaining in the age of Augustus and the Antonines that it is no particular defect in him to leave it unnoticed. Yet though the intensity of its nobler peculiarities was on the wane, many a vestige would perhaps have been apparent to so learned an eye, if his temperament and disposition had been prone to seize upon and search for them. Nor is there any adequate appreciation of the compensating element, of the force which really held society together, of the fresh air of the Illyrian hills, of that army which, evermore recruited from northern and rugged populations, doubtless brought into the very centre of a degraded society the healthy simplicity of a vital if barbarous religion.

It is no wonder that such a mind should have looked with displeasure on primitive Christianity. The whole of his treatment of that topic has been discussed by many pens, and three generations of ecclesiastical scholars have illustrated it with their emendations. Yet if we turn over this, the latest and most elaborate edition, containing all the important criticisms of Milman and of Guizot, we shall be surprised to find how few instances of definite exact error such a scrutiny has been able to find out. As Paley, with his strong sagacity, at once remarked, the subtle error rather lies hid in the sinuous folds than is directly apparent on the surface of the polished style. Who, said the shrewd archdeacon, can refute a sneer? And yet even this is scarcely the exact truth. The objection of Gibbon is, in fact, an objection rather to religion than to Christianity; as has been said, he did not appreciate, and could not describe, the most inward form of pagan piety; he objected to Christianity because it was the intensest of religions. We do not mean by this to charge Gibbon with any denial of, any overt distinct disbelief in the existence of a supernatural Being. This would be very unjust; his cold composed mind had nothing in common with the Jacobinical outbreak of the next generation. He was no doubt a theist after the fashion of natural theology; nor was he devoid of more than scientific feeling. All constituted authorities struck him with emotion, all ancient ones with awe. If the Roman empire had descended to his time, how much he would have reverenced it! He had doubtless a great respect for the 'First Cause'; it had many titles to approbation; 'it was not conspicuous,' he would have said, 'but it was potent'. A sensitive decorum revolted from the jar of atheistic disputation. We have already described him more than enough. A sensible middle-aged man in political life; a bachelor, not himself gay, but living with gay men; equable and secular; cautious in his habits, tolerant in his creed, as Porson said, 'never failing in natural feeling except when women were to be ravished and Christians to be martyred'. His writings are in character. The essence of the far-famed fifteenth and sixteenth chapters is, in truth, but a description of unworldly events in the tone of this world, of awful facts in unmoved voice, of truths of the heart in the language of the eyes. The wary sceptic has not even committed himself to definite doubts. These celebrated chapters were in the first manuscript much longer, and were gradually reduced to their present size by excision and compression. Who can doubt that in their first form they were a clear, or comparatively clear expression of exact opinions on the Christian history, and that it was by a subsequent and elaborate process that they were reduced to their present and insidious obscurity? The toil has been effectual. 'Divest,' says Dean Milman of the introduction to the fifteenth chapter, 'this whole passage of the latent sarcasm betrayed by the subsequent tone of the whole disquisition, and it might commence a Christian history, written in the most Christian spirit of candour.'

It is not for us here to go into any disquisition as to the comparative influence of the five earthly causes to whose secondary operation the specious historian ascribes the progress of Christianity. Weariness and disinclination forbid. There can be no question that the polity of the church, and the zeal of the converts, and other such things, did most materially conduce to the progress of the Gospel. But few will now attribute to these much of the effect. The real cause is the heaving of the mind after the truth. Troubled with the perplexities of time, weary with the vexation of ages, the spiritual faculty of man turns to the truth as the child turns to its mother. The thirst of the soul was to be satisfied, the deep torture of the spirit to have rest. There was an appeal to those

High instincts, before which our mortal Nature
Did tremble like a guilty Thing surprised.

The mind of man has an appetite for the truth.

Hence, in a season of calm weather
Though inland far we be,
Our Souls have sight of that immortal sea
Which brought us hither,
Can in a moment travel thither,
And see the Children sport upon the shore,
And hear the mighty waters rolling evermore.

All this was not exactly in Gibbon's way, and he does not seem to have been able to conceive that it was in anyone else's. Why his chapters had given offence he could hardly make out. It actually seems that he hardly thought that other people believed more than he did. 'We may be well assured,' says he, of a sceptic of antiquity, 'that a writer conversant with the world would never have ventured to expose the gods of his country to public ridicule, had they not been already the objects of secret contempt among the polished and enlightened orders of society.' 'Had I,' he says of himself, 'believed that the majority of English readers were so fondly attached even to the name and shadow of Christianity, had I foreseen that the pious, the timid, and the prudent would feel, or would affect to feel, with such exquisite sensibility, – I might perhaps have softened the two invidious chapters, which would create many enemies and conciliate few friends.' The state of belief at that time is a very large subject; but it is probable that in the cultivated cosmopolitan classes the continental scepticism was very rife; that among the hard-headed classes the rough spirit of English Deism had made progress. Though the mass of the people doubtless believed much as they now believe, yet the entire upper class was lazy and corrupt, and there is truth in the picture of the modern divine: 'The thermometer of the Church of England sank to its lowest point in the first thirty years of the reign of George III . . . In their preaching, nineteen clergymen out of twenty carefully abstained from dwelling upon Christian doctrines. Such topics exposed the preacher to the charge of fanaticism. Even the calm and sober Crabbe, who certainly never erred from excess of zeal, was stigmatized in those days by his brethren as a methodist, because he introduced into his sermons the motives of future reward and punishment. An orthodox clergyman (they said) should be content to show his people the worldly advantage of good conduct, and to leave heaven and hell to the ranters. Nor can we wonder that such should have been the notions of country parsons, when, even by those who passed for the supreme arbiters of orthodoxy and taste, the vapid rhetoric of Blair was thought the highest standard of Christian exhortation.' It is among the excuses for Gibbon that he lived in such a world.

There are slight palliations also in the notions then prevalent of the primitive church. There was the Anglican theory, that it was a *via media*, the most correct of periods, that its belief is to be the standard, its institutions the model, its practice the test of subsequent ages. There was the notion, not formally drawn out, but diffused through and implied in a hundred books of evidences, – a notion in opposition to every probability, and utterly at variance with the New Testament, – that the first converts were sober, hard-headed, cultivated inquirers, – Watsons, Paleys, Priestleys, on a small scale; weighing evidence, analysing facts, suggesting doubts, dwelling on distinctions, cold in their dispositions, moderate in their morals, – cautious in their creed. We now know that these were not they of whom the world was not worthy. It is ascertained that the times of the first church were times of excitement; that great ideas falling on a mingled world were distorted by an untrained intellect, even in the moment in which they were received by a yearning heart; that strange confused beliefs, Millennarianism, Gnosticism, Ebionitism, were accepted, not merely by outlying obscure heretics, but in a measure, half-and-half, one notion more by one man, another more by his neighbour, confusedly and mixedly by the mass of Christians; that the appeal was not to the questioning thinking understanding, but to unheeding all-venturing emotion; to that lower class 'from whom faiths ascend', and not to the cultivated and exquisite class by whom they are criticized; that fervid men never embraced a more exclusive creed. You can say nothing favourable of the first Christians, except that they *were* Christians. We find no 'form nor comeliness' in them; no intellectual accomplishments, no caution in action, no discretion in understanding. There is no admirable quality except that, with whatever distortion, or confusion, or singularity, they at once accepted the great clear outline of belief in which to this day we live, move, and have our being. The offence of Gibbon is his disinclination to this simple essence; his excuse, the historical errors then prevalent as to the primitive Christians, the real defects so natural in their position, the false merits ascribed to them by writers who from one reason or another desired to treat them as 'an authority'.

On the whole, therefore, it may be said of the first, and in some sense the most important part of Gibbon's work, that though he has given an elaborate outline of the framework of society, and described its detail with pomp and accuracy, yet that he has not comprehended or delineated its nobler essence, Pagan or Christian. Nor perhaps was it to be expected that he should, for he inadequately comprehended the dangers of the time; he thought it the happiest period the world has ever known; he would not have comprehended the remark, 'To see the old world in its worst estate we turn to the age of the satirists and of Tacitus, when all the different streams of evil coming from east, west, north, south, the vices of barbarism and the vices of civilization, remnants of ancient cults and the latest refinements of luxury and impurity, met and mingled on the banks of the Tiber. What could have been the state of society when Tiberius, Caligula, Nero, Domitian, Heliogabalus, were the rulers of the world? To a good man we should imagine that death itself would be more tolerable than the sight of such things coming upon the earth.' So deep an ethical sensibility was not to be expected in the first century; nor is it strange when, after seventeen hundred years, we do not find it in their historian.

Space has failed us, and we must be unmeaningly brief. The second head of Gibbon's history – the narrative of the barbarian invasions – has been recently criticized, on the ground that he scarcely enough explains the gradual but unceasing and inevitable manner in which the outer barbarians were affected by and assimilated to the civilization of Rome. Mr Congreve has well observed, that the impression which Gibbon's narrative is insensibly calculated to convey is, that there was little or no change in the state of the Germanic tribes between the time of Tacitus and the final invasion of the empire – a conclusion which is obviously incredible. To the general reader there will perhaps seem some indistinctness in this part of the work, nor is a free confused barbarism a congenial subject for an imposing and orderly pencil. He succeeds better in the delineation of the riding monarchies, if we may so term them, – of the equestrian courts of Attila or Timour, in which the great scale, the concentrated power, the very enormity of the barbarism, give, so to speak a shape to unshapeliness; impart, that is, a horrid dignity to horse-flesh and mare's milk, an imposing oneness to the vast materials of a crude barbarity. It is needless to say that no one would search Gibbon for an explanation of the reasons or feelings by which the northern tribes were induced to accept Christianity.

It is on the story of Constantinople that the popularity of Gibbon rests. The vast extent of the topic; the many splendid episodes it contains; its epic unity from the moment of the far-seeing selection of the city by Constantine to its last fall; its position as a link between Europe and Asia; its continuous history; the knowledge that through all that time it was, as now, a diadem by the waterside, a lure to be snatched by the wistful barbarian, a marvel to the West, a prize for the North and for the East; – these, and such as these ideas, are congenial topics to a style of pomp and grandeur. The East seems to require to be treated with a magnificence unsuitable to a colder soil. The nature of the events, too, is suitable to Gibbon's cursory imposing manner. It is the history of a form of civilization, but without the power thereof; a show of splendour and vigour, but without bold life or interior reality. What an opportunity for an historian who loved the imposing pageantry and disliked the purer essence of existence! There were here neither bluff barbarians nor simple saints; there was nothing admitting of particular accumulated detail: we do not wish to know the interior of the stage; the imposing movements are all which should be seized. Some of the features, too, are curious in relation to those of the historian's life; the clear accounts of the theological controversies, followed out with an appreciative minuteness so rare in a sceptic, are not disconnected with his early conversion to the scholastic church: the brilliancy of the narrative reminds us of his enthusiasm for Arabic and the East; the minute description of a licentious epoch evinces the habit of a mind which, not being bold enough for the practice of licence, took a pleasure in following its theory. There is no subject which combines so much of unity with so much of variety.

It is evident, therefore, where Gibbon's rank as an historian must finally stand. He cannot be numbered among the great painters of human nature, for he has no sympathy with the heart and passions of our race; he has no place among the felicitous describers of detailed life, for his subject was too vast for minute painting, and his style too uniform for a shifting scene. But he is entitled to a high – perhaps to a first place – among the orderly narrators of great events; the composed expositors of universal history; the tranquil artists who have endeavoured to diffuse a cold polish over the warm passions and desultory fortunes of mankind.

The life of Gibbon after the publication of his great work was not very complicated. During its composition he had withdrawn from Parliament and London to the studious retirement of Lausanne. Much eloquence has been expended on this voluntary exile, and it has been ascribed to the best and most profound motives. It is indeed certain that he liked a lettered solitude, preferred easy continental society, was not quite insensible to the charm of scenery, had a pleasure in returning to the haunts of his youth. Prosaic and pure history, however, must explain that he went abroad to *save*. Lord North had gone out of power. Mr Burke, the Cobden of that era, had procured the abolition of the Lords of Trade; the private income of Gibbon was not equal to his notion of a bachelor London life. The same sum was, however, a fortune at Lausanne. Most things, he acknowledged were as dear; but then he had not to buy so many things. Eight hundred a year placed him high in the social scale of the place. The inhabitants were gratified that a man of European reputation had selected their out-of-the-way town for the shrine of his fame; he lived pleasantly and easily among easy pleasant people; a gentle hum of local admiration gradually arose, which yet lingers on the lips of erudite *laquais de place*. He still retains a fame unaccorded to any other historian; they speak of the 'hôtel Gibbon': there never was even an *estaminet* Tacitus, or a *café* Thucydides.

This agreeable scene, like many other agreeable scenes, was broken by a great thunderclap. The French revolution has disgusted many people; but perhaps it has never disgusted anyone more than Gibbon. He had swept and garnished everything about him. Externally he had made a neat little hermitage in a gentle social place; internally he had polished up a still theory of life, sufficient for the guidance of a cold and polished man. Everything seemed to be tranquil with him: the rigid must admit his decorum; the lax would not accuse him of rigour: he was of the world, and an elegant society naturally loved its own. On a sudden the hermitage was disturbed. No place was too calm for that excitement: scarcely any too distant for that uproar. The French war was a war of opinion, entering households, disturbing villages, dividing quiet friends. The Swiss took some of the infection. There was a not unnatural discord between the people of the Pays de Vaud and their masters the people of Berne. The letters of Gibbon are filled with invectives on the 'Gallic barbarians' and panegyrics on Mr Burke: military details, too, begin to abound – the peace of his retirement was at an end. It was an additional aggravation that the Parisians should do such things. It would not have seemed unnatural that northern barbarians – English, or other uncivilized nations – should break forth in rough riot or cruel licence; but that the people of the most civilized of all capitals, speaking the sole dialect of polished life, enlightened with all the enlightenment then known, should be guilty of excesses unparalleled, unwitnessed, unheard of, was a vexing trial to one who had admired them for many years. The internal creed and belief of Gibbon was as much attacked by all this as were his external circumstances. He had spent his time, his life, his energy, in putting a polished gloss on human tumult, a sneering gloss on human piety; on a sudden human passion broke forth – the cold and polished world seemed to meet its end; the thin superficies of civilization was torn asunder; the fountains of the great deep seemed opened; impiety to meet its end; the foundations of the earth were out of course. We now, after long familiarity and in much ignorance, can hardly read the history of those years without horror; what an effect must they have produced on those whose minds were fresh, and who knew the people killed! 'Never,' Gibbon wrote to an English nobleman, 'did a revolution affect to such a degree the private existence of such numbers of the first people of a great country; your

examples of misery I could easily match with similar examples in this
country and neighbourhood, and our sympathy is the deeper, as we
do not possess, like you, the means of alleviating in some measure the
misfortunes of the fugitives.' It violently affected his views of English
politics; he before had a tendency, in consideration of his cosmopolitan
cultivation, to treat them as local littlenesses, parish squabbles; but
now his interest was keen and eager. 'But,' he says, 'in this rage
against slavery, in the numerous petitions against the slave trade, was
there no leaven of new democratical principles? no wild ideas of the
rights and natural equality of man? It is these I fear. Some articles in
newspapers, some pamphlets of the year, the "Jockey Club", have
fallen into my hands. I do not infer much from such publications; yet
I have never known them of so black and malignant a cast. I
shuddered at Grey's motion; disliked the half-support of Fox, admired
the firmness of Pitt's declaration, and excused the usual intemperance
of Burke. Surely such men as —, —, —, have talents for mischief. I
see a club of reform which contains some respectable names. Inform
me of the professions, the principles, the plans, the resources of these
reformers. Will they heat the minds of the people? Does the French
democracy gain no ground? Will the bulk of your party stand firm to
their own interest and that of their country? Will you not take some
active measures to declare your sound opinions, and separate
yourselves from your rotten members? If you allow them to perplex
government, if you trifle with this solemn business, if you do not
resist the spirit of innovation in the first attempt, if you admit the
smallest and most specious change in our parliamentary system, you
are lost. You will be driven from one step to another; from principles
just in theory to consequences most pernicious in practice; and your
first concession will be productive of every subsequent mischief, for
which you will be answerable to your country and to posterity. Do
not suffer yourselves to be lulled into a false security; remember the
proud fabric of the French monarchy. Not four years ago it stood
founded, as it might seem, on the rock of time, force, and opinion;
supported by the triple aristocracy of the church, the nobility, and the
parliaments. They are crumbled into dust: they are vanished from the
earth. If this tremendous warning has no effect on the men of
property in England; if it does not open every eye, and raise every

arm, – you will deserve your fate. If I am too precipitate, enlighten; if I am too desponding, encourage me. My pen has run into this argument; for, as much a foreigner as you think me, on this momentous subject I feel myself an Englishman.'

The truth clearly is, that he had arrived at the conclusion that he was the sort of person a populace kill. People wonder a great deal why very many of the victims of the French revolution were particularly selected; the Marquis de Custine, especially, cannot divine why they executed *his* father. The historians cannot show that they committed any particular crimes; the marquises and marchionesses seem very inoffensive. The fact evidently is that they were killed for being polite. The world felt itself unworthy of them. There were so many bows, such regular smiles, such calm superior condescension, – could a mob be asked to endure it? Have we not all known a precise, formal, patronizing old gentleman – bland, imposing, something like Gibbon? have we not suffered from his dignified attentions? If *we* had been on the Committee of Public Safety, can we doubt what would have been the fate of that man? Just so wrath and envy destroyed in France an upper-class world.

After his return to England, Gibbon did not do much or live long. He completed his *Memoirs*, the most imposing of domestic narratives, the model of dignified detail. As we said before, if the Roman empire *had* written about itself, this was how it would have done so. He planned some other works, but executed none; judiciously observing that building castles in the air was more agreeable than building them on the ground. His career was, however, drawing to an end. Earthly dignity has its limits, even the dignity of an historian. He had long been stout; and now symptoms of dropsy began to appear. After a short interval, he died on the 16th of January, 1794. We have sketched his character, and have no more to say. After all, what is our criticism worth? It only fulfils his aspiration, 'that a hundred years hence I may still continue to be abused'.

(*WB*, i, 351–94, *National Review*, 1856)

GLADSTONE

Mr Gladstone has, beyond any other man in this generation, what we may call the oratorical *impulse*. We are in the habit of speaking of rhetoric as an art, and also of oratory as a faculty, and in both cases we speak quite truly. No man can speak without a special intellectual gift, and no man can speak well without a special intellectual training. But neither this gift of the intellect nor this education will suffice of themselves. A man must not only know what to say, he must have a vehement longing to get up and say it. Many persons, rather sceptical persons especially, do not feel this in the least. They see before them an audience, – a miscellaneous collection of odd-looking men, – but they feel no wish to convince them of anything. 'Are they not very well as they are? They believe what they have been brought up to believe.' . . . Another kind of sceptic is distrustful . . . 'It is of no use; do not hope that mere arguments will impair the prepositions of nature and the steady convictions of years.' Mr Gladstone would not feel these sceptical arguments. He would get up to speak. He has the *didactic* impulse. He has the 'courage of his ideas'. He will convince the audience. He knows an argument which will be effective, he has one for one and another for another; he has an enthusiasm which he feels will rouse the apathetic, a demonstration which he thinks must convert the incredulous, an illustration which he hopes will drive his meaning even into the heads of the stolid. At any rate, he will try. He has a *nature*, as Coleridge might have said, towards his audience. He is sure, if they only knew what he knows, they would feel as he feels, and believe as he believes. And by this he conquers. This living faith, this enthusiasm, this confidence, call it as we will, is an extreme power in human affairs. One *croyant*, said the Frenchman, is a greater power than fifty *incrédules*.

(*WB*, iii, 420–21, from 'Mr Gladstone', *National Review*, 1860)

GOODNESS: SENSUAL AND ASCETIC

There are two kinds of goodness conspicuous in the world, and often made the subject of contrast there; for which, however, we seem to want exact words, and which we are obliged to describe rather vaguely and incompletely. These characters may in one aspect be called the sensuous and the ascetic. The character of the first is that which is almost personified in the poet-king of Israel, whose actions and whose history have been 'improved' so often by various writers, that it now seems trite even to allude to them. Nevertheless, the particular virtues and the particular career of David seem to embody the idea of what may be called sensuous goodness far more completely than a living being in general comes near to an abstract idea. There may have been shades in the actual man which would have modified the resemblance; but in the portrait which has been handed down to us the traits are perfect and the approximation exact. The principle of this character is its sensibility to outward stimulus; it is moved by all which occurs, stirred by all which happens, open to the influences of whatever it sees, hears, or meets with. The certain consequence of this mental constitution is a peculiar liability to temptation. Men are, according to the divine, 'put upon their trial through the senses'. It is through the constant suggestions of the outer world that our minds are stimulated, that our will has the chance of a choice, that moral life becomes possible. The sensibility to this external stimulus brings with it, when men have it to excess, an unusual access of moral difficulty. Everything acts on them, and everything has a chance of turning them aside; the most tempting things act upon them very deeply, and their influence, in consequence, is extreme. Naturally, therefore, the errors of such men are great. We need not point the moral.

> Dizzied faith, and guilt, and woe,
> Loftiest aims by earth defiled,
> Gleams of wisdom sin-beguiled,
> Sated power's tyrannic mood,
> Counsels shared with men of blood,
> Sad success, parental tears,
> And a dreary gift of years.

But, on the other hand, the excellence of such men has a charm, a kind of sensuous sweetness, that is its own. Being conscious of frailty, they are tender to the imperfect; being sensitive to this world, they sympathize with the world; being familiar with all the moral incidents of life, their goodness has a richness and a complication: they fascinate their own age, and in their deaths they are 'not divided' from the love of others. Their peculiar sensibility gives a depth to their religion; it is at once deeper and more human than that of other men. As their sympathetic knowledge of those whom they have seen is great, so it is with their knowledge of Him whom they have not seen; and as is their knowledge, so is their love: it is deep, from their nature; rich and intimate, from the variety of their experience; chastened by the ever-present sense of their weakness and of its consequences.

In extreme opposition to this is the ascetic species of goodness. This is not, as is sometimes believed, a self-produced ideal – a simply voluntary result of discipline and restraint. Some men have by nature what others have to elaborate by effort. Some men have a repulsion from the world. All of us have, in some degree, a protective instinct; an impulse, that is to say, to start back from what may trouble us, to shun what may fascinate us, to avoid what may tempt us. On the moral side of human nature this preventive check is occasionally imperious; it holds the whole man under its control, – makes him recoil from the world, be offended at its amusements, be repelled by its occupations, be scared by its sins. The consequences of this tendency, when it is thus in excess, upon the character are very great and very singular. It secludes a man in a sort of natural monastery; he lives in a kind of moral solitude; and the effects of his isolation for good and for evil on his disposition are very many. The best result is a singular capacity for meditative religion. Being aloof from what is earthly, such persons are shut up with what is spiritual; being unstirred by the incidents of time, they are alone with the eternal; rejecting this life, they are alone with what is beyond. According to the measure of their minds, men of this removed and secluded excellence become eminent for a settled and brooding piety, for a strong and predominant religion. In human life too, in a thousand ways, their isolated excellence is apparent. They walk through the whole of it with an abstinence from sense, a zeal of morality, a purity of ideal, which other men have not. Their religion has an imaginative grandeur, and their life something of an unusual impeccability. And these are obviously singular excellencies. But the deficiencies to which the same character tends are equally singular. In the first place, their isolation gives them a certain pride in themselves, and an inevitable ignorance of others. They are secluded by their constitutional δαίμων from life; they are repelled from the pursuits which others care for; they are alarmed at the amusements which others enjoy. In consequence, they trust in their own thoughts; they come to magnify both them and themselves – for being able to think and to retain them. The greater the nature of the man, the greater is this temptation. His thoughts are greater, and, in consequence, the greater is his tendency to prize them, the more extreme is his tendency to overrate them. This pride, too, goes side by side with a want of sympathy. Being aloof from others, such a mind is unlike others; and it feels, and sometimes it feels bitterly, its own unlikeness. Generally, however, it is too wrapt up in its own exalted thoughts to be sensible of the pain of moral isolation; it stands apart from others, unknowing and unknown. It is deprived of moral experience in two ways, – it is not tempted itself, and it does not comprehend the temptations of others. And this defect of moral experience is almost certain to produce two effects, one practical, and the other speculative. When such a man is wrong, he will be apt to believe that he is right. If his own judgement err, he will not have the habit of checking it by the judgement of others; he will be accustomed to think most men wrong; differing from them would be no proof of error, agreeing with them would rather be a basis for suspicion. He may, too, be very wrong, for the conscience of no man is perfect on all sides. The strangeness of secluded excellence will be sometimes deeply shaded by very strange errors. To be commonly above others, still more to think yourself above others, is to be below them every now and then, and sometimes much below. Again, on the speculative side, this defect of moral experience penetrates into the distinguishing excellence of the character, – its brooding and meditative religion. Those who see life under only one aspect, can see religion under only one likewise. This world is needful to interpret what is beyond; the seen must explain the unseen. It is from a tried and a varied and a troubled moral life that the deepest and truest ideas of God arise. The ascetic character wants these; therefore in its religion there will be a harshness of outline, a bareness, so to say, as well as a grandeur. In life we may look for a singular purity; but also, and with equal probability, for singular self-confidence, a certain unsympathizing straitness, and perhaps a few singular errors.

The character of the ascetic, or austere species of goodness, is almost exactly embodied in Milton.

(*WB*, ii, 114–17, from 'John Milton', *National Review*, 1859)

GOTHIC CLUMSINESS

The Latin language is clumsy. Light pleasure was an exotic in the Roman world; the terms in which you strive to describe it suit rather the shrill camp and the droning law-court. In English ... we have this too. Business is in our words; a too heavy sense clogs our literature: even in a writer so apt as Pope at the *finesse* of words, you feel the solid Gothic roots impede him. It is difficult not to be cumbrous. The horse may be fleet and light, but the wheels are ponderous and the road goes heavily.

(*WB*, ii, 32–3, from 'Béranger', *National Review*, 1857)

THE GREAT EXHIBITION

6 Great Coram St.
8 May 1851

My dearest Mother,

I took a start yesterday and went to see the Queen open the Exhibition. It went off very well though her Majesty looked matronly and aged and the ladies in attendance on her were an affecting spectacle. The only accurate idea that I can give you of the Exhibition is that it is a great fair under a cucumber frame: the booths very numerous and the glass case very well painted: only it must be one of the Swiss fairs where they sell everything from the best jewellery down to needles and thread. The day was most brilliant and the crowd enormous both of which were essential to the goodness of the spectacle as the palace would be cold and icy without inhabitants and sun is required for the proper apportionment of light and shade and the due appreciation of the painted roof. The form of the building is that of a cross – the long stroke from an analogy to church architecture being called the nave, and the short stroke the transept. The Queen sat in the centre with the crowd around and behind her, and I was lucky enough to get a place in the front row of one of the galleries immediately overlooking the chair of state, and almost exactly over the head of your aged and infirm friend the Duke of Wellington. The proceedings were in the nature of pantomime as I could not hear a single syllable either of the address or the answer to it, and ninety-nine hundreds of the audience were similarly circumstanced: a great majority not being able to see anything either. I fancied that I caught two or three words of the archbishop's grace or benediction but I am not sure: at any rate I heard a sermonic tone of voice which was a great satisfaction. I suppose the archbishop was inserted in the program to please the foreigners who are in the habit of consecrating railways and all sorts of secular places: otherwise I think he might as well have been left out as there was nothing there in keeping with him, – nobody minded him and the Queen looked as if she wished that he would leave off. The court looked brilliant enough as far as the men went: the foreign magnates very well got up, our Cabinet ministers like town criers and the Lord Chancellor like a Butler on the stage – There was a strong light upon them, and a tree behind – a real tree growing in the ground and just coming into leaf – which threw them out well and was original and picturesque looking. I walked about for an hour or two when the Queen went. There is an immense amount of wealth industry and ingenuity and all that sort of thing: and I suppose the best of all things that can be manufactured is there: but no one thing can make much impression in such a mass: the point of the scene is their number and the good effect of the whole. In the exact centre is a stunning fountain of glass made by the Oslers of Oxford St. The foreign departments are much behindhand: the United States especially: indeed at present nothing satisfactory can be collected except that in that country they are extremely well off for soap. They have an immense compartment all to themselves at the end of the nave and nothing hardly in it except busts in soap of the Queen and other people. It must be amusing to wash yourself with yourself and a great relief from the wretchedness of the employment. There were a great many Americans in the crowd. Quain – with whom I went – got hold of one who swore he was member in Congress for California and looked like a Smithfield drover. Otherwise there were much fewer foreigners than I expected. They were certainly not a twentieth part of the crowd. There are a good many of questionable aspect in the streets, but few I take it that abound in coin. I hear that the house-letting people are at a low ebb in consequence.

Hope you can read this scrawl. I write in a hurry as I want to go
to bed –

Yours affly

W. BAGEHOT

I shall go to Hampstead on Sunday. Love to all.

(*WB*, xii, 317–19)

The habit of common and continuous speech is a symptom of mental deficiency It proceeds from not knowing what is going on in other people's minds.

The House of Commons is a public meeting, at which more than six hundred and fifty members have a right to be present, and at which, in times like these, a great part of the six hundred and fifty are present. Anyone, who knows by experience what any other public meeting of six hundred persons is, will feel the invincible difficulty of getting it to transact any business.

How to get the obedience of men is the hard problem; what you do with that obedience is less critical.

HISTORIANS

The tendency of man is to take an interest in man, and almost in man only. The world has a vested interest in itself. Analyse the minds of the crowd of men, and what will you find? Something of the outer earth, no doubt, – odd geography, odd astronomy, doubts whether Scutari is in the Crimea, investigations whether the moon is less or greater than Jupiter; some idea of herbs, more of horses; ideas, too, more or less vague of the remote and supernatural, – notions which the tongue cannot speak, which it would seem the world would hardly bear if thoroughly spoken. Yet, setting aside these which fill the remote corners and lesser outworks of the brain, the whole stress and vigour of the ordinary faculties is expended on their possessor and his associates, on the man and on his fellows. In almost all men, indeed, this is not simply an intellectual contemplation; we not only look on, but act. The impulse to busy ourselves with the affairs of men goes further than the simple attempt to know and comprehend them: it warms us with a further life; it incites us to stir and influence those affairs; its animated energy will not rest till it has hurried us into toil and conflict. At this stage the mind of the historian as we abstractedly fancy it naturally breaks off: it has more interest in human affairs than the naturalist; it instinctively selects the actions of man for occupation and scrutiny in preference to the habits of fishes or the structures of stones; but it has not so much vivid interest in them as the warm and active man. To know is sufficient for it; it can bear not to take a part. A want of impulse seems born with the disposition. To be constantly occupied about the actions of others; to have constantly presented to your contemplation and attention events and occurrences memorable only as evincing certain qualities of mind and will, which very qualities in a measure you feel within yourself, and yet be without an impulse to exhibit them in the real world, 'which is the world of all of us'; to contemplate, yet never act; 'to have the House before you', and yet to be content with the reporters' gallery, – shows a chill impassiveness of temperament, a sluggish insensibility to ardent impulse, a heavy immobility under ordinary emotion. The image of the stout Gibbon placidly contemplating the animated conflicts, the stirring pleadings of Fox and Burke, watching a revolution and heavily taking no part in it, gives an idea of the historian as he is likely to be. 'Why,' it is often asked, 'is history dull? It is a narrative of life, and life is of all things the most interesting.' The answer is, that it is written by men too dull to take the common interest in life, in whom languor predominates over zeal, and sluggishness over passion.

(*WB*, i, 398–9, from 'Mr Macaulay', *National Review*, 1856)

HUMOUR AND WIT

A great deal of excellent research has been spent on the difference between 'humour' and 'wit'. There is, however, between them, the distinction of dry sticks and green sticks; there is in humour a living energy, a diffused potency, a noble sap; it grows upon the character of the humorist. Wit is part of the machinery of the intellect; as Madame de Stael says, '*La gaieté de l'esprit est facile à tous les hommes qui ont de l'esprit.*' We wonder Mr Babbage does not invent a punning-engine; it is just as possible as a calculating one. Sydney Smith's mirth was essentially humorous; it clings to the character of the man; as with the sayings of Dr Johnson, there is a species of personality attaching to it; the word is more graphic because Sydney Smith – that man being the man that he was, – said it, than it would have been if said by anyone else. In a desponding moment, he would have it he was none the better for the jests which he made, any more than a bottle for the wine which passed through it; this is a true description of many a wit, but he was very unjust in attributing it to himself.

(*WB*, i, 336, from 'The First Edinburgh Reviewers', *National Review*, 1855)

Impelling power and restraining wisdom are as opposite as any two things, and are rarely found together.

In all countries new wealth is ready to worship old wealth, if old wealth will only let it.

In every country the extreme party is most irritated against the party which comes nearest to itself, but does not go so far.

In happy states, the Conservative party must rule upon the whole a much longer time than their adversaries. In well-framed polities, innovation – great innovation that is – can only be occasional. If you are always altering your house, it is a sign either that you have a bad house, or that you have an excessively restless disposition – there is something wrong somewhere.

In the faculty of writing nonsense, stupidity is no match for genius.

It is by external pressure, and the resistance it elicits, that a government gains its authority, and by the absence of it that it is apt to lose it.

It is the fact, that by the constitution of society the bold, the vigorous, and the buoyant, rise and rule; and that the weak, the shrinking, and the timid, fall and serve.

It is only people who have had a tooth out, that really know the dentist's waiting room.

It is unfortunately the case that official people in England can scarcely ever be induced to make a start in the right direction till they have been beaten successively off every false scent – a process involving long delay, vast expense, much mischief, and much humiliation.

IDEAS

Dogma is a dry hard husk; poetry has the soft down of the real fruit. Ideas seize on the fanatic mind just as they do on the poetical; they have the same imperious ruling power. The difference is, that in the one the impelling force is immutable, iron, tyrannical; in the other the rule is expansive, growing, free, taking up from all around it moment by moment whatever is fit, as in the political world a great constitution arises through centuries, with a shape that does not vary, but with movement for its essence and the fluctuation of elements for its vitality.

(*WB*, ii, 21, from 'Béranger', *National Review*, 1857)

THE IMPORTANCE OF BEING QUIET

Pascal said that most of the evils of life arose from 'man's being unable to sit still in a room'; and though I do not go that length, it is certain that we should have been a far wiser race than we are if we had been readier to sit quiet – we should have known much better the way in which it was best to act when we came to act. The rise of physical science, the first great body of practical truth provable to all men, exemplifies this in the plainest way. If it had not been for quiet people, who sat still and studied the sections of the cone, if other quiet people had not sat still and studied the theory of infinitesimals, or other quiet people had not sat still and worked out the doctrine of chances, the most 'dreamy moonshine', as the purely practical mind would consider, of all human pursuits; if 'idle star-gazers' had not watched long and carefully the motions of the heavenly bodies – our modern astronomy would have been impossible, and without our astronomy 'our ships, our colonies, our seamen', all which makes modern life, modern life could not have existed. Ages of sedentary, quiet thinking people were required before that noisy existence began, and without those pale preliminary students it never could have been brought into being. And nine-tenths of modern science is in this respect the same: it is the produce of men whom their contemporaries thought dreamers – who were laughed at for caring for what did not concern them – who, as the proverb went, 'walked into a well from looking at the stars' – who were believed to be useless, if anyone could be such. And the conclusion is plain that if there had been more such people, if the world had not laughed at those there were, if rather it had encouraged them there would have been a great accumulation of proved science ages before there was. It was the irritable activity, the 'wish to be doing something', that prevented it. Most men inherited a nature too eager and too restless to be quiet and find out things; and even worse – with their idle clamour they 'disturbed the brooding hen', they would not let those be quiet who wished to be so, and out of whose calm thought much good might have come forth.

(*WB*, vii, 123, from *Physics and Politics*, 1872)

THE IMPORTANCE OF STUPIDITY

I fear you will laugh when I tell you what I conceive to be about the most essential mental quality for a free people, whose liberty is to be progressive, permanent, and on a large scale; it is much *stupidity* . . . let me take the Roman character – for, with one great exception . . . they are the great political people of history. Now, is not a certain dullness their most visible characteristic? What is the history of their speculative mind? – a blank. What their literature? – a copy. They have left not a single discovery in any abstract science; not a single perfect or well-formed work of high imagination. The Greeks, the perfection of narrow and accomplished genius, bequeathed to mankind the ideal forms of self-idolizing art – the Romans imitated and admired; the Greeks explained the laws of nature – the Romans wondered and despised . . . Throughout Latin literature, this is the perpetual puzzle – Why are we free and they slaves? . . . why do the stupid people always win, and the clever people always lose? I need not say that, in real sound stupidity, the English are unrivalled. You'll

hear more wit, and better wit, in an Irish street row than would keep
Westminster Hall in humour for five weeks . . .

What we opprobriously call stupidity, though not an enlivening
quality in common society, is nature's favourite resource for preserving steadiness of conduct and consistency of opinion. It enforces
concentration; people who learn slowly, learn only what they must.
The best security for people's doing their duty is that they should not
know anything else to do; the best security for fixedness of opinion is
that people should be incapable of comprehending what is to be said
on the other side. These valuable truths are no discoveries of mine.
They are familiar enough to people whose business it is to know
them. Hear what a dense and aged attorney says of your peculiarly
promising barrister: – 'Sharp! oh yes, yes! he's too sharp by half. He is
not *safe*; not a minute, isn't that young man.' 'What style, sir,' asked
of an East India Director some youthful aspirant for literary renown,
'is most to be preferred in the composition of official dispatches?' 'My
good fellow,' responded the ruler of Hindostan, 'the style *as we* like is
the Humdrum.' I extend this, and advisedly maintain that nations,
just as individuals, may be too clever to be practical, and not dull
enough to be free.

(*WB*, iv, 50–53, from 'On the New Constitution of France, and the
Aptitude of the French Character for National Freedom', *Inquirer*,
1852)

INTERFERENCE

All governments like to interfere; it elevates their position to make
out that they can cure the evils of mankind. And all zealots wish they
should interfere, for such zealots think they can and may convert the
rulers and manipulate the state control.

(*WB*, xi, 225, from 'The Postulates of English Political Economy',
Fortnightly Review, 1876)

INVESTMENTS

We wish somebody would write something on the *duty* of common
sense. Many divines patronize other virtues, ingenious speculators are

florid on out of the way obligations, but all neglect the duty of not
concerning oneself with affairs which one can't manage, and of
managing appropriately those which one does manage. And yet this is
worth something. The happiness of how many families, the welfare
of how many children, depend on it. 'The philosophy,' says Henry
Taylor, 'which teaches a contempt of money does not go very deep.'
If it be a difficult thing to get, it is also quite as certainly a difficult
thing to spend.

These remarks are suggested to us by the present state of the
money market. We do not in general concern ourselves minutely
with monetary affairs: removed as we are from the stimulating
atmosphere of mercantile transactions, it would be absurd in us to
write elaborately on their obscure ramifications or daily detail. As the
ancient moralist has observed, a resident at Lacedaemon should not
perplex himself as to how the Scythians should be governed; but
pecuniary affairs may be so important, mercantile obligations may be
so clear – matters in Scythia may be so patent, that, as moralists, we
may be compelled to notice them; and so we think it is at present.

'The history,' says Lord Overstone, 'of what we are in the habit
of calling the state of trade is an instructive lesson. We find it subject
to various conditions, which are periodically returning; it revolves
apparently in an established cycle. First we find it in a state of
quiescence, next improvement, growing confidence, prosperity, excitement, overtrading, CONVULSION, pressure, stagnation, distress, ending
again in quiescence.' We are now at what may be called the second or
critical stage. We have had a considerable period of quiescence: since
the conclusion of what is called the railway mania there has been a
prevalent torpidity in mercantile affairs; speculations have been
rational, enterprise calm, society at rest. It is with society itself to say
whether this tranquillity shall or shall not continue.

'John Bull,' says someone, 'can stand a great deal, but he cannot
stand TWO per cent.' This is the meaning of Lord Overstone's cycle.
After a great crisis like that of 1847 – a great destruction of credit, a
large depreciation of property – money is, as it is called, *scarce*. At the
very conclusion of the most recent panic, money could hardly be
borrowed, on the most indisputable security, at eight per cent; since
that time this rate has been, gradually, though surely, lessening. The

constant accumulations of property, the habitual savings of thrifty people, the influx of foreign capital, the discovery of colonial gold, have so crowded the pecuniary market, that money has become 'a drug'. Consols touch on 101; the rate of interest is proportionably low; on some securities it even approaches the awful limit of two per cent.

Here the moral obligation arises. People won't take two per cent; they won't bear a loss of income. Instead of that dreadful event, they invest their careful savings in something impossible – a canal to Kamchatka, a railway to Watchet, a plan for animating the Dead Sea, a corporation for shipping skates to the Torrid Zone. A century or two ago, the Dutch burgomasters, of all people in the world, invented the most imaginative occupation. They speculated in *impossible tulips*. It was quite understood that they were impossible: nobody had ever seen such species as were sold, nobody ever wished to see such species as were bought; but money was plenty. There had been originally a 'legitimate demand' for gardening-roots and soothing flowers; and out of that the whole grew. Just so with railways: some, no doubt, were required; but money was abundant. In consequence, every place was to have a railway; every railway was to pay twenty per cent, 'as safe as the Bank of England'; scrip in schemes as visionary as the most imaginary tulip were daily bought and sold. There was no toleration for secure gain for quiet pursuits, for ordinary industry; people could not stand two per cent.

We are not going to advocate simple fatalism. We do not say that in affairs like these, in a matter dependent on human resolution and determination, the same causes will, of necessity, produce the same effects precisely. We hope and trust they will not. We hope that people will be wise – that capitalists will exercise a discretion – that merchants will not over-trade – that shopkeepers will not overstock – that the nonmercantile public will bear a reduction in income – that they will efface superfluities, and endure adversity, and abolish champagne; but unless self-denial is exercised, and judgement put forth and common sense exerted, the case is hopeless. One of two alternatives must be taken. If the old, and tried, and safe investments no longer yield their accustomed returns, we must take what they do yeild, or try what is untried. We must either be poorer or less safe; less opulent or less secure.

This point is quite independent of any hypothesis as to the causes of the present state of monetary transactions. That money is abundant, is a fact; why it is abundant, is a theory. That savings are not so easily 'put out' as they were formerly, we are sure; but why they are so is an obscure and controverted topic. It may be that it is the Californian gold – that it is the Australian gold – that it is over-production – that it is a want of bank notes – that it is an excess of bank notes – that it is Free Trade – that it is the absence of Free Trade – that causes our evils. It may be (as Mr John Stuart Mill says it is) the barrenness of land, or it may be the existence of a volcano in Mount Hekla; but anyhow we have our money, and can't invest it in the way we used at the rate of a return we used to obtain for it, and this is the whole difficulty.

Nor must we be understood to speak evil of speculation in general, we only warn our readers against a feverish and irrational excitement. It is good that people are inventive – it is much to discover an industrial idea: we are grateful to those that are original. But let only those be original who can be – let those walk first whom nature intended to be first – let those only enter on new speculations who feel really and truly competent to comprehend and judge of them. People out of business should keep from untried undertakings – people in business should stick to their own line. We comprehend only our own experience, or what resembles it. Common sense teaches that booksellers should not speculate in hops, or bankers in turpentine; that railways should not be promoted by maiden ladies, or canals by beneficed clergymen; that savings should not be hazarded because they *may* yield much, or money squandered because it might be more; that families may be ruined by rashness, and children made beggars by an investment without information. In the name of common sense, let there be common sense.

(*WB*, ix, 272–5, *Inquirer*, 1852)

IRISH NATIONALISM

It is the misfortune of Ireland that it is not true of politics there that 'nothing succeeds like success', but rather, if we may be permitted the bull, that 'nothing succeeds like failure'. The Irish get impatient of the uniformity of even a prosperous agitation, and for this very good reason, that it is not so much the thing agitated for that they want, as the agitation itself. Now when it is agitation that is popular, and not the object of the agitation, it is obvious that the agitation must not remain too long in the same phase, or else it becomes monotonous, and ceases to agitate. That is, we do not doubt, the chief weakness of Irish politics. The cries are far more popular than the objects of the cries ... It is the chief blot on all political life in Ireland that there is so little seriousness in the choice of the political aims which are put forward. A great German of the last century once said in a rash moment, that if he had his choice between the eager search for truth and the possession of truth, he would prefer the former – forgetting that he could not prefer the search to the thing without dropping all earnestness out of the search itself. Just so the Irish people appear to feel in relation to political matters, even in their serious moments. They prefer the demand to the satisfaction of the demand, and thus success, or the prospect of success, instead of sobering them, as it does almost all races which are really political, only tends to make them put forth still more impracticable demands. As you see in all bargains, the disposition to compromise always implies that the eye of the person who accepts the compromise is on the *thing* bargained for, not on mere triumph in the bargain. The Irish politicians have no disposition to compromise, because, as we believe, they have not their eyes on the thing demanded, but on the sound of the demand itself.

(*WB*, viii, 130–31, from 'The Limerick Demonstration', *The Economist*, 1876)

Legislative assemblies, leading articles, easy eloquence, – such are good – very good, – useful – very useful. Yet they can be done without. We can want them. Not so with all things. The selling of figs, the cobbling of shoes, the manufacturing of nails, – these are the essence of life. And let who so frameth a constitution for his country think on these things.

'Literary men,' it has been said, 'are outcasts'; and they are eminent in a certain way notwithstanding. 'They can say strong things of their age; for no one expects they will go out and act on them.' They are a kind of ticket-of-leave lunatics, from whom no harm is for the moment expected; who seem quiet, but on whose vagaries a practical public must have its eye.

LANGUAGE AND NATIONAL CHARACTER

The invention of books has at least one great advantage. It has half-abolished one of the worst consequences of the diversity of languages. Literature enables nations to understand one another. Oral intercourse hardly does this. In English a distinguished foreigner says not what he thinks, but what he can. There is a certain intimate essence of national meaning which is as untranslatable as good poetry. Dry thoughts are cosmopolitan; but the delicate associations of language which express character, the traits of speech which mark the man, differ in every tongue, have not even cumbrous circumlocutions that are equivalent in another. National character is a deep thing – a shy thing; you cannot exhibit much of it to people who have a difficulty in understanding your language; you are in a strange society, and you feel you will not be understood.

(*WB*, ii, ii, from 'Béranger', *National Review*, 1857)

LAW AND ORDER

The first duty of every government, and more especially of every representative government – because being representative it allows violent differences of opinion – is to maintain order – that is, in plain English, to make the law so powerful that nobody thinks he can defy it with impunity. It is its first duty, *not* because the malcontents deserve punishment – they may not deserve it at all, as in the case of a rising of slaves or conquered persons – but because it has pledged itself to all the loyal that it will do it; that they shall not be hurt either in person or property except by due process of fairly executed law. If therefore discontent becomes insurrection in Ireland, or passes the limit beyond which society can be said to be protected, there will be nothing for it except to employ force, whatever the result may be. The past engagements of Government must be kept even if the fulfilment of their promises for the future should be delayed. But this 'contingency', as Mr Disraeli termed it, has not yet arisen, and decision as to the fact of its occurrence must be left to the executive Government itself. It is nearly sure to act soon enough. There is an instinct in all governments which prompts them to be somewhat over-ready in defence or 'order' – an instinct based, we believe, on a sense of the limit to their own powers, a perception that while order is maintained they will know what to do, but that if it disappears they may be called upon to deal with circumstances entirely novel, and, it may be, beyond their grasp. In Ireland more especially there is a permanent temptation to use force. Ireland, like Italy, is 'easy to govern with a state of siege', and has never for six hundred years failed to respond to the direct application of military rule by an apparent submission. But then as in Italy, so in Ireland, this submission has never been real; has never enabled the ruler to found anything; has never diminished in any way or any degree the persistent, undying dislike of the people towards the government which applies such means. If history teaches anything at all, it is that Coercion Bills for Ireland do not help to conciliate the Irish.

(*WB*, viii, 112–13, from 'The Irish Policy of the Liberal Government',

The Economist, 1870)

THE LEADERSHIP OF THE OPPOSITION

The disinclination of Mr Gladstone to undertake for the present the leadership of the Opposition, at least in its complete form, is very natural. Mr Gladstone has worked harder than any Prime Minister ever worked before; he has had five years of that work; he has earned repose as far as it is possible for labour to earn it. Every kind of temporary arrangement should be made to give it to him as far as it is possible and as far as he requires it. But such half-and-half arrangements can be but temporary. The duties of a Leader of Opposition are far too important and too peculiar to be for a long time put into commission, or to be trusted to a deputy.

We may say that these duties are three – first, there is the formal and almost ceremonial class. Very often enough the whole House of Commons and the whole country are agreed that certain things should be done. If certain kinds of arrangements have to be made about the Queen, if public honours – like the funeral of the Duke of Wellington – are to be given to a great statesman, it is customary that the Leader of the Opposition should second the motion. The act is unanimous, and the most effective mode of proving that unanimity is that the head of the government should propose it, and that the head of the party which generally opposes the government should say in a kind of official way that they concur in it. Few things are more curious or more strictly of English invention than this way of treating an organized opposition to the government as a part of the government; statesmen trained in despotisms can scarcely comprehend such a thing, but nevertheless it is most useful and full of good sense.

Secondly, there is the duty at times of regulating, and at times of intensifying the opposition to the government. It will not do to oppose the ministry equally upon everything. In old times, it is true, the opposition seems to have done something very like it. Whole volumes of the old parliamentary debates seem only to come to this, that whatever Mr Pitt said Mr Fox denied. But only a hopeless opposition, which had no chance of office, and therefore foresaw no responsibility, could act thus. An indiscriminate opposition to all measures of the existing government, if successful for the instant, would in the end be fatal, because it would land the opposition in office pledged to mischievous falsehoods in every kind of public business. Most of the measures which a ministry proposes are framed by the permanent officials, effect public improvements too long delayed, and are such as every ministry would adopt. An opposition which without care and recklessly opposes all such things as these, would, if it should reach office, reach it loaded with untenable principle. But, indeed, it would never reach it. The country tests the fitness of a party for office by its discretion in opposition; if it sees such a party opposing the obviously good measures of others, it infers that it is obviously unfit to propose good measures of its own. An indiscriminate opposition will never nowadays, in England, become a ministry. Nor will an undisciplined opposition either. Indeed, the undisciplined opposition is the worst species of the indiscriminate. Without discipline different sections of the opposition will make incessant and different rushes against different measures of the government – one set will vote and speak against one thing, another set vote and speak against another. But the whole will never combine, its entire force will never be displayed; there will be an innumerable series of petty skirmishes in Parliament, but no single pitched battle. The power of such an opposition is daily frittered away; and its evident disorganization daily diminishes its chance of office. The country says instinctively, if these people are not united enough to oppose others together, how will they ever be enough united to act together themselves? Such an opposition, too, is of no use to the public, at least not of the special use which it ought to be. The main function of an opposition is criticism; it ought to detect among the measures of the government which are the bad measures and which are the bad parts of the good measures. An occupied nation like ours cannot do this for itself; it cannot find out things for itself; it requires to have its attention effectually called to what is bad. And the only way of attracting its attention is a great struggle in Parliament. Mr Disraeli, in one of his novels, says, on the part of a government he is imagining, that 'the best repartee is a majority'; in the same way it may be said, on the part of the opposition, that the best criticism on a government is a close division. Nothing else arrests the public like that; nothing else makes people in the city and other practical places stop and think and talk. It is scarcely too much to say that the English people never care to form a judgement about a proposition which has not at least a large minority to advocate it in Parliament. They think that a measure so upheld is 'practical', but anything which is not so upheld is not. The main duty of an opposition is three or four times in a session to arrest the attention of the nation; to compel it to consider the questionable measures of the government; to form an opinion whether those measures ought or ought not to be carried. And the main duty of the Leader of Opposition is to settle which those occasions of concentration shall be; to determine, in the first place, which are, in his judgement, the worst faults of the government; and, secondly, on which of those faults he can most easily induce *all* his followers to act together. The intellectual problem is very difficult, because the detection of these faults requires a careful survey of the whole policy and whole legislation of the government; and beyond this there is the great further difficulty, that the Leader of Opposition must have such a sympathy with his followers as to feel which of these faults most of them would most like to oppose, and such an ascendancy over his followers as to induce them – in some cases against their own judgement – to oppose on these points, and to forbear opposing on other points. Probably this difficulty is the greatest within the range of constitutional government. The Leader of Opposition is set to make bricks without straw. He has to form as good an opinion as that of a minister, without access to ministerial information; and he has to guide his followers just as a minister, without the *prestige* of office and the power of present reward, both which a minister possesses.

The difficulty is indeed greater than we have yet described. There is a third class of cases which are the most difficult of any. A Leader of Opposition must not only induce on most occasions an unwilling minority of his followers to act with him as well as the willing majority, but on some occasions he must induce the majority itself to remain quiet and not to oppose the government, though many of them perhaps are wild to do so. His daily task is that of combining the whole, and occasionally he has besides the still harder task of restraining the whole. Sir Robert Peel on more than one occasion restrained his party thus. It is Mr Disraeli's best claim to particular statesmanship that during the American War he restrained most of his followers, who were eager for the recognition of the South, and whose action on that point might have landed us in disastrous difficulty. The highest and the most important capacity in the Leader of Opposition is to be able on special occasions to resist the mistaken wishes of the party which he leads. No other service which he can perform to the state is, at certain times, so valuable as this.

Besides these inevitable functions of an opposition leader, there is another which has to be performed occasionally only, that is the finding a programme for his party. Many of the most successful opposition leaders have never done this at all. On a memorable occasion Sir Robert Peel declined 'to prescribe till he was called in'; it may be doubted whether during all the years he was in opposition he ever issued anything which could at all be called a programme. The present government has succeeded to office without any announced principles, and partly because it has not announced any. Many people support it because they hope it will be wise, though they have little idea what sort of wisdom they wish for; and some at least support it from expectations which it is pretty certain will be falsified. In the present divided state of the Liberal party a long interval probably should elapse before a new manifesto should be issued. The old questions have mostly been settled; the new questions are as yet too undetermined and too vague to be dealt with in an authoritative exposition. Policies must 'grow'; they cannot be suddenly made. The last manifesto was, as we now know, an error. Mr Gladstone's proposal to repeal the income tax weakened the good wishes of many of his supporters at the last election, and the probable prospect of now retaining it diminishes their regret for his failure. Scarcely anything could be more painful to thoughtful Liberals than that the cardinal issue chosen to decide which party should remain in office should be one which had never been discussed, and on which the present generation of Liberals had never acted together. We trust that the utter failure of this manifesto will be a sufficient warning against the sudden issue of similar manifestoes hereafter. But still it is the undoubted duty of a Leader of Opposition to consider whether or not such programmes should be issued, and also on some rare occasions to issue them.

Such are the duties of the Leader of Opposition, and from them two things are at once evident – first, that they can only be properly performed by the predominant statesman of a party; that they are so difficult and peculiar as to make it impossible for any lesser person to perform them; that, though a temporary arrangement may be made for a short interval, they are so important that 'no conundrum', as we have heard it phrased, must be tried about them; that they are at least as arduous, perhaps more arduous, than those of a Prime Minister, and that only an expectant Prime Minister can be expected to perform them. Secondly, that as long as Mr Gladstone sits in the House of Commons no other person can ever perform these duties. While he has life, health, and power he is the only possible leader. He is so enormously superior to everyone else, not only in eloquence, but also in experience, in knowledge, in combativeness, that no one else can ever lead while he is present. There is no room for him as an 'independent member'. He would derange the plans of any other man if he disapproved of them, and he could not be asked to concur in the plans of any other man unless he approved of them. He has never been a man to whom it was possible to assent to the proposals of others exactly; if he has assented in life it has always been with 'a difference', and in this case that 'difference' would destroy the unity of the Opposition. If at some far 'distant time' he should wish, as he says, to 'divest himself of the responsibilities of leadership', he must retire almost entirely from public life. Greatness has 'its difficulties as well as its claims', and one of those difficulties is that it can never try to act under meaner men without depriving those meaner men of almost all their usefulness. Mr Gladstone has no doubt been already a conspicuous statesman for many years; but nevertheless his powers of labour are still very great. Very few younger men perhaps would like to do half his week's work. English public life requires a singularly sound constitution; it early kills off those who do not possess it. But with those who have that constitution, it is not unfavourable to longevity. Mr Gladstone is still many years younger than Lord Palmerston was when he began to lead the House of Commons. Many years of the greatest usefulness, we trust, are still before him, and it is only in one situation that he can be thus useful.

(*WB*, vi, 60–64, *The Economist*, 1874)

LEARNING TO READ

No one not engaged in education knows the time and labour it takes to teach a child wholly devoid of hereditary culture how to read as grown up people of the better class read, that is, without effort of any kind, and almost without consciousness; and yet, unless this power is attained, education may be said to be almost without value. It certainly cannot be acquired before ten years of age without the devotion of almost the whole time to that study and to writing; and any diversion of the mind to other subjects ends in such neglect of this one, that boys who can read at ten, at thirty can barely spell out their own names.

(*WB*, xiv, 139, from 'Mr Lowe on Education', *The Economist*, 1871)

THE LIMITATIONS OF GOVERNMENT

If you will only write a description of it, any form of government will seem ridiculous. What is more absurd than a despotism, even at its best? A king of ability or an able minister sits in an orderly room filled with memorials and returns, and documents, and memoranda. These are his world; among these he of necessity lives and moves. Yet how little of the real life of the nation he governs can be represented in an official form! How much of real suffering is there that statistics can never tell! how much of obvious good is there that no memorandum to a minister will ever mention! how much deception is there in what such documents contain! how monstrous must be the ignorance of the closet statesman, after all his life of labour, of much that a ploughman could tell him of! A free government is almost worse, as it must read in a written delineation. Instead of the real attention of a laborious and anxious statesman, we have now the shifting caprices of a popular assembly – elected for one object, deciding on another; changing with the turn of debate; shifting in its very composition; one set of men coming down to vote today, to-morrow another and often unlike set, most of them eager for the dinner-hour, actuated by unseen influences, – by a respect for their constituents, by the dread of an attorney in a far-off borough. What people are these to control a nation's destinies, and wield the power of an empire, and regulate the happiness of millions! Either way we are at fault. Free government seems an absurdity, and despotism is so too. Again, every form of law has a distinct expression, a rigid procedure, customary rules and forms. It is administered by human beings liable to mistake, confusion, and forgetfulness, and in the long run, and on the average, is sure to be tainted with vice and fraud. Nothing can be easier than to make a case, as we may say, against any particular system, by pointing out with emphatic caricature its inevitable miscarriages, and by pointing out nothing else. Those who so address us may assume a tone of philanthropy, and for ever exult that they are not so unfeeling as other men are; but the real tendency of their exhortations is to make men dissatisfied with their inevitable condition, and what is worse, to make them fancy that its irremediable evils can be remedied, and indulge in a succession of vague strivings and restless changes.

(*WB*, ii, 102–3, from 'Charles Dickens', *National Review*, 1858)

Man, being the strongest of all animals, differs from the rest; he was obliged to be his own domesticator; he had to tame himself.

Man is of all pieces of luggage the most difficult to be removed.

A man's mother is his misfortune, but his wife is his fault.

Middle-aged men, of feeble heads and half-made reputations, dislike the sharp arguments and the unsparing jests of 'boys at college'; they cannot bear the rough society of those who, never having tried their own strength, have not yet acquired a fellow-feeling for weakness.

MAHOMETAN GOVERNMENT

The more we hear of the situation in Constantinople and in Turkey generally, the more clear is it that the Mahometan power is entirely unsuited to the government of mixed populations, and that any effort to bolster it up in Europe is a serious and dangerous mistake. It is not merely that the activity of the Mahometan power really means the activity of the Mahometan idea as an aggressive idea – that no one can infuse energy into Turks, as Turks, without infusing fanaticism into Mahometans, as Mahometans. That alone is formidable enough, for good government depends at least as much on an impartial respect for the rights of all as it does on energy in enforcing respect for the authority which protects those rights. But there is much more than this. Political government in Turkey has never been an art. There has been no such thing as an administrative tradition in Turkey or a school of Turkish statesmen in which Turkish politicians could find something wherewith to supplement their religious faith. The despotism of the Commander of the Faithful has always been too complete for that. Fidelity has consisted, not in studying the art of government, but in doing his will, whether wise or foolish, safe or foolhardy. If the representative of the Prophet did not get what he liked out of one minister, he straightway removed him, and put another in his place. Hence the growth of anything like a constitutional tradition was rendered simply impossible by that military allegiance to the representative and head of the system, which was at the root of its wonderful conquests many centuries ago, and of its incapacity for improvement now. For the Mahometans, an *art* of government does not, and cannot, exist. There is nothing but a *faith* of government, and the moment anything happens to shake the government, the instinctive movement of the people's mind is towards the faith which could alone, as they no doubt rightly think, restore the energy of the governing power. And thus, whenever it is known, as it is known all over the Turkish dominions in Europe by this time, that the Turkish power is confronted by disobedience which threatens it with extinction, and Turkish finance by a discredit which promises a speedy end to any hope of hiring aid, we hear in all parts of Turkey of a stimulus given to the religious faith with which the Mahometan power is identified, and of outbreaks of ill-feeling against Christians, on very trivial pretences, which really spring not so much from any fear of violence to the Mahometan faith, as of hope from that fanaticism which is the ultimate resort of the Mahometan faith. It is then quite childish to hope in reforms of the government of the various provinces. Before you can have reforms of government you must have in a good many persons a real conviction that the malpractices complained of are bad, and a wish to substitute for them something more orderly and impartial. But that is precisely what there is not to be found within the limits of the Mahometan caste. On the contrary, the more the Mahometans are convinced that Turkey is going to pieces, the more their minds recur to what seems to them the natural remedy – the reassertion of that despotic power over the unbelievers which they fancy that in an hour of weakness, they were led to relax.

The European remedy for the misgovernment might be all very well if we could get anyone to apply it who would wield any power. But whom can the Sultan get? Christians will not trust him. They know very well that a Mahometan ruler who appointed them as his subordinates in order to satisfy his enemies and to gain time, would throw them over as soon as ever he had the chance. Mahometans would trust him, but they would not accept the principles which the European powers advocate. On the contrary, what the insurgents regard as oppression, *they* regard as the natural and legitimate subjection of the infidel to the true believer. The very emergency which renders reform necessary there, renders it also impossible. The Mahometans themselves, so far from believing in the remedy proposed, believe in the very opposite prescription, and, if left to themselves, would try and administer it. It is obvious how very hopeless it would be to govern on European principles, by the agency of a caste which is always on the look out to subvert those principles, and re-introduce the aggressive military ideas of the founder of the system. The simple truth is that the art of government, as we know it in Europe, can never be practised by the Mahometan military caste, and for that reason, if the Mahometan and the Christian populations are to go on living side by side in Europe, the government must fall into the hands of those who are not Mahometans, but who have learned to rule Mahometans with an impartiality with which Mahometans will never learn to rule those whom they regard as infidels. Of course, it is just conceivable that this change might take place without any violent change in the boundaries of the Empire now known as Turkey in Europe. A Christian ruler at Constantinople, if he were really a ruler of genius, and had the services of one or two good generals, might succeed in reducing the conflicting elements of the Turkish Empire to as much order as the British rule has introduced into India among the various Hindoo and Mahometan races. That is, we say, just conceivable. But it seems a great deal more likely that little by little the Mahometan power will lose its grasp over the subject provinces, and that partly by insurrections, partly by the interpositions of neighbouring powers, partly by the steady degeneration of Mahometan statesmanship and finance, the decay of the Empire will proceed and be replaced by the growth of smaller and more prosperous local governments of less ambitious character and very various kinds. The great danger is that Russia may resist this natural local growth of the germs of better, though rude and unpretending, governments, through her desire to prepare the way for the extension of her own empire in this direction; and we should say that the true policy to which any disinterested government at the present moment should give its moral support, would be a policy favourable to the gradual and partial dismemberment of the Ottoman Empire after the precedents of former settlements, but not favourable to any grand attempt to patch up the Turkish Empire as a whole – which will mean, we fear, in practice, its more rapid dissolution as a whole.

Lord Derby has certainly been right in refusing to join in any plan of the latter kind, such as has apparently been proposed at the Conference of Berlin. The notion of Turkey under its present ruler – or, indeed, any ruler – becoming a constitutional power is simply childish. There are no elements at hand for any change of the sort. And the notion of doing any good by an armistice, to be succeeded by a European intervention on a great scale, for the pacification of the revolutionary provinces, is so wild that it is difficult to believe it seriously entertained by any statesman of note who has given common attention to the subject. But if it be true that Lord Derby has opposed this wild scheme on the ground that he looks for a real fulfilment by Turkey of the promises made in answer to the Andrássy Note,* we doubt whether he is any wiser than the Austrian and German and French and Italian ministers whose plan he is criticizing. It is not in the power of a Mahometan government to fulfil their promises, and it is not in keeping with the true policy of England to put pressure on Montenegro and Servia and Bulgaria to make them observe a true neutrality, only in order to give Turkey a chance of recovering by military force the command of the insurgent provinces. We speak, of course, without knowing the line actually taken by Lord Derby, and

---

* Following uprisings in Bosnia and Herzegovina in 1875, Count Andrássy, the Austrian foreign minister, in 1875 unsuccessfully tried to avert war with a peace proposal which stipulated equality of Christians and Muslims, along with other reforms.

only as assuming the positions persistently attributed to him in all the various quarters where some account of the recent negotiations has leaked out. It is very possible that these positions are mistakenly attributed to him. But we must say this, that to use our influence in any way in order to restore Turkish rule where Turkish rule has been a pure evil, and has for the present ceased, would be a very bad use of that influence. The counsel which seems to us the only truly disinterested counsel in this emergency, would be of a kind tending to insulate the political problem to be solved as much as possible in the places where some immediate solution is necessary, and to deprecate any large and grandiose treatment of a question which can only be dealt with successfully if it is dealt with gradually and piecemeal.

As we have already said, we do sincerely believe that, gradually and slowly, but steadily, Mahometan government in Europe must die out. It is not only a government essentially despotic, but one which is not, and can never be, a despotism of the scientific kind, being in its very essence one of the fanatical kind. That being the case, the simplest plan obviously is to supersede it wherever it has grossly misconducted itself with as little appearance of revolution, and as little reconstruction of the 'map of Europe' as possible. Instead of imposing armistices and concurring in mixed commissions appointed to attempt impossible problems, the wise course is to supersede the direct government of the Sultan by some more popular and local government wherever Europe sees that the direct government of the Sultan is no longer advisable, but to soften the blow by making the new state thus formed a tributary to the Porte. We do not mean that England has either interest or power enough, to render a peremptory tone on this matter in opposition to the other powers, advisable. But when we are asked for advice we should give our advice frankly; and this seems to us the only kind of advice which, if followed, would tend to delay a great and most dangerous catastrophe, and to diminish the magnitude of the political crisis, whenever that catastrophe at length arrives.

(*WB*, viii, 291–5, *The Economist*, 1876)

THE MEANING AND THE VALUE OF THE LIMITS OF THE PRINCIPLE OF NATIONALITIES

The present moment is undeniably apt for analysing the meaning and for estimating the value of the principle of nationalities, for the English Government is now basing its policy upon it. The French Government has long done so. Years hence, probably, it will be considered as *the* historical feature of the last ten years that Louis Napoleon introduced this principle into practical diplomacy. He found it in his youth surging among restless and unsettled conspirators. He saw it was a vague sort of faith to vast multitudes – a vague sort of implement to some plotters. From the experience of his youth, the French Emperor has been taught to make it the cardinal feature in the policy of his age.

There is a most obvious objection to this principle. No great race has ever acted upon it, for every great country is peopled by different races. Each race has conquered weaker races right and left, and great nations have grown up from the results of these conquests. France and Spain, two most homogeneous countries, include heterogeneous elements – Basques, Bretons, Alsatian Germans, speaking a different language, differing altogether in national character: Wales, a corner of England, the Highlands, a corner of Scotland, the south of Ireland, are inhabited by a people alien in blood and in language to the mass of the English. The principle of nationalities, *as* a principle, and if it is to be pushed out in logic, cannot claim the support of history; it is, on the contrary, discountenanced by history and opposed to the consistent practice of great nations. Though, therefore, we believe the principle to have a true essence, we must be prepared for its having many erroneous accompaniments and vicious accidents, and for the necessity of a little care in winnowing the useful wheat from the useless chaff.

The interest of the world is that it should be composed of *great nations*, not necessarily great in territory, but great in merit, great in their connecting spirit, great in their political qualities, vigorous while living, famous when dead. Between a great national history like that of Rome or England and the unelevated lives of an equal number of human beings – suppose of South Sea islanders or Esquimaux wanderers – there is as great a discrepancy as between the organized world of nature and the unorganized. A great oak lives its continuous and impressive life like a great nation; a parcel of unorganized particles hustle hither and thither in the world, and leave no image which memory can retain and no story for an annalist to tell – no definite result to be written as their epitaph or claimed as their trophy. History would be a barren catalogue of isolated facts – life a discontinuous rush of human events – if great, single, continuous nations did not bind the whole together. Strike Greece and Rome from ancient, strike France and England from modern times, see how loose and aimless a secular history would become.

But a great nation is only produced by two causes. One of these – the rarest, perhaps, but not the less effectual – is the binding concentration of an external danger. Switzerland – with three races with three languages, composed of elements which differ from each other, as Italy differs from Germany, as France differs from them both – with Italian customs, and French customs, and German customs – with three languages spoken in its very Diet – maintains a vigorous, true, real, national life such as France, with its pure homogeneity and its vast size, may reasonably envy. The dread of their rich, wealthier, and aggressive neighbours, continuing through centuries, and being the haunting pain of successive generations, has knit these miscellaneous mountaineers into a firm, sympathizing, political nation.

But in the absence of such external concentrating necessity, great nations must be mainly composed of elements which have a natural tendency to confine, which have a natural affinity because they are intrinsically similar. 'Like loves like' is a very ancient proverb, and a condition of a real nation is that at the same moment it should be impelled by the same motives, excited by the same hopes, depressed by the same fears, thinking the same thoughts. It is almost part of this that it should speak the same language. So curiously are men's thoughts moulded by the words in which they are embodied, that men of different speech – except in cases of visible palpable danger – will never think the same thoughts or dream the same dreams. One will grow into one form; its neighbour into a different form. Even if men of a different speech *do* think the same, they cannot tell one another that they do so; they cannot tell it quickly enough for the swift necessities of political action. That popular opinion, so familiar, so powerful, so commonplace to us, is only possible in a nation which is almost wholly composed of a homogeneous race. It is popular, because there is a people – a set of men – at the same moment capable of feeling a single sentiment and acting on a single thought.

These remarks suggest at once the use and the limits of the principle we speak of. 'Nationalities' are useful when they create 'nations', and they are of no use for any other purpose. The accordance in sentiment, language, and manners between different parts of a great country, is a general condition for the function of a great nation. We in this age are erecting nations under the guidance of this principle and of their true elements, but we should do more harm than good if we apply it wildly and recklessly, if we do not heedfully recognize the limitations which history suggests, which common sense confirms, and which the principle itself prescribes.

First, this principle not only would not facilitate, but would prevent, the formation of great nations if it were much applied at an early stage of the world's progress. It is only in ages like this, when there is a *taste* for union among mankind, that it can be safely applied at all. In early ages *dis*union is what pleases men. Each parish wishes to set up for itself; thinks every other parish beneath it; will not endure to be coupled with it. The difficulties of communication, the want of a common literature, soon makes differences of dialect between places, and then magnify these differences of dialect into differences of language. The natural antipathy of the barbarian to his neighbour is now reinforced by the natural dislike which all men feel to other mode of manners, speech, and thought. Not a single England, but a heptarchy of discordant nations, was the choice of an Anglo-Saxon England; not a single France, but a motley assemblage of fiefs and duchies, was the choice of the medieval Frenchmen. The need of early times is a forcible union, for no other is possible. Different languages and races are scattered over the world, and a great nation is only formed out of them by the sword of the conqueror. France and England were both so made, and it would have been a calamity to the world to have kept a separate Normandy, Provence, or Brittany, instead of binding them into one France; it would have been a calamity to have kept alive a separate Wales, or Scotland, or Ireland, instead of binding them into a United Kingdom. The principle of nationalities is not a good in itself, a dogma of superstition to be pursued at all times blindly, but a means to an end, to be applied rationally and discriminately towards that end. In early times, the rough hand of the military monarch had better bind up the miscellaneous elements which will not coalesce otherwise. In the course of ages their differences will pass away, and the weltering mass will shape itself into a nation. In our day, when men prefer union, the principle of nationalities may be used to create nations; in early times it could only prevent their formation, since the passion for disunion was intense and overwhelming, and any excuse for it would have been caught at and accepted. In practice, no two provinces, or perhaps parishes, would have admitted that they belonged to the same nationality.

Secondly, it is even plainer that this principle would not be beneficial, but rather mischievous and calamitous, if it were applied to break up historical nations, which – though composite in structure, and, therefore, so far defective – yet maintain a true national spirit, have a common popular judgement and opinion, and are thoroughly capable of harmonious and conjoint action. To break the Swiss nation because it is composed of different nationalities, would be the sacrifice of an attained end for the pleasure of applying certain means which may or may not recreate it. You have already a great nation, and the luckiest application of the dogma can give you no more. You have what you want without applying it, and you may lose what you had *by* applying it.

Lastly, it is simply pernicious to apply the principle to the case of alien fragments of old races, now connected and bound up with great nations, but which, if set free, would have no other kindred nation of their own to combine with, and which, therefore, though petty, feeble, and long unused to great affairs, would have to set up for themselves. To set up the Basque nationality, or the Breton, or the Welsh, would be injurious to the Basque, the Bretons, and Welsh, even more than to Spain, France, and England. These bits of old races have no great kindred empire near them to which they are allied in spirit, whose language they speak, whose thoughts they *feel*. They had better remain as picturesque additions to old nations of another 'nationality', for they have not the position, the number, the vital energy to make a living country for themselves.

These limitations remove, perhaps, the vague and romantic charm from the principle of nationalities, but they bring it within the sphere of practice. They show us that there it is based not simply on impulsive faith, but within due limits upon sober reason. They give us, to some extent if not completely, the rule for applying a dogma, which most people feel to have much plausibility and semblance of reason, but which most are puzzled to define and distinguish so as to avoid absurd, untenable, and impracticable conclusions.

(*WB*, viii, 149–53, *The Economist*, 1864)

JOHN STUART MILL

Mr Mill belongs we think to the Aristotelic or unspiritual order of great thinkers. A philosopher of this sort starts always from considerations of pure intellect. He never assumes the teachings of conscience: he never, that is, treats as primordial facts, either the existence of a law of duty independent of consequences, nor a moral government of the world, nor a connection either between virtue and a reward, or between sin and retribution. He may have a great mastery over trains of reasoning, a great skill in applying comprehensive principles to complicated phenomena; he may have robust sense like Locke or Adam Smith, a power of exhausting a subject like Aristotle or Bentham, or subtlety like the former, or definiteness in scheming like the latter: but whatever be his merits or deficiencies, this remains as his great characteristic, that the light of his intellect is exactly what Bacon calls 'dry light'; it is 'unsteeped in the humours of the affections'; it rests on what is observed to be; it never grounds itself on any inward assurance of what ought to be; it disregards what Butler calls the 'presages of conscience', and attends only to the senses and the inductive intellect. In physical science and even in metaphysics, the views of such men may be extensive, subtle or profound: in politics also they may, and often will, excel in tracing the different kinds of administrative machinery; they will in general be excellent judges of means, though not well fitted to appreciate what a thinker of a different order would be apt to consider the highest ends of government; in morals their views will in general be vague and not seldom erroneous, for their conscience is not luminous enough to give them vivid or well-defined convictions on the subject of duty . . .

Such are the leading characteristics attaching to the school of thinkers, of whom Locke and Aristotle are perhaps the most attractive representatives, and among whom Auguste Comte is assuredly the least valuable specimen compatible with any remarkable ability. It would lead us too far from our subject to explain at length that the extreme opposite of that school of thinkers is to be found in the school of Plato, and Butler, and Kant, who practically make the conscience the ultimate basis of all certainty, who infer from its inward suggestion the moral government of the world; the connection between shame and fear, and between sin and retribution; from whose principles it may perhaps be deduced that the ground for trusting our other faculties is the duty revealed by conscience, of trusting those of them essential to the performance of the task assigned by God to man: thinkers, in short, whose peculiar function it is to establish in the minds of thoughtful persons that primitive theology which is the necessary basis of all positive revelation.

To what may be called the *moral genius* of these writers, the author before us makes no pretension. He would, we apprehend, indeed, deny that it was possible for any man to possess what we reckon as their characteristic merits. On the other hand, in all the merits of the purely intellectual class of thinkers, we must travel far back into the past before we can find anyone whom we know to be possessed of them in an equal measure.

(*WB*, xi, 160–61, from 'Principles of Political Economy', *Prospective Review*, 1848)

MODERATES

[A moderate man] does not consciously shift or purposely trim his course. He firmly believes that he is substantially consistent. 'I do not wish in this house,' he would say in our age, 'to be a party to any extreme course. Mr Gladstone brings forward a great many things which I cannot understand; I assure you he does. There is more in that bill of his about tobacco than he thinks; I am confident there is. Money is a serious thing, a *very* serious thing. And I am sorry to say Mr Disraeli commits the party very much. He avows sentiments which are injudicious. I cannot go along with him . . . Great orators are very well; but, as I said, how is the revenue? And the point is, not to be led away and to be moderate, and not to go to an extreme . . .' We may laugh at such speeches, but there have been plenty of them in every English parliament. A great English divine has been described as always leaving out the principle upon which his arguments rested; even if it was stated to him, he regarded it as far-fetched and extravagant. Any politician who has this temper of mind will always have many followers; and he may be nearly sure that all great measures will be passed more nearly as he wishes them to be than as great orators wish . . . Nine-tenths of men are more afraid of violence than of anything else; and inconsistent moderation is always popular, because of all qualities it is most opposite to violence, – most likely to preserve the present safe existence.

(*WB*, iii, 60–61, from 'Bolingbroke as a Statesman', *National Review*, 1863)

THE MONARCHY*

The use of the Queen, in a dignified capacity, is incalculable. Without her in England, the present English Government would fail and pass away. Most people when they read that the Queen walked on the slopes at Windsor – that the Prince of Wales went to the Derby – have imagined that too much thought and prominence were given to little things. But they have been in error; and it is nice to trace how the actions of a retired widow and an unemployed youth become of such importance.

The best reason why monarchy is a strong government is, that it is an intelligible government. The mass of mankind understand it, and they hardly anywhere in the world understand any other. It is often said that men are ruled by their imaginations; but it would be truer to say they are governed by the weakness of their imaginations. The nature of a constitution, the action of an assembly, the play of parties,

---

* *The English Constitution* was first published in nine parts between 1865 and 1867 in the *Fortnightly Review* and in 1867 in book form. Anthony Trollope, one of the *FR*'s founders, was among those who objected strongly to its tone. This is the first of two chapters on the monarchy.

the unseen formation of a guiding opinion, are complex facts, difficult to know and easy to mistake. But the action of a single will, the fiat of a single mind, are easy ideas: anybody can make them out, and no one can ever forget them. When you put before the mass of mankind the question, 'Will you be governed by a king, or will you be governed by a constitution?' the inquiry comes out thus – 'Will you be governed in a way you understand, or will you be governed in a way you do not understand?' The issue was put to the French people; they were asked, 'Will you be governed by Louis Napoleon, or will you be governed by an assembly?' The French people said, 'We will be governed by the one man we can imagine, and not by the many people we cannot imagine.'

The best mode of comprehending the nature of the two governments, is to look at a country in which the two have within a comparatively short space of years succeeded each other.

'The political condition,' says Mr Grote, 'which Grecian legend everywhere presents to us, is in its principal features strikingly different from that which had become universally prevalent among the Greeks in the time of the Peloponnesian war. Historical oligarchy, as well as democracy, agreed in requiring a certain established system of government, comprising the three elements of specialized functions, temporary functionaries, and ultimate responsibility (under some forms or other) to the mass of qualified citizens – either a Senate or an Ecclesia, or both. There were, of course, many and capital distinctions between one government and another, in respect to the qualification of the citizen, the attributes and efficiency of the general assembly, the admissibility to power, &c.; and men might often be dissatisfied with the way in which these questions were determined in their own city. But in the mind of every man, some determining rule or system – something like what in modern times is called a *constitution* – was indispensable to any government entitled to be called legitimate, or capable of creating in the mind of a Greek a feeling of moral obligation to obey it. The functionaries who exercised authority under it might be more or less competent or popular; but his personal feelings towards them were commonly lost in his attachment or aversion to the general system. If any energetic man could by audacity or craft break down the constitution, and render himself permanent ruler according to his own will and pleasure, even though he might govern well, he could never inspire the people with any sentiment of duty towards him: his sceptre was illegitimate from the beginning, and even the taking of his life, far from being interdicted by that moral feeling which condemned the shedding of blood in other cases, was considered meritorious: he could not even be mentioned in the language except by a name (τύραννος, *despot*) which branded him as an object of mingled fear and dislike.

'If we carry our eyes back from historical to legendary Greece, we find a picture the reverse of what has been here sketched. We discern a government in which there is little or no scheme or system, still less any idea of responsibility to the governed, but in which the mainspring of obedience on the part of the people consists in their personal feeling and reverence towards the chief. We remark, first and foremost, the king; next, a limited number of subordinate kings or chiefs; afterwards, the mass of armed freemen, husbandmen, artisans, freebooters, &c.; lowest of all, the free labourers for hire and the bought slaves. The king is not distinguished by any broad, or impassable boundary from the other chiefs, to each of whom the title *Basileus* is applicable as well as to himself: his supremacy has been inherited from his ancestors, and passes by inheritance, as a general rule, to his eldest son, having been conferred upon the family as a privilege by the favour of Zeus. In war, he is the leader, foremost in personal prowess, and directing all military movements; in peace, he is the general protector of the injured and oppressed; he offers up moreover those public prayers and sacrifices which are intended to obtain for the whole people the favour of the gods. An ample domain is assigned to him as an appurtenance of his lofty position, and the produce of his fields and his cattle is consecrated in part to an abundant, though rude hospitality. Moreover he receives frequent presents, to avert his enmity, to conciliate his favour, or to buy off his exactions; and when plunder is taken from the enemy, a large previous share, comprising probably the most alluring female captive, is reserved for him apart from the general distribution.

'Such is the position of the king in the heroic times of Greece – the only person (if we except the herald and priests, each both special and subordinate) who is then presented to us as clothed with any individual authority – the person by whom all the executive functions, then few in number, which the society requires, are either performed or directed. His personal ascendancy – derived from divine countenance bestowed both upon himself individually and upon his race, and probably from accredited divine descent – is the salient feature in the picture: the people hearken to his voice, embrace his propositions, and obey his orders: not merely resistance, but even criticism upon his acts, is generally exhibited in an odious point of view, and is indeed never heard of except from some one or more of the subordinate princes.'

The characteristic of the English monarchy is that it retains the feelings by which the heroic kings governed their rude age, and has added the feelings by which the constitutions of later Greece ruled in more refined ages. We are a more mixed people than the Athenians, or probably than any political Greeks. We have progressed more unequally. The slaves in ancient times were a separate order; not ruled by the same laws, or thoughts, as other men. It was not necessary to think of them in making a constitution: it was not necessary to improve them in order to make a constitution possible. The Greek legislator had not to combine in his polity men like the labourers of Somersetshire, and men like Mr Grote. He had not to deal with a community in which primitive barbarism lay as a recognized basis to acquired civilization. *We have*. We have no slaves to keep down by special terrors and independent legislation. But we have whole classes unable to comprehend the idea of a constitution – unable to feel the least attachment to impersonal laws. Most do indeed vaguely know that there are some other institutions besides the Queen, and some rules by which she governs. But a vast number like their minds to dwell more upon her than upon anything else, and therefore she is inestimable. A republic has only difficult ideas in government; a constitutional monarchy has an easy idea too; it has a comprehensible element for the vacant many, as well as complex laws and notions for the inquiring few.

A *family* on the throne is an interesting idea also. It brings down the pride of sovereignty to the level of petty life. No feeling could seem more childish than the enthusiasm of the English at the marriage of the Prince of Wales. They treated as a great political event, what, looked at as a matter of pure business, was very small indeed. But no feeling could be more like common human nature as it is, and as it is likely to be. The women – one half the human race at least – care fifty times more for a marriage than a ministry. All but a few cynics like to see a pretty novel touching for a moment the dry scenes of the grave world. A princely marriage is the brilliant edition of a universal fact, and as such, it rivets mankind. We smile at the *Court Circular,* but remember how many people read the *Court Circular*! Its use is not in what it says, but in those to whom it speaks. They say that the Americans were more pleased at the Queen's letter to Mrs Lincoln, than at any act of the English Government. It was a spontaneous act of intelligible feeling in the midst of confused and tiresome business. Just so a royal family sweetens politics by the seasonable addition of nice and pretty events. It introduces irrelevant facts into the business of government, but they are facts which speak to 'men's bosoms' and employ their thoughts.

To state the matter shortly, royalty is a government in which the attention of the nation is concentrated on one person doing interesting actions. A republic is a government in which that attention is divided between many, who are all doing uninteresting actions. Accordingly, so long as the human heart is strong and the human reason weak, royalty will be strong because it appeals to diffused feeling, and republics weak because they appeal to the understanding.

Secondly, the English monarchy strengthens our government with the strength of religion. It is not easy to say why it should be so. Every instructed theologian would say that it was the duty of a person born under a republic as much to obey that republic as it is the duty of one born under a monarchy to obey the monarch. But the mass of the English people do not think so; they agree with the oath of allegiance; they say it is their duty to obey the 'Queen'; and they have but hazy notions as to obeying laws without a queen. In former times, when our Constitution was incomplete, this notion of local holiness in one part was mischievous. All parts were struggling, and it was necessary each should have its full growth. But superstition said one should grow where it would, and no other part should grow without its leave. The whole Cavalier party said it was their duty to obey the king, whatever the king did. There was to be 'passive obedience' to him, and there was no religious obedience due to anyone else. He was the 'Lord's anointed', and no one else had been anointed at all. The Parliament, the laws, the press were human institutions; but the monarchy was a divine institution. An undue advantage was given to a part of the Constitution, and therefore the progress of the whole was stayed.

After the Revolution this mischievous sentiment was much weaker. The change of the line of sovereigns was at first conclusive. If there was a mystic right in anyone, that right was plainly in James II; if it was an English duty to obey anyone whatever he did, he was the person to be so obeyed; if there was an inherent inherited claim in any king, it was in the Stuart king to whom the crown had come by descent, and not in the Revolution king to whom it had come by vote of Parliament. All through the reign of William III there was (in common speech) one king whom man had made, and another king whom God had made. The king who ruled had no consecrated loyalty to build upon; although he ruled in fact, according to sacred theory there was a king in France who ought to rule. But it was very hard for the English people, with their plain sense and slow imagination, to keep up a strong sentiment of veneration for a foreign adventurer. He lived under the protection of a French king; what he did was commonly stupid, and what he left undone was very often wise. As soon as Queen Anne began to reign there was a change of feeling; the old sacred sentiment began to cohere about her. There were indeed difficulties which would have baffled most people; but an Englishman whose heart is in a matter is not easily baffled. Queen Anne had a brother living and a father living, and by every rule of descent, their right was better than hers. But many people evaded both claims. They said James II had 'run away', and so abdicated, though he only ran away because he was in duresse and was frightened, and though he claimed the allegiance of his subjects day by day. The Pretender, it was said, was not legitimate, though the birth was proved by evidence which any court of justice would have accepted. The English people were 'out of' a sacred monarch, and so they tried very hard to make a new one. Events, however, were too strong for them. They were ready and eager to take Queen Anne as the stock of a new dynasty; they were ready to ignore the claims of her father and the claims of her brother, but they could not ignore the fact that at the critical period she had no children. She had once had thirteen, but they all died in her lifetime, and it was necessary either to revert to the Stuarts or to make a new king by Act of Parliament.

According to the Act of Settlement passed by the Whigs, the crown was settled on the descendants of the 'Princess Sophia' of Hanover, a younger daughter of a daughter of James I. There were before her James II, his son, the descendants of a daughter of Charles I, and elder children of her own mother. But the Whigs passed these over because they were Catholics, and selected the Princess Sophia, who, if she was anything, was a Protestant. Certainly this selection was statesmanlike, but it could not be very popular. It was quite impossible to say that it was the duty of the English people to obey the House of Hanover upon any principles which do not concede the right of the people to choose their rulers, and which do not degrade monarchy from its solitary pinnacle of majestic reverence, and make it one only among many expedient institutions. If a king is a useful public functionary who may be changed, and in whose place you may make another, you cannot regard him with mystic awe and wonder: and if you are bound to worship him, of course you cannot change him. Accordingly, during the whole reigns of George I and George II the sentiment of religious loyalty altogether ceased to support the Crown. The prerogative of the king had no strong party to support it; the Tories, who naturally would support it, disliked the actual King; and the Whigs, according to their creed, disliked the king's office. Until the accession of George III the most vigorous opponents of the Crown were the country gentlemen, its natural friends, and the representatives of quiet rural districts, where loyalty is mostly to be found, if anywhere. But after the accession of George III the common feeling came back to the same point as in Queen Anne's time. The English were ready to take the new young prince as the beginning of a sacred line of sovereigns, just as they had been willing to take an old lady, who was the second cousin of his great-great-grandmother. So it is now. If you ask the immense majority of the Queen's subjects by what right she rules, they would never tell you that she rules by parliamentary right, by virtue of 6 Anne, c. 7. They will say she rules by 'God's grace'; they believe that they have a mystic obligation to obey her. When her family came to the Crown it was a sort of treason to maintain the inalienable right of lineal sovereignty, for it was equivalent to saying that the claim of another family was better than hers; but now, in the strange course of human events, that very sentiment has become her surest and best support.

But it would be a great mistake to believe that at the accession of George III the instinctive sentiment of hereditary loyalty at once became as useful as now. It began to be powerful, but it hardly began to be useful. There was so much harm done by it as well as so much good, that it is quite capable of being argued whether on the whole it was beneficial or hurtful. Throughout the greater part of his life George III was a kind of 'consecrated obstruction'. Whatever he did had a sanctity different from what anyone else did, and it perversely happened that he was commonly wrong. He had as good intentions as anyone need have, and he attended to the business of his country, as a clerk with his bread to get attends to the business of his office. But his mind was small, his education limited, and he lived in a changing time. Accordingly, he was always resisting what ought to be, and prolonging what ought not to be. He was the sinister but sacred assailant of half his ministries; and when the French Revolution excited the horror of the world, and proved democracy to be 'impious', the piety of England concentrated upon him, and gave him tenfold strength. The monarchy by its religious sanction now confirms all our political order; in George III's time it confirmed little except itself. It gives now a vast strength to the entire Constitution, by enlisting on its behalf the credulous obedience of enormous masses; then it lived aloof, absorbed all the holiness into itself, and turned over all the rest of the polity to the coarse justification of bare expediency.

A principal reason why the monarchy so well consecrates our whole state is to be sought in the peculiarity many Americans and many utilitarians smile at. They laugh at this 'extra', as the Yankee called it, at the solitary transcendent element. They quote Napoleon's saying, 'that he did not wish to be fatted in idleness', when he refused to be grand elector in Sieyès' Constitution, which was an office copied, and M. Thiers says, well copied, from constitutional monarchy. But such objections are wholly wrong. No doubt it was absurd enough in the Abbé Sieyès to propose that a new institution, inheriting no reverence, and made holy by no religion, should be created to fill the sort of post occupied by a constitutional king in nations of monarchical history. Such an institution, far from being so august as to spread reverence around it, is too novel and artificial to get reverence for itself; if, too, the absurdity could anyhow be augmented, it was so by offering an office of inactive uselessness and pretended sanctity to Napoleon, the most active man in France, with the greatest genius for business, only not sacred, and exclusively fit for action. But the blunder of Sieyès brings the excellence of real monarchy to the best light. When a monarch can bless, it is best that he should not be touched. It should be evident that he does no wrong. He should not be brought too closely to real measurement. He should be aloof and solitary. As the functions of English royalty are for the most part latent, it fulfils this condition. It seems to order, but it never seems to struggle. It is commonly hidden like a mystery, and sometimes paraded like a pageant, but in neither case is it contentious. The nation is divided into parties, but the crown is of no party. Its apparent separation from business is that which removes it both from enmities and from desecration, which preserves its mystery, which enables it to combine the affection of conflicting parties – to be a visible symbol of unity to those still so imperfectly educated as to need a symbol.

Thirdly, the Queen is the head of our society. If she did not exist the Prime Minister would be the first person in the country. He and his wife would have to receive foreign ministers, and occasionally foreign princes, to give the first parties in the country; he and she would be at the head of the pageant of life; they would represent England in the eyes of foreign nations; they would represent the government of England in the eyes of the English.

It is very easy to imagine a world in which this change would not be a great evil. In a country where people did not care for the outward show of life, where the genius of the people was untheatrical, and they exclusively regarded the substance of things, this matter would be trifling. Whether Lord and Lady Derby received the foreign ministers, or Lord and Lady Palmerston, would be a matter of indifference; whether they gave the nicest parties would be important only to the persons at those parties. A nation of unimpressible philosophers would not care at all how the externals of life were managed. Who is the showman is not material unless you care about the show.

But of all nations in the world the English are perhaps the least a nation of pure philosophers. It would be a very serious matter to us to change every four or five years the visible head of our world. We are not now remarkable for the highest sort of ambition; but we are remarkable for having a great deal of the lower sort of ambition and envy. The House of Commons is thronged with people who get there merely for 'social purposes', as the phrase goes; that is, that they and their families may go to parties else impossible. Members of Parliament are envied by thousands merely for this frivolous glory, as a thinker calls it. If the highest post in conspicuous life were thrown open to public competition, this low sort of ambition and envy would be fearfully increased. Politics would offer a prize too dazzling for mankind; clever base people would strive for it, and stupid base people would envy it. Even now a dangerous distinction is given by what is exclusively called public life. The newspapers describe daily and incessantly a certain conspicuous existence; they comment on its characters, recount its details, investigate its motives, anticipate its course. They give a precedence and a dignity to that world which they do not give to any other. The literary world, the scientific world, the philosophic world, not only are not comparable in dignity to the political world, but in comparison are hardly worlds at all. The newspaper makes no mention of them, and could not mention them. As are the papers, so are the readers; they, by irresistible sequence and association, believe that those people who constantly figure in the papers are cleverer, abler, or at any rate, somehow higher, than other people. 'I wrote books,' we heard of a man saying, 'for twenty years, and I was nobody; I got into Parliament, and before I had taken my seat I had become somebody.' English politicians are the men who fill the thoughts of the English public; they are the actors on the scene, and it is hard for the admiring spectators not to believe that the admired actor is greater than themselves. In this present age and country it would be very dangerous to give the slightest addition to a force already perilously great. If the highest social rank was to be scrambled for in the House of Commons, the number of social adventurers there would be incalculably more numerous, and indefinitely more eager.

A very peculiar combination of causes has made this characteristic one of the most prominent in English society. The middle ages left all Europe with a social system headed by courts. The government was made the head of all society, all intercourse, and all life; everything paid allegiance to the sovereign, and everything ranged itself round the sovereign – what was next to be greatest, and what was farthest least. The idea that the head of the government is the head of society is so fixed in the ideas of mankind that only a few philosophers regard it as historical and accidental, though when the matter is examined, that conclusion is certain and even obvious.

In the first place, society as society does not naturally need a head at all. Its constitution, if left to itself, is not monarchical, but aristocratical. Society, in the sense we are now talking of, is the union of people for amusement and conversation. The making of marriages goes on in it, as it were, incidentally, but its common and main concern is talking and pleasure. There is nothing in this which needs a single supreme head; it is a pursuit in which a single person does not of necessity dominate. By nature it creates an 'upper ten thousand'; a certain number of persons and families possessed of equal culture, and equal faculties, and equal spirit, get to be on a level – and that level a high level. By boldness, by cultivation, by 'social science' they raise themselves above others; they become the 'first families', and all the rest come to be below them. But they tend to be much about a level among one another; no one is recognized by all or by many others as superior to them all. This is society as it grew up in Greece or Italy, as it grows up now in any American or colonial town. So far from the notion of a 'head of society' being a necessary notion, in many ages it would scarcely have been an intelligible notion. You could not have made Socrates understand it. He would have said, 'If you tell me that one of my fellows is chief magistrate, and that I am bound to obey him, I understand you, and you speak well; or that another is a priest, and that he ought to offer sacrifices to the gods which I or anyone not a priest ought not to offer, again I understand and agree with you.

But if you tell me that there is in some citizen a hidden charm by which his words become better than my words, and his house better than my house, I do not follow you, and should be pleased if you will explain yourself.'

And even if a head of society were a natural idea, it certainly would not follow that the head of the civil government should be that head. Society as such has no more to do with civil polity than with ecclesiastical. The organization of men and women for the purpose of amusement is not necessarily identical with their organization for political purposes, any more than with their organization for religious purposes; it has of itself no more to do with the State than it has with the Church. The faculties which fit a man to be a great ruler are not those of society; some great rulers have been unintelligible like Cromwell, or brusque like Napoleon, or coarse and barbarous like Sir Robert Walpole. The light nothings of the drawing-room and the grave things of office are as different from one another as two human occupations can be. There is no naturalness in uniting the two; the end of it always is, that you put a man at the head of society who very likely is remarkable for social defects, and is not eminent for social merits.

The best possible commentary on these remarks is the history of English royalty. It has not been sufficiently remarked that a change has taken place in the structure of our society exactly analogous to the change in our polity. A republic has insinuated itself beneath the folds of a monarchy. Charles II was really the head of society; Whitehall, in his time, was the centre of the best talk, the best fashion, and the most curious love affairs of the age. He did not contribute good morality to society, but he set an example of infinite agreeableness. He concentrated around him all the light part of the high world of London, and London concentrated around it all the light part of the high world of England. The Court was the focus where everything fascinating gathered, and where everything exciting centred. Whitehall was an unequalled club, with female society of a very clever and sharp sort superadded. All this, as we know, is now altered. Buckingham Palace is as unlike a club as any place is likely to be. The court is a separate part, which stands aloof from the rest of the London world, and which has but slender relations with the more amusing part of it.

The first two Georges were men ignorant of English, and wholly unfit to guide and lead English society. They both preferred one or two German ladies of bad character to all else in London. George III had no social vices, but he had no social pleasures. He was a family man, and a man of business, and sincerely preferred a leg of mutton and turnips after a good day's work, to the best fashion and the most exciting talk. In consequence, society in London, though still in form under the domination of a court, assumed in fact its natural and oligarchical structure. It, too, has become an 'upper ten thousand'; it is no more monarchical in fact than the society of New York. Great ladies give the tone to it with little reference to the particular court world. The peculiarly masculine world of the clubs and their neighbourhood has no more to do in daily life with Buckingham Palace than with the Tuileries. Formal ceremonies of presentation and attendance are retained. The names of levée and drawing-room still sustain the memory of the time when the king's bed-chamber and the queen's 'with-drawing room' were the centres of London life, but they no longer make a part of social enjoyment: they are a sort of ritual in which nowadays almost every decent person can if he likes take part. Even court balls, where pleasure is at least supposed to be possible, are lost in a London July. Careful observers have long perceived this, but it was made palpable to everyone by the death of the Prince Consort. Since then the court has been always in a state of suspended animation, and for a time it was quite annihilated. But everything went on as usual. A few people who had no daughters and little money made it an excuse to give fewer parties, and if very poor, stayed in the country, but upon the whole the difference was not perceptible. The queen bee was taken away, but the hive went on.

Refined and original observers have of late objected to English royalty that it is not splendid enough. They have compared it with the French court, which is better in show, which comes to the surface everywhere so that you cannot help seeing it, which is infinitely and beyond question the most splendid thing in France. They have said, 'that in old times the English court took too much of the nation's money, and spent it ill; but now, when it could be trusted to spend well, it does not take enough of the nation's money. There are arguments for not having a court, and there are arguments for having a splendid court; but there are no arguments for having a mean court. It is better to spend a million in dazzling when you wish to dazzle, than three-quarters of a million in trying to dazzle and yet not dazzling.' There may be something in this theory; it may be that the court of England is not quite as gorgeous as we might wish to see it. But no comparison must ever be made between it and the French court. The Emperor represents a different idea from the Queen. He is not the head of the state; he *is* the state. The theory of his government is that everyone in France is equal, and that the Emperor embodies the principle of equality. The greater you make him, the less, and therefore the more equal, you make all others. He is magnified that others may be dwarfed. The very contrary is the principle of English royalty. As in politics it would lose its principal use if it came forward into the public arena, so in society if it advertised itself it would be pernicious. We have voluntary show enough already in London; we do not wish to have it encouraged and intensified, but quieted and mitigated.

Our court is but the head of an unequal, competing, aristocratic society: its splendour would not keep others down, but incite others to come on. It is of use so long as it keeps others out of the first place, and is guarded and retired in that place. But it would do evil if it added a new example to our many examples of showy wealth – if it gave the sanction of its dignity to the race of expenditure.

Fourthly, we have come to regard the Crown as the head of our *morality*. The virtues of Queen Victoria and the virtues of George III have sunk deep into the popular heart. We have come to believe that it is natural to have a virtuous sovereign, and that the domestic virtues are as likely to be found on thrones as they are eminent when there. But a little experience and less thought show that royalty cannot take credit for domestic excellence. Neither George I, nor George II, nor William IV were patterns of family merit; George IV was a model of family demerit. The plain fact is, that to the disposition of all others most likely to go wrong, to an excitable disposition, the place of a constitutional king has greater temptations than almost any other, and fewer suitable occupations than almost any other. All the world and all the glory of it, whatever is most attractive, whatever is most seductive, has always been offered to the Prince of Wales of the day, and always will be. It is not rational to expect the best virtue where temptation is applied in the most trying form at the frailest time of human life. The occupations of a constitutional monarch are grave, formal, important, but never exciting; they have nothing to stir eager blood, awaken high imagination, work off wild thoughts. On men like George III, with a predominant taste for business occupations, the routine duties of constitutional royalty have doubtless a calm and chastening effect. The insanity with which he struggled, and in many cases struggled very successfully, during many years, would probably have burst out much oftener but for the sedative effect of sedulous employment. But how few princes have ever felt the anomalous impulse for real work; how uncommon is that impulse anywhere; how little are the circumstances of princes calculated to foster it; how little can it be relied on as an ordinary breakwater to their habitual temptations! Grave and careful men may have domestic virtues on a constitutional throne, but even these fail sometimes, and to imagine that men of more eager temperaments will commonly produce them, is to expect grapes from thorns and figs from thistles.

Lastly, constitutional royalty has the function which I insisted on at length in my last essay, and which, though it is by far the greatest, I need not now enlarge upon again. It acts as a *disguise*. It enables our real rulers to change without heedless people knowing it. The masses of Englishmen are not fit for an elective government; if they knew how near they were to it, they would be surprised, and almost tremble.

Of a like nature is the value of constitutional royalty in times of transition. The greatest of all helps to the substitution of a cabinet government for a preceding absolute monarchy, is the accession of a king favourable to such a government, and pledged to it. Cabinet government, when new, is weak in time of trouble. The Prime Minister – the chief on whom everything depends, who must take responsibility if anyone is to take it, who must use force if anyone is to use it – is not fixed in power. He holds his place, by the essence of the government, with some uncertainty. Among a people well accustomed to such a government, such a functionary may be bold; he may rely, if not on the parliament, on the nation which understands and values him. But when that government has only recently been introduced, it is difficult for such a minister to be as bold as he ought to be. His power rests too much on human reason, and too little on human instinct. The traditional strength of the hereditary monarch is at these times of incalculable use. It would have been impossible for England to get through the first years after 1688 but for the singular ability of William III. It would have been impossible for Italy to have attained and kept her freedom without the help of Victor Emmanuel; neither the work of Cavour nor the work of Garibaldi were more necessary than his. But the failure of Louis Philippe to use his reserve power as constitutional monarch is the most instructive proof how great that reserve power is. In February, 1848, Guizot was weak because his tenure of office was insecure. Louis Philippe should have made that tenure certain. Parliamentary reform might afterwards have been conceded to instructed opinion, but nothing ought to have been conceded to the mob. The Parisian populace ought to have been put down, as Guizot wished. If Louis Philippe had been a fit king to introduce free government, he would have strengthened his ministers when they were the instruments of order, even if he afterwards discarded them when order was safe, and policy could be discussed. But he was one of the cautious men who are 'noted' to fail in old age: though of the largest experience, and of great ability, he failed and lost his crown for want of petty and momentary energy, which at such a crisis a plain man would have at once put forth.

Such are the principal modes in which the institution of royalty by its august aspect influences mankind, and in the English state of civilization they are invaluable. Of the actual business of the sovereign – the real work the Queen does – I shall speak in my next paper.

(*WB*, v, 226–41)

Nations touch at their summit. It is always the highest class which travels most, knows most of foreign nations, has the least of the territorial sectarianism which calls itself patriotism, and is often thought to be so.

No educated mind can, without experience, divine the ideas of the uneducated.

No government is bound to permit a controversy which will annihilate it.

Nothing is more unpleasant than a virtuous person with a mean mind.

Nothing is so transitory as second-class fame.

Nowadays the diffusion of physical science – even of popular physical science – has partly taught us that much truth is dull and complex, and that the most interesting parts of truth can only be understood by those who have mastered that dull and complex part. But even now we do not remember this half enough.

NAPOLEON III

[Louis Napoleon] has one excellent advantage over other French statesmen – he has never been a professor, nor a journalist, nor a promising barrister, nor, by taste, a *littérateur*. He has not confused himself with history; he does not think in leading articles, in long speeches, or in agreeable essays. But he is capable of observing facts rightly, of reflecting on them simply, and acting on them discreetly. And his motto is Danton's, *De l'audace et toujours de l'audace*.

(*WB*, iv, 34, from 'The Dictatorship of Louis Napoleon', *Inquirer*, 1852)

NATION-MAKING

In the last essay I endeavoured to show that in the early age of man – the 'fighting age' I called it – there was a considerable, though not certain, tendency towards progress. The best nations conquered the worst; by the possession of one advantage or another the best competitor overcame the inferior competitor. So long as there was continual fighting there was a likelihood of improvement in martial virtues, and in early times many virtues are really 'martial' – that is, tend to success in war – which in later times we do not think of so calling, because the original usefulness is hid by their later usefulness. We judge of them by the present effects, not by their first. The love of law, for example, is a virtue which no one now would call martial, yet in early times it disciplined nations, and the disciplined nations won. The gift of 'conservative innovation' – the gift of *matching* new institutions to old – is not nowadays a warlike virtue, yet the Romans owed much of their success to it. Alone among ancient nations they had the deference to usage which combines nations, and the partial permission of selected change which improves nations; and therefore they succeeded. Just so in most cases, all through the earliest times, martial merit is a token of real merit: the nation that wins is the nation that ought to win. The simple virtues of such ages mostly make a man a soldier if they make him anything. No doubt the brute force of number may be too potent even then (as so often it is afterwards): civilization may be thrown back by the conquest of many very rude men over a few less rude men. But the first elements of civilization are great military advantages, and, roughly, it is a rule of the first times that you can infer merit from conquest, and that progress is promoted by the competitive examination of constant war.

This principle explains at once why the 'protected' regions of the world – the interior of continents like Africa, outlying islands like Australia or New Zealand – are of necessity backward. They are still in the preparatory school; they have not been taken on class by class, as No. II, being a little better, routed and effaced No. I; and as No. III, being a little better still, routed and effaced No. II. And it explains why western Europe was early in advance of other countries, because there the contest of races was exceedingly severe. Unlike most regions, it was a tempting part of the world, and yet not a corrupting part; those who did not possess it wanted it, and those who had it, not being enervated, could struggle hard to keep it. The conflict of nations is at first a main force in the improvement of nations.

But what *are* nations? What are these groups which are so familiar to us, and yet, if we stop to think, so strange; which are as old as history; which Herodotus found in almost as great numbers and with quite as marked distinctions as we see them now? What breaks the human race up into fragments so unlike one another, and yet each in its interior so monotonous? The question is most puzzling, though the fact is so familiar, and I would not venture to say that I can answer it completely, though I can advance some considerations which, as it seems to me, go a certain way towards answering it. Perhaps these same considerations throw some light, too, on the further and still more interesting question why some few nations progress, and why the greater part do not.

Of course at first all such distinctions of nation and nation were explained by original diversity of race. They *are* dissimilar, it was said, because they were created dissimilar. But in most cases this easy supposition will not do its work. You cannot (consistently with plain facts) imagine enough original races to make it tenable. Some half-dozen or more great families of men may or may not have been descended from separate first stocks, but sub-varieties have certainly not so descended. You may argue, rightly or wrongly, that all Aryan nations are of a single or peculiar origin, just as it was long believed that all Greek-speaking nations were of one such stock. But you will not be listened to if you say that there were one Adam and Eve for Sparta, and another Adam and Eve for Athens. All Greeks are evidently of one origin, but within the limits of the Greek family, as of all other families, there is some contrast-making force which causes city to be unlike city, and tribe unlike tribe.

Certainly, too, nations did not originate by simple natural selection, as wild varieties of animals (I do not speak now of species) no doubt arise in nature. Natural selection means the preservation of those individuals which struggle best with the forces that oppose their race. But you could not show that the natural obstacles opposing human life much differed between Sparta and Athens, or indeed between Rome and Athens; and yet Spartans, Athenians, and Romans differ essentially. Old writers fancied (and it was a very natural idea) that the direct effect of climate, or rather of land, sea, and air, and the sum total of physical conditions varied man from man, and changed race to race. But experience refutes this. The English immigrant lives in the same climate as the Australian or Tasmanian, but he has not become like those races; nor will a thousand years, in most respects, make him like them. The Papuan and the Malay, as Mr Wallace finds, live now, and have lived for ages, side by side in the same tropical regions, with every sort of diversity. Even in animals his researches show, as by an object-lesson, that the direct efficacy of physical conditions is over-rated. 'Borneo,' he says, 'closely resembles New Guinea, not only in its vast size and freedom from volcanoes, but in its variety of geological structure, its uniformity of climate, and the general aspect of the forest vegetation that clothes its surface. The Moluccas are the counterpart of the Philippines in their volcanic structure, their extreme fertility, their luxuriant forests, and their frequent earthquakes; and Bali, with the east end of Java, has a climate almost as arid as that of Timor. Yet between these corresponding groups of islands, constructed, as it were, after the same pattern, subjected to the same climate, and bathed by the same oceans, there exists the greatest possible contrast, when we compare their animal productions. Nowhere does the ancient doctrine – that differences or similarities in the various forms of life that inhabit different countries are due to corresponding physical differences or similarities in the countries themselves – meet with so direct and palpable a contradiction. Borneo and New Guinea, as alike physically as two distinct countries can be, are zoologically as wide as the poles asunder; while Australia, with its dry winds, its open plains, its stony deserts and its temperate climate, yet produces birds and quadrupeds which are closely related to those inhabiting the hot, damp, luxuriant forests which everywhere clothe the plains and mountains of New Guinea.' That is, we have like living things in the most dissimilar situations, and unlike living things in the most similar ones. And though some of Mr Wallace's speculations on ethnology may be doubtful, no one doubts that in the archipelago he has studied so well, as often elsewhere in the world, though rarely with such marked emphasis, we find like men in contrasted places, and unlike men in resembling places. Climate is clearly not *the* force which makes nations, for it does not always make them, and they are often made without it.

The problem of 'nation-making' – that is, the explanation of the origin of nations such as we now see them, and such as in historical times they have always been – cannot, as it seems to me, be solved without separating it into two: one, the making of broadly marked races, such as the negro, or the red man, or the european; and the second, that of making the minor distinctions, such as the distinction between Spartan and Athenian, or between Scotchman and Englishman. Nations, as we see them, are (if my arguments prove true) the produce of two great forces: one the race-making force which, whatever it was, acted in antiquity, and has now wholly, or almost, given over acting; and the other the nation-making force, properly so called, which is acting now as much as it ever acted, and creating as much as it ever created.

The strongest light on the great causes which have formed and are forming nations is thrown by the smaller causes which are altering nations. The way in which nations change, generation after generation, is exceedingly curious, and the change occasionally happens when it is very hard to account for. Something seems to steal over society, say of the Regency time as compared with that of the present Queen. If we read of life at Windsor (at the cottage now pulled down), or of Bond Street as it was in the days of the loungers (an extinct race), or of St James's Street as it was when Mr Fox and his party tried to make 'political capital' out of the dissipation of an heir apparent, we seem to be reading not of the places we know so well, but of very distant and unlike localities. Or let anyone think how little is the external change in England between the age of Elizabeth and the age of Anne compared with the national change. How few were the alterations in physical condition, how few (if any) the scientific inventions affecting human life which the later period possessed, but the earlier did not! How hard it is to say what has caused the change in the people! And yet how total is the contrast, at least at first sight! In passing from Bacon to Addison, from Shakespeare to Pope, we seem to pass into a new world.

In the first of these essays I spoke of the mode in which the literary change happens, and I recur to it because, literature being narrower and more definite than life, a change in the less serves as a model and illustration of the change in the greater. Some writer, as was explained, not necessarily a very excellent writer or a remembered one, hit on something which suited the public taste: he went on writing, and others imitated him, and they so accustomed their readers to that style that they would bear nothing else. Those readers who did not like it were driven to the works of other ages and other countries – had to despise the 'trash of the day', as they would call it. The age of Anne patronized Steele, the beginner of the essay, and Addison its perfecter, and it neglected writings in a wholly discordant key. I have heard that the founder of *The Times* was asked how all the articles in *The Times* came to seem to be written by one man, and that he replied – 'Oh, there is always some one best contributor, and all the rest copy.' And this is doubtless the true account of the manner in which a certain trademark, a curious and indefinable unity, settles on every newspaper. Perhaps it would be possible to name the men who a few years since created the *Saturday Review* style, now imitated by another and a younger race. But when the style of a periodical is once formed, the continuance of it is preserved by a much more despotic impulse than the tendency to imitation – by the self-interest of the editor, who acts as *trustee*, if I may say so, for the subscribers. The regular buyers of a periodical want to read what they have been used to read – the same sort of thought, the same sort of words. The editor sees that they get that sort. He selects the suitable, the conforming articles, and he rejects the non-conforming. What the editor does in the case of a periodical, the readers do in the case of literature in general. They patronize one thing and reject the rest.

Of course there was always some reason (if we only could find it) which gave the prominence in each age to some particular winning literature. There always is some reason why the fashion of female dress is what it is. But just as in the case of dress we know that nowadays the determining cause is very much of an accident, so in the case of literary fashion, the origin is a good deal of an accident. What the milliners of Paris, or the *demi-monde* of Paris, enjoin our English ladies, is (I suppose) a good deal chance; but as soon as it is decreed, those whom it suits and those whom it does not all wear it. The imitative propensity at once ensures uniformity; and 'that horrid thing we wore last year' (as the phrase may go) is soon nowhere to be seen. Just so a literary fashion spreads, though I am far from saying with equal primitive unreasonableness – a literary taste always begins on some decent reason, but once started, it is propagated as a fashion in dress is propagated; even those who do not like it read it because it is there, and because nothing else is easily to be found.

The same patronage of favoured forms, and persecution of disliked forms, are the main causes too, I believe, which change national character. Some one attractive type catches the eye, so to speak, of the nation, as servants catch the gait of their masters, or as mobile girls come home speaking the special words and acting the little gestures of each family whom they may have been visiting. I do not know if many of my readers happen to have read Father Newman's celebrated sermon, 'Personal Influence the Means of Propagating the Truth'; if not, I strongly recommend them to do so. They will there see the opinion of a great practical leader of men, of one who has led very many where they little thought of going, as to the mode in which they are to be led; and what he says, put shortly and simply, and taken out of his delicate language, is but this – that men are guided by *type*, not by argument; that some winning instance must be set up before them, or the sermon will be vain, and the doctrine will not spread. I do not want to illustrate this matter from religious history, for I should be led far from my purpose, and after all I can but teach the commonplace that it is the life of teachers which is *catching*, not their tenets. And again, in political matters, how quickly a leading statesman can change the tone of the community! We are most of us earnest with Mr Gladstone; we were most of us *not* so earnest in the time of Lord Palmerston. The change is what everyone feels, though no one can define it. Each predominant mind calls out a corresponding sentiment in the country: most feel it a little. Those who feel it much express it much; those who feel it excessively express it excessively; those who dissent are silent or unheard.

After such great matters as religion and politics, it may seem trifling to illustrate the subject from little boys. But it is not trifling. The bane of philosophy is pomposity: people will not see that small things are the miniatures of greater, and it seems a loss of abstract dignity to freshen their minds by object lessons from what they know. But every boarding-school changes as a nation changes. Most of us may remember thinking, 'How odd it is that this "half" should be so unlike last "half": now we never go out of bounds, last half we were always going: now we play rounders, then we played prisoner's base'; and so through all the easy life of that time. In fact, some ruling spirits, some one or two ascendant boys, had left, one or two others had come; and so all was changed. The models were changed, and the copies changed; a different thing was praised, and a different thing bullied. A curious case of the same tendency was noticed to me only lately. A friend of mine – a Liberal Conservative – addressed a meeting of working men at Leeds, and was much pleased at finding his characteristic, and perhaps refined points, both apprehended and applauded. 'But then,' as he narrated, 'up rose a blatant Radical who said the very opposite things, and the working men cheered him too, and quite equally.' He was puzzled to account for so rapid a change. But the mass of the meeting was no doubt nearly neutral, and, if set going, quite ready to applaud any good words without much thinking. The ringleaders changed. The radical tailor started the radical cheer; the more moderate shoemaker started the moderate cheer; and the great bulk followed suit. Only a few in each case were silent, and an absolute contrast was in ten minutes presented by the same elements.

The truth is that the propensity of man to imitate what is before him is one of the strongest parts of his nature. And one sign of it is the great pain which we feel when our imitation has been unsuccessful. There is a cynical doctrine that most men would rather be accused of wickedness than of *gaucherie*. And this is but another way of saying that the bad copying of predominant manners is felt to be more of a disgrace than common consideration would account for its being, since *gaucherie* in all but extravagant cases is not an offence against religion or morals, but is simply bad imitation.

We must not think that this imitation is voluntary, or even conscious. On the contrary, it has its seat mainly in very obscure parts of the mind, whose notions, so far from having been consciously produced, are hardly felt to exist; so far from being conceived beforehand, are not even felt at the time. The main seat of the imitative part of our nature is our belief, and the causes predisposing us to believe this, or disinclining us to believe that, are among the obscurest parts of our nature. But as to the imitative nature of credulity there can be no doubt. In *Eöthen* there is a capital description of how every sort of European resident in the East, even the shrewd merchant and 'the post-captain', with his bright, wakeful eye of command, comes soon to believe in witchcraft, and to assure you, in confidence, that there 'really is something in it'. He has never seen anything convincing himself, but he has seen those who have seen those who have seen those who have seen. In fact, he has lived in an atmosphere of infectious belief, and he has inhaled it. Scarcely anyone can help yielding to the current infatuations of his sect or party. For a short time – say some fortnight – he is resolute; he argues and objects; but, day by day, the poison thrives, and reason wanes. What he hears from his friends, what he reads in the party organ, produces its effect. The plain, palpable conclusion which everyone around him believes, has an influence yet greater and more subtle; that conclusion seems so solid and unmistakable; his own good arguments get daily more and more like a dream. Soon the gravest sage shares the folly of the party with which he acts, and the sect with which he worships.

In true metaphysics I believe that, contrary to common opinion, unbelief far oftener needs a reason and requires an effort than belief. Naturally, and if man were made according to the pattern of the logicians, he would say, 'When I see a valid argument I will believe, and till I see such argument I will not believe.' But, in fact, every idea vividly before us soon appears to us to be true, unless we keep up our perceptions of the arguments which prove it untrue, and voluntarily coerce our minds to remember its falsehood. 'All clear ideas are true', was for ages a philosophical maxim, and though no maxim can be more unsound, none can be more exactly conformable to ordinary human nature. The child resolutely accepts every idea which passes through its brain as true; it has no distinct conception of an idea which is strong, bright, and permanent, but which is false too. The mere presentation of an idea, unless we are careful about it, or unless there is within some unusual resistance, makes us believe it; and this is why the belief of others adds to our belief so quickly, for no ideas seem so very clear as those inculcated on us from every side.

The grave part of mankind are quite as liable to these imitated beliefs as the frivolous part. The belief of the money market, which is mainly composed of grave people, is as imitative as any belief. You will find one day everyone enterprising, enthusiastic, vigorous, eager to buy, and eager to order: in a week or so you will find almost the whole society depressed, anxious, and wanting to sell. If you examine the reasons for the activity, or for the inactivity, or for the change, you will hardly be able to trace them at all, and as far as you can trace them, they are of little force. In fact, these opinions were not formed by reason, but by mimicry. Something happened that looked a little good, on which eager sanguine men talked loudly, and common people caught their tone. A little while afterwards, and when people were tired of talking this, something also happened looking a little bad, on which the dismal, anxious people began, and all the rest followed their words. And in both cases an avowed dissentient is set down as 'crotchety'. 'If you want,' said Swift, 'to gain the reputation of a sensible man, you should be of the opinion of the person with whom for the time being you are conversing.' There is much quiet intellectual persecution among 'reasonable' men; a cautious person hesitates before he tells them anything new, for if he gets a name for such things he will be called 'flighty', and in times of decision he will not be attended to.

In this way the infection of imitation catches men in their most inward and intellectual part – their creed. But it also invades men – by the most bodily part of the mind – so to speak – the link between soul and body – the manner. No one needs to have this explained; we all know how a kind of subtle influence makes us imitate or try to imitate the manner of those around us. To conform to the fashion of Rome – whatever the fashion may be, and whatever Rome we may for the time be at – is among the most obvious needs of human nature. But what is not so obvious, though as certain, is that the influence of the imitation goes deep as well as extends wide. 'The matter,' as Wordsworth says, 'of style very much comes out of the manner.' If you will endeavour to write an imitation of the thoughts of Swift in a copy of the style of Addison, you will find that not only is it hard to write Addison's style, from its intrinsic excellence, but also that the more you approach to it the more you lose the thought of Swift. The eager passion of the meaning beats upon the mild drapery of the words. So you could not express the plain thoughts of an Englishman in the grand manner of a Spaniard. Insensibly, and as by a sort of magic, the kind of manner which a man catches eats into him, and makes him in the end what at first he only seems.

This is the principal mode in which the greatest minds of an age produce their effect. They set the tone which others take, and the fashion which others use. There is an odd idea that those who take what is called a 'scientific view' of history need rate lightly the influence of individual character. It would be as reasonable to say that those who take a scientific view of nature need think little of the influence of the sun. On the scientific view a great man is a great new cause (compounded or not out of other causes, for I do not here, or elsewhere in these papers, raise the question of freewill), but, anyhow, new in all its effects, and all its results. Great models for good and evil sometimes appear among men, who follow them either to improvement or degradation.

I am, I know, very long and tedious in setting out this; but I want to bring home to others what every new observation of society brings more and more freshly to myself – that this unconscious imitation and encouragement of appreciated character, and this equally unconscious shrinking from and persecution of disliked character, is the main force which moulds and fashions men in society as we now see it. Soon I shall try to show that the more acknowledged causes, such as change of climate, alteration of political institutions, progress of science, act principally through this cause; that they change the object of imitation and the object of avoidance, and so work their effect. But first I must speak of the origin of nations – of nation-making as one may call it – the proper subject of this paper.

The process of nation-making is one of which we have obvious examples in the most recent times, and which is going on now. The most simple example is the foundation of the first state of America, say New England, which has such a marked and such a deep national character. A great number of persons agreeing in fundamental disposition, agreeing in religion, agreeing in politics, form a separate settlement; they exaggerate their own disposition, teach their own creed, set up their favourite government; they discourage all other dispositions, persecute other beliefs, forbid other forms or habits of government. Of course a nation so made will have a separate stamp and mark. The original settlers began of one type; they sedulously imitated it; and (though other causes have intervened and disturbed it) the necessary operation of the principles of inheritance has transmitted many original traits still unaltered, and has left an entire New England character – in no respect unaffected by its first character.

This case is well known, but it is not so that the same process, in a weaker shape, is going on in America now. Congeniality of sentiment is a reason of selection, and a bond of cohesion in the 'West' at present. Competent observers say that townships grow up there by each place taking its own religion, its own manners, and its own ways. Those who have these morals and that religion go to that place, and stay there; and those who have not these morals and that religion either settle elsewhere at first, or soon pass on. The days of colonization by sudden 'swarms' of like creed is almost over, but a less visible process of attraction by similar faith over similar is still in vigour, and very likely to continue.

And in cases where this principle does not operate all new settlements, being formed of 'emigrants', are sure to be composed of rather restless people, mainly. The stay-at-home people are not to be found there, and these are the quiet, easy people. A new settlement voluntarily formed (for of old times, when people were expelled by terror, I am not speaking) is sure to have in it much more than the ordinary proportion of active men, and much less than the ordinary proportion of inactive; and this accounts for a large part, though not perhaps all, of the difference between the English in England, and the English in Australia.

The causes which formed New England in recent times cannot be conceived as acting much upon mankind in their infancy. Society is not then formed upon a 'voluntary system' but upon an involuntary. A man in early ages is born to a certain obedience, and cannot extricate himself from an inherited government. Society then is made up, not of individuals, but of families; creeds then descend by inheritance in those families. Lord Melbourne once incurred the ridicule of philosophers by saying he should adhere to the English Church *because* it was the religion of his fathers. The philosophers, of course, said that a man's fathers' believing anything was no reason for his believing it unless it was true. But Lord Melbourne was only uttering out of season, and in a modern time, one of the most firm and accepted maxims of old times. A secession on religious grounds of isolated Romans to sail beyond sea would have seemed to the ancient Romans an impossibility. In still ruder ages the religion of savages is a thing too feeble to create a schism or to found a community. We are dealing with people capable of history when we speak of great ideas, not with prehistoric flint-men or the present savages. But though under very different forms, the same essential causes – the imitation of preferred characters and the elimination of detested characters – were at work in the oldest times, and are at work among rude men now. Strong as the propensity to imitation is among civilized men, we must conceive it as an impulse of which their minds have been partially denuded. Like the far-seeing sight, the infallible hearing, the magical scent of the savage, it is a half-lost power. It was strongest in ancient times, and *is* strongest in uncivilized regions.

This extreme propensity to imitation is one great reason of the amazing sameness which every observer notices in savage nations. When you have seen one Fuegian, you have seen all Fuegians – one Tasmanian, all Tasmanians. The higher savages, as the New Zealanders, are less uniform; they have more of the varied and compact structure of civilized nations, because in other respects they are more civilized. They have greater mental capacity – larger stores of inward thought. But much of the same monotonous nature clings to them too. A savage tribe resembles a herd of gregarious beasts; where the leader goes they go too; they copy blindly his habits, and thus soon become that which he already is. For not only the tendency, but also the power to imitate, is stronger in savages than civilized men. Savages copy quicker, and they copy better. Children, in the same way, are born mimics; they cannot help imitating what comes before them. There is nothing in their minds to resist the propensity to copy.

Every educated man has a large inward supply of ideas to which he can retire, and in which he can escape from or alleviate unpleasant outward objects. But a savage or a child has no resource. The external movements before it are its very life; it lives by what it sees and hears. Uneducated people in civilized nations have vestiges of the same condition. If you send a housemaid and a philosopher to a foreign country of which neither knows the language, the chances are that the housemaid will catch it before the philosopher. He has something else to do; he can live in his own thoughts. But unless she can imitate the utterances, she is lost; she has no life till she can join in the chatter of the kitchen. The propensity to mimicry, and the power of mimicry, are mostly strongest in those who have least abstract minds. The most wonderful examples of imitation in the world are perhaps the imitations of civilized men by savages in the use of martial weapons. They learn the *knack*, as sportsmen call it, with inconceivable rapidity. A North American Indian – an Australian even – can shoot as well as any white man. Here the motive is at its maximum, as well as the innate power. Every savage cares more for the power of killing than for any other power.

The persecuting tendency of all savages, and, indeed, of all ignorant people, is even more striking than their imitative tendency. No barbarian can bear to see one of his nation deviate from the old barbarous customs and usages of their tribe. Very commonly all the tribe would expect a punishment from the gods if any one of them refrained from what was old, or began what was new. In modern times and in cultivated countries we regard each person as responsible only for his own actions, and do not believe, or think of believing, that the misconduct of others can bring guilt on them. Guilt to us is an individual taint consequent on choice and cleaving to the chooser. But in early ages the act of one member of the tribe is conceived to make all the tribe impious, to offend its peculiar god, to expose all the tribe to penalties from heaven. There is no 'limited liability' in the political notions of that time. The early tribe or nation is a religious partnership, on which a rash member by a sudden impiety may bring utter ruin. If the state is conceived thus, toleration becomes wicked. A permitted deviation from the transmitted ordinances becomes simply folly. It is a sacrifice of the happiness of the greatest number. It is allowing one individual, for a moment's pleasure or a stupid whim, to bring terrible and irretrievable calamity upon all. No one will ever understand even Athenian history, who forgets this idea of the old world, though Athens was, in comparison with others, a rational and sceptical place, ready for new views, and free from old prejudices. When the street statues of Hermes were mutilated, all the Athenians were frightened and furious; they thought that they should *all* be ruined because some *one* had mutilated a god's image, and so offended him. Almost every detail of life in the classical times – the times when real history opens – was invested with a religious sanction; a sacred ritual regulated human action; whether it was called 'law' or not, much of it was older than the word 'law'; it was part of an ancient usage conceived as emanating from a superhuman authority, and not to be transgressed without risk of punishment by more than mortal power. There was such a *solidarité* then between citizens, that each might be led to persecute the other for fear of harm to himself.

It may be said that these two tendencies of the early world – that to persecution and that to imitation – must conflict; that the imitative impulse would lead men to copy what is new, and that persecution by traditional habit would prevent their copying it. But in practice the two tendencies co-operate. There is a strong tendency to copy the most common thing, and that common thing is the old habit. Daily imitation is far oftenest a conservative force, for the most frequent models are ancient. Of course, however, something new is necessary for every man and for every nation. We may wish, if we please, that tomorrow shall be like today, but it will not be like it. New forces will impinge upon us; new wind, new rain, and the light of another sun; and we must alter to meet them. But the persecuting habit and the imitative combine to ensure that the new thing shall be in the old fashion; it must be an alteration, but it shall contain as little of variety as possible. The imitative impulse tends to this, because men most easily imitate what their minds are best prepared for – what is like the old, yet with the inevitable minimum of alteration; what throws them least out of the old path, and puzzles least their minds. The doctrine of development means this – that in unavoidable changes men like the new doctrine which is most of a 'preservative addition' to their old doctrines. The imitative and the persecuting tendencies make all change in early nations a kind of selective conservatism, for the most part keeping what is old, but annexing some new but like practice – an additional turret in the old style.

It is this process of adding suitable things and rejecting discordant things which has raised those scenes of strange manners which in every part of the world puzzle the civilized men who come upon them first. Like the old head-dress of mountain villages, they make the traveller think not so much whether they are good or whether they are bad, as wonder how anyone could have come to think of them; to regard them as 'monstrosities', which only some wild abnormal intellect could have hit upon. And wild and abnormal indeed would be that intellect if it were a single one at all. But in fact such manners are the growth of ages, like Roman law or the British Constitution. No one man – no one generation – could have thought of them – only a series of generations trained in the habits of the last and wanting something akin to such habits, could have devised them. Savages *pet* their favourite habits, so to say, and preserve them as they do their favourite animals; ages are required, but at last a national character is formed by the confluence of congenial attractions and accordant detestations.

Another cause helps. In early states of civilization there is a great mortality of infant life, and this is a kind of selection in itself – the child most fit to be a good Spartan is most likely to survive a Spartan childhood. The habits of the tribe are enforced on the child; if he is able to catch and copy them he lives; if he cannot he dies. The imitation which assimilates early nations continues through life, but it begins with suitable forms and acts on picked specimens. I suppose, too, that there is a kind of parental selection operating in the same way probably tending to keep alive the same individuals. Those children which gratified their fathers and mothers most would be most tenderly treated by them, and have the best chance to live, and as a rough rule their favourites would be the children of most 'promise', that is to say, those who seemed most likely to be a credit to the tribe according to the leading tribal manners and the existing tribal tastes. The most gratifying child would be the best looked after, and the most gratifying would be the best specimen of the standard then and there raised up.

Even so, I think there will be a disinclination to attribute so marked, fixed, almost physical a thing as national character to causes so evanescent as the imitation of appreciated habit and the persecution of detested habit. But, after all, national character is but a name for a collection of habits more or less universal. And this imitation and this persecution in long generations have vast physical effects. The mind of the parent (as we speak) passes somehow to the body of the child. The transmitted 'something' is more affected by habits than it is by anything else. In time an ingrained type is sure to be formed, and sure to be passed on if only the causes I have specified be fully in action and without impediment.

As I have said, I am not explaining the origin of races, but of nations, or, if you like, of tribes. I fully admit that no imitation of predominant manner, or prohibitions of detested manners, will of themselves account for the broadest contrasts of human nature. Such means would no more make a Negro out of a Brahmin, or a Red Man out of an Englishman, than washing would change the spots of a leopard or the colour of an Ethiopian. Some more potent causes must co-operate, or we should not have these enormous diversities. The minor causes I deal with made Greek to differ from Greek, but they did not make the Greek race. We cannot precisely mark the limit, but a limit there clearly is.

If we look at the earliest monuments of the human race, we find these race-characters as decided as the race-characters now. The earliest paintings or sculptures we anywhere have, give us the present contrasts of dissimilar types as strongly as present observation. Within historical memory no such differences have been created as those between Negro and Greek, between Papuan and Red Indian, between Esquimau and Goth. We start with cardinal diversities; we trace only minor modifications, and we only see minor modifications. And it is very hard to see how any number of such modifications could change man as he is in one race-type to man as he is in some other. Of this there are but two explanations; *one*, that these great types were originally separate creations, as they stand – that the Negro was made so, and the Greek made so. But this easy hypothesis of special creation has been tried so often, and has broken down so very often, that in no case, probably, do any great number of careful inquirers very firmly believe it. They may accept it provisionally, as the best hypothesis at present, but they feel about it as they cannot help feeling as to an army which has always been beaten; however strong it seems, they think it will be beaten again. What the other explanation is exactly I cannot pretend to say. Possibly as yet the data for a confident opinion are not before us. But by far the most plausible suggestion is that of Mr Wallace, that these race-marks are living records of a time when the intellect of man was not as able as it is now to adapt his life and habits to change of region; that consequently early mortality in the first wanderers was beyond conception great; that only those (so to say) haphazard individuals throve who were born with a protected nature – that is, a nature suited to the climate and the country, fitted to use its advantages, shielded from its natural diseases. According to Mr Wallace, the Negro is the remnant of the one variety of man who without more adaptiveness than then existed could live in interior Africa. Immigrants died off till they produced him or something like him, and so of the Esquimau or the American.

Any protective habit also struck out in such a time would have a far greater effect than it could afterwards. A gregarious tribe, whose leader was in some imitable respects adapted to the struggle for life, and which copied its leader, would have an enormous advantage in the struggle for life. It would be sure to win and live, for it would be coherent and adapted, whereas, in comparison, competing tribes would be incoherent and unadapted. And I suppose that in early times, when those bodies did not already contain the records and the traces of endless generations, any new habit would more easily fix its mark on the heritable element, and would be transmitted more easily and more certainly. In such an age, man being softer and more pliable, deeper race-marks would be more easily inscribed and would be more likely to continue legible.

But I have no pretence to speak on such matters; this paper, as I have so often explained, deals with nation-making and not with race-making. I assume a world of marked varieties of man, and only want to show how less marked contrasts would probably and naturally arise in each. Given large homogeneous populations, some Negro, some Mongolian, some Aryan, I have tried to prove how small contrasting groups would certainly spring up within each – some to last and some to perish. These are the eddies in each race-stream which vary its surface, and are sure to last till some new force changes the current. These minor varieties, too, would be infinitely compounded, not only with those of the same race, but with those of others. Since the beginning of man, stream has been a thousand times poured into stream – quick into sluggish, dark into pale – and eddies and waters have taken new shapes and new colours, affected by what went before, but not resembling it. And then on the fresh mass, the old forces of composition and elimination again begin to act, and create over the new surface another world. 'Motley was the wear' of the world when Herodotus first looked on it and described it to us, and thus, as it seems to me, were its varying colours produced.

If it be thought that I have made out that these forces of imitation and elimination be the main ones, or even at all powerful ones, in the formation of national character, it will follow that the effect of ordinary agencies upon that character will be more easy to understand than it often seems and is put down in books. We get a notion that a change of government or a change of climate acts equally on the mass of a nation, and so are we puzzled – at least, I have been puzzled – to conceive how it acts. But such changes do not at first act equally on all people in the nation. On many, for a very long time, they do not act at all. But they bring out new qualities, and advertise the effects of new habits. A change of climate, say from a depressing to an invigorating one, so acts. Everybody feels it a little, but the most active feel it exceedingly. They labour and prosper, and their prosperity invites imitation. Just so with the contrary change, from an animating to a relaxing place – the naturally lazy look so happy as they do nothing, that the naturally active are corrupted. The effect of any considerable change on a nation is thus an intensifying and accumulating effect. With its maximum power it acts on some prepared and congenial individuals; in them it is seen to produce attractive results, and then the habits creating those results are copied far and wide. And, as I believe, it is in this simple but not quite obvious way, that the process of progress and of degradation may generally be seen to run.

(*WB*, vii, 64–80, from *Physics and Politics*, 1869)

Of all pursuits ever invented by man for separating the faculty of argument from the capacity of belief, the art of debating is probably the most effectual.

The ordinary human mind finds a great rest in fixing itself on a concrete object, but neither the metaphysician nor the stock jobber have any such means of repose. Both must make their minds ache by fixing them intently on what they can never see, and by working out all its important qualities and quantities. A stock jobber loses money, and in the end is ruined, if he omits any, or miscalculates any. If any man of business is to turn abstract thinker, this is the one who should do so.

Other things being equal, yesterday's institutions are by far the best for today; they are the most ready, the most influential the most easy to get obeyed, the most likely to retain the reverence which they alone inherit, and which every other must win.

ON THE EMOTION OF CONVICTION

What we commonly term Belief includes, I apprehend, both an Intellectual and an Emotional element; the first we more properly call 'assent', and the second 'conviction'. The laws of the Intellectual element in belief are 'the laws of evidence', and have been elaborately discussed; but those of the Emotional part have hardly been discussed at all, indeed, its existence has been scarcely perceived.

In the mind of a rigorously trained inquirer, the process of believing is, I apprehend, this: – First comes the investigation, a set of facts are sifted, and a set of arguments weighed; then the intellect perceives the result of those arguments, and, as we say, assents to it. Then an emotion, more or less strong sets in, which completes the whole. In calm and quiet minds the intellectual part of this process is so much the strongest that they are hardly conscious of anything else; and as these quiet, careful people have written our treatises, we do not find it explained in them how important the emotional part is.

But take the case of the Caliph Omar, according to Gibbon's description of him. He burnt the Alexandrine Library, saying, 'All books which contain what is not in the Koran are dangerous; all those which contain what is in the Koran are useless.' Probably no one ever had an intenser belief in anything than Omar had in this. Yet it is impossible to imagine it preceded by an argument. His belief in Mahomet, in the Koran, and the sufficiency of the Koran came to him probably in spontaneous rushes of emotion; there may have been little vestiges of argument floating here and there, but they did not justify the strength of the emotion, still less did they create it, and they hardly even excused it.

There is so commonly some considerable argument for our modern beliefs, that it is difficult nowadays to isolate the emotional element, and therefore, on the principle that in Metaphysics 'egotism is the truest modesty', I may give myself as an example of utterly irrational conviction. Some years ago I stood for a borough in the West of England, and after a keen contest was defeated by seven. Almost directly afterwards there was accidentally another election, and as I would not stand, another candidate of my own side was elected, and I of course ceased to have any hold upon the place, or chance of being elected there. But for years I had the deepest conviction that I should be 'Member for Bridgwater'; and no amount of reasoning would get it out of my head. The borough is now disfranchised; but even still, if I allow my mind to dwell on the contest, – if I think of the hours I was ahead in the morning, and the rush of votes at two o'clock by which I was defeated, – and even more, if I call up the image of the nomination day, with all the people's hands outstretched, and all their excited faces looking the more different on account of their identity in posture, the old feeling almost comes back upon me, and for a moment I believe that I shall be Member for Bridgwater.

I should not mention such nonsense, except on an occasion when I may serve as an intellectual 'specimen', but I know I wish that I could feel the same hearty, vivid faith in many conclusions of which my understanding says it is satisfied that I did in this absurdity. And if it should be replied that such folly could be no real belief, for it could not influence any man's action, I am afraid I must say that it did influence my actions. For a long time the ineradicable fatalistic feeling, that I should some time have this constituency, of which I had no chance, hung about my mind, and diminished my interest in other constituencies, where my chances of election would have been rational, at any rate.

This case probably exhibits the maximum of conviction with the minimum of argument, but there are many approximations to it. Persons of untrained minds cannot long live without some belief in any topic which comes much before them. It has been said that if you can only get a middle-class Englishman to think whether there are 'snails in Sirius', he will soon have an opinion on it. It will be difficult to make him think, but if he does think, he cannot rest in a negative, he will come to some decision. And on any ordinary topic, of course, it is so. A grocer has a full creed as to foreign policy, a young lady a complete theory of the sacraments, as to which neither has any doubt whatever. But in talking to such persons, I cannot but remember my Bridgwater experience, and ask whether causes like those which begat my folly may not be at the bottom of their 'invincible knowledge'.

Most persons who observe their own thoughts must have been conscious of the exactly opposite state. There are cases where our intellect has gone through the arguments, and we give a clear assent to the conclusions. But our minds seem dry and unsatisfied. In that case we have the intellectual part of Belief, but want the emotional part.

That belief is not a purely intellectual matter is evident from dreams, where we are always believing, but scarcely ever arguing; and from certain forms of insanity, where fixed delusions seize upon the mind and generate a firmer belief than any sane person is capable of. These are, of course, 'unorthodox' states of mind; but a good psychology must explain them, nevertheless, and perhaps it would have progressed faster if it had been more ready to compare them with the waking states of sane people.

Probably, when the subject is thoroughly examined, 'conviction' will be proved to be one of the intensest of human emotions, and one most closely connected with the bodily state. In cases like the Caliph Omar it governs all other desires, absorbs the whole nature, and rules the whole life. And in such cases it is accompanied or preceded by the sensation that Scott makes his seer describe as the prelude to a prophecy:

> 'At length the fatal answer came,
> In characters of living flame, –
> Not spoke in word, nor blazed in smoke,
> But borne and branded on my soul.'

A hot flash seems to burn across the brain. Men in these intense states of mind have altered all history, changed for better or worse the creed of myriads, and desolated or redeemed provinces and ages. Nor is this intensity a sign of truth, for it is precisely strongest in those points in which men differ most from each other. John Knox felt it in his anti-Catholicism; Ignatius Loyola in his anti-Protestantism; and both, I suppose, felt it as much as it is possible to feel it.

Once acutely felt, I believe it is indelible; at least, it does something to the mind which it is hard for anything else to undo. It has been often said that a man who has once really loved a woman never can be without feeling towards that woman again. He may go on loving her, or he may change and hate her. In the same way, I think, experience proves that no one who has had real passionate conviction of a creed, the sort of emotion that burns hot upon the brain, can ever be indifferent to that creed again. He may continue to believe it, and to love it; or he may change to the opposite, vehemently argue against it, and persecute it. But he cannot forget it. Years afterwards, perhaps, when life changes, when external interests cease to excite, when the apathy to surroundings which belongs to the old begins all at once, and to the wonder of later friends, who cannot imagine what is come to him, the grey-headed man returns to the creed of his youth.

The explanation of these facts in metaphysical books is very imperfect. Indeed, I only know one school which professes to explain the emotion, as distinguished from the intellectual element in belief.

Mr Mill (after Mr Bain) speaks very instructively of the 'animal nature of belief', but when he comes to trace its cause, his analysis seems, to me at least, utterly unsatisfactory. He says that 'the state of belief is identical with the activity or active disposition of the system at the moment with reference to the thing believed'. But in many cases there is firm belief where there is no possibility of action or tendency to it. A girl in a country parsonage will be sure 'that Paris never can be taken', or that 'Bismarck is a wretch', without being able to act on these ideas or wanting to act on them. Many beliefs, in Coleridge's happy phrase, slumber in the 'dormitory of the mind'; they are present to the consciousness, but they incite to no action. And perhaps Coleridge is an example of misformed mind in which not only may 'Faith' not produce 'works', but in which it had a tendency to prevent works. Strong convictions gave him a kind of cramp in the will, and he could not act on them. And in very many persons much-indulged conviction exhausts the mind with the at-tached ideas; teases it, and so, when the time of action comes, makes it apt to turn to different, perhaps opposite, ideas, and to act on them in preference.

As far as I can perceive, the power of an idea to cause conviction, independently of any intellectual process, depends on three properties.

1st. *Clearness*. The more unmistakable an idea is to a particular mind, the more is that mind predisposed to believe it. In common life we may constantly see this. If you once make a thing quite clear to a person, the chances are that you will almost have persuaded him of it. Half the world only understand what they believe, and always believe what they understand.

2nd. *Intensity*. This is the main cause why the ideas that flash on the minds of seers, as in Scott's description, are believed; they come mostly when the nerves are exhausted by fasting, watching, and longing; they have a peculiar brilliancy, and therefore they are believed. To this cause I trace too my fixed folly as to Bridgwater. The idea of being member for the town had been so intensely brought home to me by the excitement of a contest, that I could not eradicate it, and that as soon as I recalled any circumstances of the contest it always came back in all its vividness.

3rd. *Constancy*. As a rule, almost everyone does accept the creed of the place in which he lives, and everyone without exception has a tendency to do so. There are, it is true, some minds which a mathematician might describe as minds of 'contrary flexure', whose particular bent it is to contradict what those around them say. And the reason is that in their minds the opposite aspect of every subject is always vividly presented. But even such minds usually accept the *axioms* of their district, the tenets which everybody always believes. They only object to the variable elements; to the inferences and deductions drawn by some, but not by all.

4thly. On the *Interestingness* of the idea, by which I mean the power of the idea to gratify some wish or want of the mind. The most obvious is curiosity about something which is important to me. Rumours that gratify this excite a sort of half-conviction without the least evidence, and with a very little evidence a full, eager, not to say a bigoted one. If a person go into a mixed company, and say authoritatively 'that the Cabinet is nearly divided on the Russian question, and that it was only decided by one vote to send Lord Granville's despatch', most of the company will attach some weight more or less to the story without asking how the secret was known. And if the narrator casually add that he has just seen a subordinate member of the Government, most of the hearers will go away and repeat the anecdote with grave attention, though it does not in the least appear that the lesser functionary told the anecdote about the Cabinet, or that he knew what passed at it.

And the interest is greater when the news falls in with the bent of the hearer. A sanguine man will believe with scarcely any evidence that good luck is coming, and a dismal man that bad luck. As far as I can make out, the professional 'Bulls' and 'Bears' of the City *do* believe a great deal of what they say, though, of course, there are exceptions, and though neither the most sanguine 'bull' nor the most dismal 'bear' can believe *all* he says.

Of course, I need not say that this 'quality' peculiarly attaches to the greatest problems of human life. The firmest convictions of the most inconsistent answers to the everlasting questions 'whence?' and 'whither?' have been generated by this 'interestingness' without evidence on which one would invest a penny.

In one case, these causes of irrational conviction seem contradictory. Clearness, as we have seen, is one of them; but obscurity, when obscure things are interesting, is a cause too. But there is no real difficulty here. Human nature at different times exhibits contrasted impulses. There is a passion for sensualism, that is, to eat and drink; and a passion for asceticism, that is, not to eat and drink; so it is quite likely that the clearness of an idea may sometimes cause a movement of conviction, and that the obscurity of another idea may at other times cause one too.

These laws, however, are complex, – can they be reduced to any simpler law of human nature? I confess I think that they can, but at the same time I do not presume to speak with the same confidence about it that I have upon other points. Hitherto I have been dealing with the common facts of the adult human mind, as we may see it in others and feel it in ourselves. But I am now going to deal with the 'prehistoric' period of the mind in early childhood, as to which there is necessarily much obscurity.

My theory is, that in the first instance a child believes everything. Some of its states of consciousness are perceptive or presentative, – that is, they tell it of some heat or cold, some resistance or non-resistance then and there present. Other states of consciousness are representative, – that is, they say that certain sensations could be felt, or certain facts perceived, in time past or in time to come, or at some place, no matter at what time, then and there out of the reach of perception and sensation. In mature life, too, we have these presentative and representative states in every sort of mixture, but we make a distinction between them. Without remark and without doubt, we believe the 'evidence of our senses', that is, the facts of present sensation and perception; but we do not believe at once and instantaneously the representative states as to what is non-present, whether in time or space. But I apprehend that this is an acquired distinction, and that in early childhood every state of consciousness is believed, whether it be presentative or representative.

Certainly at the beginning of the 'historic' period we catch the mind at a period of extreme credulity. When memory begins, and when speech and signs suffice to make a child intelligible, belief is almost omnipresent, and doubt almost never to be found. Childlike credulity is a phrase of the highest antiquity, and of the greatest present aptness.

So striking, indeed, on certain points, is this impulse to believe, that philosophers have invented various theories to explain in detail some of its marked instances. Thus it has been said that children have an intuitive disposition to believe in 'testimony', that is, in the correctness of statements orally made to them. And that they do so is certain. Every child believes what the footman tells it, what its nurse tells it, and what its mother tells it, and probably every one's memory will carry him back to the horrid mass of miscellaneous confusion which he acquired by believing all he heard. But though it is certain that a child believes all assertions made to it, it is not certain that the child so believes in consequence of a special intuitive predisposition restricted to such assertions. It may be that this indiscriminate belief in all sayings is but a relic of an omnivorous acquiescence in all states of consciousness, which is only just extinct when childhood is plain enough to be understood, or old enough to be remembered.

Again, it has been said much more plausibly that we want an intuitive tendency to account for our belief in memory. But I question whether it can be shown that a little child *does* believe in its memories more confidently than in its imaginations. A child of my acquaintance corrected its mother, who said that 'they should never see' two of its dead brothers again, and maintained, 'Oh yes, mamma, we shall; we shall see them in heaven, and they will be so glad to see us.' And then the child cried with disappointment because its mother, though a most religious lady, did not seem exactly to feel that seeing her children in that manner was as good as seeing them on earth. Now I doubt if that child did not believe this expectation quite as confidently as it believed any past fact, or as it could believe anything at all, and though the conclusion may be true, plainly the child believed not from the efficacy of the external evidence, but from a strong rush of inward confidence. Why, then, should we want a special intuition to make children believe past facts when, in truth, they go farther and believe with no kind of difficulty future facts as well as past?

If on so abstruse a matter I might be allowed a graphic illustration, I should define doubt as 'a hesitation produced by collision'. A child possessed with the notion that all its fancies are true, finds that acting on one of them brings its head against the table. This gives it pain, and makes it hesitate as to the expediency of doing it again. Early childhood is an incessant education in scepticism, and early youth is so too. All boys are always knocking their heads against the physical world, and all young men are constantly knocking their heads against the social world. And both of them from the same cause, that they are subject to an eruption of emotion which engenders a strong belief, but which is as likely to cause a belief in falsehood as in truth. Gradually under the tuition of a painful experience we come to learn that our strongest convictions may be quite false, that many of our most cherished ones are and have been false; and this causes us to seek a 'criterion' which beliefs are to be trusted and which are not; and so we are beaten back to the laws of evidence for our guide, though, as Bishop Butler said, in a similar case, we object to be bound by anything so 'poor'.

That it is really this contention with the world which destroys conviction and which causes doubt is shown by examining the cases where the mind is secluded from the world. In 'dreams', where we are out of collision with fact, we accept everything as it comes, believe everything and doubt nothing. And in violent cases of mania, where the mind is shut up within itself, and cannot, from impotence, perceive what is without, it is as sure of the most chance fancy, as in health it would be of the best proved truths.

And upon this theory we perceive why the four tendencies to irrational conviction which I have set down survive, and remain in our adult hesitating state as vestiges of our primitive all-believing state. They are all from various causes 'adhesive' states – states which it is very difficult to get rid of, and which, in consequence, have retained their power of creating belief in the mind, when other states, which once possessed it too, have quite lost it. *Clear* ideas are certainly more difficult to get rid of than obscure ones. Indeed, some obscure ones we cannot recover, if we once lose them. Everybody, perhaps, has felt all manner of doubts and difficulties in mastering a mathematical problem; at the time, the difficulties seemed as real as the problem, but a day or two after he has mastered it, he will be wholly unable to imagine or remember where the difficulties were. The demonstration will be perfectly clear to him, and he will be unable to comprehend how anyone should fail to perceive it. For life he will recall the clear ideas, but the obscure ones he will never recall, though for some hours, perhaps, they were painful, confused, and oppressive obstructions. *Intense* ideas are, as everyone will admit, recalled more easily than slight and weak ideas. *Constantly* impressed ideas are brought back by the world around us, and if they are so often, get so tied to our other ideas that we can hardly wrench them away. *Interesting* ideas stick in the mind by the associations which give them interest. All the minor laws of conviction resolve themselves into this great one: 'That at first we believe all which occurs to us – that afterwards we have a tendency to believe that which we cannot help often occurring to us, and that this tendency is stronger or weaker in some sort of proportion to our inability to prevent their recurrence.' When the inability to prevent the recurrence of the idea is very great, so that the reason be powerless on the mind, the consequent 'conviction' is an eager, irritable, and ungovernable passion.

If this analysis be true, it suggests some lessons which are not now accepted.

1. They prove that we should be very careful how we let ourselves believe that which may turn out to be error. Milton says that 'error is but opinion', meaning true opinion, 'in the making'. But when the conviction of any error is a strong passion, it leaves, like all other passions, a permanent mark on the mind. We can never be as if we had never felt it. 'Once a heretic, always a heretic', is thus far true, that a mind once given over to a passionate conviction is never as fit as it would otherwise have been to receive the truth on the same subject. Years after the passion may return upon him, and inevitably small recurrences of it will irritate his intelligence and disturb its calm. We cannot at once expel a familiar idea, and so long as the idea remains its effect will remain too.

2. That we must always keep an account in our minds of the degree of evidence on which we hold our convictions, and be most careful that we do not permanently permit ourselves to feel a stronger conviction than the evidence justifies. If we do, since evidence is the only criterion of truth, we may easily get a taint of error that may be hard to clear away. This may seem obvious, yet if I do not mistake, Father Newman's 'Grammar of Assent' is little else than a systematic treatise designed to deny and confute it.

3. That if we do, as in life we must sometimes, indulge a 'provisional enthusiasm', as it may be called, for an idea, – for example, if an orator in the excitement of speaking does not keep his phrases to probability, and if in the hurry of emotion he quite believes all he says, his plain duty is on other occasions to watch himself carefully, and to be sure that he does not as a permanent creed believe what in a peculiar and temporary state he was led to say he felt and to feel.

Similarly, we are all in our various departments of life in the habit of assuming various probabilities as if they were certainties. In Lombard Street the dealers assume that 'Messrs Baring's acceptance at three months' date is sure to be paid', and that 'Peel's Act will always be suspended at a panic'. And the familiarity of such ideas makes it nearly impossible for any one who spends his day in Lombard Street to doubt of them. But, nevertheless, a person who takes care of his mind will keep up the perception that they are not certainties.

Lastly, we should utilize this intense emotion of conviction as far as we can. Dry minds, which give an intellectual 'assent' to conclusions which feel no strong glow of faith in them, often do not know what their opinions are. They have every day to go over the arguments again, or to refer to a note-book to know what they believe. But intense convictions make a memory for themselves, and if they can be kept to the truths of which there is good evidence, they give a readiness of intellect, a confidence in action, a consistency in character, which are to be not had without them. For a time, indeed, they give these benefits when the propositions believed are false, but then they spoil the mind for seeing the truth, and they are very dangerous, because the believer may discover his error, and a perplexity of intellect, a hesitation in action, and an inconsistency in character are the sure consequences of an entire collapse in pervading and passionate conviction.

(*WB*, xiv, 46–56, paper given to the Metaphysical Society, 1870)

ORATORY

The oratorical impulse is a *disorganizing* impulse. The higher faculties of the mind require a certain calm, and the excitement of oratory is unfavourable to that calm. We know that this is so with the hearers of oratory; we know that they are carried away from their fixed principles, from their habitual tendencies, by a casual and unexpected stimulus. We speak commonly of the power of the orator. But the orator is subject himself to much the same calamity. The force which carries away his hearers must first carry away himself. He will not persuade any of his hearers unless he has first succeeded, for the moment at least, in persuading his own mind. Every exciting speech is conceived, planned, and spoken with excitement. The orator feels in his own nerves, even in a greater degree, that electric thrill which he is to communicate to his hearers. The telling ideas take hold of him with a sort of *seizure*. They fasten close upon his brain. He has a sort of passionate impulse to tell them. He hungers, as a Greek would have said, till they are uttered. His mind is full of them. He has the vision of the audience in his mind. Until he has persuaded these men of these things, life is tame, and its other stimulants are uninteresting. So much excitement is evidently unfavourable to calm reflection and deliberation. Mr Pitt is said to have thought more of the manner in which his measures would strike the House than of the manner in which, when carried, they would work. Of course he did – every great orator will do so, unless he has a supernatural self-control. An ordinary man sits down – say to make a budget: he arranges the accounts; adds up the figures; contrasts the effects of different taxes; works out steadily hour after hour their probable incidence, first of one, then of another. Nothing disturbs him. With the orator it is different. During that whole process he is disturbed by the vision of his hearers. How they will feel, how they will think, how they will like his proposals, – cannot but occur to him. He hears his ideas rebounding in the cheers of his hearers, he is disheartened at fancying that they will fall tamely on an inanimate and listless multitude. He is subject to two temptations; he is turned aside from the conceptions natural to the subject by an imagination of his audience; his own eager temperament naturally inclines him to the views which will excite that audience most effectually. The tranquil deposit of ordinary ideas is interrupted by the sudden eruption of volcanic forces. We know that the popular instinct suspects the judgment of great orators; we know that it does not give them credit for patient equanimity; and the popular instinct is right.

(*WB*, iii, 429–30, from 'Mr Gladstone', *National Review*, 1860)

OWNERSHIP

The ownership of land by individuals is the best incentive to diffused industry and continued improvement by those individuals which a political society can possess. The face of a country will be changed by nothing so quick as by the detailed division of labour over the land. Tell each individual, 'If you improve the plot of land you work upon, you shall have that plot with all the improvements you make in it', and a barren desert will, under the continual industry of a crowded population, become soon a garden of Eden.

(*WB*, x, 256, from 'Sir Charles Wood's Despatch Recommending the Perpetual Settlement of the Land Revenue of India', *The Economist*, 1862)

The peace of the world is preserved by a habit – nearly unconscious – of constant subordination.

Perhaps there is nothing in the world which average men and women – very little which even the most educated men and women – understand less than their own liability to mistake, and there is nothing which it is more difficult to teach them.

Persecute a sect and it holds together, legalize it and it splits and resplits, till its unity is either null or a non-oppressive bond.

Philosophers may be divided into seers on the one hand, and into gropers on the other.

The place of nearly everybody depends on the opinion of everyone else.

Politicians, as has been said, live in the repute of the commonalty. They may appeal to posterity; but of what use is posterity? Years before that tribunal comes into life your life will be extinct. It is like a moth going into Chancery.

A practised advocate learns to believe in his brief. A subordinate statesman in a popular government soon accepts the measures of his party. The pressure of circumstances is far greater upon him than upon the advocate, and the insensible bias is the same. No mode of life can be conceived more unfavourable to originality of thought.

A public department is very apt to be dead to what is wanting for a great occasion till the occasion is past.

The pyramids of Egypt once built, no one cared about the builders.

LORD PALMERSTON

Lord Palmerston only died on Wednesday, and already the world is full of sketches and biographies of him. It is very natural that it should be so, for he counted for much in English politics: his personality was a power, and it is natural that everyone should at his death seek to analyse what we used to have, and what we have now lost. We will do so, but remembering how often the tale has been told, we will be as brief as possible.

Lord Derby happily said that *he* was born in the 'pre-scientific' period, and Lord Palmerston was so even more. He was, it is true, a boarder at Dugald Stewart's, and we believe transcribed at least a part of the lectures on political economy of that philosopher, lately published. But the combined influence of interior nature and the surrounding situation was too strong. His real culture was that of living languages and the actual world. He was the best French scholar among his contemporaries, – so much so that when he went to Paris in 1859, the whole society which fancied he was an imperious and ignorant Englishman, was charmed by the grace of his expression. His English in all his speeches was sound and pure, and in his greater efforts almost fastidiously correct. The *feeling* for language, which is one characteristic of a great man of the world, was very nice in Lord Palmerston and very characteristic.

It was from the actual knowledge of men – from close specific contact – that Lord Palmerston derived his data. We have heard grave men say with surprise, 'He always has an anecdote to cap his argument.' He begins, 'I knew a man once,' and the anecdotes had no trace of the garrulity of age: they were real illustrations of the matter in hand. They were the chosen instances of a man who thought in instances. Some men think, as the philosophers say, by 'definition'; others by 'type'; Lord Palmerston, like an animated man, used to the animated world, thought in examples, and hardly realized abstract words.

It was because of this that in international matters – the only ones for which in youth he cared – he was a great practical lawyer. He knew, what hardly anyone knows, the subject-matter. He knew the *cases* with which during a long life he had to deal. To most men international law is a matter of precedent and words; to him it was a matter of personal adventure and reality. Some people, not unqualified to judge, have said that his opinion on such matters was as good as any law officer's. He might not have studied Vattel or Wheaton so closely as some; but he had, which is far better, followed with a keen interest the actual and necessary practice of present nations.

It was this sort of worldly sympathy and worldly education which gave Lord Palmerston his intelligibility. He was not a common man, but a common man might have been cut out of him. He had in him all that a common man has and something more. And he did not at all despise, as some philosophers teach people to do, the common part of his mind. He was profoundly aware that the common mass of plain sense is the great administrative agency of the world, and that if you keep yourself in sympathy with this you win, and if not you fail. Sir George Lewis used to say that just as Demosthenes declared action to be the first, second, and third thing in a statesman, so intelligibility is the first, second, and third thing in a constitutional statesman. It is to us certainly the first, second, and third thing in Lord Palmerston. This is not absolutely eulogistic. No one resembled less than Lord Palmerston the fancied portrait of an ideal statesman laying down in his closet plans to be worked out twenty years hence, and to be appreciated twenty years hence. He was a statesman for the moment. Whatever was not wanted now, whatever was not practicable now, whatever would not *take* now, he drove quite out of his mind. The prerequisites of a constitutional statesman have been defined as the 'powers of a first-rate man, and the creed of a second-rate man'. The saying is harsh, but it is expressive. Lord Palmerston's creed was never the creed of the far-seeing philosopher; it was the creed of a sensible and sagacious, but still commonplace man. His objects were common objects: what was uncommon was the will with which he pursued them.

No man was better in action, but no man was more free from the pedantry of business. People, he has been heard to say, have different minds. 'When I was a young man, the Duke of Wellington made an appointment with me at half-past seven in the morning, and someone asked me, "Why, Palmerston, how will you keep that engagement?" "Oh," I said, "of course, the easiest thing in the world. I shall keep it the last thing before I go to bed."' He knew that the real essence of work is concentrated energy and that people who really have that in a superior degree by nature, are independent of the forms and habits and artifices by which less able and active people are kept up to their labour.

Lord Palmerston prided himself on his foreign policy, on which we cannot now pronounce a judgement. But it is not upon this that his fame will rest. He had a great difficulty as a foreign minister. He had no real conception of any mode of life except that with which he was familiar. His idea, his fixed idea, was that the Turks were a highly-improving and civilized race, and it was impossible to beat into him their essentially barbaric and unindustrial character. He would hear anything patiently, but no corresponding ideas were raised in his mind. A man of the world is not an imaginative animal, and Lord Palmerston was by incurable nature a man of the world. Keenly detective in what he could realize by experience – utterly blind, dark, and impervious to what he could not so realize. Even the best part of his foreign policy was alloyed with this defect. The mantle of Canning had descended on him, and the creed and interests of Canning. He was most eager to use the strong influence of England to support free institutions – to aid 'the Liberal party' was the phrase in those days – everywhere on the Continent. And no aim could be juster and better; it was the best way in which English strength could be used. But he failed in the instructed imagination and delicate perception necessary to its best attainment. He supported the Liberal party when it was bad and the country unfit for it, as much as when it was good and the nation eager for it. He did not define the degree of his sympathy, or apportion its amount to the comparative merits of the different claims made on it. According to the notions of the present age, too, foreign policy should be regulated by abstract, or at least comprehensive principles, but Lord Palmerston had no such principles. He prided himself on his exploits in Europe, but it is by his instincts in England that he will be remembered.

It was made a matter of wonder that Lord Palmerston should begin to rule the House of Commons at seventy, and there is no doubt he was very awkward at first in so ruling it. Sir James Graham, and other judges of business management, predicted that 'the thing would fail', and that a new government would have to be formed. But the truth is, that though he had been fifty years in the House of Commons, Lord Palmerston had never regularly attended it, and even still less attended *to* it. His person had not been there very much, and his mind had been there very little. He answered a question on his own policy, or made a speech, and then went away. Debate was not to him, as to Mr Pitt, or Mr Gladstone, a matter of life and pleasure. Mr Canning used to complain, 'I can't get that three-decker Palmerston to bear down.' And when he was made Leader of the House, it came out that he hardly knew, if he did know, the forms of the House. But it was a defect of past interest, not a defect of present capacity. He soon mastered the necessary knowledge, and as soon as he had done so, the sure sagacity of his masculine instincts secured him an unconquerable strength.

Something we wished to say more on these great gifts, and something, too, might be said as to the defects by which they were alloyed. But it is needless. Brevity is as necessary in a memorial article as in an epitaph. So much is certain: – We shall never look upon his like again. We may look on others of newer race, but his race is departed. The merits of the new race were not his merits; their defects are not his. England will never want statesmen, but she will never see in our time *such* a statesman as Viscount Palmerston.

(*WB*, iii, 275–8, *The Economist*, 1865)

SIR ROBERT PEEL

Sir Robert Peel was once said to know how to 'dress up a case for Parliament' better than anyone else. And in this art there are two secrets. The first is always to content yourself with the minimum of general maxims, which will suit your purpose and prove what you want. By doing so you offend as few people as possible, you startle as few people as possible, and you expose yourself to as few retorts as possible. And the second secret is to make the whole discussion very uninteresting – to leave an impression that the subject is very dry, that it is very difficult, that the department had attended to the dreary detail of it, and that on the whole it is safer to leave it to the department, and a dangerous responsibility to interfere with the department. The faculty of disheartening adversaries by diffusing on occasion an oppressive atmosphere of businesslike dullness is invaluable to us parliamentary statesmen.

(*WB*, iii, 572, from 'Mr Lowe as Chancellor of the Exchequer', *The Economist*, 1871)

PITT THE YOUNGER

The exact description of Mr Pitt is, that he had in the most complete perfection the faculties of a great administrator, and that he added to it the commanding temperament, though not the creative intellect, of a great dictator. He was tried by long and prosperous years, which exercised to the utmost his peculiar faculties, which enabled him to effect brilliant triumphs of policy and of legislation: he was tried likewise by a terrible crisis, with which he had not the originality entirely to cope, which he did not understand as we understand it now, but in which he showed the hardihood of resolution and a consistency of action which capitivated the English people, and which impressed the whole world.

(*WB*, iii, 126, from 'William Pitt', *National Review*, 1861)

POST-PANIC

The crisis is all over and everybody has *too* much money. It is really a very ridiculous world. The last few times I have been here everybody was on their knees asking for money – now you have nearly to go on your knees to ask people to take it. Neither of these two extremes is very pleasant. Being besought is not unagreeable intrinsically – but when a man is very earnest for money, you begin to suspect he is 'in difficulties' and ought not to have it, and in the other case it seems demeaning the majesty of the money to ask – or beseech – human beings to take it. You look at a hard-eyed bill-broker and think what is this man created for, if *not* to take money. Still, the present state of things has the advantage that there is no tension of mind in managing your business while it lasts. You need not follow a man with your eyes when he takes away your money and think '*Will* he ever pay me?' – I own I like the *sensation* of safety.

(*WB*, xiii, 456–7, from a letter to Eliza, 1858)

POST-WAR GLOOM

The years immediately succeeding the great peace were years of sullenness and difficulty. The idea of the war had passed away; the thrill and excitement of the great struggle were no longer felt. We had maintained, with the greatest potentate of modern times, a successful contest for existence; we had our existence, but we had no more; our victory had been great, but it had no fruits. By the aid of pertinacity and capital, we had vanquished genius and valour; but no visible increase of European influence followed. Napoleon said, that Wellington had made peace as if he had been defeated. We had delivered the Continent; such was our natural idea: but the Continent went its own way. There was nothing in its state to please the everyday Englishman. There were kings and emperors; 'which was very well for foreigners, they had always been like that; but it was not many kings could pay ten per cent income-tax'. Absolutism, as such, cannot be popular in a free country. The Holy Alliance, which made a religion of despotism, was scarcely to be reconciled with the British constitution. Altogether we had vanquished Napoleon, but we had no pleasure in what came after him. The cause which agitated our hearts was gone; there was no longer a noise of victories in the air; continental affairs were dead, despotic, dull; we scarcely liked to think that we had made them so; with weary dissatisfaction we turned to our own condition.

This was profoundly unsatisfactory. Trade was depressed; agriculture ruinous; the working classes disaffected. During the war, our manufacturing industry had grown most rapidly; there was a not unnatural expectation that, after a general peace, the rate of increase would be accelerated. The whole Continent, it was considered, would be opened to us; Milan and Berlin decrees no longer excluded us; Napoleon did not now interpose between 'the nation of shopkeepers' and its customers; now he was at St Helena, surely those customers would buy? It was half-forgotten that they could not. The drain of capital for the war had been, at times, heavily felt in England; there had been years of poverty and discredit; still our industry had gone on, our workshops had not stopped. We had never known what it was to be the seat of war, as well as a power at war. We had never known our burdens enormously increased, just when our industry was utterly stopped; disarranged as trading credit sometimes was, it had not been destroyed. No conscription had drained us of our most efficient consumers. The Continent, south and north, had, though not everywhere alike, suffered all these evils; its population were poor, harassed, depressed. They could not buy our manufactures, for they had no money. The large preparations for a continental export lay on hand; our traders were angry and displeased. Nor was content to be found in the agricultural districts. During the war, the British farmer had inevitably a monopoly of this market; at the approach of peace, his natural antipathy to foreign corn influenced the legislature. The Home Secretary of the time had taken into consideration, whether 76s. or 80s. was such a remunerating price as the agriculturist should obtain, and a corn-law had passed accordingly. But no law could give the farmer famine-prices, when there was scarcity here and plenty abroad. There were riots at the passing of the 'bread-tax', as it was; in 1813, the price of corn was 120s.; the rural mind was sullen in 1816, when it sunk to 57s. The protection given, though unpopular with the poor, did not satisfy the farmer.

The lower orders in the manufacturing districts were, of necessity, in great distress. The depression of trade produced its inevitable results of closed mills and scanty employment. Wages, when they could be obtained, were very low. The artisan population was then new to the vicissitudes of industry: how far they are, even now, instructed in the laws of trade, recent prosperity will hardly let us judge; but, at that time, they had no doubt that it was the fault of the State, and if not of particular statesmen, then of the essential institutions, that they were in want. They believed the government ought to regulate their remuneration, and make it sufficient. During some straitened years of the war, the name of 'Luddites' became known. They had principally shown their discontent by breaking certain machines, which they fancied deprived them of work. After the peace, the records of the time are full of 'Spencean Philanthropists', Hampden Clubs', and similar associations, all desiring a great reform – some of mere politics, others of the law of property and all social economy. Large meetings were everywhere held, something like those of the year 1839: a general insurrection, doubtless a wild dream of a few hot-brained dreamers, was fancied to have been really planned. The name 'Radical' came to be associated with this discontent. The spirit which, in after-years, clamoured distinctly for the five points of the Charter, made itself heard in mutterings and threatenings.

Nor were the capitalists, who had created the new wealth, socially more at ease. Many of them, as large employers of labour, had a taste for Toryism; the rule of the people to them meant the rule of their workpeople. Some of the wealthiest and most skilful became associated with the aristocracy; but it was in vain with the majority to attempt it. Between them and the possessors of hereditary wealth, there was fixed a great gulf; the contrast of habits, speech, manners, was too wide. The two might coincide in particular opinions; they might agree to support the same institutions; they might set forth, in a Conservative creed, the same form of sound words: but, though the abstract conclusions were identical, the mode of holding them – to borrow a subtlety of Father Newman's – was exceedingly different. The refined, discriminating, timorous immobility of the aristocracy was distinct from the coarse, dogmatic, keep-downishness of the manufacturer. Yet more marked was the contrast, when the opposite tendencies of temperament had produced, as they soon could not but do, a diversity of opinion. The case was not quite new in England. Mr Burke spoke of the tendency of the first East Indians to Jacobinism. They could not, he said, bear that their present importance should have no proportion to their recently acquired riches. No extravagant fortunes have, in this century, been made by Englishmen in India; but Lancashire has been a California. Families have been created there, whose names we all know, which we think of when we mention wealth; some of which are now, by lapse of time, passing into the hereditary caste of recognized opulence. This, however, has been a work of time; and, before it occurred, there was no such intermediate class between the new wealth and the old. 'It takes,' it is said that Sir Robert Peel observed, 'three generations to make a gentleman.' In the meantime, there was an inevitable misunderstanding; the new cloth was too coarse for the old. Besides this, many actual institutions offended the eyes of the middle class. The state of the law was opposed both to their prejudices and interests: that you could only recover your debts by spending more than the debt, was hard; and the injury was aggravated, the money was spent in 'special pleading'– 'in putting a plain thing so as to perplex and mislead a plain man'. 'Lord Eldon and the Court of Chancery,' as Sydney Smith expressed it, 'sat heavy on mankind.' The existence of slavery in our colonies, strongly supported by a strong aristocratic and parliamentary influence, offended the principles of middle-class Christianity, and the natural sentiments of simple men. The cruelty of the penal law – the punishing with death sheep-stealing and shop-lifting – jarred the humanity of that second order of English society, which, from their habits of reading and non-reading, may be called, *par excellence*, the scriptural classes. The routine harshness of a not very wise executive did not mitigate the feeling. The *modus operandi* of government appeared coarse and oppressive.

We seemed to pay, too, a good deal for what we did not like. At the close of the war, the ten per cent income-tax was of course heavily oppressive. The public expenditure was beyond argument lavish; and it was spent in pensions, sinecures ('them idlers' in the speech of Lancashire), and a mass of sundries, that an economical man of business will scarcely admit to be necessary, and that even now, after countless prunings, produce periodically 'financial reform associations', 'administrative leagues', and other combinations which amply testify the enmity of thrifty efficiency to large figures and muddling management. There had remained from the eighteenth century a tradition of corruption, an impression that direct pecuniary malversation pervaded the public offices; an idea true in the days of Rigby or Bubb Dodington, but which, like many other impressions, continued to exist many years after the facts in which it originated had passed away. Government, in the hands of such a man as Lord Liverpool, was very different from Government in the hands of Sir Robert Walpole: respectability was exacted: of actual money-taking there was hardly any. Still, especially among inferior officials, there was something to shock modern purity. The size of jobs was large: if the Treasury of that time could be revived, it would be depressed at the littleness of whatever is perpetrated in modern administration. There were petty abuses too in the country – in municipalities – in charitable trusts – in all outlying public moneys, which seemed to the offended man of business, who saw them with his own eyes, evident instances confirming his notion of the malpractices of Downing Street. 'There are only five little boys in the school of Richester; they may cost £200, and the income is £2,000, and the trustees don't account for the balance; which is the way things are done in England: we keeps an aristocracy,' &c. The whole of this feeling concentrated into a detestation of rotten boroughs. The very name was enough: that Lord Dover, with two patent sinecures in the Exchequer and a good total for assisting in nothing at the Audit Office, should return two members for one House, while Birmingham, where they made buttons, – 'as good buttons as there are in the world, sir,' – returned no members at all, was an evident indication that Reform was necessary. Mr Canning was an eloquent man; but 'even *he* could not say that a decaying stump was the *people*'. Gatton and Old Sarum became unpopular. The source of power seemed absurd, and the use of power was tainted. Side by side with the incipient Chartism of the Northern operative, there was growing daily more distinct and clear the Manchester philosophy, which has since expressed itself in the Anti-Corn-Law League, and which, for good and evil, is now an element so potent in our national life. Both creeds were forms of discontent. And the counterpoise was wanting. The English Constitution has provided that there shall always be one estate raised above the storms of passion and controversy, which all parties may respect and honour. The King is to be loved. But this theory requires, for a real efficiency, that the throne be filled by such a person as can be loved. In those times it was otherwise. The nominal possessor of the crown was a very old man, whom an incurable malady had long sequestered from earthly things. The actual possessor of the royal authority was a voluptuary of overgrown person, now too old for healthy pleasure, and half-sickened himself at the corrupt pursuits in which, neverthe-less, he indulged perpetually. His domestic vices had become disgrace-fully public. Whatever might be the truth about Queen Caroline, no one could say she had been well treated. There was no loyalty on which suffering workers, or an angry middle class, could repose: all through the realm there was a miscellaneous agitation, a vague and wandering discontent.

(*WB*, iii, 159–64, from 'Lord Brougham', *National Review*, 1857)

PRESS

The influence of the Press, if you believe writers and printers, is the one sufficient condition of social well-being. Yet newspaper people are the only traders that thrive upon convulsion. In quiet times, who cares for the paper? In times of tumult, who does not? . . . Take in *The Times*, and you will see it assumed that every year ought to be an era. 'The government does nothing', is the indignant cry, and simple people in the country don't know that this is merely a civilized *façon de parler* for 'I have nothing to say'.

(*WB*, iv, 71–2, from 'The French Newspaper Press', *Inquirer*, 1852)

THE PROPOSED COLLEGE FOR WOMEN*

While some of our contemporaries are discussing, perhaps a little unprofitably, the intellectual and moral equality or inequality of women and men, and whether the constitution of the family be monarchical or not, – a delicate question which we should call one of fact rather than of speculative reason, – we feel more concerned to promote the discovery – it is unfortunate that it should still be a matter so completely undiscovered – of what women's special qualifica-tions *are* for practical life, by doing all in our power to develop those feminine powers which have hitherto lain idle for want of culture. The proposal which has been made by some energetic reformers to

---

* Bagehot liked women; George Eliot was a close friend whom he greatly admired. At this time he was coming to the conclusion that there was no good argument against giving qualified women the vote.

establish a genuine college for women, not a mere high-class boarding school, but a college where the students shall have that freedom to study in their own private rooms without fussy supervision which young men enjoy at Oxford and Cambridge, seems to us to be one of the most valuable steps yet made in this direction; and we heartily concur in the views laid down by the Rev. Llewellyn Davies in *Macmillan's Magazine* for June, and in the prospectuses which have been issued to solicit subscriptions for the new college by Miss Emily Davies and her coadjutors.

It has often been remarked, and we do not doubt that the remark points to a real difference of constitution between men and women, that very few women indeed have so far succeeded in any of the higher branches of literature, science, or art, as to gain the reputation of original and creative genius. Except in the department of prose fiction, not one branch can be named in which women can pretend to the first rank. Even in music, in which women's education has probably been less neglected than any other, no great composers' names are the names of women. Now we do not deny that such facts as these are fairly accepted as indicating a certain actual inferiority of creative power in women as compared with men. At the same time we believe that the difference, great as it actually is, may not turn out to be so great as it appears. That girls have in *all* countries till quite recently been habitually far worse taught than boys is matter of notoriety, but it is not to the mere inferiority of the teaching that we now wish to draw attention. What girls have had no experience at all of, as compared with boys, is the effort at independent study. The close supervision which naturally enough has influenced their domestic life has been extended into their intellectual education. If lads are too seldom encouraged to grope their own way through difficult subjects without being prompted and led at every turn, we may say that girls are never encouraged to do anything of the sort at all – nay, that they scarcely ever have the opportunity of doing so, since the habit of their intellectual as of their moral education has been the attitude of *dependence*, instead of the attitude of original inquiry and research. A great deal of this has been doubtless due to the disposition of masculine teachers to help and prompt their female pupils; but a great deal more is due to the unfavourable circumstances under which girl's education, whether at boarding schools or at home, is mostly pursued. No schoolmistresses and few mothers ever think of providing a study for each girl where she can be really free from interruption and puzzle out her own way through intellectual difficulties which she knows that she is expected to solve for herself if she can. There has been, and is still, an idea that a girl is more 'feminine' if she waits passively to be 'told' her way through a difficulty, than if she applies her whole energies to unravel it for herself; and everything, both in her external surroundings and her moral relations, is usually adapted to increase and deepen this sense of dependence, which almost ranks indeed as a feminine virtue. Now, we do not wish at all to enter on the thorny ground of the monarchical character of the family and the related questions, but it seems reasonable to suggest that *all* intellectual culture, so far as it is really intellectual, aims at removing this absolute dependence upon authority, and at teaching the intellect to trust laws rather than persons. If it be contended that women should be kept intellectually dependent on men, that is only another way of saying they should not be educated at all. Moreover, education will probably be given, as we all know, to some hundreds of thousands of women in every generation who will find no man to be dependent on, and for these, at least, the virtue (if it be one) of intellectual dependence or confidence in arbitrary authority, can only be a misfortune. On the whole, therefore, we cannot but think that the rise of an institution intended to give women the opportunity, not merely of *learning*, but of a very different art – *studying* – is a matter of the first importance, and we heartily hope that the 30,000*l.* requisite to build the proposed college – of which we regret to see that only about 2,000*l.* have as yet been received – may soon be forthcoming.

What we should expect from the multiplication of such experiments for encouraging young women to cultivate independent thought and study, is not so much that we should make them rivals of the originality of men in the same fields of science, art, and literature, as that they would develop an unexpected amount of originality in many fields wherein men have hitherto done little, and to which their powers have usually seemed but poorly adapted. Certainly, the tendency of the movement for opening various professions – such as that of medicine – to women, seems to show that women are creating for themselves special departments for which they are peculiarly well adapted, and which have hitherto been cursorily treated, or in great measure neglected, by professional men; and we should be inclined to expect that if women were trained in habits of greater intellectual independence, the same result might show itself in the fields of pure intellectual research. As we have seen so much feminine genius stream towards the region of prose fiction for which the minute style of 'miniature-painting on ivory' (as Miss Austen described her own great literary talent) seems peculiarly fitted, so we suspect that there would be special departments of investigation and execution in science, and art, and scholarship, for which we should find that feminine powers, once taught to be self-reliant, would be remarkably adapted; – and thus we might have not so much a crowd of new rivals in the old fields as a crowd of new explorers in fields hitherto more or less neglected. What we have called the marked want of creative power, of originality, shown by women in music, and painting, and poetry, and other departments of intellectual conception which have hitherto been regarded as properly feminine, is we suspect less due to the intellectual deficiency of individual genius, than to the moral deficiency of class-training. You may see in many women the germs of what would undoubtedly be genius if there had been enough perseverance, self-confidence, habit of initiative, to give their powers a fair chance of growth and ripening. But in women genius is constantly wasted, solely from the confirmed habit of waiting upon others in all things. The few women who have risen to fame have usually done so (like George Eliot, Miss Brontë, and in a less degree Mrs Browning) through the aid of circumstances which have thrown them wholly on themselves, and forced them into self-reliance and self-culture. It is unquestionable that much intellectual faculty, which is of the highest calibre, turns out to be sterile for want of some very simple moral qualifications; and we have a good deal of reason to think that this is, partly at least, the reason why women have hitherto shown so little creative force. What they need are the moral conditions of creative force more than the intellectual conditions – the habit of sounding their own mental problems for themselves, of judging rapidly for themselves in emergencies, of relying upon themselves to prosecute a train of thought or study once begun. Now, it is because the separate studies of a genuine college, the solitude it permits, the voluntary collision of thought between student and student which it encourages, the comparative intellectual freedom which it secures, seem to us to be elements so specially valuable in female education that we earnestly desire to see this experiment fairly made. If it were to succeed it would open a new prospect for female intellect; and we believe that in the hands into which it has fallen, – the Bishop of St David's, and other men of the highest eminence have given their names and authority to the scheme, – this experiment is likely to be fairly tried under such conditions as to superintendence and discipline as will secure it against abuses, and yet provide also for its students a genuine collegiate life.

(*The Economist*, 1868)

PUBLIC SERVANTS

The trained official hates the rude, untrained public. He thinks that they are stupid, ignorant, reckless – that they cannot tell their own interest – that they should have the leave of the office before they do anything.

(*WB*, v, 328, from *The English Constitution*, 1867)

A really sensible press, arguing temperately after a clean and satisfactory exposition of the facts, is a great blessing in any country.

The Reform question approaches one of those stages, so common in real business when, after a prolonged and half-understood discussion, the board of directors, or the meeting of shareholders (as the case may be), out of weariness and necessity, accept some solution which satisfies all immediate needs, but which leaves the higher necessities of the case unsatisfied, and throws over the future a great shade.

REFERENDA

A plebiscitum is the extreme form of universal suffrage, and it has therefore a secret charm for almost all democrats; and there is some reason to believe that all democracies tend towards a trial of this tremendous weapon ... Even in England and among politicians men will vote against government on a special proposal who will vote for them and for that proposal if it is made a question of confidence, and the plebiscitum is a wider application of the same practice. It may in fact be used to annul the vote of the very people who vote it. The plebiscitum is not only inconsistent with parliamentary government, but is of necessity almost hostile – tends not to confirm but rather to reverse parliamentary decisions.

(*WB*, iv, 139–41, from 'The Emperor's Proclamation', *The Economist*, 1870)

THE 1867 REFORM ACT

Altogether the Liberals, or at least the extreme Liberals, were much like a man who has been pushing hard against an opposing door, till, on a sudden, the door opens, the resistance ceases, and he is thrown violently forward. Persons in such an unpleasant predicament can scarcely criticize effectually, and certainly the Liberals did not so criticize.

(*WB*, v, 171, from Introduction to the second edition of *The English Constitution*, 1872)

REFORMING ZEAL

We are familiar with the aberrations of the ex-Chancellor; we forget how bold, how efficacious, how varied was the activity of Henry Brougham.

There are several qualities in his genius which make such a life peculiarly suited to him. The first of these is an aggressive impulsive disposition. Most people may admit that the world goes ill; old abuses seem to exist, questionable details to abound. Hardly anyone thinks that anything may not be made better. But how to improve the world, to repair the defects, is a difficulty. Immobility is a part of man. A sluggish conservatism is the basis of our English nature. '*Learn*, my son,' said the satirist, 'to bear tranquilly the calamities of others.' We easily learn it. Most men have a line of life, and it imposes certain duties which they fulfil; but they cannot be induced to start out of that line. We dwell in 'a firm basis of content'. 'Let the mad world go its own way, for it will go its own way.' There is no doctrine of the English Church more agreeable to our instinctive taste than that which forbids all works of supererogation. 'You did a thing without being obliged,' said an eminent statesman; 'then that must be wrong.' We travel in the track. Lord Brougham is the opposite of this. It is not difficult to him to attack abuses. The more difficult thing for him would be to live in a world without abuses. An intense excitability is in his nature. He must 'go off'. He is eager to reform corruption, and rushes out to refute error. A tolerant placidity is altogether denied to him.

And not only is this excitability eager, it is many-sided. The men who have in general exerted themselves in labours for others, have generally been rather of a brooding nature; certain ideas, views, and feelings have impressed themselves on them in solitude; they come forth with them among the crowd: but they have no part in its diversified life. They are almost irritated by it. They have no conception except of their cause; they are abstracted in one thought, pained with the dizziness of a heated idea. There is nothing of this in Brougham. He is excited by what he sees. The stimulus is from without. He saw the technicalities of the law-courts; observed a charitable trustee misusing the charity moneys; perceived that George IV oppressed Queen Caroline; went to Old Sarum. He is not absorbed in a creed: he is pricked by facts. Accordingly his activity is miscellaneous. The votary of a doctrine is concentrated, for the logical consequences of a doctrine are limited. But an open-minded man, who is aroused by what he sees, quick at discerning abuses, ready to reform anything which he thinks goes wrong, – will never have done acting. The details of life are endless, and each of them may go wrong in a hundred ways.

Another faculty of Brougham (in metaphysics it is perhaps but a phase of the same) is the faculty of easy anger. The supine placidity of civilization is not favourable to animosity. A placid Conservative is perhaps a little pleased that the world is going a *little* ill. Lord Brougham does not feel this. Like an Englishman on the Continent, he is ready to blow up anyone. He is a Jonah of detail; he is angry at the dust of life, and wroth with the misfeasances of *employés*. The most reverberating of bastinadoes is the official mind basted by Brougham. You did *this* wrong; why did you omit *that*? document C ought to be on the third file; paper D is wrongly docketed in the ninth file. Red tape will scarcely succeed when it is questioned; you should take it as Don Quixote did his helmet, without examination, for a most excellent helmet. A vehement industrious man proposing to untie papers and not proposing to spare errors is the terror of a respectable administrator. 'Such an unpracticable man, sir, interfering with the *office*, attacking private character, messing in what cannot concern him.' These are the jibes which attend an irritable anxiety for the good of others. They have attended Lord Brougham through life. He has enough of misanthropy to be a philanthropist.

(*WB*, iii, 171–2, from 'Lord Brougham', *National Review*, 1857)

RELIGIOUS EDUCATION

Actual contact in early youth with persons of a different religion is an essential ingredient, and one of the most potent ingredients, in the good training of the human mind. We believe that those who miss it in youth lose what nothing can afterwards replace to them. We believe that they will never learn what others think unless they learn it then; that they will never know what is in their own minds unless they learn it then; that no matter what their nominal creed may be they will not understand it really; that they will not *feel* its relation to other creeds; that most likely their minds will be full of vague ideas, and undetected errors, and vicious certainties, which argument cannot touch, and which nothing save the collision with living doubt can destroy. The peculiarity of mixed education which makes Catholics dislike it, is exactly that for which we at least most prize it.

(*WB*, viii, 116, from 'The Essence of the Irish University Bill', *The Economist*, 1873)

REPLACING THE PILOT

Under a cabinet constitution at a sudden emergency this people can choose a ruler for the occasion. It is quite possible and even likely that he would not be ruler *before* the occasion. The great qualities, the imperious will, the rapid energy, the eager nature fit for a great crisis are not required – are impediments – in common times. A Lord Liverpool is better in everyday politics than a Chatham – a Louis Philippe far better than a Napoleon. By the structure of the world we often want, at the sudden occurrence of a grave tempest, to change the helmsman – to replace the pilot of the calm by the pilot of the storm. In England we have had so few catastrophes since our Constitution attained maturity, that we hardly appreciate this latent excellence. We have not needed a Cavour to rule a revolution – a representative man above all men fit for a great occasion, and by a natural, legal mode brought in to rule. But even in England, at what was the nearest to a great sudden crisis which we have had of late years – at the Crimean difficulty – we used this inherent power. We abolished the Aberdeen Cabinet, the ablest we have had, perhaps, since the

Reform Act – a Cabinet not only adapted, but eminently adapted, for every sort of difficulty save the one it had to meet – which abounded in pacific discretion, and was wanting only in the 'daemonic element'; we chose a statesman, who had the sort of merit then wanted, who, when he feels the steady power of England behind him, will advance without reluctance, and will strike without restraint. As was said at the time, 'We turned out the Quaker, and put in the pugilist.'

(*WB*, v, 222, from *The English Constitution*, 1867)

REVIEWERS

The essence of civilization, as we know, is dullness. In an ultimate analysis, it is only an elaborate invention, or series of inventions for abolishing the fierce passions, the unchastened enjoyments, the awakening dangers, the desperate conflicts, to say all in one word, the excitements of a barbarous age, and to substitute for them indoor pleasures, placid feelings, and rational amusements. That a grown man should be found to write reviews is in itself a striking fact. Suppose you asked Achilles to do such a thing, do you imagine he would consent? It would be interesting (if unintelligible) to experience the admirable Greek in which he would repudiate the proposal ... And yet this employment is the last result of modern civilization. It is the employment to which society devotes its very best minds, for no one is superior to ourselves, and we are, it is clear, the persons who are performing it. Yet, how torpid it is! It is nearly as bad as being in literary society; to hear 'that Mr Carlyle contemplates a new work'; 'that there was an article of his in one of the Reviews, but in which I don't recollect'; to be asked in five following sentences if you have read five successive publications; to have to say of each, 'No, but I am told it is a pleasing work'; – and yet this is to many of us a daily immolation.

(*WB*, xiv, 179–80, from 'Matthew Arnold's *Empedocles on Etna*',
Inquirer, 1853)

REVIEWING

Review-writing is one of the features of modern literature. Many able men really give themselves up to it. Comments on ancient writings are scarcely so common as formerly; no great part of our literary talent is devoted to the illustration of the ancient masters; but what seems at first sight less dignified, annotation on modern writings was never so frequent. Hazlitt started the question, whether it would not be as well to review works which did not appear, in lieu of those which did – wishing, as a reviewer, to escape the labour of perusing print, and, as a man, to save his fellow-creatures from the slow torture of tedious extracts. But, though approximations may frequently be noticed – though the neglect of authors and independence of critics are on the increase – this conception, in its grandeur, has never been carried out. We are surprised at first sight, that writers should wish to comment on one another; it appears a tedious mode of stating opinions, and a needless confusion of personal facts with abstract arguments; and some, especially authors who have been censured, say that the cause is laziness – that it is easier to write a review than a book – and that reviewers are, as Coleridge declared, a species of maggots, inferior to bookworms, living on the delicious brains of real genius. Indeed it *would* be very nice, but our world is so imperfect. This idea is wholly false. Doubtless it is easier to write one review than one book: but not, which is the real case, many reviews than one book. A deeper cause must be looked for.

In truth review-writing but exemplifies the casual character of modern literature. Everything about it is temporary and fragmentary. Look at a railway stall; you see books of every colour, blue, yellow, crimson, 'ring-streaked, speckled, and spotted', on every subject, in every style, of every opinion with every conceivable difference, celestial or sublunary, maleficent, beneficent – but all small. People take their literature in morsels, as they take sandwiches on a journey. The volumes at least, you can see clearly, are not intended to be everlasting. It may be all very well for a pure essence like poetry to be immortal in a perishable world; it has no feeling; but paper cannot endure it, paste cannot bear it, string has no heart for it. The race has made up its mind to be fugitive, as well as minute. What a change from the ancient volume! –

That weight of wood, with leathern coat o'erlaid,
Those ample clasps, of solid metal made;
The close-press'd leaves, unclosed for many an age,
The dull red edging of the well-fill'd page;
On the broad back the stubborn ridges roll'd,
Where yet the title stands in tarnish'd gold.

And the change in the appearance of books has been accompanied – has been caused – by a similar change in readers. What a transition from the student of former ages! – from a grave man, with grave cheeks and a considerate eye, who spends his life in study, has no interest in the outward world, hears nothing of its din, and cares nothing for its honours, who would gladly learn and gladly teach, whose whole soul is taken up with a few books of 'Aristotle and his Philosophy', to the merchant in the railway, with a head full of sums, an idea that tallow is 'up', a conviction that teas are 'lively', and a mind reverting perpetually from the little volume which he reads to these mundane topics, to the railway, to the shares, to the buying and bargaining universe. We must not wonder that the outside of books is so different, when the inner nature of those for whom they are written is so changed.

(*WB*, i, 309–11, from 'The First Edinburgh Reviewers', *National Review*, 1855)

REVISIONIST HISTORY

Even simple readers are becoming aware that historical investigation, which used to be a sombre and respectable calling, is now an audacious pursuit. Paradoxes are very bold and very numerous. Many of the recognized 'good people' in history have become bad, and all the very bad people have become rather good. We have palliations of Tiberius, eulogies on Henry VIII, devotional exercises to Cromwell, and fulsome adulation of Julius Caesar and of the first Napoleon.

(*WB*, iii, 123, from 'William Pitt', *National Review*, 1861)

RUMOUR

Nothing can exceed the torture of being constantly told 'on the best authority' a vast variety of inconsistent rumours, the mass of which must be lies, but some one of which may possibly have some truth in it. Every person of any influence in such matters knows that the truth at the moment is imparted only to a very few persons – who are generally reticent, and selected because they are reticent – and that therefore the mass of grave and plausible persons who affect to know so much are usually impostors, and know nothing.

(*WB*, xiv, 153–4, from 'The Restoration of Mr Gladstone to Power',
The Economist, 1873)

A schoolmaster should have an atmosphere of awe, and walk wonderingly, as if he was amazed at being himself.

Selling is of course desirable, but it is only desirable if the purchase money is paid.

Sensible men have a well-founded suspicion of those who repeat the same unvarying dogma under many varying circumstances.

Snobbishness is an insidious endemic, but it is rarely a mortal malady.

Some extreme sceptics, we know, doubt whether it is possible to deduce anything as to an author's character from his works. Yet surely people do not keep a tame steam-engine to write their books; and if those books were really written by a man, he must have been a man who could write them; he must have had the thoughts which they express, have acquired the knowledge they contain, have possessed the style in which we read them. The difficulty is a defect of the critics. A person who knows nothing of an author he has read, will not know much of an author whom he has seen.

So strong are the combative propensities of man, that he would rather fight a losing battle than not fight at all.

SHADOW MINISTERS

In the composition of Cabinets little attention should be paid to information acquired on particular subjects on the Opposition benches. There can be no doubt that those benches are very imperfect as means of instruction, and very efficient as *foci* of error. A cynical Minister once said that 'the Opposition is sure to hear the wrong story about everything'. Most governments do most of their work rightly, but in so doing they inevitably offend many persons. Many of them, especially the less sensible, take their 'grievances', as they call them, to the Opposition, in the hope that they may be mentioned, and the decision of the administration perhaps reversed, in Parliament. An active member of Parliament who is accessible to such things will soon hear innumerable foolish complaints of all our great departments. If a man is known to take an interest in, and to be ready to make himself the mouthpiece of, any particular sort of such grievances – say, those against the Admiralty – he will be incessantly crammed with foolish rumours about the Admiralty business; and if he abandons his mind to them he is sure to form the worst possible opinions about the Admiralty, which, if he is a ready speaker, he will constantly express in the House. By so doing, he will get the credit of attending to the Admiralty business, and will at a political crisis be apt to be named, in what are called 'political circles', as likely to succeed to Admiralty office. But, in fact, no one is less likely; the experienced statesmen who make Cabinets know that no one can be less fit. It is an evil in parliamentary government that at intervals the administration of great departments should be committed to men who are untrained for them. Still, experience shows that a man of unprejudiced mind and great ability, who makes an efficient use of the skilled counsel he receives from the permanent part of the department, may, even without the advantage of previous training, do good service to the State. But the case is hopeless if he is not only untrained but *mis*trained; if he enters the office not with no opinions but with wrong opinions; if not merely he is ignorant of the correcting and guiding opinions of the office but if he is fixed on heresies and fallacies opposed to those opinions. A person that does not know a language may hope, if he takes pains, to learn to pronounce it; but if has once learnt to mispronounce it, he will never be able to do so. And the same principle has its application in other pursuits. A wise framer of Cabinets will select for responsible situations men of as much sense as he can find, and will leave office to train them; he will avoid those who have acquired prejudices and expressed errors in the misleading atmosphere of Opposition.

(*WB*, xiv, 169–70, from 'The Structure of the New Government',
The Economist, 1874)

SHELLEY

Shelley's political opinions were . . . the effervescence of his peculiar nature. The love of liberty is peculiarly natural to the simple impulsive mind. It feels irritated at the idea of a law; it fancies it does not need it; it really needs it less than other men. Government seems absurd – society an incubus. It has hardly patience to estimate particular institutions: it wants to begin again – to make a *tabula rasa* of all which men have created or devised; for they seem to have been constructed on a false system, for an object it does not understand. On this *tabula rasa* Shelley's abstract imagination proceeded to set up arbitrary monstrosities of 'equality' and 'love', which never will be realized among the children of men.

(*WB*, i, 454–5, from 'Percy Bysshe Shelley', *National Review*, 1856)

SLAVERY

Slavery is the one institution which effectually counteracts the assimilative force to which all new countries are subject, – that force which makes all men alike there, and which stamps upon the communities themselves so many common features. In such countries men are struggling with the wilderness; they are in daily conflict with the rough powers of nature, and from them they acquire a hardness and a roughness somewhat like their own. They cannot cultivate the luxuries of leisure, for they have no leisure. They must be mending their fences, or cooking their victuals, or mending their clothes. They cannot be expected to excel in the graces of refinement, for these require fastidious meditation and access to great examples, and neither of these are possible to hard-worked men at the end of the earth. A certain democracy in such circumstances rises like a natural growth of the soil. An even equality in mind and manners, if not in political institutions, is inevitably forced upon those whose character is pressed upon by the same rude forces, who have substantially the same difficulties, who lead in all material points the same life. All are struggling with the primitive difficulties of uncivilized existence, and all are retarded by that struggle at the same low level of instruction and refinement.

Slavery breaks this dead level, and it is the only available device that does so. The owner of a few slaves, partly employed in the service of his house and partly in the cultivation of his land, has a good deal of leisure, and is not exposed to any very brutalizing temptation. It is his interest to treat his slaves well, and in ordinary circumstances he does treat them well. They give him the means of refinement, and the opportunities of culture: they receive from him good clothing, a protective surveillance, and some little moral improvement. Washington was such a slave-owner, and it is probable that at Mount Vernon what may be called the temptation of slavery presented itself in its strongest and most attractive form. At all events, it is certain that, by the irresistible influence of superior leisure and superior culture, the Virginian slave-owner acquired a singular pre-eminence in the revolutionary struggle, moved the bitter jealousy of all his contemporaries, and bestowed an indefinite benefit upon posterity. But even this beneficial effect of slavery, momentary as it was, was not beneficial to the Union as such: it did not strengthen, but weakened the uniting bond; it introduced an element of difference between state and state, which stimulated bitter envy, and suggested constant division. In the correspondence of the first race of Northern statesmen, a dangerous jealousy of the superior political abilities of the South is frequently to be traced.

The immense price, however, which has been paid for the shortlived benefit of slavery has been immeasurably more dangerous to the Union than the benefit itself. As we all perceive, it is tearing it in two. In the progress of time slave-owning becomes an investment of mercantile capital, and slaves are regarded, not as personal dependents, but as impersonal things. The necessities of modern manufacture require an immense production of raw material, and in certain circumstances slaves can be beneficially employed on a large scale to raise that material. The evils of slavery are developed at once. The owner of a few slaves whom he sees every day will commonly treat them kindly enough; but the owner of several gangs, on several different plantations, has no similar motive. His good feelings are not much appealed to in their favour; he does not know them by name, he does not know them by sight; they are to him instruments of production, which he bought at such and such a price, which cost so many dollars, which must be made to yield so many dollars. He is often brutalized by working them cruelly; he is still oftener brutalized in other ways by the infinite temptations which a large mass of subject men and subject women inevitably offer to tyranny and to lust.

(*WB*, iv, 294–5, from 'The American Constitution at the Present Crisis', *National Review*, 1861)

SYDNEY SMITH AND JONATHAN SWIFT

The whole genius of the two writers is emphatically opposed. Sydney Smith's is the ideal of popular, buoyant, riotous fun; it cries and laughs with boisterous mirth; it rolls hither and thither like a mob, with elastic and commonplace joy. Swift was a detective in a dean's wig: he watched the mob; his whole wit is a kind of dextrous indication of popular frailties; he hated the crowd; he was a spy on beaming smiles, and a common informer against genial enjoyment. His whole essence was a soreness against mortality; show him innocent mirth, he would say, How absurd! He was painfully wretched, no doubt, in himself: perhaps, as they say, he had no heart; but his mind, his brain had a frightful capacity for secret pain; his sharpness was the sharpness of disease; his power the sore acumen of morbid wretchedness. It is impossible to fancy a parallel more proper to show the excellence, the unspeakable superiority of a buoyant and bounding writer.

(*WB*, i, 337, from 'The First Edinburgh Reviewers', *National Review*, 1855)

THE SPECIAL DANGERS OF HIGH COMMERCIAL DEVELOPMENTS

At a time when we are all somewhat disposed to blame commercial men for what we call their speculative indiscretions, people are too apt to forget how much excuse there is in the high development which modern commerce has assumed, for the sort of restless activity which, whether you blame it or not, is almost certain to result in indiscretions. Political economy has to a certain extent misled literary men – and, therefore, popular opinion, which of course takes its tone very much from what the newspapers say – as to the kind of faculty needed in commerce. There can be no question that that kind of faculty – we speak of course of that engaged in the higher departments of productive and distributive industry – is of a very rare and a very remarkable, though also, of course, of a very narrow kind; and that literary men who are always repeating the old formula of economical science, about the 'wages of superintendence', 'the reward of abstinence', 'the cost of insurance', as if these three phrases adequately described the faculty needed for conducting either a large manufacturer's, or a large merchant's, or a large banker's, or bill discounter's business, simply throw dust in their own eyes. The qualities required in the higher departments of commerce are to the qualities required in the lower departments very much what the qualities needed by a great strategist, who has to handle armies of half a million of men, and to calculate exactly where they should be distributed, are to the qualities needed by the soldier or the non-commissioned officer, who has nothing more to do than to go through with his own little and well-learned task of obedience to orders, and the exact transmission of them.

Now, let anybody once realize this, and realize it fully, and it will be matter for very little wonder that the commercial men who have the power requisite, or think they have it, for great combinations, are not always willing to confine themselves within the limits which strict prudence requires. For prudence, of course, in these matters *means* incurring no obligation which there is not a very strong presumption that they will be able to meet. In other words, prudence is strictly limited by the capital at the disposal of these men. Now, when a man has a great capacity for many wide combinations, it is not unnatural that his intellectual interests and calculations should far outrun the means at his disposal, and that he should, without any ignoble or unworthy unscrupulousness – though of course not without fault – be eager to avail himself of any advantage which the confidence of others may give him for extending his operations.

We often talk as if the haste to be rich, the mere desire of wealth, were the only motive power in these great speculative transactions which, when they fail, cause so much misery and so much scandal. But no mistake can be greater. We do not for a moment mean that the desire to be rich, the passion for making wealth, is not far too great – and in a considerable measure the cause of the speculative rashness we see. But it is not by any means the sole cause, hardly, perhaps, even the chief cause. We find as a rule that the men who can handle, or who think they can handle, large armies well are apt to favour war when any international question arises which involves war; and if this be so – and the bias to war must almost always, even in this case, be unconscious, for nobody knows so well as great generals what misery war involves – how much more natural it is that those who can handle, or who think they can handle, great commercial combinations well, and who of course anticipate from them, not the misery which war always causes even to the victor, but the satisfaction and enjoyment which useful commercial enterprises bring hardly less to the mere agents who conduct them and to the passive population of consumers to whose advantage they are ultimately to conduce than to the authors of them, should feel a bias of which they are unconscious in favour of the exercise of their faculty, and against the timid counsels which would have them keep within the strictest limits of prudence. Our belief is that it is quite as much the natural heat of imaginative faculty – for however odd the word 'imaginative' may sound in connection with the enterprises of the manufacturer or the merchant, it is an imaginative faculty of a particular kind, and nothing short of it, which fits a man for the conception and execution of those great commercial operations – which leads men to embark in transactions larger than their resources will properly admit, as the haste to be rich, which, however, no doubt mingles with and vivifies that imaginative faculty. Commerce in the present day is as difficult and full of problems which interest and fascinate the intellect in a certain somewhat narrow way, as war or politics.

No doubt there is not the same public recognition of these problems and of the kind of power needed to solve them. But that only makes the matter worse. Where a pursuit is one which not only occupies the keenest intellect, but success in which wins considerable admiration and fame on its own account, and without regard at all to the pecuniary rewards it brings, a part of the charm of it consists in the social honour enjoyed. But though the rich commercial man enjoys plenty of honour on account of his riches, there is hardly any public appreciation of the faculty which enabled him to win those riches, and yet in all probability it is that, and not the rewards it has gained him, on which he really prides himself. And the less his peculiar ability is really recognized in the world, the more it is to him in secret, and the more eager he is to find himself the kind of work in which he takes delight, and in which he realizes the consciousness of his own power. We are, indeed, persuaded that very much speculation indeed is due to this nobler excuse for it – the natural tendency of compressed force to expand and make itself fairly visible at least to the mind which wields it. Just as the born mathematician or musician will find himself mathematical or musical work to do, even at the sacrifice of worldly prospects which are of very considerable importance to him, so the manufacturer or merchant, born with a genius for the sort of combination which is needed in the higher commerce, will find himself employment for his faculty even at the risk of a failure far more painful to him than mere wealth could ever be delightful. Men of the world do not recognize this, for they do not know the sort of faculty needed in commerce, and even the ablest commercial men, when out of their special element, will seem as stupid and devoid of life as a great mathematician will often appear when he is condemned to listen to gossip, or a great musician when he hears of nothing but politics. The sleepy-looking commercial man, who hardly knows what literature means, and never heard of Mr Mill, or Mr Darwin, or the spectroscope, has often beneath that dull outside an intelligence as wakeful and restless as that of a French wit. And it is this eager intelligence of his, conscious of great power, or of the misleading symptoms of great power, which, quite as much as any mere thirst for wealth, leads him into operations extending beyond the scope of his legitimate means.

We are anxious that this should be fairly recognized, because we are quite sure that the world does injustice to the magnates of the City when it accuses the unfortunate among them of lightly playing with what is not their own to spend, in mere greediness and avarice. There is greediness and avarice enough, no doubt; but, probably, hardly more in the City than in the West End. The chief difference is that, in the City, such greediness as there is enters so completely into the chief work of life that no man can really tell where it is that his intellectual interest in his work ends, and his craving for wealth begins. As far as we can see, by far the best check on this intense vitality and recklessness of the commercial intelligence would result from such wider culture as would give these men other keen intellectual interests as well as those which are identified with their occupations. It is not the widely cultivated men who are the most eager in their commercial enterprises. They have other channels for their intellectual life and energy, and accordingly they can afford to limit the energy of their commercial enterprise within the bounds of prudence. It is the men who have no other intellectual life except the life of commercial enterprise who are the truly dangerous men – not dangerous because they are generally less scrupulous, but because they are more eager for the full employment of their powers, than their better educated contemporaries. The energy of commerce runs with a strong current, in part at least because it runs between such very narrow banks. Let it find a number of different mouths, a delta instead of a single opening, and it will not rush on with the same dangerous velocity. Culture always diminishes intensity. And in the commercial world we could well afford to favour that result.

(*WB*, x, 45–8, *The Economist*, 1875)

SUCCESS AND FAILURE

Certain of the ungodly may, notwithstanding the Psalmist, flourish even through life like a green bay-tree; for providence, in external appearance (far differently from the real truth of things, as we may one day see it), works by a scheme of averages. Most people who ought to succeed, do succeed; most people who do fail, ought to fail. But there is no exact adjustment of 'mark' to merit; the competitive examination system appears to have an origin more recent than the creation of the world; – 'on the whole', 'speaking generally', 'looking at life as a whole', are the words in which we must describe the providential adjustment of visible good and evil to visible goodness and badness.

(*WB*, ii, 61, from 'The Waverley Novels', *National Review*, 1858)

SUMMITS

The summits of the various kinds of business are, like the tops of mountains, much more alike than the parts below – the bare principles are much the same; it is only the rich variegated details of the lower strata that so contrast with one another. But it needs travelling to know that the summits *are* the same. Those who live on one mountain believe that *their* mountain is wholly unlike all others.

(*WB*, v, 331, from *The English Constitution*, 1867)

SWORDS FOR LEDGERS

We see so much of the material fruits of commerce that we forget its mental fruits. It begets a mind desirous of things, careless of ideas, not acquainted with the niceties of words. In all labour there should be profit, is its motto. It is not only true that we have 'left swords for ledgers', but war itself is made as much by the ledger as by the sword. The soldier – that is, the great soldier – of today is not a romantic animal, dashing at forlorn hopes, animated by frantic sentiment, full of fancies as to a lady-love or a sovereign; but a quiet, grave man, busied in charts, exact in sums, master of the art of tactics, occupied in trivial detail; thinking, as the Duke of Wellington was said to do, *most* of the shoes of his soldiers; despising all manner of *éclat* and eloquence; perhaps, like Count Moltke, 'silent in seven languages'. We have reached a 'climate' of opinion where figures rule, where our very supporter of divine right, as we deemed him, our Count Bismarck, amputates kings right and left, applies the test of results to each, and lets none live who are not to do something. There has in truth been a great change during the last five hundred years in the predominant occupations of the ruling part of mankind; formerly they passed their time either in exciting action or inanimate repose. A feudal baron had nothing between war and the chase – keenly animating things both – and what was called 'inglorious ease'. Modern life is scanty in excitements, but incessant in quiet action. Its perpetual commerce is creating a 'stock-taking' habit – the habit of asking each man, thing, and institution, 'Well, what have you done since I saw you last?'

(*WB*, v, 363, from *The English Constitution*, 1867)

Thackeray is like the edited and illustrated edition of a great dinner.

That an Englishman should grumble is quite right, but that he should grumble at gravity is hardly right. He is rarely a lively being himself, and he should have a sympathy with those of his kind.

There is a kind of hot-headedness in the pursuit of very abstract truth; a mind which has once made the painful puzzling effort will not allow a question as to the value of the result. In a little while a man's system becomes part of himself; he has so ingrained his mind with the repetition of a single argument that to doubt his own theory seems like doubting his own understanding.

There is an ordinance of nature at which men of genius are perpetually fretting, but which does more good than many laws of the universe which they praise: it is, that ordinary women ordinarily prefer ordinary men.

There is no method by which men can be both free and equal.

There is one thing which no one will permit to be treated lightly – himself. And so there is one too which a sovereign assembly will never permit to be lessened or ridiculed – its own power.

This is the highest attainment of art: to be at the same time nature and something more than nature.

To get through the necessary work of a great department – to attend the House of Commons with official watchfulness and regularity – to achieve the mere correspondence of minister (omitting all the exhausting *social* claims on such a man) – are each of them terrifying tasks. Putting them together, we may rather wonder (for myself I constantly wonder) how men's nerves and brains contrive to get through them.

To tell a mob how their condition may be improved is talking hydrostatics to the ocean.

TEACHING

I have but slight opinion of the practice of teaching, as a discipline for the mind of the teacher. There is no collision in it with an equal mind. The only opponent is an inferior in years and standing, who is conscious of his own ignorance, who wishes his tutor's good opinion, who may particularly need his good word; and it is absurd to support that there can be in such circumstances any fair clash of mind with mind, any of that fair competition of intellect with intellect, such as we find in other pursuits. It will not be often that searching and trying questions will occur to the student, and even if they do, no one who has got common sense will venture to ask many. Lecturers are men, and no one likes being reduced to a difficulty; the way to please them, is to ask them a question that will be an excuse for saying their lecture, or a part of it, over again; they like to hear their own voices, and the old tune; do this, and especially if they be advanced in years, they will contemplate you with venerable kindness, and speak of you as 'not so quick as some (perhaps quickness is overrated nowadays), but an attentive young gentleman, and most anxious to improve'.

(*WB*, xiv, 191–2, from 'The Universities', *Inquirer*, 1854)

TOLERANCE

Tolerance is learned in discussion, and, as history shows, is only so learned. In all customary societies bigotry is the ruling principle. In rude places to this day anyone who says anything new is looked on with suspicion, and is persecuted by opinion if not injured by penalty. One of the greatest pains to human nature is the pain of a new idea. It is, as common people say, so 'upsetting'; it makes you think that, after all, your favourite notions may be wrong, your firmest beliefs ill-founded; it is certain that till now there was no place allotted in your mind to the new and startling inhabitant, and now that it has conquered an entrance you do not at once see which of your old ideas it will or will not turn out, with which of them it can be reconciled, and with which it is at essential enmity. Naturally, therefore, common men hate a new idea, and are disposed more or less to ill-treat the original man who brings it. Even nations with long habits of discussion are intolerant enough. In England, where there is on the whole probably a freer discussion of a greater number of subjects than ever was before in the world, we know how much power bigotry retains. But discussion, to be successful, requires tolerance. It fails wherever, as in a French political assembly, anyone who hears anything which he dislikes tries to howl it down. If we know that a nation is capable of enduring continuous discussion, we know that it is capable of practising with equanimity continuous tolerance.

(*WB*, vii, 110, from *Physics and Politics*, 1872)

TRAINING

I occasionally read denunciatory eloquence to the effect that the only end of educational training is the abstract improvement of the individual in and for himself, and that it degrades the dignity of the art to consider whether it fits or unfits for the mercenary callings of mankind. 'Stimulate the thought,' it is said, 'cultivate the taste, fashion the intellect, strengthen the reason, store the memory, teach a young man to know, and, a hard task, to love the greatest works of the greatest thinkers, and you will have done him an enormous service.' I say you will have done him irreparable injury if you have disqualified him for his necessary duties, and his inevitable life . . . the better man will be, not the one who has received the highest and most extreme discipline, not he who in the language of the rhetorician is most familiar with 'what Plato meditated and Socrates discussed', but he who is most able to apply his intellect efficiently to what is around him, to form a correct judgement of the matter on which he must judge, to act rightly where he is compelled to act, to follow with the routine which he must follow, who, if I may say so, can transact best his necessary existence.

(*WB*, xiv, 193–4, from 'On the Extension of the Universities', *Inquirer*, 1854)

TYPES OF SOCIETY

There are three methods in which a society may be constituted. There is the equal system, which, with more or less of variation, prevails in France and in the United States. The social presumption in these countries always is that everyone is on a level with everyone else. In America, the porter at the station, the shopman at the counter, the boots at the hotel, when neither a Negro nor an Irishman, is your equal. In France *égalité* is a political first principle. The whole of Louis Napoleon's *régime* depends upon it: remove that feeling, and the whole fabric of the Empire will pass away. We once heard a great French statesman illustrate this. He was giving a dinner to the clergy of his neighbourhood, and was observing that he had now no longer the power to help or hurt them, when an eager *curé* said, with simple-minded joy, 'Oui, monsieur, maintenant personne ne peut rien, ni le comte, ni le prolétaire.' The democratic priest so rejoiced at the universal levelling which had passed over his nation, that he could not help boasting of it when silence would have been much better manners. We are not now able – we have no room and no inclination – to discuss the advantages of democratic society; but we think in England we may venture to assume that it is neither the best nor the highest form which a society can adopt, and that it is certainly fatal to that development of individual originality and greatness by which the past progress of the human race has been achieved, and from which alone, it would seem, all future progress is to be anticipated. If it be said that people are all alike, that the world is a plain with no natural valleys and no natural hills, the picturesqueness of existence is destroyed, and, what is worse, the instinctive emulation by which the dweller in the valley is stimulated to climb the hill is annihilated and becomes impossible.

On the other hand, there is the opposite system, which prevails in the East, – the system of irremovable inequalities, of hedged-in castes which no one can enter but by birth, and from which no born member can issue forth. This system likewise, in this age and country, needs no attack, for it has no defenders. Everyone is ready to admit that it cramps originality by defining our work irrespective of our qualities and before we were born; that it retards progress by restraining the wholesome competition between class and class, and the wholesome migration from class to class, which are the best and strongest instruments of social improvement.

And if both these systems be condemned as undesirable and prejudicial, there is no third system except that which we have, – the system of *removable inequalities*, where many people are inferior to and worse off than others, but in which each may *in theory* hope to be on a level with the highest below the throne, and in which each may reasonably, and without sanguine impracticability, hope to gain one step in social elevation, to be at last on a level with those who at first were just above them. But, from the mere description of such a society, it is evident that, taking man as he is, with the faults which we know he has, and the tendencies which he invariably displays, some poison of 'snobbishness' is inevitable. Let us define it as the habit of 'pretending to be higher in the social scale than you really are'. Everybody will admit that such pretension is a fault and a vice, yet every observant man of the world would also admit that, considering what other misdemeanours men commit, this offence is not inconceivably heinous; and that, if people never did anything worse, they might be let off with a far less punitive judgement than in the actual state of human conduct would be just or conceivable. How are we to hope men will pass their lives in putting their best foot foremost, and yet will never boast that their better foot is farther advanced and more perfect than in fact it is? Is boasting to be made a capital crime? Given social ambition as a propensity of human nature; given a state of society like ours, in which there are prizes which every man may seek, degradations which everyone may erase, inequalities which everyone may remove, – it is idle to suppose that there will not be all sorts of striving to cease to be last and to begin to be first, and it is equally idle to imagine that all such strivings will be of the highest kind. This effort will be, like all the efforts of our mixed and imperfect human nature, partly good and partly bad, with much that is excellent and beneficial in it, and much also which is debasing and pernicious. The bad striving after unpossessed distinction is snobbishness, which from the mere definition cannot be defended, but which may be excused as a natural frailty in an emulous man who is not distinguished, who hopes to be distinguished, and who perceives that a valuable means of gaining distinction is a judicious though false pretension that it has already been obtained.

(*WB*, ii, 307–9, from 'Sterne and Thackeray', *National Review*, 1864)

THE ULTIMATE END OF FENIANISM

Tinsley's Magazine, a new publication, of a very light kind, contains this month a paper of importance. It is a statement by a leading Fenian, whose character and position are evidently known to the editor, of Fenian policy and designs; and though tainted with that grandiloquence which no Irishman seems quite able to avoid, is manly and straightforward enough in tone. The main object of the writer is to announce a fact well known to politicians, but frequently forgotten by the public, that the object of Fenianism is not the redress of Irish grievances, the abolition of the Church, or the resettlement of tenures, but the establishment of Irish independence. The American Irish, says the writer, suffer no grievances, are moved by no hatred of parsons, no hunger for land, yet they are of all Irishmen the most vehemently bitter against England. Their impulse is the passion known of late as that of nationality, and they are determined not to rest until they have made of the island an independent Irish Republic like Switzerland, and, probably, though the writer does not say so, with a cantonal organization. To this end they will work on steadily, trusting to find their opportunity when England is involved in war, and meanwhile keeping up a fever of excitement in Great Britain itself, whereby they hope to exhaust the government, and obtain the adhesion of a section of the English democracy.

We are not about, of course, to point out either the folly or the wickedness of these views, to analyse the differences between the position of Ireland and the position of Poland, or to expatiate on the resistless physical power of Great Britain as compared with Ireland. It is useless to tell Irishmen that all this has been said and tried a hundred years ago, that in this very paper there are traces of disunion in the Fenian ranks, that in 'carrying the war into England', they are simply giving tone to British institutions, bitterness to British sentiment towards Ireland. It is not to Fenian advantage, but to Fenian disadvantage, that our garrison should be strengthened, our police armed, our populace accustomed to the use of the revolver; but that is not the point. Our object is to point out to the Irish Americans, in the interest of the Irish themselves, that they are seeking the unattainable; that, granting the possibility of separating Ireland from England, that separation would not involve Irish independence. Accepting for a moment the Fenian point of view, and allowing that their movement is a 'Red' one – a protest at once against modern society and the subjection of one nation to another – the Fenians still make one very evident and very serious mistake. They always treat Ireland as if Ireland were filled by a nation, which, let alone, would live like Switzerland – very quiet, very peaceable, and very well to do. They conceal from themselves, and, in a great measure, from the American public, that Ireland contains *two* peoples – one Irish, or, if they like that word better, Fenian, and another which, though calling itself by many names, is, in character, in creed, and in social circumstances, substantially Scotch. Not only is there no unity between these races, but there is no possibility of any. The hatred of a Venetian for an Austrian is feeble compared with the hatred of a Tipperary peasant for a northerner; the pride of a Virginian to a Negro is gentleness compared with the pride of a Protestant of Ulster to any 'native' whatsoever. The two peoples differ radically in race, creed, and civilization, in their fundamental theories of land, in the tendencies of their dreams, in their notions of social organization – in everything, in short, which has ever divided mankind. They have waged an internecine war for six hundred years, during which they have built up a popular literature of hostility; they renew this war in streets and alleys every year, and they are ready at this moment as ever to fight it out, if only England would let them, 'to the bitter end'. It is a certainty, if anything in politics is certain, that the independence of Ireland would be the signal for a civil war, which would be a struggle at once of races, of creeds, and of civilizations, and would end only in the subjugation or expulsion of one or the other side. The Fenians, probably, think their superiority not doubtful; but some of them, at least, have read something, and we ask them to ponder carefully these facts. The northerners in Ireland are relatively as strong against the southerners as ever the Scotch were in their contest of centuries with England, and England never won. They are quite as favourably situated, for England never conquered even the Lowlands; they are not liable to be betrayed by their own leaders; they are the richer of the two Irish peoples; and they possess, we will not say the higher but the more efficient civilization. They possess, moreover, by the confession of all men, one special quality which the Scotch had not – a quality often found in very inferior but never in feeble races – the faculty of governing, of keeping energetically and continuously at the top. No race exists so disposed towards strict military organization; and we do not doubt that within a month of independence, Ulster would be a strong military state, governed by men with a distinct plan for ruling the island, with an army based on the Prussian system, and able to hire auxiliaries from all the world. It is more than probable that they would reconquer the island, and allying themselves with England on their own terms, restore nearly the state of affairs which existed before emancipation. France, the Fenian leaders may say, would prevent that. We see no earthly reason why France should, for Ireland would be a terrible embarrassment to her, enabling England, in every European convulsion, to compel her to exert her whole strength to defend a colony divided by four hundred miles of sea; but supposing that France did, Ireland, as O'Connell is said to have foreseen clearly, would not then be an independent republic but a French dependency. That may be a very happy fate – we are not arguing that – but it is not the fate the Fenians avowedly desire. Then there is America? Well, we ask the American Irish themselves, on what grounds they believe that the United States, if they interfered at all, would interfere on their side? The freeholders of the States are not Catholics. They would have no special interest, English power once abolished, in helping one side more than another. They have no sentimental love for the Fenian character, considered by itself. The Scotch have as strong a hold in America as the Irish, the Germans are stronger yet, and the true Yankees the strongest of all, and each of those three classes would be impelled, by every peculiarity in their characters, to side with the stern domineering Teutonic Puritans, then under process of extirpation by Celtic Catholics, of greater number than themselves. That latent, but very strong dislike between the Americans and the Irish, which comes up in every riot, would, in all probability, break into a flame, and Ireland, if Americanized at all, would be Americanized after the Puritan, and not after the Fenian fashion. Anyhow, it would not be an independent republic of the Swiss kind which the Fenians would have formed, but a dependent republic of the American kind. Grant everything the Fenians imagine to be true, and still their favourite dream would be as far off as ever, much further off than it would be if they were again a colony of Great Britain. The real analogy of their position is not Poland or Venetia, but Bohemia, where four millions of Czechs, controlled by an immutable geographical position, vainly try to destroy the power of the million and a quarter of Germans quartered among them, and dream dreams of winning their autonomy by the aid of a race whose political creed is summed up in their own proverb, 'in Heaven one God; on earth one Czar'.

(*WB*, viii, 89–92, *The Economist*, 1867)

UNDERWRITERS (À PROPOS A HARBOUR IN CORNWALL)

I suppose we ought to think much of the courage with which sailors face such dangers, and of the feelings of their wives and families when they wait the return of their husbands and fathers; but my City associations at once carried me away to the poor underwriter who should insure against loss at such a place. How he would murmur, 'Oh! my premium,' as he saw the ship tossing up to the great black rock and the ugly breakwater, and seeming likely enough to hit both. I shall not ask at Lloyd's what is the rate for Boscastle rocks, for I remember the grave rebuke I once got from a serious underwriter when I said some other such place was pretty. 'Pretty! I should think it was,' he answered; 'why, it is lined with our money!'

(*WB*, xiv, 117, from 'Boscastle', *Spectator*, 1866)

UNIVERSITY EDUCATION

In England at least a university education does one thing – namely, emancipates men from any excess of appreciation of its importance, such as the ablest men who have not passed through it, are inclined to attach to it. It would seem as if it took a university education to teach a man that, excellent as it is, it is not all that the outside world supposes, and may, under certain unfavourable conditions, be even rather mischievous than otherwise.

> (*WB*, vii, 447–8, from 'The Public Bewilderment about Higher Education', *The Economist*, 1876)

THE UNSEEN WORK OF PARLIAMENT

Some persons, and even some important organs of liberal opinion, have censured the programme of the session as uninviting. It has seemed to them that there is not enough of promise in it. It has seemed to them that so elaborate, and in some respects so cumbrous, an apparatus as the English Parliament should this year do more than pass a few laws of unattractive usefulness. They have wished for something more exciting, and as the subject is very important, it may be as well to examine whether such wishes are reasonable.

We believe that, when all the necessary circumstances are duly taken account of, they are in an extreme degree unreasonable. We believe that the true working of the representative government very much depends on the fact that the nation is not inclined to require excitement from it. We are confident that if, as has been the case in some foreign countries where the representative experiment has been tried unsuccessfully, the country should ever look on the proceedings of Parliament as an intellectual and theatrical exhibition, no merit in our laws, no excellence in our national character, could save our institutions from very serious danger.

The reason of this is, in truth, plain and familiar. It is not possible that every year should be a constitutional era; and, even if it were possible, it would not be desirable. Large changes in our fundamental institutions are grave tasks: they can only be proposed when the public mind has been thoroughly familiarized with their necessity;

when the evil to be remedied is keenly experienced; when the preliminary discussion has been sufficient and effectual. These conditions can rarely be satisfied. Great evils are rare: effectual discussion is slow: the public mind does not readily apprehend anything new. Moreover, a constitution is but a means to an end; it is only important in so far as it is an instrument of good government. No machine can work well if subjected to incessant alteration, and if we impair the efficiency of an institution by the frequency of our innovations, we are sacrificing the end to the means. We are purchasing a satisfactory constitution at the price of a satisfactory government.

The public mind of England is sufficiently familiar with these arguments. We feel from our long experience and from our practical habits that we must not make changes for the sake of a change – that we must know what we are doing when we do so change – that we must regard the Imperial Parliament not as a theatrical exhibition or an intellectual stimulant, but as a practical machine. Perhaps, however, we do not sufficiently bear in mind how much Parliament really does. We have had for many years a vast number of important legislative measures which have occupied exclusive attention. We have not, perhaps, sufficiently thought of the *unseen work* of Parliament, nor adequately considered how needful it is to prevent that work from being impaired by pompous suggestions and by unnecessary attempts at showy legislation.

The first part of the duty of Parliament is the choice of the Cabinet who are to administer the affairs of the country. It is upon the Cabinet, as we all know, that everything which is important in our public business rests and must rest. They are the executive committee – the board of directors of the English nation: if they administer well, our affairs will be well; and if they administer badly, all our affairs will go wrong. And with the increasing complexity of the world, the difficulty of administration, as well as its importance, is rapidly on the increase. All this is easily comprehended. But on certain occasions it is for the most part overlooked. Because the choice of a ministry is an occasional act, done once and not repeated for a considerable interval, it is not counted as one of the habitual functions of Parliament, it is not taken account of in reckoning the results of each session. No error, however, could be more complete on this subject. The constant proximity of Parliament is the real force which makes ministers what they are – which prevents their being arbitrary – which prevents their being negligent – which prevents their being eccentric – which ensures their attending to public opinion – which enforces a substantial probity throughout the administration. It may sound like a rhetorical illustration, but it is literally true, that it would be a sufficient account of the laborious sittings of a long session if it were found that by those labours a good ministry had been kept in for the whole time. Burke said that the end of the British Constitution was to bring twelve men into the jury box; it would be truer to say that it was to bring fifteen good men into a dingy room in Downing Street.

Again, Parliament has a function of its own which is distinct from legislation, but which in the present state of the world is at least as important. It has an *expressive* function. An immense and most miscellaneous mass of topics are brought before the English nation every year; the stupendous growth of our trade, the extension of our empire, the increase of our philanthropy, the refinement of our public spirit, and an augmented national intelligence, increase these subjects year by year. On all these it has an opinion, and it needs an organ for expressing it. Parliament is that organ. Whatever be the defects in its constitution (and a theorist will find many), it thoroughly expresses the substantial opinion of the average Englishman. Its voice is not the voice of Lord John Russell, nor the voice of Mr Disraeli, nor of Lord Palmerston – nor the expression of any casual individual or of any eccentric idiosyncrasy, but of the English nation. It is this which gives it such a singular efficiency in foreign countries. England *thinks aloud*, and her voice is heard in all the world. Nor is it a paradox to say that Parliament performs this expressive function better in consequence of what might at first seem to be its principal defects. We grieve over the commonplace loquacity of ordinary members, and certainly some of it performs no useful purpose and might well be immediately dispensed with, but much of this loquacity is really useful. It shows by the best evidence that opinions so expressed are not the solitary judgements of great statesmen, nor the long-sighted anticipations of forecasting minds, but the average judgements of ordinary men. And for this purpose bad speaking is more effectual than the very best. Mr

Gladstone is the greatest orator in Parliament, but there is something which Mr Gladstone is less able to express than anyone else, and that is the simple opinion of ordinary men. His reputation for originality is an insuperable obstacle: whatever he says is suspected of being his own. On all occasions if he is cited as a witness to public opinion, the answer is ready, 'Oh, *that* is Mr Gladstone.' At any rate, no one will impute excessive originality to ordinary members of Parliament: what they say is a nearly perfect test of the average English opinion, for they are themselves excellent specimens of the average Englishman.

It is not, of course, our object to depreciate or to speak lightly of the legislative duties of Parliament. They are so well understood and so obvious, that we are apt to think of them as its only duties. We should expect from Parliament every year, *not* indeed astonishing reforms, *not* statutes that will be an era in the history of our legislation, but an adequate supply of moderately useful measures – we should expect some business either of actual legislation, or of inquiries that may result in legislation from each session – but then we must remember that *this* business will have the qualities of *all* business. It will look dull and uninviting; it will administer no excitement; every part of it will be entirely untheatrical. 'Tedious usefulness' is said to be 'the acme of civilization'; it certainly is one of the most important functions of Parliament.

(*WB*, vi, 45–8, *The Economist*, 1861)

We all come down to dinner, but each has a room to himself.

We are nowadays little alone, and when we are we read in books the thoughts of others. We are dependent (and it is good that we should be so) on others perpetually. Strife face to face with men is unknown to all save a professed class who are systematized so as to annihilate as much as possible individual will in all save the commander. Accordingly in our days characters are becoming more and more uniform, and eccentricity less and less common; the qualities common to all men are acquiring a greater prominence, those peculiar to a few obtaining less and less of importance and regard.

We have so many little discussions that we get no full discussions; we eat so many sandwiches that we spoil our dinner.

We must remember that the evil of sectarianism is one of the crying sins of human nature. One of the most common defects of half-instructed minds is to think much of that in which they differ from others, and little of that in which they agree with others. The special dogmas of their individual creed are to a certain class much more important than the truths of religion and Christianity as mankind at large believes them.

Whenever there is an important trial involving any complex point of engineering, twelve engineers will give evidence upon oath, and doubtless with perfect sincerity, in the affirmative – and twelve others, with equal sincerity and upon oath also, in the negative.

While the Liberal turn of mind denotes the willingness to admit new ideas, and the perfect impartiality with which those ideas, when admitted, are canvassed and considered, the Conservative turn of mind denotes adhesiveness to the early and probably inherited ideas of childhood, and a very strong and practically effective distrust of novel intellectual suggestions which come unaccredited by any such influential association.

Without a hard ascent you can rarely see a great view.

The worst families are those in which the members never really speak their minds to one another; they maintain an atmosphere of unreality, and everyone always lives in an atmosphere of suppressed ill-feeling. It is the same with nations.

Writing for posterity is like writing on foreign post-paper: you cannot say to a man at Calcutta what you would say to a man at Hackney; you think 'the yellow man is a very long way off; this is fine paper, it will go by a ship'; so you try to say something worthy of the ship, something noble, which will keep and travel.

WALTZING

I have added what *I* call waltzing to my other accomplishments. It differs from what other people call by that name, not only in the step which is of my own invention, but also in its having no relation whatever to the music, and by preserving its rotatory motion in a great measure by collisions with the other couples. It's very amusing running small French girls against some fellow's elbow, it's like killing flies years ago. There is, however, the inconvenience that one does not like to ask the same girl twice; she might say she had not insured her life, but if you are careful to select a fresh subject for each experiment, the pastime will succeed. I do not fancy it pleases the girls; he dances *tout seul* ('all by himself') I heard one of them say with great indignation to her female friends, as if a fellow of my age could be expected to keep time with her or with the music either, and it pleases me, it being a new, if not humane excitement, and is better than talking feeble philosophy in out of the way corners.

(*WB*, xii, 330–31, from a letter to Edith Bagehot, 1851)

WAR

There never was a worse blunder than the supposition that the more states there are to suffer by a sanguinary quarrel, the sooner will the motives prevail for bringing it to a conclusion. Let the belligerents spare the neutrals in every possible way, if they do not want to be fighting for ever. It is in the interests of those who remain at peace that the principles regulating the natural limitations of war should be considered and decided on; not in the interests of those who are eager to inflict the most injury they can, in the shortest time, on their antagonist. That, no doubt, is the real object of war; but then, who will deny that even when at war a nation has, and ought to have, a great many other even more important objects than the object of striking a crushing blow at his enemy? It is usually much more important even for a belligerent nation not to cut itself from its fellowship with other nations than even to make its antagonist succumb. And if it were not so, it is certainly much more important for the nations which remain at peace to be allowed to profit to the full by that peace, than it is for those who are at war to inflict the greatest possible damage, in the shortest possible time, on those with whom they are at war. It may not be possible always to reconcile the immediate interest of a belligerent with the best interest of the neutrals. But when that is impossible, the best interests of the neutrals ought to prevail. And even if it were true, instead of false, that the worse the injury war inflicts, the sooner it is likely to come to an end, even in that case, a war of somewhat longer duration, which does not ruin neutrals as well as belligerents, would be a less evil to the world than a war of shorter duration which had inflicted on pacific peoples almost as much suffering as on those which were at strife.

(*WB*, viii, 73–4, from 'The Declaration of Paris', *The Economist*, 1877)

THE WHIGS

In truth Whiggism is not a creed, it is a character. Perhaps as long as there has been a political history in this country there have been certain men of a cool, moderate, resolute firmness, not gifted with high imagination, little prone to enthusiastic sentiment, heedless of large theories and speculations, careless of dreamy scepticism; with a clear view of the next step, and a wise intention to take it; a strong conviction that the elements of knowledge are true, and a steady belief that the present world can, and should be, quietly improved.

These are the Whigs.

(*WB*, i, 318–19, from 'The First Edinburgh Reviewers', *National Review*, 1855)

WINNING A SEAT

If you want to represent a constituency, you must not go down to them and say, 'See, I have all these new ideas, of which you have no notion: these new plans, which you must learn and study – all this new knowledge, of which neither you nor your fathers ever heard.' If you hint at anything like this you will be rejected at once. But, on the contrary, you must say what they think only perhaps a little better than they could say it; advocate the schemes they wish advocated; be zealous for the party's tradition which you and they have in common. The cleverer you can be in doing this, the more you can please them with their own thoughts and make them happy with their own inventions, the better they will like you. But (exceptions apart) you must not try to teach them. They want a representative, not a tutor; a man who will vote as they wish, not one who will teach them what they ought to wish for.

(*WB*, vi, 58–9, from 'The Advantages and Disadvantages of Becoming a Member of Parliament', *The Economist*, 1874)

WRITING

The art of narration is the art of writing in hooks-and-eyes. The principle consists in making the appropriate thought follow the appropriate thought, the proper fact the proper fact; in first preparing the mind for what is to come, and then letting it come. This can only be achieved by keeping continually and insensibly before the mind of the reader some one object, character, or image, whose variations are the events of the story, whose unity is the unity of it.

(*WB*, i, 423, from 'Mr Macaulay', *National Review*, 1856)

You cannot calm the passions of men by defining their words.

You do not expect a plain cook to turn philosophical chemist; and it is as little rational to expect a barrister of cases and instances to be changed on a sudden to a judge of great principles and broad doctrines.

You may talk of the tyranny of Nero and Tiberius; but the real tyranny is the tyranny of your next door neighbour. What law is so cruel as the law of doing what he does? What yoke is so galling as the necessity of being like him? What *espionage* of despotism comes to your door so effectually as the eye of the man who lives at your door? Public opinion is a permeating influence, and it exacts obedience to itself; it requires us to think other men's thoughts, to speak other men's words, to follow other men's habits.

MORE BAGEHOT

The Collected Works of Walter Bagehot (fifteen volumes, edited by Norman St John-Stevas, London, 1965–1986) is splendidly comprehensive and abounds with interesting assessments of Bagehot in his various intellectual manifestations by experts in their field.

They are organized as follows:

Literary Essays (volumes I and II)
Historical   (III and IV)
Political   (V–VIII)
Economic   (IX–XI)
Letters   (XII and XIII)
Miscellany   (XIV and XV)

Many of Bagehot's best writings are on unlikely or superficially uninteresting subjects, so avoid being repelled by off-putting titles or topics.

Below is a list of some of the highlights in each volume, with an asterisk beside my favourites; I indicate also some useful assessments of various facets of Bagehot's writing.

I Substantial essays on Bishop Butler, *The First Edinburgh Reviewers (including Sydney Smith), Macaulay, Walter Scott, Shakespeare and *Shelley; a short biography of Bagehot by St John-Stevas and a literary appreciation by Sir William Haley.

II Substantial essays on *Dickens, Milton, *Lady Mary Wortley Montagu and *Nassau Senior ('Senior's Journals').

III Substantial essays on *Bolingbroke, *Lord Brougham, Gladstone, *Sir Robert Peel, Pitt, Adam Smith and *James Wilson; short illuminating appreciations of contemporary politicians, including John Bright, Gladstone and *Lord Lyndhurst; *Jacques Barzun on 'Bagehot as Historian'.

IV *Letters on the French *coup d'état* of 1851 (of which Bagehot was an eyewitness), 'The "Monroe Doctrine"', *'The Emperor Napoleon', 'The Evil and Good in the American Civil War', * 'Cardinal Antonelli'.

V *The English Constitution*, St John–Stevas on 'The Political Genius of Walter Bagehot'.

VI 'Competitive Tests for the Public Service', *'Average Government', *'Thinking Government', 'Intellectual Conservatism', 'The Special Danger of Men of Business as Administrators', *'The Defect of America: Presidential and Ministerial Governments Compared', 'The History of the Unreformed Parliament, and its Lessons', 'The Suffrage for Women'.

VII *Physics and Politics*, 'The Necessary Consequences of Government by a Minority', 'Lord Derby on Working Class Conservatism', *'The Chances for a Long Conservative Régime in England', 'Bad Lawyers or Good?', *Lord Amberley on Sunday Recreation', 'Oxford', *'The Women's Degrees', 'Mr John Morley on Education'.

VIII *'Count Your Enemies and Economise Your Expenditure', *'The Limerick Demonstrations', *'The Irish Viceroyalty', *One Difference Between France and England', *'Do the Conditions Requisite for a Stable Government Exist in France?', 'Prince Bismarck's Foreign Policy', 'What should be our Present Policy in the East'.

IX *Lombard Street*, R. S. Sayers on 'Bagehot as an Economist'.

X 'The Panic', 'The Advantages that would Accrue from an Ownership of the Railways by the State', 'The Railways and the Government'.

XI 'The Postulates of English Political Economy', 'Adam Smith and Our Modern Economy', 'Malthus', *'Ricardo', Robert Giffen on 'Bagehot as an Economist'.

XII and XIII In these volumes letters to his intimates are generally the most enjoyable, particularly those to his parents, Thomas and

Edith Bagehot, to Eliza Wilson (later his wife) during their courtship, and to Richard Holt Hutton.

XIV 'The Metaphysical Basis of Toleration', 'The Ignorance of Man', 'Aristocratic and Unaristocratic Statesmen', ★'The Logic of Banking', 'The Liberal Creed as to Government by the Sword', 'The Trash of the Day', 'Lord Stanhope's Life of Pitt', ★'The Danger of Quiet Times', ★'The State of Europe', ★'Aesthetic Twaddle *versus* Economic Science', ★'The Merchant's Function'.

XV On Bagehot: Henry Sawtell's Letter of 1882, ★Richard Holt Hutton's memoir, Woodrow Wilson, ★Augustine Birrell, St John-Stevas on 'Walter Bagehot's Conversation'.

For an excellent bibliography of works by and on Bagehot, see *WB*, xv, pp. 426–42. Of the biographies, that by his sister-in-law Mrs Russell Barrington (*The Life of Walter Bagehot*, London, 1914) is the most moving, William Irvine's (*Walter Bagehot*, London, 1939) is the most stimulating and Alastair Buchan's (*The Spare Chancellor. The Life of Walter Bagehot*, London, 1959) the most efficient. Ruth Dudley Edwards's *The Pursuit of Reason: The Economist, 1843–1993* (London, 1993) deals with Bagehot's career from the perspective of his editorship of, and long-term influence on, *The Economist*.

SOURCES

(In the text, sources are given for longer extracts. Sources for short untitled pieces and aphorisms are given below, with page references and numbers denoting the order of extracts on the page.)

Sources

INDEX

Index

Index

Index

Index

Index